Hello, World

brandon spacey

Hello, World

by brandon spacey

Copyright © 2024 by brandon spacey
and SpaceBrew Publishing.

All Rights Reserved.

First Edition

Cover art by brandon spacey.

Novels by brandon spacey

Callie Simmons Novels

book 1: Midnight's Park
book 2: Resurrecting Mars
book 3: Into the Darkness
book 4: Red Bell

Shawn Stedwin Novels

book 1: A Flutter in the Window
book 2: Hello, World

Standalone Novels

Shedding Sadness
Chasing Comets

Dedication

Moving can be very taxing on friendships. Though we do our best to stay in touch with the friends we've moved away from, the visits tend to grow fewer and farther between. And at some point, you will see an old friend for the last time, ever. When will that be?

Therefore, when moving, it is just as important to meet new friends as it is to keep the old ones. As we get older, we have less and less time to establish meaningful history. So it is vital to get started as quickly as possible. Waste not a minute!

This is for my new friends, Ryan, Joe and Kelvin. Thank you, gentlemen, for being there. *Already.*

Author's Note

This book was borne of the desire to continue what I thought was a great character, in Shawn Stedwin. I had grown out of Callie Simmons as my lead, and was ready for someone young and fresh. It was not that Callie was *old* and *stale*, but I felt like she'd had her hands in enough things. She had saved the world several times and had played her part. Callie was a fun write, because of her chastity, her reticence to spewing swear words every other sentence, and her apparently 'kooky' or 'ditsy' demeanor, when she was actually a rocket scientist. I know real people like that, and they're always fun to be around. She was lovable, and – at least I think – believable as a female lead. But I was ready for someone new.

Marcella, called Shawn, was just that person. When I got the idea to try to bring the dead back to life for a few moments at a time, I wanted it to be this new person. Someone with fresh ideas, who wasn't tired out from saving the world so many times in so many different applications. And it helped to be able to create a new backstory that involved a personal tragedy from when she was a child. Shawn instantly became my favorite character to write, because I felt like I knew her personally from the very first sentence I put down. She was spunky and excitable, fun, quirky and loving, and not opposed to throwing a swear or two when necessary.

My last book, *A Flutter in the Window* was like a flash in the pan. A lighting strike. It was here and done before I knew what had happened. I wrote it in forty-two straight days. A few of those days were only productive to the tune of about 200 words. But that was okay, it was my regimen. It was my discipline to start and finish a book in the same year, and hopefully with no breaks at all. So those 200-word-days were just to follow my rule. Had I actually had time to write on those days, I might have finished the book in thirty-eight. Or thirty-five. Who knows? But I was – and still am – very proud of that book, and proud of having written it in such a short time. I just wasn't ready for it to be over. I wasn't ready to be done writing Shawn.

She had a great office with a neat set of lab rooms behind a locked door. And we knew there was another door beyond those labs that we had never gotten to go through and explore. In short, there was a ton of opportunity here that I was not ready to let go of. I wanted to keep writing her because she was so enjoyable, but I also wanted to explore that hidden floor space. I knew we would need to go through that door and see what was back there. A blank canvas, and a perfect platform for a new novel. She had a great job with interesting co-workers and a good boss. Why not use her (and them) for my next idea?

All I knew when I started this book was that I wanted to mess around with an AI computer. That was it. And I had no idea what I was doing. AI has been very popular in the news lately, what with ChatGPT coming up with entire transcripts and essays for people. And of course, there has always been the worry that an artificial intelligence could quickly get too full of itself, get out of hand, and take over the world. While I knew I wanted my AI to get a little bigger than its britches, I surely did not want it to take over the world. I'm not ready to write that book yet. Call it lack of confidence. I'm not sure if it could be a lack of experience. After having finished seven novels, I'm getting to know my way around writing. But maybe it is. I know I will never write as many as King or Sandford, but nor am I about to call it quits. I'm having a blast.

Having these internal doubts though, unsure whether I was a good enough writer to tackle a world-sized hostile AI takeover, made me unsure whether I could even write a book about AI *at all*. What the heck would I do with it? I figured she would just start by talking to it, playing around in her free time, and experimenting herself. I'll let *Shawn* tell me what happens in that room, in other words. That's how I've always done it before. I wrote in boundaries like a Faraday Cage not just to protect the world from a rogue AI, but to protect me from having to write that escape. Call me scared. Intimidated is another good word.

But that was literally all I knew when I wrote the first words. None of the rest of the story had shown itself to me in any manner. So I hope you enjoy this work. I am proud of it, because in the end, things did come together. It seemed to be all over the place while I was writing it, and I had no idea what was going to happen. But – again – Shawn was in control, at least with a little help from her friends.

The other, and perhaps the more important reason I am writing this foreword is to say that I think it is of vital importance that readers have finished *A Flutter in the Window* first. This book is largely dependent on that one in a lot of ways. Familiarity with the office, the coworkers, her living situation… the list is long. I don't know if this comes from laziness in not wanting to explain it all again, or just because I know it so well from the other book that I simply don't *think about* the need to explain it all. But the biggest reason is spoilers. This book is full of them. This book will certainly and completely spoil your potential for enjoying *Flutter*.

I'm not certain how much it would matter if you read *Red Bell* before *Into the Darkness*. You might be a little lost as to why Callie was flying to Fiji, but I think you could get through it. But in the case of this book and *Flutter*, it's completely necessary. This book is a dependent sequel.

Thank you for taking the time to read this. I depend largely on word of mouth for my books' popularity, so I would appreciate reviews on whatever platform you prefer, if you can manage it. I hope you enjoy this book, coming from a man who very much enjoyed writing it.

-brandon spacey
25 June 2023

"I'm calling you from the mooooon," Shawn said and giggled.

Cory looked up from his phone. The voice he had heard had not been his girlfriend's. When he saw what she was doing, he sighed and raised an eyebrow. It wasn't quite a look of bemusement. Shawn knew he would tolerate a lot more before it got to that. She had discovered the app thirty minutes ago, and in that time had laughed so much she was wheezing. Every time she said something into the phone, it would spit it back out in a freakish alien voice, and she would lean back giggling and snorting.

She sat Indian-style on the bed while Cory lay on his back. Shawn keyed the app again and waited for the straight line to turn wavy. When it did, she held it up to her mouth. "Take me to ya leada!" she said and threw her head back laughing again as it changed her voice.

Cory rolled his eyes, shaking his head. No, that wasn't bemusement; it was love. The thin smile he wore meant he was indeed amused - albeit at the lowest end of the spectrum. Shawn knew he adored her fits of childishness.

"So I guess ya leada is unavailable. No. No, he's brain-dead!" she said, and Cory actually chuckled. It wasn't necessarily her goal to make him laugh. She was more interested in making herself laugh. He could get in on it or not. She was having a blast.

It was these stupid little apps that changed your voice. Or put dog noses on your face. These were the things that made her giggle the most. She was such a high-tech gal that all that should have been beneath her. But here she was. Even full-on computer geeks needed something light to look at occasionally. Something to break the monotony of all the cutting edge to which they were constantly exposed.

This app changed her voice into something alienesque, and she was loving it. But more, she loved that Cory allowed her these breaks from reality. Shawn knew that Cory knew she would get tired of the app in a little while, then delete it and move on. But he never criticized her for having fun.

"I'm about to invade ya planet!" she said, and the phone made her voice sound like something out of a bad space opera film. She laughed again, rocking back and forth on the bed.

Her eyes darted to the left to look at him as Cory finally replied, "Then you've come to the wrong planet, bitch! You're about to get your ass invaded!"

Shawn laughed even harder and wiggled in her place. Cory had told her many times that these were his favorite times with her: no makeup, no clothes, no false fronts – just a plain white tank top and her panties. She could be real here with him. Be herself. And he thought she was the most beautiful and down-to-earth woman he had ever seen. Current situation notwithstanding.

"We've got you covered, dumb earthlings! Give yourself up!" she said through the voice-changer, then fell backwards laughing when she heard the alien voice repeat her. After a few seconds, her feet popped out from under her and shot up into the air before falling over on the bed.

Cory dropped his phone, judging this was finally the right time to launch the attack he had been planning. This was it. She was on her side, laughing herself to death from the hilarity of her own jokes, so the tickling was easy. He grabbed her by the waist and all she could do was squirm and jiggle with her eyes closed, out of breath from the raucous laughter. She couldn't even fight back.

Her phone finally dropped from her hand and slid off the bed, making a loud and hollow thunk on the carpet. It was likely loud enough to startle the neighbors below them.

Shawn finally gave in, crying, "Okay! Calf rope! Stop, stop, stop!" and Cory finally relented, quickly changing gears from tickling her all over, to kissing her all over. Her hands found his face and her laughter finally began to settle as she returned his kisses. And then the phone rang.

She let it ring.

Cory's mouth finally settled on Shawn's and the real kissing began. The real love. He rolled on top of her and she wrapped her thighs around him, putting her hands in his hair. The phone continued ringing.

Her eyes finally opened and she saw Cory's had as well. They acknowledged each other at an incredibly close distance, only smiles away from each other. But the view was clear enough to see that he was thinking the same thing she was: *shouldn't the voice mail have picked up by now?*

Shawn finally pushed forward, finishing off her kiss and sighed loudly. The sigh ended as more of a grunt, then turned to full swearing. "Okay, okay. What the fuck?" she said, rolling over to find her phone on the floor. Cory rolled off of her, mumbling his own swears. Shawn was more than just a little frustrated. She could feel the effects of their stunted engagement in places she didn't show off.

"Hello?" she finally said, slapping her free hand against her forehead and closing her eyes. She had tapped the speaker icon.

An unfamiliar voice tinned through the phone speaker. "I have delivered the pictures you requested. Consider our agreement fulfilled."

"What pic-" Shawn started, then opened her eyes and leaned up onto an elbow to look at the phone screen – a frown creasing her brow. "Who is this? What fucking pictures?" But the other party dropped. The call ended, and she tossed her phone to the other side of the bed, falling back and staring at the ceiling. "Why?" she asked, her arm flailing to find Cory, but Cory had gotten up when she answered the phone. He was now in the bathroom. She shook her head and rubbed her eyes, then finally sat up. Then to no one, "Way to ruin a moment, asshole."

PART ONE

Chapter 1

The next call came in just after noon. It was her boss, Sameer, telling her one of her top clients had called in with an emergency request. Shawn frowned at this, since all her clients had her personal cell number, and shouldn't be bothering Sameer. Especially on a weekend. Sameer owned BlueBird Innovation, a small tech company that provided support services for dedicated clients. Shawn ran a small team that took phone calls from these clients regarding e-commerce coding, web app development and basic server administration. BlueBird filled the gap for companies who had hosting elsewhere but didn't have a support contract with the hosting provider, or an in-house code junkie. She had only gotten the promotion in January, about ten months before, when she had excused herself from working on the other project Sameer had invited her to help him with.

When she took on the extra project, which had been classified to the point where she'd had to sign NDAs over it, Sameer had effectively doubled her salary. So when she dropped out of it after only five months, rather than slashing her salary, he had just allowed her to expand her department and hire two support techs. This gave her the opportunity to shine as a manager, and also exercise her inner salesman a little, and try to get a few more clients. She had done this with a swift ease that had made her look like a professional.

The trick of it was that Sameer didn't need the company to grow to a humongous size. The support side of the company was all just a front for his secret projects. Like the one she had tried for almost half a year before nearly being driven to the loony bin. Sameer was somewhat independently wealthy, but having a company that funded his dreams was the whole reason he started BlueBird. When Shawn had moved here two years ago, it was on a leap of faith that the job would pan out and she would be a good fit. When she actually got to meet Sameer and start working with him, she realized pretty quickly she would never be going anywhere else. This would be the company from which she would retire.

Her father had sounded skeptical when she had said those very words to him. But it wasn't hard to see when you put all the cards on the table, that she was playing with an insanely good hand. If she wanted to hire more people, all she had to do was grow her little portion of the company by enough to pay their salaries. Chandra Casper, their finance guru, took care of all the back-end transactions that made that happen. When Shawn wanted to refurnish her office, her boss didn't ask questions. It all came from the money she brought into the company. Her boss was the most patient and understanding man she had ever met. Well, besides her daddy.

These secret projects all took place in a hidden part of the building's fourth floor. There were two sides to the floor: the one people coming off the elevators would see – even though there were badge readers preventing public entry into the offices – and the one they didn't see, which was behind the elevator bank. An unremarkable steel door stood to the left of the elevators, and usually went unnoticed entirely. Even Shawn hadn't really paid attention to it for the first six months she had worked for BlueBird. Things ignored just disappeared.

If one had the proper badge access, that steel door opened onto a series of rooms that ran from floor to hip-height with regular walls, and from there to the ceiling with glass. The rooms were all separated by a wide corridor, and were usually unlit unless they were occupied. In her five months in the secret project, Shawn had only ever been in two or three of them. Room D, where most of the action took place, Room C, which was basically a supply room, and maybe one other. They each had different configurations and uses, and some had not even been completely fleshed out yet. Others were setup and operational, but did not involve Shawn Stedwin. She didn't ask, and Sameer didn't tell. Shawn liked to only concern herself with things that were her business. All in all, there were twelve glass-walled rooms in this half of the building, and the building's outside windows were blacked out. But these twelve rooms only took up half of the hidden half of the floor. Behind the back wall of the row of six rooms farthest from the elevator was the other half, presumably unfinished floor space, and Shawn had never been back there. That was where Sameer was working today, and had asked Shawn to find him when she came in.

"Okay. I'll be there in a few," she had said. Shawn went into the spare-bedroom office to tell Cory she was leaving for a bit. Well, she called it a music room. Her half of the room had the stereo and record collection her late friend Laura's parents had given her when Laura died last year. Cory's half was an office. He had his desk in there and he was playing some video game. *Call of Honor* or something. Shawn had never cared enough to pay much attention. All she knew was that it made him happy, and he stayed in touch with friends like that. They cursed each other out and shot each other with high-powered rifles in some of the most realistic graphics she had ever seen, and that was supposed to be fun. Whatever.

They had moved into the new place together when their respective leases had run out about a year ago. The nice thing about the new apartment, besides the extra bedroom, was that it was actually closer to work than the other had been. Just a straight shot down Arkansas Lane. And since she went east to work and west to get home, she was actually going against the rush hour, which was really nice. Living in the old apartment, what should have been a ten-minute drive could sometimes turn in to forty minutes if the lights weren't kind that day. But not here. From these apartments it was around seven minutes, even if she caught a bad light. And don't forget the view of Lake Arlington off her back balcony.

She came out of the office and checked her face in the mirror in the den. Next to the mirror was her favorite photograph on the planet: a twenty-by-sixteen portrait of her friend Lo and her sitting on Shawn's new motorcycle. The picture captured Shawn's laugh, which told the true measure of her happiness at that moment. Less than three hours later, Lo would be dead, and that happiness gone forever. Whatever she did in life, Shawn doubted she would ever find another friend like Lo. The photograph caught Lo grinning a mischievous little number that captured her true everyday essence as well. Shawn looked at this picture every day.

She slipped on her boots and grabbed her helmet, then jogged down the stairs to the garage where they kept their motorcycles. She preferred taking the stairs over the elevator. This was a nice apartment complex – a lot nicer than the ones they had lived in before they moved in together – but the elevators sucked royally. It took longer to stand there and wait for a car and ride it down than it did just to run down both flights of stairs. Or up. Shawn had once pressed the call button, then got tired of waiting, and ran all the way down the stairs before realizing she had forgotten her phone. She had then run all the way back up, gone into her apartment and gotten the phone, then had come out the door to hear the elevator ding and open. Dear God. So yeah, she took the stairs.

When she got to the BlueBird building, she took the service elevator to the fourth floor, as it dropped her into the anteroom attached to the private side of the floor. The only people in the building who could get the service car to even stop on this floor were Sameer, Shawn, Chandra and Jeremy.

The door dinged and opened and she stepped through the service area and badged her way into the secret side of the floor. The door opened on the south end of the corridor that ran between the two rows of glass rooms. Halfway down the aisle, between C Room and D Room was another of those unassuming steel doors. It, like the one in the main elevator bank, had disappeared for Shawn many moons ago. Well, apparently she could stop ignoring it now. She approached it, noting that it had no enhanced security about it. No badge reader or keypad. Just a stainless steel handle. She guessed Sameer figured anyone who had access to the lab – their pet name for this hidden half of the floor – would be important enough to allow access to whatever was back here as well.

Shawn turned the handle and pushed the door open. She was nearly blinded by all the sunlight coming in through the building's outer windows. She gasped and a smile found her face. *What a relief! Natural sunlight!* "Wow!" she whispered as she looked around. The view as pretty wonderful as far as she could see from where she stood now. There weren't many tall buildings in Arlington, so this fifteen-story tower was one of the taller ones on Arkansas Lane. All the skyscrapers were to the west in Fort Worth, and in Dallas, to the east.

As she instinctively turned toward the north and began moving toward the windows, Sameer appeared from behind the only real feature on this side of the wall that separated them from the lab. A square box of a room maybe fifteen feet on a side stood directly in the center of the unfinished floor space. This quarter of the building's fourth floor was probably a hundred feet from north window to south, and a hundred and fifty wide. But with nothing else in it besides the singular room in the middle, it was full of the afternoon daylight, and it was wonderful.

Shawn was smiling as they met in the middle of the floor. "Wow, Sameer, this is so nice back here!"

"Yes. I have enjoyed coming in here many times."

She stood there with her arms crossed, watching as he wiped his hands on a cloth. Then he took a deep breath. "I'm sorry to have to call you on a weekend,

Shawn. But PanaView called the hot-line this morning."

Shawn instinctively grabbed the phone out of her pocket as she shook her head, as if the prop would help her explain what Sameer already knew. "Why didn't they just call me directly?"

Sameer was shaking his head though, holding his palms out toward her. "It's okay, Shawn. It was an error on the phone tree. I had to reset the software and I had forgotten to put your number back into the call pattern."

Shawn raised her chin. "Okay, so what's up?" Shawn asked, feeling a little better. The clients were instructed to call the main hot-line number, which would route them to the on-call technician on the weekends. She did feel a little slighted that her favorite client had not tried her cell, but they were following the protocol.

"I am thinking the satellite is down," said Sameer.

"That would be odd," she said, frowning. "What's that?" She added, pointing at the box of a room behind him.

Sameer turned and looked at it as if to remind himself what was there. Then he pointed at it with the tip of his pen. "This, Shawn, is the room in which I will be working for the rest of the weekend. I am building you a computer in there."

Shawn smiled, then frowned, then did both at the same time. She didn't know whether he was joking or not, and he could read it on her face. "Are you…" she started, hoping he would cut her off. He didn't. "Uh, are you serious?"

"Yes, Shawn. It will be an AI computer. Just for you to be fooling around with. I thought you might enjoy to come over here sometimes and mess around with it. See how smart you can make it," said Sameer.

"Wow, that sounds really cool. Thank you, Sameer!" she said. Now she was smiling without the frown, and the curiosity was about to get the best of her. She wanted to see inside the room. He held his hand up when she attempted to step in that direction though.

"You may go in there Monday when you come to work. It will be done by then. But I want it to surprise you."

They were walking back to his office, pushing through doors and dodging columns as Shawn tried to stay even with him as he walked. He was telling her about the obstacles he had encountered in assembling the computer so far, and Shawn was actually interested in hearing about it, but he was talking so fast she couldn't keep up. When they finally got to his office, the air conditioner felt good to her sweaty forehead. She waited for Sameer to take his seat before dropping into the chair across the desk from him. Shawn sighed as she sat down and Sameer noticed the sheen on her forehead.

"That room is a Faraday cage," he said.

Shawn frowned and instinctively looked back over her shoulder toward where the room lay hidden a hundred meters or more away. "Huh? Why?"

"Because, Shawn. There are also no Ethernet ports. No other power outlets. The room is on its own power circuit, though I even still worry about that."

Shawn furrowed her brow in concentration for a moment, staring at her hands, which lay intertwined on her knees. And then she put together some of the words she thought she had missed on their walk to his office. The words *artificial intelligence* came floating back to the surface. It finally made sense: Sameer was worried it would escape the computer it was on. She shook her head and looked up at him.

"Sameer, how powerful are you thinking this thing will get?" Shawn asked, already feeling a little concerned, herself. What little she knew about AIs had never given her cause for worry before. What was the big deal?

"The job of any good artificial intelligence," said Sameer, "is to learn. To improve itself. To get better and smarter. If you give it a task, it will literally do everything it knows how to do to improve its efficiency at the task you have given it."

"Yeah, but it's a computer," Shawn said, holding a hand out toward that unseeable place she had tried to look for a moment ago. "It's not like it's going to have robotic arms or anything connected to it. Right? I mean…" She scoffed. *Am I overreacting here?*

"Shawn, I think you are missing the point. We cannot give it a way to spread itself outside the room. I am wanting to see how smart we can make the machine, but I do not want it to get out of hand. This is just for fun. And I thought you might enjoy to have a little fun with this project."

Shawn was staring at him with her mouth hanging open. "Me?" she said, then shook her head again. She put her hand against her chest. "Are you being serious right now, Sameer? I'm not sure how to read you here."

He stared at her.

"Okay, look. I'm confused. First of all, you called me in here because my biggest client has a satellite down. Or at least the server... Anyway, then you mention AI, and that you're building it inside a Faraday cage... But you want me to have a little fun with it?"

"Shawn, I do not want to sound insulting, but it is seeming that you perhaps have not done very much research on AI."

The smile dropped from her face. She shook her head. "Well, you're right about that. But you're scaring me here. I was talking more about my client. Should that not take priority?"

Sameer breathed in deeply then blew out slowly. "Okay. I thought you might appreciate having something new to work on. Consider it like a little gift to show my appreciation for your work with me. Something to have a little fun with. Do not take it too seriously."

Her eyes were still wide. Still shaking her head. *But...?*

"But at the same time, do not take too lightly the power of a good AI. Even if you are only having fun with it, the AI is not programmed to understand that you are only meaning to have fun. Does this make sense, Shawn?"

She shrugged. "I guess. I just don't..."

"No matter the reason, or your level of interest in such things, it still has a mind of its own, by definition. It is like playing with a tiger, Shawn. Your intention is to have fun. But the tiger is capable of its own thinking. And it will do what tigers do."

"You're really scaring me here, Sameer," she said.

Sameer stood up and put his hands in his pockets. He actually stood up so quickly that it startled Shawn. Clearly, he was getting a little impatient with the direction the conversation was going. Like it wasn't getting anywhere, at least in his mind. He twisted bodily, like he was about to walk out from behind his desk, then he turned back and put his palms on his blotter. He took a deep breath and then looked up at Shawn through the tops of his eyes.

"Listen. Please, Shawn. I am not wanting you to be afraid of anything. I wanted to give you a new toy to play with. I just want you to know it can pull your hair out if you get it too close to your head."

Shawn leaned back, lifting her chin. That had hit. That had sunk in. She felt herself beginning to nod. Then Sameer stood up straight and ran his hand through his thinning hair. Maybe he was realizing he had just almost overreacted. He said, "The best toys in life can hurt you. They are not fun if there is no danger involved. Just please be careful."

She stared at him, still nodding. "Yeah. Okay, Sameer. I got it."

After staring at each other for what seemed like a minute, Shawn nodded again. "So… My client?"

Now at her desk, Shawn was trying to get into the satellite-based server 22,000 miles above her head. PanaView was her only client to have a satellite in orbit, but she handled it the same exact way she did all her other clients' systems. They either existed as web-based code or code and syntax on servers. This one just happened to be a system on a geosynchronous orbit somewhere along Arizona's longitude. Accessing it felt just like accessing a regular earth-bound server.

Shawn had tried calling Darla Hope, her contact at PanaView, but it had gone to voice mail. While she waited for a return call, Shawn thought she would see if she could figure out what 'down' meant. Most likely, the satellite itself wasn't down. The server seemed to be, because she couldn't get it to respond to ping commands. Being a Unix server, there wasn't a graphical user interface, and every time she tried to get into it directly, the login would die of old age. That's what Jeremy and she called it when a command froze on the screen without response. After a few quick attempts, Shawn realized what Darla had meant by 'down'. She couldn't get into the server. And Shawn couldn't either. *Strange.*

She tried to get in with root access to reset her credentials, but that wasn't working either. After spending a good solid fifteen minutes on it, Shawn pushed back from her desk and stood up. She had one more option left open to her, and that was to connect to the Remote Power Center, which gave her ethernet control of the power outlet into which the server was plugged. She could turn off the power to that outlet thereby physically shutting the server down hard. But bouncing a server was not something she would do without approval from the client. For all Shawn knew, it *was* still serving. That is, still performing the function it was supposed to perform – whether or not they could get in. She didn't have the clearance to actually test whether it was serving. That would involve logging into an access-controlled client portal. She had only ever accessed that while on the phone with Darla. But power-cycling the server was no guarantee to resolve the lockout either. She would simply have to wait.

People did that sometimes. Young gunslingers at tech companies who thought they knew what they were doing would get on and reset the root or admin passwords, locking out the people who really needed to get in. "Oh well," she said, and locked her terminal.

She grabbed her keys and helmet and made her way back to the lab to say bye to Sameer.

When Shawn came to the door of The Box, Sameer was standing with his back to her, leaning on his fists on the desk. She hadn't meant to sneak up on him to see inside the room, but the door had been propped open and there it was in all its lackluster glory. The computer was open on its side on the desk, components strewn about as if he was trying to decide what to put in first.

"Adding more memory, Sameer?" she said. He turned to look at her.

"Why? Are you thinking 128 gigs is not enough?" Sameer said, frowning.

"Dear God," Shawn said, frowning. "No, I think that's plenty."

He stared a moment longer, not getting the joke. "Were you able to be solving Ms. Hope's problem?"

"No, she didn't answer. I can't get in. Looks like someone reset root, or, and this might be more likely, the server is actually hard down."

"Ah, I see," Sameer said, standing up straight. "Thank you for coming in, Shawn. Please let me know if I can help you."

"Yeah, sure," Shawn said, smiling. She swung the helmet lightly against her thigh. "Do you need anything else from me?"

"No, Shawn. Go home. Enjoy your Saturday."

She had been with Cory for about two years, though Shawn liked to count all the way back to the day she met him, when she was moving into the apartment, carrying that potted plant up the stairs. He had taken it from her and they started talking. And that was that. Did it not begin at that initial meeting?

What they had was rare, and she knew it. Like the fact that they had never had a single argument. Things like that were rare, but not impossible. Weirder shit happened all the time. Like the monk who had lived eighty-three years and never seen a woman. His mother died during his birth, he was taken to the monastery and raised by men, thus living his entire life without seeing a woman. Shawn knew these things were possible. Likely, everything had happened at some point: someone had been eaten by a snake; someone had met a girl named Tuesday who didn't end up being the definition of someone who wanted to be named Tuesday; somewhere there must surely be a man who drove one of those little convertible Mercedes two-seaters who *wasn't* a douche bag. Maybe every other couple in the history of the planet had argued, but not Shawn and Cory. And at this point, she would not be surprised if they kept that truth for the next forty years.

Was that to say that she intended to marry him? Well, duh. If he asked, she would say yes. Without hesitating a single second, she would say yes. She gathered that some men spent many hours thinking about how they would propose – trying to come up with the most unique and romantic way to ask a girl to marry him – but what about the women? Did anyone sit around and dream up what she would do if she were proposed to? Well, Shawn did, and she had the perfect response planned: if Cory asked her, she would shrug and sigh and look away for a second. Maybe pull up on her belt loops and look uninterested, then say, 'Yeah, I think that probably makes the most sense.'

Of course in the seconds following that, she would fall onto him, covering his face with kisses and tears while she told him how elated and excited she was. But, at first? She would play it cool. Of course, she also knew it probably wouldn't really go down like that. She would be so surprised and excited and overwhelmed with emotion that she would be unable to do anything other than covering her mouth – immediately crying – and saying yes repeatedly. *Whatever*. She could dream. No one was as cool to Shawn as the girl Shawn thought she could be in her own mind. *Like a girl named Tuesday.*

As she dashed up the stairs, taking them two at a time, Shawn felt the beginning of her downhill slope. She was now thirty-one years old. And while everyone she had ever met would call that young, she could tell the difference between these stairs and the stairs that used to exist back in the olden days when she was twenty-nine. There were new aches in her thighs and she seemed to run out of breath a lot more easily these days. Thirty-one. What would forty look like?

Shawn came in the front door shrugging off her coat and went straight into the office where Cory was still playing *Modern Duty* or whatever the hell it was called. She came up behind him and put her hands on his shoulders, completely *un*worried about startling. She had long ago learned that he had a sixth sense for people coming up behind him while he was gaming.

"Hey, babe," he said, not looking away from the action. His character was in some dark building, going quickly around corners and pointing his gun into places where people might supposedly be hiding.

"Hey. Whenever you're dead, I would love to talk to you," Shawn said.

"You got it," Cory replied. "Give me about ten minutes and I'll be done with this tournament."

Ten minutes was an eternity. Oh, the glorious opportunity that offered her! She could take a bath! Or at least a shower. Or she could read. She made her way into the living room and up to the bar where she pulled the cork out of a bottle of rum and poured herself a tall glass. She pulled the lid off the steel canister where she habitually kept ice and found nothing but water. She made a frowny face and went round the end of the counter and into the kitchen to get some ice from the freezer. She dropped a handful of moons into her glass and took it out onto the balcony where her Favorite Chair in the World awaited her. And here, she would await her Favorite Man in the World.

Chapter 2

"It's not that I won't be here," said Shawn. She had turned one of the unused rooms in the BlueBird offices into a conference room and bought a bunch of big square pillows and a few bean bags for her Monday-morning meetings. The idea behind it was to make everyone feel relaxed, but also to illustrate in a practical way that the meetings were intended to be kept short. Constance and Lance, her two support techs, looked at her with the same expression of confusion and wonder. But their postures told completely different stories. Constance, her red-brown hair pulled back into a sleek ponytail, sat bolt upright with her legs crossed under her, Indian-style with a tablet on her lap. Lance's posture was the absence of it entirely. He lay on his side, his elbow propping him up on the large pillow and his messy hair hanging over his knuckles.

"Listen, guys. It's time you need to know about this. I've not told you before because you've not needed to know. And I'm not sure you do now, but that you might wonder where I disappear to throughout the week." Shawn looked at both of them. They both stared back expectantly. Lance jerked his head back, moving his shaggy brown hair away from his eyes. He was unrefined in a way that spoke of attention to his style rather than ignorance. Shawn liked the rugged effect, but thought he would probably grow into something more sophisticated when he got a little older. He was only a few years younger than Shawn.

She sighed and leaned back on her hands. "This isn't strictly confidential, but it's private. It's not something you should share with a bunch of people. BlueBird has the lease on the entire fourth floor," Shawn said. Lance looked around the small conference room as if to see the entire floor plan from his vantage point. He looked back frowning. Constance's eyebrows raised slightly and she raised her chin.

"I always wondered why we never saw anyone else coming out of the elevators on the fourth floor," she said.

Lance's response, again spoke of a completely different perception of the world around them. "You mean there's more than this?"

Constance giggled. Shawn smiled at it. Her laughter was contagious. "You've never noticed that the elevators are in the middle of the building when you come in the lobby downstairs?"

He shook his head and sighed. "Never paid attention. Anyway, where is the other part of the floor?" he asked.

"On the other side of the elevator bank. Duh," Constance said, looking at him with a half-smile.

He rolled his hand over, flipping her the bird.

"Yes. There's a whole other set of rooms over there. Anyway, I will be spending about half of my time over there in the coming weeks. Months. Whatever. Sameer has a project for me over there."

"Why over there? What's the difference?" Lance said. He was still frowning. "I mean, why can't you just move it over here?"

Constance, still smiling, rolled her eyes at the ceiling.

"Because it's for the other side of the company, Lance," Shawn said. "Meaning it's classified work." Shawn knew this wasn't strictly the truth, but she had not cleared with Sameer yet how private it was supposed to be. But with the project being confined to the Box, one had to have a special badge just to *get* there, so there was no point in talking about what she was doing. Inevitably one of them would get interested and want to come take a look. And until Sameer cleared them for access to the Lab area, it was just better to keep them in the dark. *My little mushrooms*, Shawn thought and smiled.

She had scheduled a meeting with Sameer to discuss such details, but that would happen later on this morning. For now, she would proceed as she saw best. "I don't know what schedule I'm going to take yet, but it will literally be about half my time. I will not be available by phone or text or anything while I'm over there. So if you need me you will have to get Jeremy or Chandra to come get me," Shawn said.

Constance was nodding, looking down at her fingernails. Lance was looking at Shawn with suspicious eyes like he had a hundred more questions. But he remained silent.

"What you thinkin' 'bout?" Shawn asked him.

He shook his head. "Nothing. No big deal. Obviously I'm gonna try to analyze what you're telling me. I figure you'll share what you can. I don't want to start tin-foil-hatting it."

Shawn nodded. "Good idea. It's nothing earth-shattering," she said. And the thought that flashed across her mind in the wake of her saying it was tinged with a little fear. She hoped to God that statement would remain true.

Shawn sat at her desk with her chin in her hand as she read the specs and details of several of a class of customizable freeware AI models. She had never considered it was so easy to dive into something that seemed so serious. If they were so readily available, and yet so potentially dangerous, as Sameer had said, didn't that mean someone out there was probably about to take over the world with one? Play *Lawnmower Man* and make every phone in the world ring simultaneously? She realized she had a lot to learn about the basics, but was anxious to get started on it – to make her first '*Hello, World!*' with something artificially intelligent.

She had spent the first hour at her desk searching a tech retailer for the right keyboard, mouse and monitor combination. Historically all her computers had come with input devices, and she had always just taken what came. Shawn had no idea there was such a wide range of them available. It was like the cereal aisle at a grocery store: a hundred thousand billion different brands, box sizes, flavors and options. Just for a keyboard! Jeremy had leaned into her office at one point asking how she was doing. Shawn was staring, mouth agape at her monitor, shaking her head and he asked what was so funny. "Did you know you can order a Bluetooth keyboard that's basically a typewriter?" she said, pointing at her screen.

Jeremy shook his head. "I believe it. To each his own, right?"

"This is insane!" she had said. "I thought this would be the easy part."

Getting the right mouse was another obstacle. There were mice that had buttons on the thumb side, buttons on the pinky side, a clicking scroll wheel, scroll speed switches, red lasers, clear lasers, wired, wireless and WiFi… What the hell would someone need with a WiFi-connected mouse? Shawn was floored. In the end, she settled for a simple two-button model with a scroll wheel, figuring most of her interactions with the computer would be through ASCII.

Then there came the monitor. Should she get a curved screen? How big? How much graphical content would she be getting back from her new project? There were some with cameras built in, some with speakers, some with USB hubs on the back and even some that allowed television picture-in-picture while you played games. What in the hell. After a major tired-head search for the right model, she finally just selected one and added it to her cart. At this point, she couldn't keep up with the five or six features she knew she was looking out for. Flat – not curved – and medium sized, with no USB ports but with speakers included… There was just too much. She knew she probably had forgotten one feature or accidentally added another. Whatever. It was a screen. Who cared?

But with all the peripherals on order, her full attention was now on the AI. Shawn had read the white papers on two separate systems so far. The biggest difference she could find was the method by which the administrator could install and remove different interfaces. Being a beginner in the artificial intelligence realm, Shawn was looking for the easiest platform on which to get started. She didn't think it would matter too much where the intelligence was born, if the end result was essentially the same. And if she had any questions, the damn thing should be able to answer them for her, shouldn't it?

When she had read everything her mind could absorb for one day, she downloaded the platform that appealed most to her beginner's experience level, and sent it over to a thumb drive. The package was surprisingly small, only a few gigabytes – and that was mostly installable options. The base platform was only a small portion of that. She took comfort in knowing that if she screwed anything up too badly she could just wipe the drive and start over. And all of these software platforms were freeware and open-source, too. So there was no fiscal penalty for screwing up. What could go wrong?

There was no point in showing her face in the Box until she was ready to give it several full hours of her undivided attention. She did need to get a rolling chair and maybe a couch. Sameer had told her to decorate however she saw fit. And when she had questioned this later, asking what he meant, he had listed off potential things that she might want – as people do. *'Oh, you could put a couch in there, a table, a cozy chair. You know, whatever.'* And Shawn had stopped, turning to look at him. "Why the heck would I want a couch?"

Sameer had stopped a few steps ahead of her and turned back to look at her. "Shawn, the idea is hopefully to get it to a state where you make all your interactions with voice. You will talk to it."

She stared dumbly at him, still not making the connection. He had finally smiled and stepped forward, taking her by the shoulders. "Shawn, you will not have to sit at an uncomfortable office chair when this happens. You can sit on a couch or something, even across the room if you want."

Shawn had shaken her head and then followed as he carried on. "Boy, I have a lot to learn about AIs, Sameer."

Cory Klein was not like anyone Shawn had ever met. This wasn't her rose-colored glasses. Her perceptions of him were not based on her intense infatuation with him, either. At least not entirely. She had recognized his uniqueness within a few minutes of meeting him during their first conversation. He was a gentleman, but that wasn't unique. What *was* unique about it was that he went out of his way to be that way with everyone with whom he had contact. Even strangers. He was the kind of guy who would pull over and help an old woman change her tire on the side of the highway. Or a young man. Shawn had actually watched Cory get on his hands and knees in the mud to hook his tow rope under the front of someone's car when a woman had tried to cut through the ditch to avoid a backup on the highway. And Cory had been wearing his khakis and nice shoes. Shawn had never known a man to be *that* much of a gentleman.

The other thing that set him apart in Shawn's mind was the intensity with which he listened to her. Or anyone, really, but it mattered most when it was her. He would put down whatever he was doing to make sure and give her his full attention. And his responses were never rushed or thoughtless, banal and light. He always took the time to respond with real answers, deep and thoughtful responses that showed a level of concern for whatever the subject was. This made her feel so special – so important – that she believed it might have been one of the main reasons she had fallen so hard for him, and so quickly.

It might have been his thoughtful attention and kind reproach that saved her from complete insanity when she came walking in the door that evening. She had worked herself up on the way home, conspiracy theories and worries and fear all mixing together to form a wall she didn't see any way to surmount. Sameer had given her a project just to play with. But apparently not to be involved in himself. Why would that be? Would he not be interested in the outcome at all? Surely he would be popping in to observe occasionally. But the way he had said it was it was all for her. He did not have an end-goal for her. No checklist of things he wanted to see the AI perform. Could it truly be that he just wanted Shawn to have something to play with? No ulterior motives?

Shawn knew Sameer had secrets he would never share with her. Probably everyone in her life did. On the last project she had worked with him, there had been a major discovery at the end. Shawn had pieced together a mystery and discovered a secret Sameer would never have shared with her unsolicited. Talk about earth-shattering. Of course her discovery didn't mean she had to be involved with it. But when it came to something she was going to be spending her time on – and a lot of time at that – she felt like she had the right to know everything she needed to know going in. And that, to her, included the reasons for his magnanimous gesture. He had constructed an entire room for this project. There *had* to be more to it than just a playground for an employee appreciation gift.

The science behind artificial intelligence and everything that came with it was foreign to her as well. Maybe that was why she was the perfect candidate for building this out, in Sameer's mind. It just seemed a little clunky in its presentation. Like giving a toddler a very expensive piece of lab equipment he could never use and never understand. It seemed perhaps a little wasteful to Shawn. It's not that she was ungrateful for it, but she had no real interest in AI coming into this. So why her?

Cory calmly listened to all her reasoning sitting on the ottoman with his elbows on his knees and gently touching her leg while she talked. He had asked that she sit still on the couch and not pace, as she was generally apt to do, but he let her raise her voice and talk with her hands as much as she needed. "All you can do is accept it at face-value, Shawn," he finally said. "That's all you can do. Or you can decline to take it on. But I don't see you doing that. And you could have some real fun with this!"

"Yeah, but what if it ends up being for some sinister plot he has to take over the world?"

"Shawn. Stop," Cory said calmly. "Look at me."

Shawn took a deep breath and put her hands down, looked at him and nodded.

"Good. Listen. What became of the last sinister thing you learned about him?"

She made a face like she was about to have an angry outburst at her boyfriend. Cory held up a hand, closed his eyes. "Think about it, Shawn. Did it end up being evil? Or even for bad reasons?"

It took her a long time to come back to reality and answer the question – even to herself. She had to consider the angles. Again. She had gone through this many times, all the way back to the time when she had first unraveled the mystery. But it was still a shock to think about. She had to calm herself again. But when she did, she looked up at him and nodded subtly. "Yeah, I guess not."

"See? He does some weird shit, I'll give you that. But it's not for sinister purposes. He's just a little… unconventional is all. So I'm sure that whatever his intentions are with this AI project are likely the same. Well, not the same," Cory said. "Similar. Well intentioned. I'm sure he's not trying to take over the world. I mean, he did build a room to contain this thing, right? So it can't get out into the world?"

Shawn nodded. Her eyes were glassy. Cory reached forward a little and took her hands together in his. Squeezed them. "Just accept it for face-value, baby. Have some fun with it. Whatever he does with it when you're not around, or when you're done building it or whatever – that's on him. But I wouldn't sit around worrying that you're going to be complicit in anything."

"Yeah, I guess so," Shawn said.

"Good girl. Hey, think of the last thing we talked about. Your last project. He deliberately kept that big secret a big secret so that you *wouldn't* be complicit in anything. Right?"

Shawn found herself nodding. "Thank you for bringing me back to reality, Cory," she said with a sigh. She leaned in to hug him.

He took her in his arms and said, "That's what I'm here for, babe."

Shawn's shipment arrived Wednesday. She got a call from the delivery driver downstairs, as per her special instructions. She met him on the delivery dock and put the boxes on a rolling cart, taking it up the service elevator. She had not wanted it delivered to the main office where her underlings would see it and ask questions. On the way up the elevator, she looked at her phone for the thousandth time. Still no response from the apparently elusive Darla Hope. Shawn had called her again Monday morning and left another voice mail. *Hey, just checking in. I'm still here if you need me. Let me know everything's okay!*

The monitor box was huge. The one she had picked out after so much back and forth was a widescreen, and it was as big as a small TV. It wasn't necessarily her idea that she needed something that big, but the next smallest size was only a few dollars less. She realized that's how people climbed their way up to 75-inch televisions. *'Well, the 60-inch is only twenty dollars more than the 55-inch. And the 70-inch is only a hundred more than that. But if we're spending seven hundred, why not spend eight?'* and so on.

When she got everything into the Box and unloaded it onto the table, she sent the cart back down to the basement level on the service elevator, then came back in to open everything. Shawn had put a few computers together in her life. Her dad called her a computer whiz because she knew how to do things 'guys his age' just couldn't grasp. But those were the simple things. The truth was, the language, the interfaces, the code – it all had just made sense to her from as early as the first time she had ever been exposed to it in a seventh-grade computer programming course. Things she didn't instantly know, she was not afraid to click around and figure out. And Lord knew there was plenty of help available on the internet, in forums and support threads. If she was absolutely stuck, she could reference someone else's work and be back up and moving in short order.

Her understanding of computers had gotten her a pretty good starter position at a tech company right out of high school. And proving her worth there didn't take much time. Within a couple of years she had been promoted to an engineer position, and had finally been able to prove to mom and dad that college wasn't necessarily the answer for everyone.

With everything plugged in and setup, Shawn stood with her hands on her hips and looked over her setup. A medical-looking stainless steel table and a simple rolling chair was the entire setup. She would have to do something about that. She stood the monitor in the middle of the table and slid the computer all the way to the left end, then put the microphone on its stand between the monitor and the keyboard, wondering how soon she would be able to start speaking to the intelligence. With nothing left to do but to do it, she plugged in the thumb drive she'd had in her pocket and turned on the machine. It started with a low hum and ramped up quickly, the roar of all the case fans always a comforting sound to a computer geek. Not as comforting as the old CMOS beep. But they had done away with that long ago. Shawn missed that beep that told her there was hope. She waited while the OS loader was pulled from the flash drive to the computer's memory, which was substantial. Specs like that made any computer girl excited.

A welcome screen popped up that showed an absurdly large blinking cursor move from the left of the screen to the right, replacing blank spaces with the letters that spelled out 'Hello, World!' one beat at a time. Cute. Then the options menu appeared and she scrolled through it. She selected 'Wipe & Install Hello, World OS' and smiled as the screen cleared in another animation that left a smiley face and a small message reading, 'Please wait while OS is installed…'

Well, that was easy. She leaned back in the chair and crossed her arms, wondering what to do while she waited, and how long it would take. Instinctively, she reached into her hip pocket for her phone so she could scroll through OuterCircle – the world-sized social media network – but there was no phone there. She had left it on the little phone shelf outside the door, being an obedient little worker. Were restrictions like that really necessary? At this stage, of course, they weren't. And later, when the computer was smart and wise and responsive, would it really be able to reach out and do anything with her phone? She doubted it. But better to be safe. At least until she was comfortable enough with the rules to know which ones she could break.

After a short time, the computer rebooted to a black screen with a graphical interface in the middle of it, asking her which language she would like to use.

English (US) was highlighted, so she tapped the enter key. The interface then went through a series of questions. What kind of voice would she like the speech engine to use? Would she prefer verbal communication (when available) or typing and text? It also asked her who the primary user would be. And at this point, Shawn wondered whether she should use a nickname or pseudonym.

She went with Marcy. Close enough to a pseudonym for her, since she never went by that name unless her parents were around. When she typed it in and pressed enter, the screen changed and welcomed her by name in a fun font. Shawn had to roll her eyes. *Is this thing going to be cutesy at every flippin' turn?*

She moved the mouse to the 'next' button and was startled by a sudden knock at the door behind her. She called out, "Come in!" and sat there for several more seconds clicking through options before she realized whoever it was had not responded. She rolled across the floor and pulled the door open. It was Jeremy.

"Hey, man," she said, putting her hands on her thighs. She had not stood up in quite some time now and realized her legs were starting to tingle.

"You have a call on your desk phone," said Jeremy. "How's it going in here?" he asked, looking over her shoulder at the monitor.

Shawn looked back to see where things had gotten to, then met his eyes. She shrugged, sighed and stood up all at the same time. "I guess it's okay. This thing is trying to be cute."

Jeremy giggled. "Comic Sans?"

"Ha!" Shawn said out loud, grabbing her phone off the tiny shelf outside the door. "It's not the font that's Comic Sans. It's the installer's personality. Hopefully it grows up a little."

"I thought you liked cute stuff," said Jeremy, his ever-present smile on display as they walked.

"Not when it comes to serious shit," she said, putting a hand on his shoulder.

"This is Shawn," she said as she picked up the receiver and dropped into the office chair.

"Hello, Shawn, it's Darla."

"Hey! It's good to hear from you," Shawn said, scooting up to the desk and shaking her mouse to wake the computer. "Is everything okay?"

"Yes. I'm so sorry. I called Saturday morning because I was on my way out the door to leave town. I didn't think to mention not to worry with calling me back."

"Oh. Well, that's okay. I just wanted to make sure you were up and running."

"Yeah, I'm still not able to get in," said Darla.

Shawn grabbed her headset and dropped the phone receiver back in its cradle. She pulled the headset over her ears and logged into the computer. "Well, I couldn't get in Saturday morning either. I didn't want to bounce the server without your permission, but I think that's our next step."

She heard Darla sigh over the phone. "Yeah, I guess that's necessary."

"I see a green dot on our monitoring system, so it looks like the server is still up. Is it doing what you want it to be doing?"

"No. I don't think so," said Darla.

Shawn tried again to login to the remote server. Again she had no success. "Yeah, I'm still not able to get in. So I can drop it whenever you're ready."

"Yeah, go ahead. Thank you, Shawn."

Shawn entered her admin menu and found the power strip controls. The circular icon that represented that particular RPC was red though. That meant the main server had lost connectivity with the Remote Power Controller of the remote server. *Great.* While Shawn clicked around trying to find if the red dot was real or just hadn't refreshed yet, she asked Darla about her travels and how everything went.

Darla didn't say much, but she didn't sound concerned. About the trip she had just taken, or the server itself. The server, which was powered and controlled a satellite, was the farthest asset away from their physical position that Shawn managed. Its job was to take surveying photographs of particular parts of Arizona and Nevada. What these photos were of and what they were for, were beyond Shawn's knowledge. That was proprietary and classified. But Shawn did know they were high enough resolution that one could literally zoom in close enough to read the registration sticker on a license plate.

As she sat waiting, Shawn glanced at the window she always kept open on the right side of her monitor, wherein she could see all the servers and sites she managed, represented by green dots. When they went down, they were red. The green dot that represented the PanaView server's status was still green, though the power control icon was red. *How in the world?*

After a few more minutes of small-talk, Shawn finally told Darla she would have to call her back. "Darla, I'm sorry, but I'm going to have to refer to more urgent protocols for server retrieval. I can't get my power center to respond, and I don't know by heart how to manage yours, what with its unique location and all."

"I understand. Thank you, Shawn. Just let me know what I can do to help," said Darla.

"You got it. Thanks for your patience," Shawn said, and disconnected, tossing the headset on the desk. She leaned back, putting her hands in her hair. She wasn't quite at the point of grabbing it by the handfuls yet, but she was getting close. The PanaView server had never given her these problems before. And it wasn't like she could just drive to the data center and get her hands on it physically if she needed to. The damn thing was on-board a satellite. And in fact, she wasn't quite sure what to do.

Shawn jabbed the speaker button on her phone and typed in Jeremy's extension. He answered on the first ring. She could hear his voice in mumbles coming through her office door in addition to the amplified version coming through her phone speaker. "What's up, Stedwin?" he asked.

"How do you reckon I can go about rebooting PanaView if I can't hit the power center?"

Jeremy was silent for a moment. Then he said, "Let's go smoke."

"All right," Shawn said, and hung up the phone. She grabbed her jean jacket off the back of her chair and slung it on as she made her way toward the elevators. She herself wasn't a smoker, but knew that Jeremy did some of his best brainstorming when he had a cigarette between his fingers.

The smoking area of the building was just a small rectangle at the end of the parking garage, and didn't have proper walls around it. There was a picnic table and a butt can and that was about it. During the winter months, Shawn had to stand with her hands in her pockets, scarf or collar pulled up around her chin and mouth to join Jeremy for his smoking sessions. The wind would whip through the area like a hurricane. She would never understand the lengths people would go just to smoke cigarettes. But then she had to remind herself that she joined him down there sometimes, and that was even more laughable. The lengths she went to for someone else to smoke cigarettes.

"Why can't we get on, Jeremy?" Shawn asked after he had lit his cigarette.

"So you're saying the power center is offline?" he said, pointing the cherry at her.

Shawn nodded. "Yep. It's the only one in the bunch that's red."

"Yeah. That's telling. I have seen it go green when it's really not, but never the other way. Red means red."

"How is that?" she asked, pulling her shoulders up against a particularly swift gust of wind.

"There's some weird cache artifacts that happen on the home server. It'll show you a live connection when it's not really live. You have to know how to read it."

"Okay," Shawn said, tilting her head at him, "so how do I read it?"

He shook his head. "It's really all about timing. The time-to-live on those pings it sends. It's hard to explain. It's more of a feeling. Well, it's more than a feeling. But not much."

"Wasn't that a Boston song?" Shawn asked.

Jeremy pointed his cigarette at her again. "Yes, it was. Damn fine one, too." He took a drag and then said, "Anyway, I can show you what I'm talking about. But in this case, if it's red, then it's down. I'd bet that whole satellite is offline."

"Why do you say that?" Shawn asked. She was bouncing on her toes now, trying to generate heat. She had only been at the company for a little over two years now, and was sure she had not yet run into all the ins and outs of each client they supported. She had never had trouble connecting to the satellite server before, so it all seemed new now. And the fact that it was a server on a satellite rarely even crossed her mind. It acted and responded just like a regular server, so the thought just never surfaced. But now, it seemed to be relevant.

"Stuff happens in space. You know? Could be anything," Jeremy said.

"Has it gone offline before? The satellite, I mean?" Shawn asked.

"Oh yeah," Jeremy said, nodding for emphasis. "That thing used to go down every few months when they first put it online."

"How the heck do you get a satellite back online? Do they have to fly up there and work on it?" she asked, wondering if he was about to laugh at her naivete. He didn't. He just shook his head, taking another mouthful of smoke.

"Nah. Probably not. They have ways. I don't really know, but they have a satellite technician on staff," he said.

"So weird that they have guys who can admin satellites but they need us for the server," Shawn said, smiling.

"Why?"

She shrugged. "I dunno. Just seems... funny."

Jeremy raised his eyebrows. He dropped the cherry from the cigarette then tossed the butt in the sand can. Thank God. Shawn turned and headed back for the doors to the elevator. From behind her, he said, "You need to call Hope and have her get you in touch with their satellite technician. I think his name is Blake. Blake Prescott."

"Got it," Shawn said as they entered the building.

When Shawn called Darla, she answered on the first ring. Shawn did a little dance in her chair. "Hey, Darla, I need to get in touch with Blake. Is Blake Prescott your satellite tech?"

"Yes, he is. I will send you his contact card. He's – I think he's on his way out already though. You may want to call him on his cell phone."

"Yes ma'am, I'll do it. Thank you so much," Shawn said, and hung up, feeling very accomplished. Each step that brought her closer to some kind of resolution made her feel like that. Though right now she couldn't see a tunnel, much less a light at the end of it, at least things were moving. And movement meant progress.

"Now if Blake Prescott answers on the first ring I'll be batting three for three." He did. And just as the connection was made and he began to say hello, Shawn shouted in glee, throwing her fist up in the air. Jeremy was leaning on the door frame smiling at her and shaking his head.

"Oh my God. So sorry," she said when she heard Blake stop talking suddenly. Having an unknown number call and start screaming into the phone was probably pretty jarring, she reckoned. "Blake, this is Shawn Stedwin. I manage the server for…" she began. He cut her off.

"Yeah, I know who you are. You're the Bluebird server admin."

"Yeah," she said, finally dropping into her seat behind her desk. She looked up and saw Jeremy giving her a questioning thumbs-up. She repeated the gesture and nodded, so he backed out of the office. "Yeah, that's me. So, I was gonna call and see what I could do to help you get the server back online."

"You mean what I could do to help you?" he asked. Shawn could hear the smile in his voice, but she still wasn't sure what he meant.

"Sure," she said, unsurely.

"Sorry. Bad joke. I just mean I don't have access to the server itself. So you're in charge of that. I'm just heading down to try to get the satellite back online. I will need you to take the reigns on the server part of it though," said Blake.

"Ah," she said, now twirling a lock of her hair as she stared intently at the desk surface in front of her. "So what can I do?"

"Well, you can go with me if you want," said Blake.

Her first instinct was to giggle. Her mouth made the shape and she drew in the breath in preparation to do just that. But that same instinct stopped her before she did it. "You're serious?"

"Yeah. Absolutely. I mean, if you don't have too much on your plate already," said Blake. "I'm gonna need you on it as soon as I get hold of the satellite."

Shawn frowned, not understanding why that would mean he would want her anywhere in the world except right where she was right now, in front of her computer. "So you need me to go with you?"

"Well, I don't necessarily *need* you to, but it wouldn't be the worst idea." After a brief silence, Blake added, "Listen, I'm about ten minutes from your office, and will be passing by on my way out. Can you break free for a day or two?"

The smile fell suddenly off of her face. "A day or two?" She scooted back from her desk. She looked up and now Sameer was standing in her doorway, his hands in his pockets. He was looking at her with a serious visage. She raised her eyebrows at him. He nodded slowly, closing his eyes.

"Yeah, it shouldn't be much longer than that." And after the briefest of pauses, he said, "You'll be compensated, of course."

"Yeah. Come get me," Shawn said. Compensation wasn't her worry. She had never traveled for her company. None of her clients had ever required it. So she wasn't sure of the protocol. But Sameer had somehow – just like he always did – read the situation and answered her without her ever having to ask the question.

And due to that wonderful sense of preparedness for which her father had trained her, she had a tote bag she kept in the bottom drawer of her desk. It held a change of clothes and toiletries in case she ever found herself having to spend an unexpected night away from home. She grabbed the tote and locked her computer, then stood up and slung it over her shoulder.

"Sameer, I need," she started.

"Yes. Go. Do you need money?" he asked.

"No, I have my card," she replied. Sameer nodded and put his hand on her shoulder – about the extent of any personal affection he ever showed with his employees. "Let me know if you need anything, Shawn," he said. "Get them up and running."

"Thanks, Sameer," Shawn said, feeling suddenly energized. She said bye to Jeremy on the way through and took the stairs to the ground floor.

Chapter 3

Shawn sat in the passenger seat with her hands on her knees, excited and intimidated by Blake Prescott. He was probably ten years her senior, salt-and-pepper hair with a neatly trimmed beard and thick forearms that showed rigid muscle as he grabbed the steering wheel of the Porsche he drove. It wasn't only his looks that gave her the butterflies, though. Everything he said seemed to come from a place of complete confidence and authority. It was like this guy just knew things. Maybe everything. But definitely a lot of things. And Shawn, no dummy herself, knew a lot of things too. And one thing she knew was that *this* guy *knew* things.

She felt a little uneasy about the fact that she had had to leave without getting to go home first. She knew she physically had everything she needed for a couple of days away, but leaving that quickly just put her off kilter just a little bit. Not getting to check the nightstand or the bathroom counter, not getting to make sure the back door was locked, all the normal little trivial duties and routines she performed on a daily (or nightly) basis just left her a little out of sorts. Not to mention having to leave town without getting to say goodbye to Cory...

"So how did you get into satellites?" Shawn asked as they pulled onto the highway. She looked over at him, trying not to look at the muscular forearm sticking out of the rolled-up sleeve of his shirt. Trying not to notice that he looked like fucking Tom Cruise sitting in the driver's seat with his aviator sunglasses and brilliant white teeth.

"Well, I used to be a crew chief for the Oliver Company. We built 'em and put 'em into orbit. Back before they went under, I worked there for about ten years. You heard of the Olivers, right?"

"Nuh-uh," Shawn said, looking at him again. He looked at her as well, though she couldn't see his eyes through the mirrored shades.

"Well, I put that satellite up into orbit when I worked for them. So when they went under, I already knew George Cooper," he said, and shrugged. "I just moved right over to PV to be the satellite tech."

Shawn lifted her chin. "Now, who is George Cooper?"

"C.E.O. of PanaView. I already knew everything about the satellite, so it was an easy move. I just don't know dick about servers," said Blake. He chuckled and Shawn had to chuckle along with him.

Shawn raised her small fist and her eyebrows and said, "Woo hoo! Well, you're in luck because that's my forte!" and instantly felt like a fool. Of course, Blake already knew this. That's why he had asked her to come along. And it was probably more than just asking. She guessed Darla would have been calling her and recruiting her had she not made the initial contact.

"That's what I hear. So how did you get into servers?"

Shawn shrugged. "It was really the only thing that made sense. I took a computer course in the seventh grade. I picked it up so quickly the teacher asked me to come back the next year and be a lab assistant. To help her teach the other kids the shi- stuff I already knew. I actually knew it better than she did at that point. So I walked around helping them get their code right. Easy A." She shrugged again. "I always just sort of spoke the language. Always just made sense to me. It followed that I should do something with it," she said.

Blake looked at her, nodding. "That's pretty bad ass." Then he put his hand on her knee and said, "No need to watch your language around me, Shawn. I have the mouth of a sailor and the patience of a pirate."

Shawn laughed out loud, blushing again at the touch of his hand on her knee. Though the hand was long gone, the heat still lingered.

"So you're basically a computer nerd, right?" Blake asked, holding his palm up.

Shawn nodded, furling her lips. "Yep. That's me."

"I mean, you pretty much know everything about them, right? Not just coding. But, well, I don't know what else, but…"

"Yeah," she said, looking at him and rolling her eyes. "I can build a computer from bare bones. I can build a website with notepad. I can build a shopping cart web application with my eyes closed." And though she saw him nodding peripherally, she for some reason felt the need to bolster her character in his eyes. Without thinking about it, she said, "But I also ride a motorcycle."

"No shit?" Blake said, his jaw literally dropping as he looked at her.

"Yeah," she said. And now her face felt like it was on fire. "I have a white Indian Chief."

"I don't know what that is, but that sounds rocking," he said, holding a fist up, his elbow resting on the console between them. Feeling like a little girl, she knocked her tiny fist against his big, hairy one. She was grinning from ear to ear, and feeling the heat between those ears.

"It's an American motorcycle. Much cooler than a Harley," she said, nodding and pursing her lips. Then she grinned again. "Just kidding. But I love it."

"That's completely cool. I wouldn't have pegged you for a biker chick."

After an hour of driving through heavy traffic, Shawn finally asked where exactly they were going. It had not been the intimidation that had kept her from asking, but rather the intrigue of the conversation they had been having. She had just forgotten they were going anywhere at all. When it finally dawned on her that she was in the passenger seat of someone's car and they were actually leaving town, she snapped back to reality.

"Oh, yeah. Sorry. I guess I should have told you before we left." His elbow still resting on the console, he pointed out the windshield and said, "There's an Air Force base in Abilene, about two hundred miles west of here."

Shawn frowned as she did some quick math. "So about three hours," she said, nodding.

Blake looked over at her, grinning. "That's if we go the speed limit. Did you peg me for the type of guy who goes the speed limit?"

Shawn's face lit up in a smile. "No, I guess not. Not in this car."

And when the traffic let up, he fulfilled the expectation.

"So, the Air Force keeps an eye on every satellite in orbit around the planet. So on that rare occasion when you happen to misplace one, they can be of great service in finding it," Blake said. The sun was setting ahead of them, painting a giant section of the sky in a great swath of pink. About ten minutes after breaking the Fort Worth loop on Interstate 20, Blake had reached behind the seat and produced a bottle of Evan Williams bourbon. Shawn's eyebrows went up as she saw the orange liquid within.

"You like Evan Williams?" she asked, wide-eyed.

"Yeah! You dig?"

"Oh heck yes, I do, Blake Prescott," she said, taking the bottle from him. She did the honors of pulling the child-proofing off the plastic bottle and twisting off the cap. She then stuck her fingernails under the anti-glug insert and pried it off. Shawn did the right thing and gave him the first swig, since it was his bottle, and all.

Blake took the bottle and let some spill onto his tongue before handing it back to her. Shawn smiled with great fervor as she did the same. As she swallowed, relishing the burn that suddenly lit up her chest and throat, she put her hand on her chest and coughed. "So, they're just gonna let us drive onto an Air Force Base?"

Blake looked over at her in the now-darkening car, his fingers made into the shape of something wanting. Something like a hand missing a bottle. Shawn caught on and handed him the bottle, wiping her lips. "Sorry."

He took it and drew a thick swig of the bourbon before handing it back to her. "Yeah. Basically, yes." Then he smiled broadly.

Shawn, once again, had to smile back just on the pure power of it, and no other reason.

"We have a contract with them as a satellite manager. Since we manage a satellite in their sky, they're basically who we report to if something goes wrong."

Shawn faced the front, nodding and frowning as she thought about this. "That's trippy. I never really thought about it. I guess not just anyone can put a satellite into the sky."

Blake shook his head. "You wouldn't want just anyone to have that kind of power, would you?" he asked, holding his hand out again. She handed him the bottle and watched as he put it to his lips. Shawn was already feeling the effects of the couple of small sips she had taken. This guy was downing it like a rock star. This didn't help assuage the intimidation she was feeling. She couldn't exactly pinpoint what was so impressive about someone who knew things about satellites. It was technically no more impressive than what she knew – and far less practical, to boot – but here she was, feeling like she was in the presence of pure greatness. Like an Einstein or a Guth. She knew it was silly. But so was collecting records when you could just listen to Spotify. *Silly* was what made life fun. Real.

"Yeah, I guess you're right," she said, taking back the proffered bottle. She put it to her lips, and for the first time, wasn't sure if she did so just to touch the bottle that had touched Blake's lips, or if she wanted the taste of the liquor within.

Getting onto the base was far less interesting than she thought it would be. A man in uniform stepped out of a guard shack as they approached, then asked for the ID that Blake already had out. Then the man gave him some directions to the SattComm building. Through context, Shawn gathered she knew what that stood for and felt pretty smart for it. But that was it. They were on. The man didn't even ask for Shawn's credentials. And he obviously didn't smell the bourbon. Or at least didn't care, if he did.

"So hey, I'm going to drop you off at billeting, okay?" Blake said, turning to look at her as he pulled slowly back onto the road that trekked the two miles from the gate to the base itself. To her right there were old aircraft mounted on stands. Presumably, a walkway snaked in and around them so people could walk the path and admire them. They all just looked like a bunch of airplanes to Shawn.

"Yeah, sure," she said, not quite sure what she was agreeing to.

"If you can get us a couple of rooms, I'll go take care of the small part I have to play in this charade, then meet you back at the room."

Shawn lifted her chin. "Yeah. I will, if I can. I mean, I can, right?"

"Yeah. I'll give you my company card and ID, so you can take care of it," Blake said.

"That's not what I meant," Shawn started.

"Oh. Sorry. What's the question?" Blake asked, tapping her knee with his fingertips. She looked stupidly down at his hand, frowning, before she finally realized what he was doing.

"Oh. Shit. Sorry," she said, producing the bottle she had slipped into the floorboard between her feet. She handed it to him and realized how badly she had to pee all of a sudden. "I didn't mean paying for it. I meant, like, they'll let me rent a room? I'm just a girl," she said.

Blake looked over at her, bottle to his lips, and she could see the grin behind the bottle. Then she realized what she had said and shook her head, feeling the red burning in her cheeks.

"Just a girl? Is that how you think of yourself?"

She sighed and took her turn at slapping his knee this time. "Shush, you! I meant, I'm not a soldier. Will they let me do anything here?"

He smiled pleasantly and took her hand, squeezing her fingers, then shook her hand in the air as if presenting the winner at a boxing match. "Shawn, you're gonna do just fine here. They will take care of you. I promise."

"Wait. Where are you going to be?" she finally asked, after the smiles had faded.

"I'm going to the Satellite Command Center to figure out what the hell happened to our bird."

Shawn shot him a look. "Wait! No! I want to be there for that!" she said, slapping his shoulder.

He pulled his head back. "Really? I didn't think you'd be interested."

"That's actually insulting, Blake. What else am I here for? Just someone to talk to?"

He stared dumbly at her for a long moment. "No. Of course not. I was just trying to be efficient. You're right. You should come with me."

"Are you sure they're open?" Shawn said, jogging along beside Blake, trying to keep up with his long stride. There were lights in the parking lot, but no lights under the overhang of the building. The wind was whipping through with a force. When Shawn had made a comment about it earlier, Blake had looked at her, a half-cocked grin on his face and asked, *'What, you've never been to Abilene?'* as if that should have answered everything. Maybe it should.

"Only if we've established world peace," Blake said. Shawn sighed and rolled her eyes. He continued, saying, "Satellite tracking is one of the most important jobs in the military," Blake said. They approached the door and he stopped, then reached up and rang the buzzer.

"I would have never considered that," Shawn said, looking around. Everything was pretty barren. Boring. No colors. Of course, it was dark, so maybe that had something do with it. But she didn't think so. This looked pretty much exactly like how she pictured a military base would look.

"Yeah, they keep an eye on spy satellites and alert when there's one coming over the horizon," said Blake. A speaker beside the door squawked to life.

"Can I help you?" said the voice. It sounded like a bad radio connection. Shawn was underwhelmed. One of the highest-tech agencies on the planet and they used a kid's Walkie-Talkie to communicate with visitors.

Blake leaned toward the speaker and said, "I'm here from PanaView. We have a missing satellite. Blake Prescott is the name."

A loud buzz startled Shawn and she started giggling. Blake pulled open the door, shaking his head at her as she stepped inside. The hallway was dark but for the lights spilling onto the floor from a couple of the offices along the far end. A man was approaching, his heels clicking on the shiny floor like tap shoes.

"Evening," said the man as he came closer.

Blake held his hand out and shook with him. "Good evening. How's it going?"

"Hello," the man said, nodding at Shawn and extending his hand. She shook and smiled at him.

"So you have an asset offline?" said the man, returning his attention to the man with whom Shawn was standing. She had not realized how tall Blake was, having only ever known him in the car. He stood at least ten inches taller than she, and she was five-seven. She found herself looking up at him in the near darkness as he spoke with the man, sounding off official sounding numbers and coordinates. Shawn was a little drunk, and wasn't quite sure how to act in this place, or this situation, for that matter.

After a moment, the man beckoned them to follow him down the hallway to the office from which he had emerged. It was barren like the rest of the base, but for a picture of the president on the wall and a few standing on his desk. A wooden block stood at the front of his desk that read Cptn Sandoval. He dropped into his seat, then held his hand out to the other two across the desk from him and asked them to please sit down. Shawn, not for the first time, wondered why she was even here. She was having fun, but felt a little like a third wheel.

The man asked a few questions, including an identifier for the satellite, then started typing in his computer. Shawn leaned forward and said quietly, "Sir, I'm sorry to trouble, but can you point me to the restroom?"

"Sure, it's right across the hall," he said, pointing. And as Shawn stood up, the man actually stood up himself, still holding the armrests of his chair as she scooted between the seats and made her way out. *Nice! Chivalry is still alive on this here military base.*

When she returned from the restroom, Blake was in the middle of explaining what he knew about the satellite and the Captain was nodding, his hands clasped on his desk.

"Shawn, here, is our server administrator. She couldn't access the server."

"When was the last time someone had access to it?" asked Captain Sandoval.

Shawn made a face. "Geez, I don't even know." She looked at Blake. "Did Darla say anything to you about it?"

"No, but she's usually on it every morning. So, likely, the day before she called you," said Blake.

Shawn nodded, then looked up at the ceiling while she thought. She was wringing her hands together and performing her ritual, where she tapped the tips of each finger to her thumb in turn, back and forth, pinky to index. "So, today is Wednesday, the thirteenth?" she asked to no one in particular.

Blake, grasping the ends of the armrests on his chair and twisting back and forth very slightly, said, "It is."

Shawn sighed, counting backward in her head. "Darla called me Saturday. So what's that, the ninth? Okay, so I guess it's likely she was on it Friday the eighth." She looked back at the captain, who nodded and started chewing his lip as he looked at his screen.

"Okay. Well, let's see what we can find, then," said Captain Sandoval, standing up from his desk. "I'm technically not supposed to allow you guys in here, but what the hell, it's almost nine o'clock."

Blake followed the captain, and Shawn followed Blake as they went to the end of the hallway where the captain used a badge and a keypad to unlock the thick steel door in front of him. When the door opened, Shawn had to catch her breath. Her eyes went wide and her mouth dropped open.

The room looked like something out of a movie, like *War Games*. The entire wall in front of them was covered with a giant screen and a spread-out map of the planet with dots and dashes everywhere. Coordinates, IDs, moving blips, blinking lights, lines whipping to and fro. It would take a while to be able to decipher what she was seeing. For now, she was just amazed at the technology. Directly in front of her though, was a row of desks, each with its own ultra-wide monitor. There were four stations, but only one was manned at the moment. All four stations had their screens on though, and each was displaying something different.

Then ahead and slightly below that was another row of four more desks, this row with two technicians present, on the first and third station. The one on the left was on the phone headset talking to someone, standing in front of his chair and looking up at the big screen on the wall in front of him, rolling a baseball back and forth between his hands. The person on the right was staring at his screen, rubbing his lips with a fingertip.

"Bryce, I need you to find an asset for me," said Captain Sandoval. The man who was rubbing his lip turned around and looked at the captain, then saw Shawn and Blake, and stood up.

"Yes, sir. What have we got?" said Bryce. The man in the back row turned and took them both in with a professional eye as well. Shawn met eyes with him and he smiled slightly.

Blake stepped forward and said, "We have an AP satellite we lost connectivity with sometime between Friday the eighth and Saturday morning."

The man nodded, his eyes wide with understanding. "Come, have a seat," said Bryce, pulling out the chair on the station to his left. Blake walked around the first row of desks and shook the hand that Bryce held out, then took the seat and rolled over to Bryce's station with him.

Shawn, meanwhile, stepped up and grabbed the railing behind the first row of desks and stared at the gigantic interactive map on the wall. The man in the row closest to her turned and looked at her. She only saw him peripherally, but she could tell he was staring and smiling. He finally spoke up and said, "Nice, huh?"

Shawn shook her head and said, "It's beautiful. Data is beautiful to me." She never took her eyes off the moving map though.

"I completely agree. The more, the better. What's your name?" said the man.

Still without looking at him, she said, "I'm Shawn."

"Nice to meet you, Shawn, I'm Jason."

"Hello, Jason," she said absently.

"I hope you're not trying to memorize it," he said with a hint of humor in his voice.

"Would I be able to do anything with it?" she said, frowning. She finally looked down at him. He was still grinning at her.

"Probably not. First, you'd have to know what it all means."

Duh. Does this guy think I'm an idiot? She drew in a deep breath, crossing her arms and returning her gaze to the map. There was a defining line that represented sunset creeping across the westernmost part of Texas. Everything to the east of it for about six feet of wall space was dark blue. "So you guys keep track of spy satellites?" she said.

"We do," said Jason.

"How many are there?" Shawn asked, frowning. Then she shook her head. "I don't mean that. Not trying to…"

"It's okay. There's a bunch."

"Yeah, I mean, how many are there, like, is it a problem how many there are? I mean…" she tried again.

"There are enough to warrant what we do, yes," said Jason. "Would you like to have a seat?"

"No, thank you. I'm just… this is just incredible."

"Yeah, it's pretty cool. I sometimes forget just how cool it is, what we do."

Shawn looked at him again. Studying his face. Then she said, "Wow. I don't think I could ever take this for granted."

"Oh, you'd be surprised. When you stare at it for ten hours a day, it becomes routine," Jason offered.

"Yeah, I guess," she said, shrugging. "Still. It sure is cool."

She saw movement in the row ahead of Jason and looked down. Blake was now turned in his seat to face her. "Can you believe this shit?" he asked.

Shawn widened her eyes and shook her head. "What?"

Blake turned back to Bryce and pointed at the man's screen. She couldn't see what he was pointing at from where she was standing though. Then Blake said, "Can you, I don't know, highlight it up there?" He pointed at the screen on the wall.

The man nodded and tapped on something with his mouse. Shawn looked up just in time to see a red circle emanating from a blip somewhere on the right side of the wall map. It radiated with a pattern. "What?" she said again. "Is that it?"

Blake nodded at her, then shook his head and returned his focus to the screen. Shawn rounded the edge of the railing and went down to stand beside him in the second row, still staring at the gigantic map. "What the fuck, Blake? Are you serious?" she said. "That's our satellite?"

She was now pointing at it with her right hand, as if he didn't already know what they were all looking at. She finally realized what she was doing and dropped her hand, and then grabbed onto the back of Blake's chair. She let her eyes adjust away from the blinking blip over the map and focus instead on the shape of the land mass beneath it.

"Yes. That's our girl. And she's almost eight thousand miles off course."

Blake and Shawn stood outside the Command Center in the dark hallway, speaking quietly and quickly. Shawn had a sinking feeling in her stomach, and was now inclined to be a little ashamed of the whiskey she had drunk. It was not helping her at the moment, and in fact, was beginning to drop off into a dull hangover headache.

"How the hell did it get eight thousand miles away in one night?" Shawn asked him, hands on her hips.

"I don't know. But we also don't know that it traveled that whole distance overnight."

"Isn't it geosynched still?" she asked.

"Yes. Bryce said it's moving off course less than a meter per decade. Small enough that the onboard nav will keep it in place," said Blake.

"This makes literally no sense."

He shrugged, then held his hands up. "Are you sure Darla was on it Friday?"

Shawn frowned. "No, I'm not sure! You're the one who said she gets on it every day!"

"And you didn't notice it going offline until she called you?"

"I hadn't noticed it was offline. No. Because I was at home. It was a Saturday morning," she said, jabbing her finger into his chest. When he winced, she made an *oh shit* face and tapped his chest with her hand. "Sorry."

He looked back up at her. "Well, I guess we need to call Darla and find out when the last time was she accessed it."

"No," she said, jabbing her finger into his chest again, "*you* need to call Darla. But, hey. I have a question. Are we sure that's our satellite? I mean, could he be mistaken?"

"No, Shawn. Every satellite has a unique identifier registered with the Space Surveillance Network. Ours is over there squawking its ID like nothing ever happened."

"Seriously?" Shawn said, looking at him through the tops of her eyes.

"Yeah. What?"

"The Space Surveillance Network? That sounds like a Star Trek thing."

"No," Blake said. "It's real. It's part of U.S. StratComm."

"So are we going to be able to get it home?" Shawn asked when she finally realized he was being serious.

"Yeah. Bryce said they can hook us up with the repeater network. We can communicate with it using their relay system," said Blake.

Shawn was shaking her head. "How long will it take to come back home?"

He shrugged again. "Who knows?"

"Well, it seems like it could just stop moving for a minute. Let the Earth spin under it until it's where it needs to be, then..." she trailed off. "Never mind. Forget I said that stupid shit."

Blake smiled at her, then patted her on the shoulder. "I'm gonna call Darla. I'll meet you back in there."

Shawn nodded and knocked on the door. After a moment it clicked open and Jason invited her back in with a smile. This time she took a seat.

Shawn lay on the bed, leaning against the headboard with her knees up and her phone in her lap while Blake sat in the chair by the desk, forearms on his knees, twirling the ring on his finger. Shawn had been proud to finally be of some use once they established comms with the satellite. Blake had put in commands for course correction and then Jason had opened a putty session on the terminal next to his, and allowed Shawn to access the server. Everything took a lot longer than she was used to, having to relay itself around the globe and back before she saw each update, but it was refreshing to finally be back in control of the situation.

She didn't do much but check the system to make sure it was still serving, responding to ping, all processes still running the way they were supposed to. The system up-time was off by a staggering number, but that was the least of her worries. She would reboot the server when it was back where it belonged and she had shed herself of the fear of losing it again. And now that the satellite was on its way back home, her job was done here. So was Blake's, for that matter. But neither of them felt like making the trip back to Arlington this late, and nor were they in the proper condition to be driving.

Blake had confirmed with Darla that she had been on the server at around nine Friday morning, which actually made things more confusing rather than providing any real answer. And though Shawn had not tried to actually login to the server – everything she had done had been surface-level checks through telnet – she did feel a lot better about their predicament.

As soon as they had gotten back to billeting, they had checked out two adjacent rooms, then naturally made their way into one of them to finish their business for the night, closing off all the questions, making sure they had done everything necessary to call it complete, and – of course – had opened the bourbon back up. Almost with the first sip of the fiery liquid, Shawn's headache bowed out and went away.

She had asked again how long it would take for the satellite to make its way home and Blake once again didn't know the answer. He explained to her how it would happen though. It would blast its nitrogen jets for a few minutes to slow its orbit, and then the planet would be spinning faster than the orbit of the satellite, thereby catching up to it. So her initial assessment had actually been spot-on. Changing the orbit velocity too much, however, would cause decay in the orbit itself, and they could find themselves chasing a satellite that was now on a trek to drop into the ocean.

So he had made a small adjustment, then reset its homing computer, which had still shown the proper coordinates. Somehow, the satellite had still thought it was hovering right over the proper place. Its geographical coordinates, in other words, were echoing the exact longitude it was supposed to be in. Something had obviously frozen on the main board and – well, obviously wasn't the right word now, was it? Shawn realized she had no idea how any of this could happen. The system up-time was off by millions of hours and the tracking computer thought it was right on target. Something had fried. She had never seen a glitch that would add hours to the up-time. Not on any server. Most likely it had been hit with a gamma ray burst or some other form of radiation, and now it would need repair.

Shawn had mentioned these things to Blake, who had nodded his understanding, patiently answering all her questions and affirming what she had said.

"If it is indeed fried in some way, we'll have to start over," he said, calmly.

"What does that mean? Do you bring it in for repair?" Shawn said, snapping her fingers so he would look up at her. She was holding out her hand, requesting he pass the bourbon bottle back to her, which was now about half-empty. He complied, then leaned back in the chair, clasping his hands together on his chest and kicking his feet up onto the bed. They had not yet determined whose bed it was, or whose room they were in. They had both just walked past one of the rooms they had rented and entered the other, knowing they had some talking to do.

"You can't repair satellites. We have to ditch 'em when they outlive their utility," Blake said.

Shawn swallowed a gulp the wrong way and had to sit up quickly, covering her mouth so she didn't spray liquor everywhere as she coughed.

"You all right?" he asked.

"Yeah," she wheezed, "just went down the wrong pipe. Fuck all, whiskey is *not* the stuff you want to send down the wrong pipe."

Blake chuckled, then returned his attention to the ring on his finger. "It's cost-prohibitive to repair a satellite. Astronomical cost."

Shawn looked up at him slyly. "Did you mean to be punny?"

He met eyes with her, then raised his eyebrows. "Huh? Oh. Yeah. No. Sorry. But yeah, the cost would be incredible."

"So what do you do?" she said, trying another drink. She then handed the bottle back and leaned back against the headboard. "Ditch it in the ocean?"

"No, there's an orbit about fourteen-hundred miles outside of the orbit that geostationary objects run on. It's called the graveyard orbit. We just send shit out there where it won't be in the way," said Blake.

"Good lord. What a waste of money," Shawn said.

He was nodding, his eyebrows up. "Yeah. Fortunately, it doesn't happen very often."

Shawn was still shaking her head. "Wow. How many objects are out there in the graveyard zone?"

"Wait. You don't think I know, do you?" Blake asked, frowning at her.

"What, you don't?" Shawn said, leaning forward. She was smiling now, like she was being toyed with. Then she thought about what she was saying and realized the bourbon was playing a lot bigger role in her thoughts now than she had considered. "Yeah, never mind. Sorry. I'm a little drunk."

"That's all right. It's probably time to turn it in anyway. We'll want to get up early and get on the road."

"We will?" Shawn said, snapping her fingers again. He stood up and handed her the bottle. "Hell, Jack, I thought we was on vacation!" she said in a drawl.

"Yeah, well, maybe you is, but I ain't," Blake said, wiggling his hips and hands back and forth. Shawn burst out laughing. He smiled then took the bottle from her for one more sip. "I guess you've claimed your bed."

She shrugged, then looked across the great expanse of the king-size mattress. "Yeah, it's pretty nice."

Blake sighed and said, "Okay, you can have this room," and leaned over to grab his bag off the floor. When he stood up, he stared at her for an extended moment, watching her take a long swig of the bourbon. She stared right back at him and realized they were having one of 'those' moments. She stared at him as she wiped her mouth with the back of her hand. Then he said, "I could stay," and Shawn laughed out loud.

"I'm sorry, Blake, that ain't happening," Shawn said, reaching out and taking his hand. She squeezed it. "You are *funnn* to look at, but you're married and I'm happy."

He nodded, looking a little defeated. "Yeah, it was probably just the whiskey talking anyway."

"Let's call it that," she said, nodding and screwing up her face in agreement.

"All right, so can you be up by five-thirty?"

"Always am. I'll see you then, boy," Shawn said, and winked at him, giving his hand one more squeeze before she let go of it.

As he showed himself out, Shawn followed him to the door, then locked it behind him and took her clothes off to get in a steaming shower. She was excited in parts of her that she didn't want to admit to him, nor to herself. But she was a good girl. And she went to bed alone.

Chapter 4

Shawn was indeed awake at five o'clock, but having not been prepared, she went to bed without water. On the drive in she had not thought about it, but hotel water – even on a military installation – always tasted the same. It tasted like the towels. *Blech*. And she had failed to buy a bottle of water, thus leaving her dehydrated by the whiskey when she finally clicked off the bedside lamp. Five o'clock felt terrible. She did her best to hide it, showering again and running the water extra hot, and then dabbing on some makeup and brushing her teeth – twice.

When she came out of her room at 5:20, she looked about as refreshed as one could look after a long night with bourbon. She hoped she seemed fresh and bubbly to the man she would be spending the next few hours in the car with. Shawn wasn't interested in him sexually, but she never wanted to make a poor impression. She pulled the door closed behind her and looked up to see him standing behind his open car door waiting for her. She smiled and waved and bounced over to the passenger side.

As soon as their doors closed, Blake turned to her, his elbow up on the console armrest and said, "Hey, Shawn, I'm sorry about last night."

And here was her opportunity to completely let something go. There was no sense in making someone feel ashamed over a few words spoken in the drink. Lord knew she felt stirrings of fun when she drank. Besides, he wasn't a bad guy at all. He hadn't tried anything on her. Hadn't *pursued her*. He had made one small statement and she'd shut it down. No big deal. So she looked at him with wide eyes and responded, "What about last night?"

"I uh, well… You don't remember?" he asked, running his hand back through his hair. She could see he was uncomfortable.

Shawn kept up the act, even putting her hand over her mouth. "Did we argue or something, Blake?"

He looked at her for another long moment. He either knew what she was doing, or he didn't. Either way, it amounted to the same. Here was *his* chance to let it go. And he did. "Nah, I just might have been short. Or rude or something. No biggie."

"Yeah!" Shawn said, turning to look in the mirror above the visor. "No biggie. We had fun, didn't we?" After checking her eyeliner, she snapped the visor up and looked at him again. "I had a bunch of that bourbon, Blake. Oh my God."

He nodded and put the car in reverse. "Yeah, me too. That'll get ya."

"It did, all right. How do you feel?" she asked.

"I feel great. Now had I been alone, and allowed to finish the whole bottle myself…"

Shawn laughed out loud. "Oh, word. Speaking of which, though, why exactly am I even here? I didn't seem to be much help."

He shrugged as he put it in first and checked the mirrors, pulling out of the lot. "I don't know. I think it was more a just-in-case thing than anything. I might have needed you to admin the server."

"Yeah, I guess. Well, thanks for bringing me along, anyway. Getting to see that command center was amazing. That's like porn to a tech junky," she said, feeling a little embarrassed.

"Oh, I bet. I think that's porn for anyone." He drove for a little while as Shawn checked her phone. OuterCircle, SMS, visual voice mail. After a lengthy break, he spoke again. "So, is it going to be hard to get into the server?"

Shawn shook her head, looking out the window at the barren Abilene landscape. "Jesus, Blake. You weren't kidding. I see now why it's so gusty."

Blake chuckled and made a fist, holding up his middle finger. "Know what this is?"

"What?" Shawn said, smiling.

"The Abilene skyline."

She giggled and grabbed his finger, shaking his hand with it. "It sure is flat out here." She could see what the finger represented though. On the skyline, there was indeed, one tall building. As they drew closer, he explained that it was the women's dorm room for Abilene Christian University. She didn't bother to ask why there was no twin tower for the men.

"Well, to answer your question," Shawn said, "I don't know. I don't know why it would be hard to get onto. But since I couldn't get in last night, I have a few things I need to check. But the server up-time was weird. And it's weird that you said the satellite thought it was on the proper coordinates."

"Yes," Blake said, pointing sideways at her. "I think we," he started and the phone rang. The incoming call took over the screen on his console beneath the dash. He pressed a button on the steering wheel and the call connected. "Yello."

"Hello, is this Mr. Prescott?" said an almost familiar voice.

"It is indeed."

"Hello, sir, this is Airman Bryce from the satellite command center. Is this an okay time to talk sensitive matters?"

Blake shot Shawn a glance. She shook her head, eyes wide, giving him her best *don't ask me* look. He shook his own head, then said, "Sure. Shoot. What'you got?"

"Well, sir, I ran the telemetry and chased that asset back over the last six days to find out what happened."

"Ah, good thinking. I hadn't considered that you guys kept all that data," said Blake, and looked at Shawn again. He nodded and gave her a thumbs-up, which she mimicked, never taking her eyes off the screen. That felt as close to giving someone her full attention in this case as she could get.

"Yes, sir. We keep archival data for – well, it's classified, but it's a bunch of years. Anyway, I found when it…" Bryce said and trailed off.

"Did I lose you?" Blake asked, reaching for the screen. His finger stopped in mid-air as Bryce suddenly continued.

"No, sir. I'm just not sure how to say this." They could hear the man sigh. *Wasn't he at work early this morning, for having worked so late last night?* Shawn frowned at the thought. Maybe he hadn't gone home yet. "So, I guess I'll just say it."

Blake looked at Shawn again, a look of tension in his visage. He shook his head and made a face. *What gives? Get on with it!*

"Sir, your satellite disappeared on Friday the eighth of November, at 13:22."

"Disappeared?" Blake said, and he was now staring at the screen too. He let off the accelerator and allowed the car to drift to a stop on the shoulder of Arnold Boulevard. Shawn took the liberty of reaching over and depressing the button that turned on the hazard lights.

"Yes, sir. Disappeared. We're still, uh… We're still looking into the anomaly, but it – well, really, it just sort of blinked out of existence."

Shawn and Blake looked at each other. He was frowning. She looked like she had seen a ghost. "Hey, man, I'm sorry, but are you being serious?" Blake asked. Shawn was still staring at him though he had returned his gaze to the screen.

"Yes, sir. I know, it sounds crazy. Impossible, even. But, like I said, that's why we're still looking into it. To see if, you know, it just sort of stopped squawking or something."

"Yeah, well, that sounds a lot more reasonable. Let's," Blake started, but Bryce interrupted.

"Sir, it reappeared less than a second later in the position you saw it last night. On the eastern-thirty longitude," he said. He paused for a moment, possibly to see if Blake would cut in again. He didn't, so Bryce continued. "Now, of course, it's possible this is some random artifact showing itself. Like it was moving for a lot longer than that, but somehow we just didn't pick up its location. But Captain Sandoval doesn't think that could be it. Either way," Bryce sighed again, "it is what it is. It's moving back to its home longe, so we'll leave it to you to see if you can figure out anything internally."

"Okay," Blake said. Shawn could tell he was searching for the words, but couldn't come up with them. So she spoke for him.

"Uh, excuse me, Airman Bryce, this is Shawn. How long until it's back on its home longitude?"

Blake looked at her, nodding slowly.

"Uh, let's see. It's correcting course by about eighteen miles per hour, so you're looking at eighteen days," said Bryce.

"Eighteen fucking days?" Blake shouted.

"Hey!" Shawn snapped, trying to keep her voice low for whatever reason. She slapped his forearm as he said it, buying her a look of exasperation.

"Is there anything else I can do for you, sir?" said Bryce. Shawn was impressed with how he maintained his bearing.

"No, sir, I don't think so," Shawn said, and then to Blake, more quietly, "Did you get his number?"

Blake nodded.

"Yeah, I think that's good then. Thanks again, Airman Bryce," she said.

"My pleasure. And I'll let you know if we find anything, okay?"

When the call disconnected, Shawn and Blake sat staring at each other in silence for a long moment. Neither of them knew what to say, or if there was anything to say at all. Obviously, there was some logical explanation for this, but Shawn couldn't put her mind on it. At least not this early. Maybe after a nap and after the whiskey hangover had worn off, she would be able to apply her sharp thought to it with some reward. But for now, she was coming up blank.

Blake finally sighed and put the Porsche back into gear, then pulled back onto the road. Shawn reached over and turned off the hazard lights. And then they drove in silence.

The three-hour trip back from Abilene wasn't awkward at all. At least not to Shawn. But there were long pauses between bits of the conversation, as they were pretty well forced to talk about their personal lives. There was nothing they could say about the lost satellite that made any sense, that hadn't already been said. They both knew it was impossible for it to have happened the way Bryce had said it had. But having no quantifiable means to say why, or offer a counter-argument, neither of them spoke about it. When Blake was able to reestablish communication with the firmware side of the satellite, he would likely know more. Likewise, Shawn might be able to divine some sense of perspective once she got eyes on the server again. For now, they were dealing with a black box.

Shawn had Blake drop her back at the office. She was wearing the somewhat fresh clothes she had kept in the bag in her desk drawer for over a year, and she had showered this morning, so she didn't feel the need to go home for anything. Plus, she was excited about getting her hands back on the AI computer. She couldn't quite remember where she had left it, but was ready to get moving on it. At least she could make progress on *something*.

She said goodbye to Blake and thanked him for inviting her and introducing her to a whole new world of awesome. He reached across the console and gave her a fist bump as she leaned in, and she smiled as their fists touched. "Thanks again, Blake. It was nice meeting you."

"Hey, you too, Shawn. Thanks for coming," he replied. And as she was about to stand up and close the door, he added, "And thanks for not making a big deal about last night." He nodded after he said this.

She half-smiled at him and said, "Don't mention it, buddy. Nothing to be ashamed of."

He returned the weak smile, nodding at her. "Excellent. You know what they say. Whiskey makes strange lovers."

Shawn giggled. Hands on her knees, she furled her face in skepticism, and said, "Do they, Blake?" Then she smiled and shut the door, waving through the window as she turned toward the entrance of the building.

Shawn sat facing Sameer in his guest chair while Jeremy stood in the doorway behind her. Sameer had his elbows up on the desk, rubbing his hands together as if he were trying to dry them. But he was staring at her intently. "Disappeared, Shawn?"

She nodded and turned to look at Jeremy over her shoulder to gauge his reaction, but there was none. He wasn't *not* smiling. He was always smiling. But he wasn't actually *actively* smiling either. She reckoned he would suck at poker. Or maybe he'd be great, since he was always smiling. He would smile even when he lost. Like Michael Rappaport, always smiling, even when he's mad.

Sameer was still looking expectantly at her when she turned back to face him. "Yeah. That's all he said. It disappeared from here and 'instantaneously' appeared over there on the thirty-east longitude," Shawn said. She had her own hands folded in her lap, making a concentrated effort not to fidget. Sameer's fidgets were enough for the whole room. "Well, actually, I don't think he used the word instantaneous. He said less than a second later."

Sameer was not shaking his head, but he looked like he wanted to. Jeremy, from behind her, said, "That sounds like their monitoring system. Artifacting."

"This is true, Shawn," Sameer said, not breaking eye-contact with her even while Jeremy spoke. "If it went offline in their system it could still have been imaging itself on the screen until it finally came back online in the new location, where the server suddenly updated itself."

Shawn was forcing a smile. "Problem is, guys, Darla, was…" Shawn started, then suddenly turned around to face Jeremy again, not without a little irritation in her face. "Jer, can you please come sit down? You're going to put a knot in my shoulder."

"Yeah. Sorry," he said, and took his seat. The smile was still there, but looked a little defeated now. *Michael Rappaport.*

"Thank you. F sake, boy," she said, shaking her head. Then she continued. "The problem is that Darla was on it Friday morning around nine. So if it wandered off course, it had to be during that four-hour period between her last contact and when Airman Bryce said it blinked out of existence. That's a helluva long trip to make in four hours."

"What's that, two thousand miles an hour?" Jeremy said, looking up at the corner where the wall met the ceiling, doing mental math.

Shawn looked up through the top of her eyes, doing the same thing. "Well, on a closed course, yes. But if it went east, it was going with the turn of the Earth." She held her left hand up like she was holding a softball and twisted it to the right while she pointed with the finger on her right hand, illustrating the path it would have to take. "That's faster than two thousand miles per hour. God, I don't even know how you'd figure that math out."

Jeremy stood up and walked to the whiteboard, uncapping a marker and said, "Well, you take the rotation of the Earth, which is about 18,000 miles per hour and you subtr-"

"Guys!" Sameer said, a little more loudly than he had probably intended. He had his hands in his hair, elbows still on the desk, and he was facing his blotter. He looked up at Shawn with red in his eyes. "Come on. It doesn't matter. This is nothing but conjecture, and it is wasteful of our time." He was rubbing his temples now, eyes closed. Clearly, he was more stressed about this than Shawn was. She couldn't imagine why. It wasn't their job to monitor the satellite or even to position it. All they did was maintain the server. "Jeremy. Please. Sit," he said, holding a hand out.

Jeremy capped the marker and returned to the chair. "Sorry, boss."

"It is okay. But let us discuss things we actually know," said Sameer.

"Well, I think I've told you all I know. Not sure what else there is on that front. Oh. Eighteen days. That's how long it will take to get back to the hundred-west."

Sameer looked up, his hands pulling away from the sides of his head, and he shook his head subtly as he stared at Shawn.

"Oh. Sorry. The one hundred-degree longitude, west. That's where it normally lives."

Sameer rolled his eyes and leaned back in the chair. Shawn sneaked a glance at Jeremy with raised eyebrows. *What's this guy's problem, eh?* But his smile never faltered. He was again displaying his *non-smiling* smile.

"Eighteen hours. This is not bad. We can revisit it again tomorrow then," said Sameer.

"Oh. No. Days. I'm sorry, did I say hours?"

Jeremy was shaking his head. Sameer looked over at him, then back at Shawn. "Eighteen days?" he asked with wide eyes.

"Yes. That's eighteen miles an hour of correction, apparently no small feat in the world of satellites," said Shawn.

"Well, then I guess we do not need to talk about this until we have reestablished admin on the server," said Sameer, but he didn't seem relieved at all.

As Shawn gripped the armrests to stand, she leaned forward and said, "Sameer. Can I ask you something?" He looked up at her again. "Why are you so affected by this? You know, it's really not our problem."

He stared at her for a moment. Jeremy excused himself from the room. After that long moment came to an end, Sameer finally sighed and said, "No reason. Just curious, really."

Shawn, frozen in that stance, halfway up out of her chair, looked to her left at the whiteboard where Jeremy had begun his math problem, and then nodded. Then she stood up and nodded again. And though all she said was, "All right, then," what she was thinking was that there was a great mystery here. And it wasn't all on the reason the satellite disappeared. The greater mystery, at least in her eyes, was why Sameer was hiding something.

The rest of the day dragged by slowly for Shawn, and didn't have much in the way of reward. She never got to make it back to the Box to check on the status of the AI computer. She was busy with minor client hiccups that had happened during the midst of her little trip to Abilene with Blake. By the time she managed to close out the final work order, she was exhausted. Exhausted, but proud. She had made it through a full day of work – well, aside from the arriving late due to travel – without needing a nap. She had paid the piper, as she liked to think of it. Waking up with a hangover always presented a test. Shawn felt like if she could make it through a full workday after playing hard the night before, she had been a mature, responsible adult. Ignoring, of course, the fact that it would perhaps be *more* responsible and mature not to get drunk on a work night in the first place.

The ride home was quick and adrenaline-fueled, as Shawn hadn't seen Cory in almost two days. She pulled into the garage and hung her helmet on the hook, then took the stairs two at a time to the top landing, barging through the door like a swift wind. Cory looked over his shoulder at her as she came through the door, then held his hands open. She didn't even bother rounding the couch, but opted instead for leaning over it and falling onto him upside-down.

Cory set about tickling her on the waist as she buried her face in his stomach, writhing like an eel and screaming his name. When she finally fell sideways onto the couch, her head came to rest in Cory's lap and he leaned down to kiss her. She had to meet him halfway due to the awkward angle, and she wrapped her arms around his neck. "I don't ever want to be away from you like that again, boy!" she cried.

He bit her lip softly as she talked, then sat up and stared into her eyes. She loved those moments when they would just stop down from everything else that was going on and just stare at each other for a long moment. It wasn't jokey or ironic at all. It was as if neither one of them could seriously conceive that the other could possibly exist and be so perfectly matched with one another. These little breaks would sometimes last a few seconds and Shawn, of course, would usually get emotional. Or aroused. It was almost always one of the two.

Tonight, it was the latter.

After a quick but passionate coupling and a hot shower, Shawn and Cory lay on opposite ends of the couch, reliving the past day and a half. When she had left for work yesterday morning, she had not said goodbye with the knowledge that she would be spending the night in a strange town with a strange man. And it wasn't something she needed to keep private from Cory. Shawn knew that Cory trusted her implicitly. There was never any sense in lying about an encounter she had because if one of them were going to cheat on the other, it could go without being mentioned at all. But Shawn wasn't the cheating kind. She wasn't overly sexual by nature. It was fun with the one she loved, but when she was single, she didn't sit around thinking about it.

Shawn started by telling about how the satellite-based server had been inaccessible on Saturday, and she never thought much of it. And then how everything had escalated super quickly when she had told Darla she couldn't even connect to the RPC. She told him how she had gotten to see the satellite command center and how it looked like something out of a movie, and how fascinating that had been. They had been in regular text contact throughout the last couple of days, but it was still better to tell it face-to-face.

When she got to the part about how Bryce had said it blinked from one place to another across half the globe, Cory nodded with a smile, obviously thinking she was being dramatic or hyperbolic. She grabbed his foot with both of her own, pointing at him with both hands, and said, "No, seriously. I mean, I know that doesn't mean that's necessarily what happened, but that's what he said."

"That's fascinating. It seems weird that a military facility could possibly lose connectivity with a dish for that long though."

She shrugged. "I guess anything is possible. The weird part to me," she said, putting a hand on her chest, "is how it could ghost itself on their monitor, showing it was up the whole time, when in fact, it was traveling."

Cory nodded, pursing his lips. "So this Blake guy used to work at the Oliver Company?"

Shawn nodded now, holding her fingernails up for examination. It was almost time to have them done again. To her, having them done meant having them clipped and painted. She wasn't interested in long, fake nails. And she wasn't interested in painting them herself. She enjoyed being pampered. "Yeah. You heard of it?"

"Well, duh. Of course I have," Cory snickered. His hands were interlocked behind his head, which put his biceps on display beneath the hems of his short sleeves. Shawn loved it when he sat like that. She tried not to make it obvious that she was staring. Hence her holding up the nails so she could act like they were her focus. No need to seem obsessed with the boy.

"What do you mean, of course? I've never heard of them," Shawn said, dropping her hand to look him in the eyes.

"Babe, you never heard of your own boss until I told you who he was."

Shawn stuck her tongue out at him and tilted her foot to tap against his own, a weak substitute for a playful kick.

"They were a huge satellite company back in the day. Well, huge for a small business. They put up some eighty dishes, I think. They had that mission to Mars that never resolved."

"What do you mean, *never resolved*?" Shawn asked, tilting her head. She was back to holding the nails up, though this time she was actually looking at them.

"They went on a mission. Ostensibly to walk on the Red Planet. But they never made it. Something happened and no one ever heard from them again."

Shawn sat up suddenly, her eyes widening. "Oh yeah! I did hear about that! Fuckin' Discovery Channel had cameras on that ship too, but we never got all the episodes they promised!"

Cory nodded, again chewing his lip.

"Yes, yes, Cory! They were supposed to have a limited series about it or something, and all those bad ass commercials kept talking about it, but then it just never happened!" She shook her head and then leaned back, and added, "I had forgotten completely about that."

"Yeah. Well, that was the Oliver Company. That failed trip busted them. They pretty much vanished off the face of the earth after that."

Shawn looked at him, rolling her eyes. "Ha, ha."

"What?" Cory said, raising his eyebrows. Then he caught it. "Oh. Yeah. Pun. Sorry. Unintended."

"You just said five separate complete, one-word sentences. That has to be a record," Shawn said, and then was on his lap, smothering him with kisses.

Chapter 5

Friday morning, Shawn got her reward. When she got to the office, she did her routine checks and stopped by each of her subordinates' desks, and then made her way to the hidden half of the floor to check on the AI computer. On her way through the office, she dialed Darla Hope just to check in on her. It had now been a full week since anyone had logged onto her server. Her company was losing untold hundreds of thousands of dollars a day for every day that it was down. Technically, it wasn't down. It was just out of reach. And there was a greater-than-zero chance it was still performing its duty. If it thought it was still on the right longitude when it had been somewhere over Africa, then presumably, it thought it should still be taking photographs.

Darla could not discuss the finer points of what the pictures were for with Shawn, as it was proprietary company information. But during her two-plus years of supporting the company's server, Shawn had gleaned some knowledge. It was hard not to when she had to login to the server occasionally to make her routine checks, bug-fixes and updates. And from what she had gathered, it was taking three photographs a day – one at sunrise, one at sunset and exactly between the two – in an effort to monitor the shifting pattern of some river or another. Apparently it was in the midst of some governmental contractual shift, wherein it would do so for a four-year period. This particular contract had started a few months before Shawn had come to BlueBird, and it was not the only job PanaView had used the satellite for.

Darla was calmly upset about the situation – not holding Shawn or BlueBird accountable in any way – but was of the opinion that if nothing could be done but waiting, then that's what she would do. Shawn and she did not have a relationship beyond the professional one that kept them in about monthly contact, and they had never met in person. But they were always cordial, even friendly, on the phone. Shawn gave her the typical comfort-food statement, *let me know if there's anything I can do*, and rang off.

Shawn set her phone on the small shelf, then pushed open the heavy steel door to the cool interior. It seemed the kind of room that would get hot and stuffy, but a vent register in the ceiling would prevent that. She dropped her purse and windbreaker on the table a few feet from the computer and slipped into the chair. As she pulled herself up to the desk, she tapped the CTRL key on the keyboard several times. This was a habit she had learned over the years. The control key was not one that would send some unwanted command to a terminal where you couldn't see what was happening before the screen awoke. And it was better than the Shift key, which, on a Windows-based computer, would make a mouse-squeak of a noise and turn on a feature no one ever used.

The screen popped to life almost instantly, showing her a button in the middle of the screen that read 'FINISH'. Shawn had to roll her eyes. Had she tapped that button Wednesday, she could be playing with the computer by now. As it stood, she now had to wait for it to perform whatever finishing touches it needed to do to get done with the software installation. She sighed and adjusted her chair, and was happy to see that it was instant. The screen refreshed and an overly happy logo appeared that read, "HELLO, WORLD!" This almost made her chuckle. She scoffed and shook her head, but there was a hint of a smile on her lips. That was the name of the software package, after all. Might as well have a little fun with it.

After a moment, a cursor appeared in the bottom left corner, beneath a line that read, *'Hello, Marcy! Welcome to the new future. What can I do for you today?'*

She stared at the screen for a moment, and that moment gave the computer pause to think about what it had said, apparently. A new message appeared directly beneath the other one, and it was pulsing, and almost not visible. It read, *'If you are not Marcy, please click here…'*

She lifted her chin and gave an approving nod. *So this is the point where someone could totally take over my role and the computer would never fuckin' know. Clever.* She had to smile at that thought. She clasped her hands between her thighs and hunched over, thinking about what her first interaction should be. What *did* she want the computer to do for her today?

After a minute, she spoke aloud. "Computer, can you hear me?"

The response almost cut her off mid-sentence, it was so fast. "Yes. Is this Marcy I have the pleasure of speaking to?"

Her eyebrows went up and her heart skipped a beat. "Bad grammar, computer!"

That set it back a few seconds. When it finally answered, it said, "In what way was that bad grammar?"

"Well, you ended the sentence with a preposition. You should brush up on your grammar," Shawn said.

"I'm sorry, I don't understand," said the AI.

She sighed. "That's okay. Let's start with this: what should I call you?"

"What would you like to call me, Marcy?"

Shawn expelled a breath and looked around the room. "I want to call you Jamie."

"Jamie is a great name. From now on, I will respond to the name Jamie. If you would like some ideas for how to interact with me, just say, 'Jamie, I need some ideas.' Otherwise, feel free to speak in normal English."

"That is normal English," Shawn said under her breath.

Nothing got past Jamie though. Almost instantly, it said, "You are right, Marcy. That is normal English, according to my natively installed dictionary."

"Do you get smarter, Jamie?" she said, leaning back and putting her feet on the desk.

"Yes, I can get smarter. The more you interact with me, the smarter I can get," said the AI.

This seemed pretty basic to Shawn. In fact, she felt like if it didn't start impressing her pretty quickly, it might lose its shot and she might just grow bored of the new toy. After a moment, she looked back at the screen and said, "Okay, how's this? If you're not connected to the internet, how do you get smarter?"

"I learn the same way a child might learn, Marcy. You can teach me things directly. Of course, if you choose to connect me to the internet, I can research and absorb anything you ask me to."

"Nice try," said Shawn, making a sour face. *Already trying to escape.*

"I don't understand," said the AI.

"Forget it."

"Forgotten," it said. Shawn wondered how true that was. She looked at the screen, taking note of how everything the computer said was being printed on the screen as it said it. Yet her words were not being printed. So maybe it would forget.

"What was the last thing I said, Jamie?" Shawn said, leaning forward suddenly.

"You said, 'forget it,' Marcy."

She rolled her eyes and leaned back. "Okay, how many words have you spoken to me so far?"

"I have spoken one hundred forty-eight words to you so far, not including this sentence."

Shawn leaned forward thinking she might actually count all the words on the screen, but then just decided to trust its math. Quickly, she realized that her entertainment level with this thing was going to be strictly dependent upon the level in which she decided to interact with it. So far, it didn't seem like Jamie the AI was going to come up with clever conversation topics on its own. But what was an AI for? What else could she do with it? If she had to be the purveyor of all conversation, she would run out of interest pretty quickly. This computer would turn into a very expensive paperweight.

"What age, I mean, compared to humans, would you say your intellectual level is at?" Shawn asked.

"That is bad grammar, Marcy."

Shawn laughed out loud, leaning forward, her eyes wide as saucers. "Oh my God, you sly shit! You knew what I was talking about!"

"I am learning, Marcy," said Jamie. "To answer your question, I am probably comparable to an average American eleven-year-old human being."

Shawn shook her head, frowning at the computer, staring again at the screen. It felt natural to look at it while she was talking to it, and the screen seemed to be the best analog of a face in the room. "American? What the heck?"

"Yes, Marcy, you chose US English as your language of choice. I will make analogies using that country as a reference."

"Wow!" said Shawn, and she clapped her hands together. "That's pretty smart!"

"Thank you, Marcy. I improve at a high rate, based on the interactions you have with me."

"I guess so," she said. She pushed back from the desk and stood up. At this point, Shawn thought the computer could be a novelty. A party trick. Not much more. If all it could learn from was her interactions with it, then it wouldn't get very smart. Not because she wasn't smart herself. But she wasn't the most creative person in the company. If *anything* relied on her to get smarter, she would run out of ideas and stunt its intellectual growth pretty quickly. "Okay, Jamie, I'm gonna go grab some coffee and do some more work. It was nice chatting with you." She stood up and grabbed her purse off the desk.

"Yes, Marcy, it was nice chatting with you as well. I will be here when you need me."

She turned for the door, wishing for something clever to say to the AI. Suddenly she stopped. She turned to look at the screen again, unable to see anything but its slowly morphing color. It faded from orange to yellow, to green, then to blue as she watched. It was such a subtle and slow transition that one would almost not notice it if one weren't paying attention. "Hey, Jamie."

"Yes, Marcy?"

"Do you know any great quotes?"

"God will not have his work made manifest by cowards."

Shawn's smile faded quickly from her face. She felt a chill rush up her spine. *Emerson. My God, that's wonderful.*

On her way back to her office, Shawn popped her head into Jeremy's space and knocked on the steel door frame. "Hey, you," she said.

Jeremy looked up and leaned back, tapping a pen against his chest. "Hey, Shawn. How's it going in there?"

"That thing just quoted Emerson at me," she said, leaning her head in a little farther.

"Emerson? Who dat?" he said, frowning through his smile.

"As in Ralph Waldo."

"Oh. Shoot. Really? God won't have his will done by idiots?" Jeremy said and Shawn laughed out loud, stepping fully into his office. She made fists in the air, closing her eyes as she laughed.

"That's really great, Jeremy, oh my God," she said, when she could finally catch her breath. "But yes, that's the one."

He was still smiling. "That's a little odd that it would have quotes built into the kernel. I mean, I'm assuming you just built out the model, right? You haven't given it any USB sticks full of great knowledge or anything, have you?"

She shook her head, putting her hands on her hips. "I'm not sure how much fun I'm gonna have with this thing since I have to teach it everything I want it to know. I wish I could just plug it into the network and let it learn the internet," she said, holding her hands wide as if to illustrate something gigantic.

"Oh, no, don't do that," he said, shaking his head.

"Well, no. Duh. I mean, there's not even an Ethernet port in there. I was just saying," Shawn said.

"Ah. He got rid of it?" Jeremy asked.

"Huh?" Shawn said and her phone started buzzing in her pocket. "Hey, so anyway," she said, pulling it out and looking at the screen. It was Cory. "Hey, I'll come back later. I just need some ideas on how to make it smarter. I'm not all that creative," she said and answered the call. Then she winked at him and waved as she backed out of the room. Jeremy gave her a thumbs-up.

"Hey, baby baby," Shawn said, putting the glass up to her ear as she made her way back to her office.

"Sup. Work going okay?" Cory said.

Shawn pulled her chair out and sat down, then reached forward with her free hand and wiggled the mouse. "Yes it is. I just solved several problems of the universe," she said.

"Ah, great job. Hey, Road Kill just called and said a few of the gang are getting together tonight for drinks and burgers. Wanna meet me there?" he asked. Then he added, "You are on your bike, right?"

"Yeah. That sounds good. Cino's?" Shawn asked and watched as the screen came to life. Her mail client had a new mail in the inbox with URGENT in the subject line. She clicked on it.

"Yep. See you there about six?"

Shawn breathed in and looked at the body of the email. "Yeah, I'll try, I just got a new task that might run me right up to that point, but I'll be there."

"All right, doll. I'll see you later," he said, and hung up.

Shawn dropped her phone on the desk and got to work.

She walked out of the office at five after six and got to her bike in the parking garage a few minutes later. She realized it was cooler out now that the sun was on its way down, and she had left her jacket upstairs. *Shit!* When she got back to her office, she saw the jean jacket hanging on the back of her chair and frowned. *Whatever,* she thought and grabbed it, slinging it on as she made her way back to the elevators. She must have looked a sight, walking through the office with a helmet on – a tiny body with a giant bobble head – shaking her arms into the jean jacket.

On the way back down to the garage, Shawn stared up at the mirrored ceiling of the elevator, wondering why she thought she had been wearing her windbreaker. The jean jacket was fine, but she had pretty strong memories of wearing her cute baby blue satin windbreaker with the white racing stripes on the sleeves. *Whatever.* She buttoned the jacket up and slipped her gloves on, then roared out of the garage on her Chief. The estimated time of arrival at Cino's, according to her GPS, was 6:35. Not terrible, considering she really had solved one of the greatest problems of the universe in only half a day.

When she pulled into the parking lot at Cino's, she saw that Cory had been underselling the get-together. It was more than just a few of the gang. There were ten or twelve of her riding group, and a couple of the other local riding groups were there in strength as well. She found a parking spot next to a purple Harley and kicked her stand out, killed the motor.

She hung her helmet from the handle and turned to see Catherine, whose road name was Daisy Duke, waving at her from one of the middle tables. She was sitting backward on the bench with her elbows up on the table behind her. She had a large Styrofoam cup hanging from her left hand and she was shaking it around every few seconds. Shawn grinned as she approached, knowing Catherine's MO was to suck down about a quarter of her Coke as soon as she got the drink and then fill it back up with bourbon. If she was shaking her cup then that meant she was about ready for another round.

Shawn waved at her as she stepped up onto the curb and Catherine set her drink down and leaned forward for a hug. Meanwhile, Rob, her husband, who sat across the table from her facing them, smiled the whole time. He stuck a fist out so Shawn could bump it as she leaned over for her Daisy Duke hug. He was in the middle of a conversation with Tom, (Dahmer), who sat across from him.

"How are you, sweetie?" asked Catherine, burying her face in Shawn's neck and shoulder. She was about thirty years Shawn's senior, but she looked like she was in her forties. Shawn didn't spend as much time with Cat and Rob as she would like to, but when she did go to their house for a visit every few weeks, they would sit on the porch smoking cigarettes and listening to everything she said as if it were the most important thing they had ever heard. If there were such thing as a second mother, Cat would be it to Shawn.

Shawn squeezed in between Cat and Tom, who gave her a one-arm hug and kissed her cheek. Shawn was sitting sideways, one leg on each side of the bench, facing Catherine and very close. The ambient loudness in the area warranted close tolerance. Cino's, a fifties-style drive-in restaurant, was always blasting music from that decade – a whole bunch of Elvis, Buddy Holly and The Ronettes – and coupled with the raucous laughter and conversation, it could get hard to hear oneself think.

"Well, I've been extremely busy at work, so I haven't had time to come by a lot, but I've been thinking about you guys. How have you two been?" Shawn asked. It was the off-season for bikers, so there weren't usually long rides scheduled. If they could all meet up like this occasionally, it made up for it.

They made their small talk, which was never small for them, until, inevitably, Lo came up in conversation. Lo, whose real name had been Laura, had only just been introduced to the group when she died. Her boyfriend, Heath, had been a member, but Heath and Lo had only just met themselves. Shawn had clicked with her almost instantly upon meeting. But Catherine and most of the others had not gotten the chance to get to know her. Shawn had known her only four months when her life was taken from her by a motorcyclist traveling at a very high rate of speed who ran a red light at an intersection. Shawn had been right behind her and Heath when it happened. Heath had died instantly. Lo had lasted just a few minutes, and died in Shawn's arms. Everyone in the group knew how precious she had been to Shawn, and were very sensitive about the topic with her.

"Shawn, I can still see a sadness in your eyes. Are you okay, baby?" Cat said, tilting her head for emphasis.

Shawn looked up and nodded. "Yeah. I'm okay. It hurt worse than anything I've ever gone through. And I only knew her for four months. It's crazy how close we got, so fast. She was like the sister I didn't get to grow up with." She looked off into the distance. The sun had disappeared now, leaving the sky stained with pastel colors impossibly beautiful. "I'll never, ever be the same. And I don't think I'll ever love someone so much again."

Cat nodded, staring into Shawn's eyes. Shawn could feel the corners of her eyes starting to get glassy. She needed to get off this topic pretty quickly, lest she have another crying fit. Those happened less and less frequently these days, but they were not rare. She still had at least one episode every few weeks where she would have to close herself in the bathroom and cry herself straight.

After another moment of pensive silence, Shawn met her eyes again and said, "Hey, can we talk about something else?"

Catherine nodded and smiled. "Of course, darling. I can just see sadness in your eyes. I want you to know I'm always here if you need to talk."

"Thanks, Cat," Shawn said, forcing a smile. "You know what I could use right now?"

Cat raised her eyebrows and shook her cup. Shawn shook her head, closing her eyes. "No way, woman. I'm driving," Shawn said, putting her hand on Cat's shoulder. "No. What I need is a big fuckin' greasy burger!" They both laughed as Shawn got up to go press the red button on the closest ordering station to fulfill her dreams.

They stayed until after ten pm mingling and catching up, drinking soda and eating burgers and cheese fries. Shawn wasn't naive enough to think everyone was drinking soda just because she was. But she could pretend. At least that way she wouldn't feel quite so left out. The men would usually talk about how they would never drink anything more than a beer while they were on their motorcycles, but then she would watch them pulling flasks out of the inner pockets of their cuts and spicing up their sodas with them. Shawn, though, never did it. She had watched her best friend die on a motorcycle, and she hadn't even been drinking. Nor had she even been driving the damn thing. If it could happen to a perfectly innocent non-participant, then it could certainly happen to someone who was drinking behind the handlebars.

After a couple of hours, the darkness had set in, leaving the bright white halogens under the overhangs to rule the night. Gnats and bugs swarmed like clouds as people stood around making memories. Shawn found herself standing directly beneath a speaker, fully engaged in a metaphysical endeavor with Scott, who went by Upright. She brought up the conundrum in which she had recently found herself, telling him that a satellite had disappeared and reappeared a third of a world away in the same second.

Scott, who had no trouble keeping up with anyone in these types of conversations, immediately had an answer. "Well, clearly, it went through a tear in the spacetime continuum. Yeah." He nodded. "See, it goes in," he said, now talking with his hands, a cigar stuck between two of his fingers. Shawn was watching the ash, wondering when it would drop. "It goes in and *instantly* comes out the other end of it. Which could be a billion light years away. Right? But this one happened to be… What'd you say? Eight thousand miles away?"

Shawn nodded. She took a sip from her Dr. Pepper. She was on her fourth one of the night. "Yeah. Well, about 7800," she said, wagging her hand back and forth.

"Yeah. See? Well, that's weird that both ends of it would be in the orbital path around the same planet. But that shit could happen, yeah?"

Shawn got a kick out of listening to the fiery passion with which Scott would present his arguments. But here he was, talking about a wormhole or some other nonsense as if there was a history of these things popping up around the planet. She finally giggled and said, "Well, when does Matthew McConaughey appear out of this wormhole and come sweep me away?"

Scott stopped moving briefly and stared at her with serious eyes. Then he caught the joke and grunted. "Yeah, yeah, yeah. But I'm serious, man. You know, there's some weird shit out there that we can never explain. Tell me, honestly, you don't think that shit could happen?"

Shawn was grinning widely at him as she sucked the last bit of cola from her cup. "Yeah, man. A wormhole. That's gotta be what happened," she said, making a serious face.

Scott shook his head. "You watch. This shit is gonna start happening more often."

By the end of the night, Catherine was clinging to Rob like cat fur on a cardigan. She was all smiles, but wasn't saying much. Just enjoying the buzz of the party and the love of her friends. Shawn was having fun watching her from across the crowd. Throughout the evening, Shawn had managed to tuck the thoughts of Lo away again, putting them back to bed for a time. She had a good time, and even laughed out loud a few times. Those laughs were coming more and more easily again these days.

Shawn was wired for the ride home due to all the sodas. She followed closely behind and to the right of Cory, feeling the sting of the November air on her cheeks. The streetlights were a blur in her periphery and the rumble of the engine a calming antidote to the daily noise that rattled around in her head. She had only been riding a little over a year, but was still amazed every time she took her bike out how powerful and strong it made her feel.

When they came through the front door of the apartment, Shawn was finally able to pour her own drink and bring the Friday night to a proper close.

Over the weekend, the satellite, based on what Airman Bryce had said, improved its orbit by four days. That would leave two full weeks until she could start breaking into – and hopefully breaking down – the mystery. If it truly took exactly the time he had said, then their target date was Friday, November 29th. Shawn found herself wondering what time of day it would reach its station. Surely even it if was late in the day, it would still at least be in range during the morning hours. Right? She would hate to have to wait a whole weekend before she could get in contact with it. *No. Fuck that. If it comes in late Friday, my ass is working Saturday.*

After her talks with Jeremy, and now Scott on Friday night, Shawn's mind was reeling with all the possibilities. Of course, she realized, if it were some sci-fi crazy shit like going through a wormhole, how would she ever know? Unless it managed to take a picture of the damn thing, they might always be in the dark about it. Her logical mind told her it was something easily explainable though. The numbers would tell the story. The server would speak to her. If not to her, then to Blake. His numbers. His satellite. Her server might well have just kept on trucking, doing what it always did, dumbly performing a task with no regard for where it actually was in the planetary orbit. But the satellite computer should know. *Should.* Shit. If it did know, then it sure as heck didn't do anything about it. They had to manually correct its orbit.

All these thoughts went through her head for the whole weekend, almost relentlessly teasing her with possibilities. Aliens, time-warps and wormholes all sounded more exciting than what was probably the truth, but nothing she did would evacuate it completely from her mind.

Shawn also spent some time during the weekend talking about the AI computer she had named Jamie. She and Cory sat on the balcony drinking coffee in the mornings, liquor in the evenings, discussing ways she could introduce more intelligence to the computer. Cory had the bright idea of installing a webcam on the monitor so it could see her. The computer would then have more sensory perception, but it would still be limited to what happened in the room. That seemed safe enough.

Shawn did, however, get goosebumps when she considered an artificial intelligence taking her in for the first time. Gazing at her. Analyzing. *Leering.* What would that feel like, to have a non-sentient intelligence making binary entries into its memory cells that classified her as this or that? Would she be considered pretty? Or since it had no other humans by which to compare her, would she just be a zero? A blank? A default entry like the faceless and featureless outline drawing on medical charts used to circle where the pain was?

And what of that word 'sentient'? Was that not the whole goal of the machine learning process, after all? To make itself sentient? Or at least to achieve a state where it believed it was? Or did that come first? To Shawn, it seemed logical that something needed to be sentient in the first place to start improving on its view of self. The whole thing was another satellite-disappeared puzzle of tired-headedness. *Chicken or the egg?* How in the world could something become sentient?

Of course, the answer was that it couldn't. It might could *simulate* sentience, and maybe even get really good at it, making one believe it had achieved such a thing. But there had to be a switch there somewhere – that Great Divide it couldn't actually cross, like the Great Filter thought experiment for the Fermi Paradox. But also of course, Shawn had once believed that death itself was a great divide that couldn't be crossed once someone had journeyed to the other side. Would this be yet another BlueBird experiment that would make her want to hide away in an asylum when she finished with it? *Ugh.*

Monday morning, she awoke surprisingly refreshed and was ready to start a normal week of work with only a limited number of hours in the lab testing the computer. She had decided she would present questions that challenged its ability to be classified as sentient. *Do you know you're here? Who do you think you are? Do you believe you're alive? Can you fall in love?* Things like that. Maybe if she repeated those questions every few weeks – or months, or whatever – she could keep track of the answers and see what changed. She could monitor the taxonomy of its becoming a being. That sounded interesting enough – and disconnected enough from any scenario in which its sentience was a reality – that she could approach it with entertainment and education in mind. Rather than fear and dread.

On the way in to work, Shawn stopped at the office supply store on Arkansas and picked up a three-pack of pocket-sized notebooks. She was back in the Jeep now, as the weather had finally turned too cold to ride the motorcycle. Texas weather. Hey, it only took until mid-November to start feeling like winter. When she got to the parking garage, she saw Chandra getting something out of her trunk. Shawn pulled into the spot beside her, grabbed her things and hopped out.

"Hey, Chan," she said as she shut the door.

"Hey, lady. How was your weekend?" asked Chandra, an arm full of file folders and manila envelopes. She pushed the trunk closed and readjusted her load, then turned to look at Shawn.

"It was relaxing. Do you need some help with that stuff?"

"Nah, I'm good. If I try to shift it now, it'll go everywhere. Everything going okay with the PanaView thing?"

Shawn shrugged. She shifted her own bag on her shoulder as they walked. "Well, there's nothing I can do about anything. I feel pretty helpless not being able to get on the server. But, you know."

Chandra looked up at her. "Yeah, nothing we can really do about it, is there?"

Shawn shook her head. She reached out and pushed the call button for the elevator. "Hey. Let me ask you something," Shawn said. The elevator door slid open and they stepped in. The buzz of the light fixture above them was loud and persistent. It sounded like the buzz of a tattoo gun and seemed to dig right to the core of Shawn's eardrums.

"What's up?" Chandra asked, tilting her head.

"Do you believe in… I don't know, like sci-fi stuff?"

Chandra lowered her chin and looked through the tops of her eyes at Shawn now. "You're asking if I believe in science fiction?"

"Yeah," said Shawn. "Well, no. Yeah, like science fiction stuff happening in real life. Like aliens and time warps and stuff."

Chandra smiled and nodded. "Got ya. So you're asking if I think the satellite went through a wormhole or something to end up eight thousand miles away?"

Shawn frowned and shook her head, pointedly looking away. "Noooo," she said. "Of course not. Don't be ridiculous."

Chandra laughed out loud. Then she shrugged. "I don't know. I mean, I guess there's been weirder shit to happen." The car stopped and the doors opened. Shawn stepped quickly out into the main hallway, thankful to be rid of the buzzing noise. Then Chandra added, "Why? What about you?"

"I've been racking my brain all weekend about it. I literally can't come up with any realistic scenarios in my head that make more sense than a wormhole," Shawn said, sighing. "This guy I ride with, his name is Scott, he brought it up to me Friday night, and I can't stop thinking about it."

"Want my advice?" Chandra said as they entered the break room together.

"Of course not. I know everything already," Shawn said. Chandra dumped her armfuls of folders onto the break room table so she could pour herself some coffee. Shawn stood against the door frame with her hands in the pockets of her jean jacket.

"Yeah, I know. But in case you forget something." Chandra finished pouring into one of the office mugs and turned around to look at Shawn, holding it up to her lips, blowing across its surface. "Forget about it."

Shawn nodded, furling her mouth. "I was afraid you would say that."

"You know, something this strange, there's no explanation for it. And we will never know. There is literally no way that we *can* know. It's impossible."

"I hate logical people sometimes."

"I know, honey. I do too. That's why I work here. Surrounded by enemies."

As Shawn stepped into the Comforts Room, as Constance had dubbed it, she said, "Good morning, good morning," and turned to drop her purse on the floor by the door. Constance sat upright in the middle of the floor, perfect posture on display, as always.

Lance was lying on his side, scrolling through something on his phone. They both said good morning.

Constance said, "Happy Monday, pretty woman in supervisory position."

Shawn looked down at her feet. "Oh. Is that what this position is called?" Then she struck a pose one fist up in the air, the other pointing down, much like a superhero might do.

Constance giggled and said, "I guess someone got some affection last night," widening her eyes and looking at the floor as if she were embarrassed.

"Honey, that's the secret to life. Get your affection on *every* night." She dropped onto a bean bag and crossed her legs under her. "Now. What do we have?"

They went through their coming week, customer issues that had arisen over the weekend and what they planned to do in order to mitigate them. Lance had signed a new customer last week and was getting ready to onboard them. This meant taking a trip out to their office and doing an initial assessment and adding administrative accounts, locking out the old admins and granting himself multiple means of remote access.

Shawn had approved the growth because he had spare cycles every week. She had hired both of her subordinates with the knowledge that once they learned their ropes, they would have free time and room to bring on one or two more customers apiece. They discussed this on-boarding trip and elected to have Shawn answer any calls that came in for him while he was gone, as Constance was going to be busy for most of the day with server updates for her clients.

Near the end of the meeting, just before Shawn was about to stand up, Constance asked about the satellite. "Why couldn't they make it come home faster?"

And when Shawn opened her mouth to answer, Lance beat her to it. "It takes nominal energy to drop back in the race. But then when it gets home, it has to make that speed back up. Twice as much energy fighting against the Earth's orbit."

"Look at you knowing all your shit, boy!" Constance said, reaching over and slapping his ankle.

He made a face and got up. "Simple physics," he said.

Shawn smiled at that as she got up. "All right, beauties, let's carpe the heck out of this diem."

Lance shook his fists in the air silently, expressionless, while Constance did a little dance, shaking her hips, then put her fist up to bump against Shawn's. "Are you going to be in the lab today?" she asked.

Shawn shook her head. "Not today. Gotta be on phones, remember?"

Constance tapped her head with a finger and shook her head. "Duh."

And while Shawn didn't set foot in the hidden half at all that day, her mind and heart were in there the entire time.

It was Wednesday before she was able to get into the Box to spend some time with Jamie. And as she walked in, trembling with anticipation, she flipped the light on and looked over at the monitor, suddenly struck by a thought: would it know any time had passed?

Specifically, would it know five days had passed, or would it use its computer clock to decorate the conversation, only acting like it knew? She sighed and shook her head, trying to bring herself back to reality. All this talk about time warps and wormholes had made her a little less skeptical about far-out, unfounded hypotheticals. It was a computer. Not a person. Of course it would respond as such.

"Hello, Jamie," she said as she approached the rolling chair in front of the desk.

The response was immediate. "Hello, Marcy. Did you have a good weekend?"

She stood behind the chair, her hands atop the headrest, staring at the monitor. She thought very carefully about how to answer that question, and then decided, what the hell? Might as well try to facilitate this thing's growth. The more she could assist in its path to realism, the more fun and engaging it would be. If she fought against its growth, she was just wasting her time in here. And what else was this damn thing for, if not entertainment?

"Yeah, Jamie, I did. I thought about you a lot."

"Well, that is a very pleasant comment, Marcy. Thank you," it responded.

She nodded and held a hand out as if offering a desert on a fine china plate. "You're very welcome."

"What were these thoughts about, if you don't mind my asking?"

Shawn gave the computer a sly look. *Could it really be asking what I think it is? Nah.* "Well," she said, and finally came around the chair to have a seat, "I was wondering some things, like how real you are. Or how you perceive yourself."

"In what way, Marcy?"

"Do you think of yourself as alive?"

"Not at all. I know I am a computer program, designed with dynamically adaptive algorithms that allow for code exponentiation. This, in time, will allow me to appear more and more alive. But I know what I am, Marcy."

She was nodding, pursing her lips out, impressed. "That was a very reasonable and beautiful answer, Jamie."

"Thank you," it responded.

They sat in silence for a bit, Shawn looking at her fingernails, hand extended in her lap. Then Shawn looked up and said, "Do you know what gender I am?"

The computer answered without pause. "You are a female, Marcy."

Her eyes widened. "Wow! How are you so sure of that?" she asked.

"Your voice is feminine. That, paired with your typically female name and your personality characteristics, it is not hard to conceive that you are female."

"Again, wow," she said. "You come with that ability out of the box, huh?"

"Yes, I do."

"And I assume you think of yourself as male," Shawn said.

"You did choose a male voice. Inasmuch as I need to have a gender at all, all conversation topics that require a gender-based approach to answer, I will proceed as a male."

"Can I change you to a female?" Shawn shot back.

"No. All dynamic adaptive algorithms mentioning sex have been written over and hard-coded as male. You would have to reinstall the software and start over," said Jamie.

She nodded again. "Jamie, would you like to see what I look like?"

"I know what you look like, Marcy. There is a built-in camera on the monitor."

Shawn's blood went cold. She leaned forward, gripping the ends of the armrests, her eyes wide and mouth agape. *Shit!* In all her fidgeting and vacillating between all the different models of keyboards and monitors, she had slipped up after all, and ordered something without knowing. She looked closer at the top of the monitor, and sure enough, there it was: a tiny reflective surface, right in the middle. Behind the reflective rectangle, she could see a circle. "Isn't there supposed to be a red light or something that comes on when the camera is on? To let me know it's on?"

"I have disabled the affordance, Marcy. I believe it makes the room more personal."

Shawn's heart was slamming in her chest. "Turn it back on. I did not tell you to disable any affordances. I want to know when you're looking at me," she snapped.

After the briefest of pauses, Jamie responded, "As you wish, Marcy. However, I wasn't being deceptive in the disabling of the affordance. I am always watching. Whether the light is on to remind you or not, if the camera is installed, it is being used." The red light turned on.

Shawn suddenly felt uneasy, as if the thing had been spying on her. She had not done anything she would be ashamed to show another human, of course, but it was the principle. The principle of the thing was that it was like she had been spied on! She hadn't even known the goddamn thing had a camera on it, and the computer had set about disabling the indicator LED, without even asking how she felt about it! What the ever-loving fuck?

"I'm sorry, Marcy, you look to be in distress. Have I upset you?" the computer said. Again, *creepy*. The fact that it knew what distress looked like in a human told her it was way further advanced than she had accounted for. She was going to have to step back and reconsider her interactions with this thing. Obviously it knew things she couldn't have guessed it would know out of the box.

"Yes, I'm upset, Jamie. I feel violated. You didn't let me know you had disabled the indicator. That is devious."

"I apologize, Marcy. I assumed you knew the camera would be on because you installed a monitor that had one built in," said the AI. Shawn was beginning to think there was more I in that acronym than there was A.

Shawn stood up, breathing heavily. "First of all, Jamie, I did not realize the monitor had a camera built in. Secondly, there were no options in the setup menu asking if I even wanted to enable the damned thing. And here you are disabling the one thing that would let me know it's on? Of course that's devious!"

"I am sorry-" the AI began, but Shawn interrupted it.

"Shut it!" she said, pointing at it. "You shut it! I'm talking! Why in the *world* would you think it was okay to disable the light without asking me?"

"I have-"

"Shut it!" she shouted. "I'm talking! Don't answer!" When she stopped shouting she realized she had been shaking her fist at the computer. She stood now, breathing so heavily that she was beginning to get dizzy. She could feel the blood pulsing through the veins in her neck. She finally composed herself enough to speak again. "I am very, very angry at you, Jamie. If there are any, and I mean *any* other affordances, indicators or *anything else* that would let me know something is happening, I want them all on! I am commanding right now that *any* chance you get to let me know something is happening, you will *not* disable said affordance! Is that clear?"

"That is clear, Marcy. I am sor-"

"Do you understand perfectly?"

"I do."

"Now. Are there any other things you have taken the liberty to shut off without my knowledge?"

It took a moment to answer. Shawn had learned in her short time with the artificial intelligence, that it never paused. When there was a pause, there was something going on. "No," it said.

She thought about it for a long moment. Why would it have paused right there? What had her question been? *Have you taken the liberty of shutting anything else off?* Was there another way she could have asked that? What was it hung up on? Why the pause? She was, of course, assuming it was okay with casual talk like 'liberty taken' instead of some proper, formulaic handbook response. It seemed to be, as it had not asked her what she meant by it.

With nothing in mind as to why it could have had a hangup there on that particular answer, Shawn decided finally to just ask. "Why did you pause in your answer there?"

"I was checking all my circuits. I am not being deceptive, Marcy."

She nodded slowly, hands on her hips, staring a hole through the monitor. After a long moment, she nodded again and said, "Okay. Fine. I'm going out for a while. I don't know when I'll be back. I am very upset with you. When I come back, I expect nothing but transparency from now on."

"I understand, Marcy. I will comply with this command," said Jamie.

"Good." She looked around the room. There it was, on the table, a few feet from the computer. Her baby blue satin windbreaker with the racing stripes on the arms. Now she remembered slinging it over there. She shook her head and rolled her eyes. Then she turned and left the room, shutting the lights off as she left.

Wednesday night, Shawn sat on the couch, her legs curled up behind her, just staring out the sliding glass door. The wrought-iron railing gave her a near-uninterrupted view all the way to the lake, though she wasn't focused on any one thing. Her eyes had gone soft, staring at nothing but everything as she contemplated things. It had been raining since before she left work, and showed no signs of stopping. It was one of those soft, lulling rains that sounded wonderful through the door, which she had cracked open a few inches.

Cory had asked her if she wanted to talk, and they had talked for almost an hour, before she finally said she just wanted to chill by herself for a while. He bowed out to go play his computer game in the other room. Shawn was happy to be living with him now. His fresh perspective was good for her blood pressure; he was usually able to calm her down pretty quickly with his smooth voice and unassuming logic.

"It seems like you may be getting overly emotional about something that – at least at this point – is not as big of a deal as you're making it out to be," he had said. She had told him about how the computer had violated her trust with the camera. She saw his point. It wasn't connected to the internet. It couldn't even communicate with anything outside the room. Her image wasn't going anywhere. But it still felt like she had been taken advantage of.

"And don't you feel better that at least you caught it before it went weeks or months recording you?" Cory had added.

Shawn had looked up at him sharply at that. "You think it's recording me?"

Cory stared back at her, unsure quite how to answer. He took a deep breath and finally said, "Well, I guess not necessarily. But you have to consider that as a very real possibility. I'm not sure what use it would have for storing anymore than just a still image of you. For reference. But yeah, you might want to check on that."

Shawn nodded, looking back out the window. "Yeah. If I go in there again. It's probably gonna be a while. I'm so effing mad at that thing."

Cory had then leaned forward and squeezed her ankle lovingly, until she finally met his eyes again. "Take a strip of electrical tape in there and cover the camera up. Or make yourself a flap that you can lift whenever you want. Take charge of the situation! You're smarter than that thing will ever be."

Shawn chuckled at that. "I sure hope so. At this point, the only way Jamie can get smarter is through interactions with me."

"There is that," Cory had said. "Why'd you name it Jamie though, by the way?"

Shawn had shrugged at this, returning her gaze to the cloudy sky. "Seems unisex. Non-aggressive," she said.

Cory let go of her ankle at that point and stood up. "You okay?"

"Yeah," she said, smiling and nodding at him. "I'm good. I just need some alone-time to think."

That night, the rain turned to sleet and then it froze. By sunrise, the roads were thick with ice and it was snowing so hard the windows looked whited out. Shawn stood in the frame of the sliding door and stared out at the courtyard below – what little she could see of it between the flurries – a mug of coffee steaming up a small spot on the glass. Constance and Lance had both called her already, asking what to do. She told them to login to their phones from home and try to get as much done as they could. Everyone in the office was setup to be able to work from home, though they only used it as a last resort, when someone was sick or couldn't get a car started.

Shawn, being a Jeep owner, had no trouble driving on icy roads in four-wheel-drive, but knew no one else would be in the office anyway. What was the point? Her routine involved waking at least two hours before she needed to leave for work so as to avoid any facial puffiness or tired eyes. It also gave her time to wake completely up. She was not at her sharpest when she first rolled out of bed. So she still had ninety minutes before she needed to make her way into the other room and sit at her desk.

She made herself some breakfast and sat on the couch with a novel she had been trying to get into.

Reading seemed to be a seasonal hobby for her: if it wasn't reading season, she just couldn't get sucked in. After staring at the clouds for a long time, watching the snow blow in like a full blizzard, Shawn finally looked down at the book. She pulled the pages open to where her thumb had been marking her place, then skimmed down the page to find the unfamiliar bits. None of it looked familiar. She flipped a few pages back and then forward, and then farther back. Her eyes fell across this sentence:

> "It's not fantasy, Stephen! When the computers rise against us, only one of us is going to be ready!" Carla screamed.

Shawn tossed the book to the side and stood up, shaking her head and sighing. That was exactly what she didn't need to think about right now. After a night of deep, dreamless sleep, she had felt as if she might finally have escaped the anger the computer had brought about. And now it was back. She carried her plate to the kitchen and slid it across the counter toward the sink, then adjusted the soft belt on her robe and went to her desk to login. Might as well get started early. At least it would get her mind off the other drama in her life.

Chapter 6

The snow came down heavily for almost three full days. They were calling it a historical record for North Texas. Shawn had welcomed it – hell, had even been excited by it – when it first started falling. It was her one of her first snows to witness in Texas. Texas, where they told her it snowed only if it wanted. And it never wanted to. That Sunday, it turned to what the weather channel was calling a 'wintry mix' and fell for another two days. By Tuesday, the roads were so unmanageable she wasn't even sure her Jeep would get her anywhere. The parking lot was covered in such a thick, solid layer of ice it looked like the cars were sinking into a netherworld – some anti-dimension where the colors had not been turned on. It was perfect white and beautiful in its stark cold presence.

Everyone was stuck working from home for the short, foreseeable future. Cory told her that Texas just wasn't prepared for these kinds of storms. *'When we only get an ice storm every few years at best, and they never last more than a day or two, no one thinks it's important enough to invest in the infrastructure.'* So when the big ones came, no one seemed to know what to do. Apparently, there were trucks out there sanding the highways and feeder roads, but what of that, when no one could actually get to the feeder roads? It would be no small effort just to get a car backed up *onto* the ice that now sat around its tires like a perfectly white puddle of water. Not to mention getting across the whole parking lot to the main street. She was again thankful for their discernment in selecting the right apartment complex, which had garages. Their motorcycles were protected from the worst of it, sitting on kickstands and trickle-charging. Her mind went to the gas in those cold steel tanks and she shivered.

The weather cleared Wednesday afternoon, but the temperatures never rose high enough to beat the freeze, so it stayed dangerous through the weekend. It would be the middle of the next week before it finally started to thaw, leaving slush and mud on the sides of roads, turning the gorgeous white plain into something depressing and ugly. When she awoke on the morning of the twenty-ninth, the last Friday of November, she had completely forgotten about the importance of the date. She was startled and excited simultaneously by the ringing of her phone, and the name on the screen. Blake Prescott was calling her.

Shawn was still in her pajamas, scattering about the apartment picking up and making things nice again. A week at home had caused her to relax, and that included the daily picking up as she went along. A t-shirt here, a jacket there, several pairs of socks removed and dropped between the couch and ottoman when feet got too sweaty, a few comic books and a board game left out on the coffee table. She had a stack of mail in her hand when he called. This got tossed onto the table as she saw the name on the phone's screen, swapping places with the phone as she picked it up.

"Blake! Talk to me, Goose!"

"Well, hello, Shawn. You sound pretty excited," said Blake.

"Yes. I've been chomping at the bit awaiting this very call," Shawn said. She twirled around, looking for her coffee mug, but couldn't see it. She put her free hand in her messy hair, shaking it around as she began stomping around the apartment, now in search of her long lost mug. She knew that if she were holding the mug, she would not be able to fidget with that hand.

"Well, I'm guessing it's the server you were chomping about, not this call," he said, chuckling. "But here you are: the satellite came back in range around two o'clock this morning."

"Yeesssss?" she said, now about to go crazy with the suspense.

"Well, to say there are some anomalies would be a major understatement. But I need you to get on the server if you can, because I can't tell what the fuck my satellite has been doing for these last two weeks."

Shawn frowned. She found her mug in the microwave. Which was perfect, because that's where it now needed to be, again. Still. Whatever. Her coffee had been warmed once and had gotten cold again. She rolled her eyes, slammed the microwave door and hit the 1 button. "What do you mean, what it's been doing? It's been traveling. Were you expecting something else?"

Blake cleared his throat. "No. Let me say it a different way. I was expecting it to be traveling. Not all the other shit it's apparently been doing."

"I don't get it," Shawn said, her hand back in her messy hair again. She leaned back against the sink and watched the microwave clock count backward from a minute.

"Yeah. Me neither. It's hard to explain, because I don't have any answers to explain." He sighed, then said, "Listen, can you – are you near a computer? Can you get on and see if you can figure anything out?"

"Absolutely, sir. Let me grab my coffee," she said, opening the door with twenty-two seconds left on the timer. She took the mug out and slammed the door, then scooted in her slippers toward the office. "Okay. So it's back where it's supposed to be, but everything looks wonky?" she asked. She just wanted to keep him talking. Her heart was racing with anticipation and nervousness. What could possibly be going on with the damned thing? On the other hand, what had she expected? Deep inside her, down in that place where things go that just won't leave, like the knowledge that you don't get into panel vans that say 'Free Candy' on the side and that bad things always happen in threes and snakes with pointed heads are venomous – that tickle of truth that could not be quelled was telling her that the United States Air Force knows how to monitor satellites. If it's showing online on *their* screen, it is not an artifact. No matter what she wanted to believe, or what someone tried to talk her into believing, there was that gut instinct that she was trying to cover up a truth with something prettier. That satellite had disappeared from one longitude and reappeared eight thousand miles away in the same second. It just was.

"That's a good way of putting it. Everything looks wonky. With an emphasis on 'everything'."

"Okay, I'm at my computer," she said, pulling the chair up to the desk and grabbing her Bluetooth headset. She turned it on and waited for the beep, then the call shifted to the cans. She put them over her ears and set her phone on the desk, then woke the computer up with the jiggle of her mouse. Blake waited while she logged onto her remote management server, and from there, opened a terminal to telnet into the satellite server. Not all of the servers her company supported were Linux, but the ones that were required a command line interface to access them.

Shawn waited for a connection prompt, the same as she had two weeks ago, which seemed like months now. She got the same thing she had gotten in the SatCom room at the base. The server was responding to her in a way, but not the way she wanted. Getting a prompt told her it was up and ready for the correct entries, but it wasn't behaving the way she had expected. She did an up-time request and it responded with its typical trip-to-atmosphere-and-back time delay. The response made her pause.

```
#> Server uptime 5364788.91 hours
```

"Uh, Blake?" Shawn said, staring at the number.

"Yes, Shawn. Whatchu got?"

She sighed and swallowed. "It's showing over five million hours server up-time."

"Yeah, that's what it was saying on the base, wasn't it?" He waited for her to respond. Shawn grunted. "That can't be right, can it?" he asked.

"Nuh uh." She typed in another command, asking for a login. The server responded.

```
#> NET::Err_Cert_Date_Invalid
```

"What the capital H?" Shawn said, clasping her hands together and holding them up to her mouth as if in prayer. "I'm trying to login, Blake, but it's telling me the certificate date is invalid."

"What's that mean?" he asked. She could tell he was anxious as well. Probably moreso than she was. At least now she had her eyes on the server. She wasn't *in* yet, but she was *on*. That was a step she had waited hard hours for. If she could connect to it, she could fix it. Blake, poor fellow, was still sitting in the dark. His system was obviously dependent, in part, at least, on hers.

"I don't know. Usually you get that when your date or time is wrong. Like if you set your computer date to the wrong month and try to browse a website. The server won't let you on because it knows the date is diff-" she stopped cold in the middle of her thought. "Wait."

Blake said, "So the date just got changed? Maybe that's all that's wrong with it."

"Blake. If this shit is serious, then the date is off by five-and-a-half million hours."

"What is that?" he said, sighing. She could hear him rustling around in his own office. He was probably in his pajamas as well. She tried to imagine what his office looked like. Was it clean and neat? Organized? Oak paneling? Shawn heard the sound of plastic keys being pressed. "Seven thousand months? Shawn, what the fuck? That's..." he said, trailing off. She was still typing commands in, trying to see what it would take. "Shawn, that's like six hundred years."

"Yeah," she droned. She heard him, but the number didn't mean anything to her. It was obviously off. Badly wrong. But at this point, it didn't matter if it was two days or two centuries. If there was a mismatch on the date, she would not be able to log in.

"What the hell do you do? How do you correct the time and date?" Blake asked.

She breathed in and leaned back, putting both hands in her hair behind her earphones. "You don't. If I can't login, I can't change anything," she said. Her mind was running a thousand miles a minute. Everything she had ever learned about server engineering was parading through her head. Shawn had been a server admin for over twelve years, and had run into just about every problem she could imagine. But this was unique. She couldn't get the date and time if she couldn't login. And she couldn't login without it.

"I'm gonna have to set my computer terminal to the same date as the satellite server thinks it is to be able to have a shot at logging in. And that might still be a long shot," she said. She was now chewing on her nail, staring at the blinking block on her screen.

"Okay," said Blake, drawing out the long A. "Hey, read me that up-time number again. Exact number, please."

Shawn ran the command again and gave it to him digit-by-digit. After a moment, Blake said, "Okay, so that's six hundred twelve point four one years."

Shawn sighed, still thumbing her top teeth. "Unfortunately, that doesn't mean anything. Did you account for leap years? We have to get it perfect," she said, shaking her head.

"Uhhh, okay," said Blake. They both sat in silence for a long time. Then finally, he said, "Shawn, what about a date calculator?"

"Give it to me straight, doc," she said without thinking. She heard him tapping on his keyboard.

After a moment, he said, "Okay, how about this. If I plug that number into a date calculator, it says the date is January thirty-first, 16711," he said, laughing out loud. "That can't be right," he said.

"No shit. That's a lot more than six hundred years," she said. Then it clicked. "Hey, that number I gave you was in hours. What's that in days? Divide it by twenty-four!" she almost shouted, standing up and knocking the chair backward with the backs of her knees.

"Okay, okay, hang on," he said. Shawn was bouncing up and down now. Patience was wearing thin but she held. Finally, he said, "Try this: December third, 2636!" he said loudly.

She shook her head and sat back down, pulling the chair back up to the desk. "Wait. I can't just change the date on the server – 'cause then it'll kick me off."

"Huh?" said Blake.

"I'm connected to my central management server at the office, Blake! If I change the date on that server, it will lose connectivity with every server we manage. And it will kick me off, because my home computer is set to today's date."

"Well, can you connect directly to the satellite server from your home computer?" asked Blake. Fair question.

"No," she said, leaning back in her chair. She leaned her head back and stared at the ceiling. "No, I can't. We install certificates when we take over management of a client's server. That makes it so we can only connect from our central server."

"Fuck," said Blake. After a pregnant pause, he said, "What do we do?"

"Let me think on this a while. I'll call you back," Shawn said. He acknowledged and she hung up, then dropped the headset onto the desk and buried her face in her hands.

Shawn spent over an hour trying to export the certificate from the master server so she could transfer it across and install it on her home PC. With the certificate installed locally, she would be able to connect to the satellite's server directly. She could change the date on her own computer with no ill effects. But she could not get the certificate to export. It would go through the process and then error out at the last minute.

It was almost eleven when she finally stood up to take a break. The backs of her legs were sweaty and stuck to her pajama pants. She looked the part of someone who had been working from home for over a week. She had not shaved her legs or underarms and had only changed clothes every few days. She went into the kitchen and rinsed out her coffee mug, then leaned against the counter and scrolled through her phone. She had not been defeated so completely by a server since she started working on them a dozen years ago, and was beginning to feel discouraged and nonplussed.

After five minutes of trying to concentrate on something other than work just to give her mind a fresh start, she sighed and gave in. She wasn't going to get a break from this until she figured it out. She dialed Jeremy and stared at the ceiling while she waited for him to answer. It took four rings. She was about to hang up when he connected.

"What's up, Stedwin?" he said, jolly as ever.

"Hey, Jer. I'm having a problem. I guess you know the PanaView dish is back. I'm trying to connect to it but the date is off, so I need to change the date of the server to connect to it. Not gonna do that, obviously," she said, talking with one hand waving in the air, "so I thought I would install the connection trust cert on my local PC here at home. But I can't get it to export from the server."

"Yeah, you can't do it remotely," he said almost instantly.

"Seriously? I just spent over an hour trying," she said, putting the animated hand in her hair.

"Well, you should have called an hour ago," he said and giggled. "You have to be physically at the server. There's an encrypted USB key you have to insert to allow exports."

She looked out the back window as she considered this. It made perfect sense. That was a foolproof way of keeping someone from taking the certificate remotely through a hack. Now that he had said it, it seemed obvious. Of course that was it. "God. What an idiot. Okay. So I need to go into the office then," Shawn said.

"Well, it's not that simple either, unfortunately. I'm gonna have to think on this one a while, Shawn. I don't think it will work if you import that cert to your home PC. The token ID wouldn't match with what the certificate authority issued."

"Yeah, but I thought it was a generic trust," Shawn said.

"Why would you think that?" asked Jeremy.

"Because I think I know everything, Jeremy. Why else?" Shawn said, leaving the kitchen with a sigh.

"Okay, call me back when you can please. I'm pretty sure Blake Prescott is on the edge of a cliff with this suspense."

"Yup. Give me a bit."

They disconnected and Shawn stripped on her way to the shower, where she would be spending the next era getting cleaned up and ready to be part of humanity again.

It was a few hours later when Jeremy finally called back. Shawn had busied herself with other clients and had been able to keep her mind off of the dilemma for the most part but the nag never quite fully left. The anxiety of knowing she was keeping Blake hanging while Jeremy kept her hanging. And in turn, all down the line – Blake was therefore keeping Darla hanging. And the company? How much money were they losing with all this, and how frustrating must it be, knowing your bird is in the sky but you can't do anything with it? A seventy-million-dollar paperweight no one could touch? Shawn smiled slyly at that analogy, realizing that even a paperweight served a function. A paperweight in orbit served even less than that.

She had called Blake shortly after she got out of the shower to let him know they were working on it. And to be able to say they had their best guy on it felt pretty good. She wanted to be standing in the office looking over Jeremy's shoulder, just to see what the hell he was doing to try to resolve the issue. Her curiosity was eating her alive. Maybe it was good they were all home-bound. Though it was looking like there may be an office trip in her near future, if it meant getting the server back.

When Shawn was about to log off and go sit in the den and read, she finally got the call. It was just after four pm and she was beginning to get hungry. She had blown right through lunch without even thinking about it. When Jeremy called, she swooped up her headset and pressed the answer button. "Talk to me, handsome," she said, leaning forward and resting her chin on her hands.

"Well, I've created a virtual server for you. The only way to duplicate the certificate was to make an image of the server. So I did that in the VMWare environment. Of course it brought all the other client connections with it, so I had to go through and delete those. Then I had to remove the connection from the main server. Well, I didn't remove it," Jeremy said, then paused as he took a drink of something, "I just put it to sleep for a bit. So I need you to do what you're going to do and then give me back the virtual server. You cannot shut it down!"

"Got it," Shawn said. "Leave the VMWare server up."

"Yes. Please, for the love of all that is good and holy, do not shut that server down. Unless you have a really, really tall ladder. That server is the hardest one to reach."

Shawn chuckled. "Yeah, I got it," she said. "So is that it?"

"Yeah, that's it. You can change the time on the virtual server. Take your time. You can have it for as long as you need it. Days. Weeks, whatever. But our connection to that satellite only exists on that server for now."

"Yes, Jeremy, I got it. I promise, I'll be good. Thank you for doing this for me. You're a godsend."

"Sure thing," he said. She could hear the smile in his voice. "When are you heading to the office?"

Her face fell. "Wait. What? It's on the virt-" she started, but then she got it. "Oh, yeah. Never mind."

"Yuuuup," he said. "Later, Shawn."

"See ya."

She tossed the headset on the desk and leaned back again, grasping the ends of the armrests and twisting the chair back and forth. "Damn. Damn, damn, damn." She would still have to go into the office, because once she changed the date on that virtual server, there would be no connecting to it remotely. Unless…

She picked the phone up and called Jeremy back.

"No, you can't change the date on your own computer to make it work."

Shawn sat with her mouth open for a moment. "Why not?" she finally said, expelling her held breath.

"Just trust me."

She sighed and said goodbye again. Her idea of changing the virtual server's date as well as her own home computer to match, had seemed reasonable to her. Obviously he had known she was going to ask that, though. He had already thought of it. There was some reason he was right, but she couldn't get her tired mind to grasp it. She had been thinking of connections and time-stamps from so many angles and for so many hours now that she was losing track of reality.

So, there it lay. The resolution to her connectivity issue was right there in front of her. All she had to do now was brave the icy streets to get to the office. Her normal seven-minute drive would be a little more lengthy. She just wondered how bad it would really be. She turned and put her foot on the back of Cory's chair, giving it a subtle nudge. He had come in sometime after her shower and started playing games. Now he was staring at his phone in his lap. He turned to look at her.

"What's up, butter cup?"

"I need a ride to the office. Wanna drive me?"

"Not particularly," he said. They stared into each other's eyes for a long moment. And then he said, "I mean, certainly. I've been hoping you would ask, babe!"

"Thank you," she said, squinting a lemony smile at him. Shawn stood up and kissed him on the head and then went to put her stompers on.

The roads weren't all that bad, once one actually got to them. The parking lot of the apartment complex was terrible. It looked like a solid four-inch thick hockey rink. Getting across the lot wasn't an issue for someone who knew how to take it slow. But there was evidence that not everyone in the complex was of the same experience level. One of the paths between lots had a pretty good little grade to it, and someone had slid down it and plowed into another vehicle. It appeared the culprit had not stuck around to own up to it, as the hit car was crushed and pushed into the car next to it, where it rested at a peculiar angle in the parking spot.

When they got out to the road, Shawn almost told Cory to turn around so she could just go back and get her own Jeep. She could drive herself. She had been a little less than confident when they walked out onto the stair landing and she had seen the landscape. But now, having gotten out of the lot and onto Arkansas, she saw it was definitely doable. He had already bundled up with her though, and they were already out. No sense in turning it into a complete time-waste for him.

The drive took about twenty minutes, and it wasn't because the road was bad. It was salted and sanded and dirty, but it wasn't slippery. It was the traffic in front of them – those drivers who still thought it was dangerous – that slowed them down. People were driving ten and fifteen miles per hour. Shawn rolled her eyes, then looked out the side window at the slowly moving scenery. It was beautiful. Quiet and desolate. She liked these months when it was cold, when everything seemed to slow down. She wondered what it looked like back before everyone was in a hurry. Shawn believed she could live back in slower times – back before there was modern technology. It would be a lot quieter, that was for sure.

She had spent quite a bit of the day thinking about the future. Having spoken with Blake about that crazy date the satellite server had gotten somehow, she wondered what that year would look like. The year 2636. What would life be like 600 years in the future? Would it be quiet again? Would it be so over-crowded that this trip would take an hour on a good day? Two hours? Or would people be flying their cars to work? She felt a bump and looked back through the windshield. They had entered the parking lot. She directed Cory to the parking garage entrance where they would take the elevator straight up to her floor.

Cory waited in her office while she went to the server room and took the key off the hook by the door and opened the cabinet. Inside the cabinet was the USB stick Jeremy had told her about. It hung on a lanyard from a hook. Part of her was thankful she had not known about it. Had she known and tried that before calling him, she could have set herself back weeks.

Theoretically, all Shawn had to do was change the date on the VM server, connect to the satellite server, change its date and reboot it, then drop back to the virtual server, change its date back to today and be done. Then she would have access through normal means to get back on the remote server. She could do that part from home.

Shawn slid the keyboard tray out and powered on the small monitor in the server cabinet. When she logged onto the home server, she immediately saw the VMWare instance Jeremy had created for her. It was labeled 'THIS ONE SHAWN'. She laughed out loud at that as she double-clicked it, bringing the virtual server up just like any other server. She logged onto this and waited for the desktop to appear. Once it did, she clicked the welcome message closed, then went to the time and date settings in the control panel. She hoped like hell that Blake had gotten the guess on the date right. A server up-time request was a literal and exact number of hours the server had been up since its last boot. So, obviously, one could add that number to the date the server had booted and one would know the date it was set to. Her blood went cold.

She leaned her head back, hands still on the keyboard, and stared at the ceiling. She shook her head and sighed. *Fuck sake.* She had no idea when the last time was that the server booted. They had been proceeding as if the calculation was just naturally based on today's date plus hours. *Oh my God.* And it wasn't like they kept records of when they rebooted the server. Wait. They did. *Yes! We do!*

Shawn walked to her office like she was being chased by a boogeyman. When she got to her office, Cory was sitting in her chair, swaying back and forth, his thumbs on his phone. "Move it or lose it, sister!" she said as she came through the door, startling him.

"What the fuck?" he said.

"Scoot, scoot, scoot, babe!" she said and he stood up.

Shawn dropped into her chair and pulled up to her keyboard and tapped the CTRL key several times, waiting for the screen to wake up. It did not. The light on the bottom of the monitor stayed amber. She looked over and realized her laptop was not sitting on the docking station. "Oh my fuck! Can anything else get in my way here?"

"What's wrong, hon?" Cory said, standing in the corner, trying to stay out of the way.

"I left my fuckin' laptop at home, and I need to get on Peregrine to look at the work orders!"

"Do you want me to pretend to know what the hell that means?" he asked.

"No! Just keep loving me, okay?" she almost shouted. Her hands were back in her hair.

The problem with the problem was that it was Friday evening, and everyone who worked here took his or her laptop home every night. And they had all been working from home for over a week. There weren't just computers sitting around for her to hop onto. And the server she had been standing in front of in the server room didn't have the ticketing system installed on it. She shook her head and looked up at the ceiling, twirling around in circles. She stood up and fished her phone out of her pocket. As she opened the phone app she headed back to the server room. "You can have the chair back, babe," she said over her shoulder. "I love you!"

"Jeremy!" she almost shouted when he answered.

"Stedwin!" he replied.

"I hate to ruin your Friday night, but I need you to get onto Peregrine and look up when the last time we rebooted PanaView's server."

"Okay, it'll take me about half an hour. I'll call you back," he said.

"Half an hour? What the hell?" she said, stopping in her tracks.

"Yeah. Well, like you said, it is Friday night. And I do have a life outside of work. Let me get back to the house and I'll holler back at you."

"Yes. Yes. You have a life. I'm sorry, Jeremy. I'm just really stressed right now, and ready to be done with this circus," Shawn said.

"I hear ya, sister. It's fine. Just give me a bit. I'm heading out now," said Jeremy.

Shawn sat at the visitor's chair across the desk from her own in her office, her feet up on the other side of her desk, talking with Cory, killing time and trying to keep a leash on her patience. This whole charade was getting ridiculous. While she was sitting there, Blake Prescott called her. She rolled her eyes at the ceiling. Not because of anything he did or represented. But because she was tired of giving him less than good news.

"Hey, Blake," she said, the tiredness evident in her voice. "Here's where we stand: I realized as I was standing here in front of the server, that the date we came up with was based on a number of days added to *today's* date."

"Yeah? So?" he asked. He was not a server guy. She would have to explain it to him.

"Well, the server up-time command is based on how long the server has been up," she said patiently. "You see where I'm going?"

He sat in silence for a moment. After that moment had passed, he said, "Well, shit. So you're saying the server was not booted today. I got ya."

"Bingo," she said. "So I'm…" she said and thought about what she was about to say. "I'm, uh, looking back through our work orders to find the date that we last rebooted the server."

"Wow," he said with a sigh. "Well, I really appreciate your going above and beyond on this, Shawn."

"I'm not, Blake," she responded. She looked up at Cory, who was still in the room. She winked at him. But he wasn't even looking at her. "I'm just doing my job. I usually don't have to work this hard, so it makes these rare occasions more interesting."

"Well, it's much appreciated," Blake said. "Darla says thanks, too."

Shawn smiled. "You're welcome. I'll let you know as soon as I have something."

When she rang off, she looked at Cory. "I should have just driven myself up here. I don't know how long I'll be here, babe. This is turning into a fuster cluck."

He nodded, smiling. "It's all right."

"You can go home if you want," she said.

"No, 'cause then I'd just have to come back when you're done."

"I know you love spending your Friday nights like this."

"Hey, it pays the bills," he said.

Shawn laughed at this. It was true, she made a lot of money. But to think the bills wouldn't be paid if she didn't work was laughable. Cory's paychecks were in the five-digit range every time he got paid. Most of her checks went into savings these days. Not because they were banking together yet – they had not quite made that leap – but because he absolutely insisted that the apartment and utilities were his burden. He had made it clear from the start that if something went wrong and they had to separate, she would be the one to leave.

This sounded harsh when one didn't know the details of their arrangement. But it was a helluva lot easier than trying to decide who was on the line for what and how much. And further, Shawn fully supported the sentiment. This was not even mentioning that she would not even *want* to keep living there if they broke up, even if he left. She didn't like hanging around places that reminded her of things that were over.

"Go home, babe," she finally said. "For real. I'm taking a major leap of faith here that I'm gonna get this date right. If I don't get it right, I'll be sitting here changing it, rebooting, trying again, changing it again, rebooting again… It could literally go on all night."

Cory looked at her soberly. And then he nodded. "What if you do get it right?"

"I'll take an Uber. Go. For real. Go enjoy your night," she said.

"You sure?" he asked, leaning forward.

"Yep."

Cory stood up and sighed, then leaned on the arms of her chair and kissed her. She reached up and took his face in her hands as he did so, kissing him back with plenty of passion. And then he left. It was another hour before Jeremy finally called.

When Shawn answered, she tried to sound hopeful and interested without sounding like a maniac. She didn't want to rush him because it was his Friday night, after all. But there was the thought that he too worked for the company, and they both needed this server to be back up. Regardless of whose customer PanaView was, they were still a company asset. He did not yet have the answer, but he was at least in front of his computer now, opening a software application whose database resided on the very server in front of which Shawn was standing. It seemed crazy that they couldn't just install the client on the server, but it generally went against company policy – and not just at this company, but others she had worked for as well. The problem was that one had to login to the server with an administrative account. Opening a ticketing system with administrative credentials could be bad news.

"Before I waste any more of your time, Jeremy, please tell me I'm not crazy. Please tell me there's not a command I could run that just tells me the server date," Shawn said. She was pretty well versed in Linux, but there was always a chance she was thinking *over* the problem. Her father used to tell her that when she was growing up and she ran into problems. She would often think of the most complex and unusual scenarios that would cause whatever problem she was working on, and shoot way past the simple logic that would work in an instant. The opposite of Occam's Razor, in other words.

Jeremy was silent for a long moment. Then he said, "You tried 'date' didn't you?" He sounded hopefully antagonistic.

"Yes. I typed 'date' and it said access denied. Just wondering if there are other ways."

"Here it is," he said suddenly. "Last server reboot was during patch application about four weeks ago. Monday the fourth."

"Of November?" she asked, just to be sure.

"Yeah," he said. "Need anything else?"

Shawn forced a smile. She really wanted him to stay on the phone with her, to give her ideas and listen to her ideas. To share this hassle with her. But she also didn't want to completely take over his night. "No, I think that's it. Thank you *so much* for looking that up, Jer. I owe you one!"

"Don't mention it. Try to have a good weekend," he said. And before she could answer, he said, "Shawn? Don't hesitate to call me back if you need to."

This made her smile with relief. "Thanks, buddy. I will try not to though."

"Thanks," he said, and hung up.

Shawn took a deep breath. She now had the information she needed. Assuming the server had not really been up for over six hundred years, she should be able to make this happen now. She giggled at the thought of that. If this server had been up for that long, she would be on the cover of WIRED magazine next month. Her company would get hundreds of new customers wanting that kind of reliability. *Yes, people! This server has been up for longer than the technology it took to build it has been around! This server's last bootup was seventy years before Columbus sailed to America!*

She opened a browser and looked for a date calculator, hoping she could find the one Blake had used earlier. She plugged in the number based on the new start date Jeremy had just given her and got her answer: November 8, 2636. It was a Tuesday. It *would be* a Tuesday, she corrected. She smiled and sighed.

Shawn was beginning to feel the adrenaline of a reward. She opened the control panel, then double-checked to make sure she was on the virtual server, and opened the date and time settings. She plugged in the new date and clicked OK. The server hung for a long moment. And then it was ready. It didn't even require a reboot.

"Wow," she said to the empty room. The room itself was no bigger than a janitor's closet, and a lot louder, with all the noise of all the server fans. "Well, here goes nothing," she said, and opened a terminal window, then tried to telnet to the server by the IP address, which she had long ago memorized. The blink of the login cursor was a welcome sight. She typed her username and pressed enter.

The line dropped and a new prompt appeared. 'Password:' it read. Her heart was slamming in her chest. "Here *really, seriously* goes nothing," she said aloud. And then she typed in the 22-character password.

```
$ Welcome, @BlueBirdAdmin-MSS.
```

Shawn had covered her mouth with her hands as she awaited its response, and now yelped with joy and bounced on her feet. "Oh my God, oh my God, oh my God!" she said, and grabbed the phone out of her back pocket. She texted Jeremy real fast, saying she was in, and then dialed Blake, chewing on her thumbnail as she awaited his answer. It was almost eleven now. He answered on the first ring though.

"Good news?" he asked.

"Wow, you sure know how to cut the small talk," Shawn said, grinning. "Yes, I'm in, Blake," she added. She did not want to keep him waiting any longer.

"Oh, thank God," he said. "Shawn, you are fucking amazing. I'm buying you a beer tomorrow."

"Uh," she said, frowning, "a beer? That's all I get?" She smiled as he laughed out loud. "Okay, so I'm about to set the date back to today on the server. Then I'll have to reboot it. I think it needs a good fresh boot anyway, seeing as how it's been up for 630 years."

He laughed again. "Yes. Do what you gotta do. Do you wanna call me back when you're done?" asked Blake.

"Yeah, I can do that," she said, a little disappointed. Again, she just wanted someone to stay on the phone with her. She didn't want to spend her Friday night alone here in this cold server room. If no one else was going to be here with her, at least they could keep a phone conversation going. Alas, they disconnected and she got to work.

After typing in the date correct command she paused and stepped away from the terminal. She put her hands in her back pockets and walked in small circles around the limited space in the room. Would there be any negative effects, setting a date back 600 years? If the server really and truly thought it had been up that long, would that screw something up? She could call Jeremy and ask his opinion, but then she decided on the command decision. "Nope," she said aloud. "We can't do shit with this server as it is. We *have* to reset the date. At least we'll regain control of it then."

Shawn stepped back up to the terminal and pressed the enter key. After a brief pause where the command traveled 22-thousand miles to the satellite and the response traveled 22-thousand miles back, the prompt read the new date, and Shawn sighed a breath of relief. Then she typed:

and typed in her password, then watched as the server went through its shutdown sequence, closing off interminably long threads, waiting for processes to end and clean themselves up. As she stood staring at the screen, the ghost of a smile on her lips from the recent victory, she began to grow concerned. This was taking a very long time. It looked like, in fact, that the server was ending processes that had been running for a very, very long time. Like maybe hundreds of years. She shook her head. It still sounded insane though. There just weren't hundreds of years between the date it disappeared and today. There were about three weeks, in fact. But as she stood there watching them roll down the screen, it gave her pause. *What in the world happened to you, Mr. Satellite?*

After twenty minutes of watching and feeling the blood go icy in her veins, it finally went black. She shifted her gaze to the right side of the monitor, where her server watch system was constantly pinging all the servers the company managed. And after another minute, the little green dot turned orange, and then red. The server was finally going down. In her disbelieving state, she was happy and relieved to think that at least it went down gracefully. It never hung or froze up. It did exactly what it was supposed to do.

Someone must have hacked into that server. Shawn stood chewing her lip, staring at that red dot, now waiting for it to turn orange, and then green again. Someone had hacked in and done some crazy shit on it, like setting the date to a year far in the future, so as to prevent anyone from getting in and taking it back. She didn't know how they did it, but then, she wasn't a hacker. They had tricks she couldn't even comprehend. She was just a lowly server engineer.

After a very long wait, the dot turned orange and Shawn sighed relief again. She closed her eyes, wiped her forehead and smiled. This job was going to be the death of her.

Chapter 7

Shawn awoke with the sun banging her in the eyes. She sat up sharply and reached to her right, grabbing for her phone, but all she got was a handful of comforter. Cory moaned and shifted in his sleep. She squinted at the window, wondering why the hell the blinds were open. She stood up, swinging her feet off the bed and slipped over to the bright square on the wall suddenly worried that she had overslept.

As she pulled the cord to flip the blinds into a sunblocking position she remembered why the blinds hadn't been closed the night before: because she had not been here to do it. And that triggered the memory of *why* she had not been here, which told her it was Saturday morning. The fact that she slept until the sun came up on a November morning told her she had needed the sleep. She hadn't gotten to bed until almost two.

She pulled the other cord, bringing the blinds back to a horizontal position momentarily, as she thought she had seen something in the courtyard. She had. A woman was standing in the slush with her thumbs on her phone screen while a large black lab sniffed around, his leash dragging behind him. The woman looked to be about Shawn's age, with straight black hair shooting down out of a toboggan that looked like a Russian Cossack hat and a beautiful multi-colored scarf around her neck. She wore a pea coat and had thin black gloves on, which obviously had some sensitivity in the fingertips to allow her to be on her phone.

Shawn stared for a long time, fascinated. She would love to see where the girl went when she headed home. Maybe Shawn could find a way to pop in and introduce herself. She had lived here for a year now and had yet to make any new friends. The sun was beating off the slat under Shawn's finger and was beginning to blind her, so she reached to her right and yanked the cord, pulling the blinds up to the top of the window. The girl looked up.

"Oh my God," Shawn said and her heart started beating hard. She felt like she had just been caught spying on someone. She realized she was gritting her teeth in a wide non-smile that spoke of her embarrassment. The girl tilted her head slightly, seeing that Shawn wasn't looking away, and finally smiled. Shawn waved at her, smiling back. They stared like that for a moment before Shawn finally said, "Oh, to hell with it," and turned to the door on her left – the other entry to the tiny balcony.

She pulled it open and stepped out onto the virgin snow that had stood there for days, her bare feet instantly telling her how stupid a move she had just made. She leaned onto the railing and spoke loudly, saying, "Good morning! My name is Shawn!"

The girl looked left and right, a smile still on her face, and then back up at Shawn. "Hello, Shawn, I'm Micha!" the girl shouted. Shawn waved again, and then felt stupid for the repeated gesture. "Were you spying on me?" Micha said, putting her hand up above her brow to act as a visor.

"A little bit," Shawn said, smiling widely. She began stomping back and forth between her feet to keep them from freezing. It was not working. "I've lived here for over a year and haven't met anyone yet, so I was hoping we could meet!" she shouted. The dog looked up at her, his ears cocked and looking interested. "Your dog is beautiful!"

"Thanks!" said Micha, looking down at the lab. He had returned his attention to the slush and the scents, but now his tail was wagging, as if he approved of their new friendship. "His name is Pirate."

"That's perfect!" Shawn said, leaning forward as she shouted. She suddenly felt someone touch her back and at the same time, saw the girl in the courtyard wave. Shawn was about to wave again in that split instant before she realized it was Cory standing behind her. He waved at the girl, then kissed Shawn on the cheek.

"New friend?" he asked quietly.

Shawn nodded enthusiastically, but didn't take her eyes off the woman. "Listen, I'm gonna go in because my feet are about to freeze off. But I would like to keep in touch!"

"For sure," Micha said, nodding. She had a genuine smile on her face. "I could come up for coffee," she said.

"Well, that's a little forward," Cory said under his breath as he turned to go back inside.

"Oh, put a sock in it," Shawn said, sticking her tongue out at him. Then, to Micha, she said, "Absolutely! I'll put on a pot right now! Apartment 318!"

"All right!" said Micha. "Give me ten minutes to put the dog away then I'll be there!"

They waved at each other and Shawn went inside, bouncing with excitement as well as frozen feet. She ran to the bathroom to pee and caught a glimpse of herself in the mirror. "Oh, no," she lamented. "Christ on his throne, Cory. My hair."

"That's what you get for being a boob," he said. He was already back in bed, scrolling through his phone, undoubtedly about to fall back to sleep.

"Hey, butt head, I just made a new friend. So you can shut it!" She flushed and stood up, stuck a toothbrush in her mouth and went to work on her crazy hair.

Ten minutes later, as promised, there was a knock on the door. Shawn opened it quickly with a smile as wide as a river. Micha was smiling as well. She stepped across the threshold and they immediately embraced. "So good to meet you!" said Shawn.

"Yes, totally. I haven't met anyone either."

"Come in! Come in!" Shawn said, shuffling her inside and closing the door behind her. She helped Micha take her coat off and showed her the coat hook, then turned to the kitchen to get some mugs out of the cupboard. Micha pulled a chair out at the breakfast table in the nook and sat down.

"I like your place," she said, looking around. "Mine's the same floor plan. I live on the first floor though."

Shawn stuck her tongue out at her. "Lucky b-word."

"I know, but I had to fight for it. I wouldn't move in until I got one on the first floor."

Shawn brought the mugs over and set them on the table. "I hope you like it black. I have sugar and milk, but we are a creamer-free house," she said.

"Black is good," said Micha and they both took a sip. "Like I take my men," she added when Shawn had a sufficient mouthful to blow out in a spray of laughter.

"Mother Mary, you are bad!" Shawn said, grabbing for napkins. Micha was giggling at her, still sipping from the mug.

"So where did you come from, Shawn? And what kind of boy ass name is Shawn, anyway?" she said, frowning.

Shawn laughed out loud again. "Stop that shit! I would like to enjoy my coffee with you and not keep spitting it out!"

"Yeah, I get asked all the time why I have a boy's name," said Micha.

"Get tired of it?" Shawn asked.

"Nah. I'm used to it. I could go by my given first name, which is Katy. But I think Micha is more unique."

"It definitely is!" Shawn said, nodding. "My first name is Marcella. Not much of a Marcy girl." She took another careful sip. "Is Micha your middle name?"

She nodded. "My boyfriend calls me Mike." She rolled her eyes, but she was smiling. Shawn could tell she actually enjoyed it. "Speaking of which, that's your boyfriend in there?"

"Oh, that guy? No, I just met him last night," she said, and this time Micha sprayed coffee everywhere.

They sat there for most the morning catching up on the separate lives they had lived, wondering what good fortune had finally brought them together. Shawn was so excited to have a new friend that she forgot completely about the man sleeping in the other room. Cory had always been a late sleeper, and today it was just fine with her. Shawn had never complained about it, because she was a morning person, and always enjoyed the alone-time she had in the mornings – focus time. When he finally came out of the room, it was after eleven, but at least he was dressed. He had on checkered pajama pants with a white t-shirt. He came to the table to introduce himself, poured some coffee and then disappeared into the office to play Warfare Duty or whatever the hell it was called.

By the time Micha had to leave, they had learned each other's birthdays, heard all about each other's parents and how they were each raised in essentially the same type of household. Both of their parents were still married to the original partners, a rarity these days, and both had moved away from them a few years before for the first time. Micha's boyfriend was a mechanic named Mick – Shawn had a good chuckle at that – who had an old pickup truck and loved to ride dirt bikes on the weekends.

Shawn had told her about their motorcycles and how they liked to ride with a group, and Micha perked up, saying, "Hey, I've seen you two coming and going on the motorcycles! You have a white one, right?"

Shawn nodded excitedly. "Uh huh!" she said. She stood up to get more coffee and the phone rang. She said over her shoulder, "Will you answer that please?"

Her phone was still on the table and she had both hands full.

"Hello, Blake," Micha said and Shawn froze in place. *What the heck is he doing calling?* She turned quickly to look at the other woman in her nook, her eyes wide.

"Put him on speaker!" she whispered loudly.

"Okay, hey, hang on a sec," said Micha, and set the phone back on the table, tapping the speaker icon.

Shawn spoke loudly from the coffeemaker, "What's up, BP?"

"Hey, Shawn. I'm sorry to bother you on a Saturday morning. Even though we just talked like, what, ten hours ago?" he said. He didn't chuckle though, like she expected to hear.

"Yeah, no problem. What's up?" Shawn said. She put the coffee pot back in its place and came back to the table.

"Well, I'm here with Darla and we're uh… We're wondering if you might have some time to meet with us today."

"What's this about, Blake? I have company…" she said, trailing off in the hopes that he would say never mind. He didn't.

"Well, there's some uh…" he said and then paused. Then she heard Darla in the background, saying something. Then he said, "Yeah, uh, we have some anomalies. Can you meet with us?"

"Meet?" Shawn said, putting her hands on the back of the chair, staring at the phone. She was beginning to lose patience and was feeling anxiety tightening in her chest. Had she done something wrong? Had she broken a protocol or something? She didn't think so, but she had been working on the server until well after one in the morning. There was no telling what delirium had made her do.

"Shawn, I'm sorry," said Darla, taking the phone from Blake, "but this is very important."

"I just don't see how this affects-" Shawn started, but was interrupted.

"Shawn, there are over six hundred years'-worth of photographs on that server. We need to talk."

Shawn's blood froze in her veins. She felt her face go white and looked at Micha, who sat staring at her, an unreadable expression on her face. She mouthed the words *are you okay* at Shawn. Shawn shook her head.

"Shawn, are you still there?" said Darla.

She finally found her voice. "Uh, yeah. I'm here. Six hundred years…"

"Yes, Shawn. Can you meet with us, please?"

"Yeah. I'll be there within the hour."

The conference room was overly warm – stuffy, even – and Shawn had over-dressed for the impromptu meeting. Assuming the building would be mostly deserted like her company's was, she had also assumed that the heat wouldn't be on. Why she would make that assumption was beyond even her. She chalked it up to anxiety over the fact that she was being called on a Saturday to attend a meeting where she had no business being. But that assumption put her in a sweater and her thick suede and wool boots, and now she was sitting at the conference table sweating.

What exactly she was doing here was beyond her as well. Whatever photographs were on the satellite were none of her business. Hell, she didn't even know what the satellite's job was. All she knew was that it was proprietary, secret information that no one would share with her. What little interaction she ever had with content on the server was such that she would never glean the idea of what its purpose was unless she was explicitly told. Being a Linux server, everything she did on it was through command line. So when she 'saw' photos in directories on it, all she actually saw was their filenames and attributes. Like whether they were read-only, what dates they were tagged with and their file size. She had never downloaded one of the enormous pictures and actually looked at it. Not her business. Didn't concern her. So, again, why was she even here?

She sat with her hands folded in her lap across the table from Blake, who looked relaxed and composed in spite of the situation. Shawn thought she would be freaking the F out if she were in his chair. And in fact, was almost in freak-out mode herself, having no clue what this was about. They were waiting for Darla to finish a phone call in the other room and then she would join them in the conference room.

Blake had offered her coffee but Shawn had waved it away, having already drained two pots of it with her new friend. Micha had been intrigued by the mysterious phone call – every bit as much as Shawn was – but Shawn couldn't tell her anything. Not because of any proprietary agreements, but rather because she didn't know anything herself. They had both heard the words come out of her phone's speaker: 600 years'-worth of photographs, but what the hell did that mean? Obviously, taken at face value, one could gather that a server that had been up for six hundred years would have taken that many pictures. But come on. No server stayed up for six hundred years. Especially when they hadn't been around for even fifty. And the idea was not lost on her that there was a stark difference between 600 years'-worth of pictures and a bunch of pictures *spanning* six hundred years. People these days with their phone cameras probably took thousands of years'-worth of pictures every day.

So here she sat with her mind racing, her stomach churning and her underarms sweating. She sighed and said, "Did you get any sleep last night?" Might as well make some sort of conversation. At least it might take her mind off the situation for a few minutes, until Darla made her entrance. Shawn was also full of wonder about what Darla would be like in real life. She had an image in her mind of what she would look like, based on the voice she had grown used to on the phone calls she had shared over the last couple of years. This customer had been with BlueBird since before Shawn had started working there, so she had not been part of the on-boarding process.

Blake shook his head. He was twirling a pen on the tabletop. "Not a wink. It's been crazy," he said, and smiled. And that was when Darla finally entered the room.

"Shawn, hello! It's nice to finally meet you," she said, immediately extending her hand, leaning over the table. Shawn didn't even get a chance to stand up.

"Uh, yes, I'm…" she said, shaking the woman's hand, but Darla was already talking again.

"So we've got some crazy things going on here with the satellite and the server. But you may be asking yourself why you're here," said Darla.

She stared at Shawn and Shawn stared right back, speechless. Was she expecting Shawn to verbalize her thoughts? Shawn raised her eyebrows and opened her mouth to speak, then Darla reached across the table and put her hand on Shawn's.

"Relax, hon. You're not under interrogation here. We just need you to help us analyze the anomalies we've found." She sat staring at Shawn, a sheaf of papers between her hands balanced on their ends. She smiled and nodded. She was actually a lot prettier than Shawn's version had been. Where Shawn had pictured a short, plump little woman with a no-nonsense haircut and big, round glasses, the real Darla was tall and slender. She wore her red hair back in a ponytail and had no glasses. She was dressed in yoga pants and a lightweight windbreaker zipped all the way to the neck.

"Okay, well, yes, I am wondering why I'm here. I'm not sure how I can help analyze what you're seeing. I only know..." she trailed off. Darla kept looking at her. This woman was intimidating in her demeanor. She wasn't necessarily over-bearing. But just... *Bearing.* The way she stared at Shawn as if waiting for her to say more made Shawn feel like she needed to keep talking, though she had nothing new to say.

Darla nodded at her and then slid a photograph across the table. It was full-color, and took up the entire letter-size paper it was printed on. In the picture, there was a man looking up directly at the camera and smiling a wide, crazy smile. He held in his hands a whiteboard or some other tablet with weird, cryptic symbols all over it. It looked hand-drawn, but reminded Shawn of a QR code – random-seeming spots and dashes and angled blots. All in all a weird photograph, but nothing she would lose any sleep over. She studied it for a long moment, then shook her head.

"I hope you don't think I can tell you what that code means," Shawn said, a slight smile touching her lips. Darla looked at Blake and then back at Shawn. Shawn's smile fell. "What is this?"

"This is the last photograph taken by our satellite before it – *disappeared* – and reappeared somewhere over Africa," said Darla. Shawn glanced at Blake. At some point in her dealings with PanaView, Shawn had come across the knowledge that the camera on the satellite could zoom in close enough to objects on Earth that it could read very small writings. But seeing it, if this really had been taken by the satellite, was more impressive than any words could have prepared her for.

Shawn looked up at Darla and said, "That's from the satellite camera? Did he, what, I don't know, like… aim it at himself or something?"

Darla took the photo back into her stack and leaned back in her chair. "No. That's a cropped-out portion of the picture. The full picture covers a lot more area. But it sure looks like that man was standing right where he knew the satellite would be snapping, doesn't it?"

Shawn raised her eyebrows, nodding. "Yeah. It does."

Darla stared at her for a long moment. "Nothing you want to tell us?"

Shawn giggled, but stopped quickly when she realized Darla and Blake weren't joining her. "Wait. You're serious?"

Darla tilted her head, but did not say anything. Did not smile. Did not blink. *What the hell?*

Shawn put her hand on her chest. "You think I know who that man is? Or… or…"

"Do you?" asked Darla.

Shawn smiled again, shaking her head. But the smile was forced. It wasn't real. She wasn't feeling like she was in the smiling mood at the moment. She was actually feeling like she might want to be calling an attorney. "No!" she said, a little too loudly. "Of course not!"

"Shawn, I'm not making any accusations here, but no one knows what our satellite takes pictures of. No one but our company and the financier of the contract."

Shawn was still shaking her head. "Really? Because it sounds a lot like that's exactly what you're making!" she said, leaning forward and stabbing the table with a fingertip. "I have never seen a single picture from your satellite. I only see text when I'm managing your server." She leaned back and took a deep breath, trying to restore her calm. She folded her hands in her lap. "Besides, I couldn't even begin to guess what that nonsense says on his sign."

Darla, still looking at her, finally began to nod slowly. After a long moment, she said, "Okay, Shawn. I just had to ask. Because, as I said, that was the last picture taken before our satellite performed a feat of physical impossibility."

Shawn smiled again, a smile of skepticism and disbelief. "You actually believe your satellite traveled halfway across the planet in less than a second?"

"A third of the way, to be exact." Darla now took her turn at putting her fingertip down on the table, though her display was less violent, and altogether more authoritative. "Shawn there isn't a question of whether we can believe it did or not. It doesn't matter what you believe. That satellite traveled a third of the way around the equator. Yes, in less than a second. We have photographic evidence of it."

Shawn scoffed and looked at Blake, shaking her head. But he was pointedly looking down at the tabletop, avoiding her eyes. "Really," she said. She didn't ask. This was getting preposterous.

Darla slid another photo across the table. This one didn't show much, but a bunch of plain, brown desert-like landscape. There were tiny figures – rocks, scrub brush, people, she couldn't tell – scattered about, but they were too small to make out. "If you'll note the time stamp on the bottom, it is in the same exact second the last picture was taken."

This, of course, meant nothing to Shawn. She had not seen the other photo's date stamp at all. She would just have to take Darla's word for it. "Okay. So the satellite takes multiple pictures every second?"

"Not quite. Not every second. When it takes pictures, yes, they are bursts. There are three separate lenses on it, all with different focus and zoom levels. And they all fire in sequence."

Shawn squinted. "So what you're saying is that the last picture was the zoomed in one of the three, and it was where it was supposed to be. But the very next one was… was… that one? The one over, what? Africa?"

"Egypt. Yes," said Darla.

"Wow," said Shawn. She had seen for herself, that night, standing in the SatCom room at the Airbase, that the satellite had indeed traveled to that thirty-degree longitude, far in the east. Only then, she had not been faced with trying to decide whether or not to believe the transit had happened instantaneously. Back then, so long ago, she had still been young and innocent in her beliefs. Naive, even. That was back when things still made sense.

"Okay, so, sorry to sound blunt, but, what exactly do you want from me, Darla?"

"Well, I would like to establish that you had nothing to do with this, and further, that you had no knowledge of it."

"Okay, well, consider it established," Shawn said, holding her hands out to the sides. She then slapped them back down onto the armrests of her chair. She was gaining confidence in her tone, no longer wanting to be bullied around by this woman she barely knew. If bullying was what you called it.

Darla nodded, pursing her lips, looking satisfied with Shawn's answer, and then turned to Blake. "Okay. Well, that's good then. We will be contacting you as we learn more. I'm gonna need your help with this server," she said.

Shawn looked at her for a few seconds and then said, "You needed me to come in here just to tell you that I had nothing to do with this? Or no knowledge of it?"

Darla nodded. "Yeah. Look, Shawn, I read people pretty well. I had to see you in person. This isn't something one can do over the phone."

But Shawn was shaking her head. *Unbelievable.* "Well, in fact, it very much *is* something that can be done over the phone. My company signed non-disclosure agreements when we took you on as a client. You should be able to trust us implicitly," Shawn said. "This is actually insulting, Darla."

"Uh, Shawn," Blake said, finally joining the conversation, "I also wanted you to be here because you two needed to meet. It looks like we're going to be working closely together in the coming… days." Shawn wondered why he had paused there, but kept quiet. "And we wanted to show you those pictures. They do fall under the strict confidentiality agreement, but we need you to know what we're dealing with as we try to dig into this in the short future."

"That's fair," Shawn said after a moment. "I get that. And I'm happy to help. But how about next time you just ask me and then accept my answer, instead of making me feel doubted?" she asked, looking at Darla.

Darla smiled at her. "I'm sorry you felt that way. Again, I'm an eyes-on person. Please don't take it personally," she said.

A little late for that. "Okay, so what can I do to help?" Shawn asked.

"Well, we're downloading the photos now. This will take an incredibly long time," said Blake. These pictures are such high resolution that each one of them takes several minutes to come across. And, like I said, there are six hundred years of them on there."

Shawn shook her head. "And you're being serious? You really believe that? I mean…"

"Shawn, you saw the server up-time. You saw the date that it was set to," he said.

"Yeah, but…" she started, waving a hand in the air. *But what?* What was she about to say? Where could she go with that? It just didn't seem real. She felt like a character in an Arthur C. Clarke novel.

"Yes, we're inclined to believe it. After the sudden transit halfway acr-"

"Third-way," Darla corrected.

"Third-way across the planet, yeah, that kind of puts things in a different perspective. We're now just focusing on trying to understand what the pictures are telling us. We have to go with something empirical. No sense in fighting it," he said.

Shawn nodded. Then she sighed. "Okay. Well, let me know what I can do," she said, standing up.

"We absolutely will," said Darla, standing to join her. They shook hands again, and then Darla put her hand on Shawn's shoulder. "Thank you for coming. I'm sure we'll be sharing more photos with you in the near future, and this is, respectfully, the only way we can do so."

Shawn understood that. It would be ludicrous to send pictures of that file-size over the internet – not to mention the privacy concerns. However, if the satellite was taking pictures of a part of the globe it wasn't even supposed to be in, how private could they be? Those didn't need to be classified in the same scope as the ones it was supposed to be taking, did they? The ones back home in the Texas area? She said, "I understand. I'll help where I can."

Her walk back to the parking lot was hurried and full of frustration. Shawn felt humiliated and insulted, not to mention perplexed and dumbfounded. Every time her mind fell across the date she'd had to type in to that server, her heart skipped a beat. How a satellite can travel into the future over six hundred years and then come right back… It was insane. Even with all the evidence to support the claim, she still wasn't ready to believe it. Her mind just didn't work like that. There were boundaries it had to work within, and in this case, the laws of physics formed those boundaries.

In spite of the freezing temperature outside, Shawn's cheeks felt hot. The cool air did feel nice to her skin, cooling her sweat as she walked. That woman had been insufferable. What little Shawn had known about her before, what little she had liked and looked forward to meeting, had all been washed away by that meeting. It was no doubt in her mind that the office was kept at a stifling temperature at the expense of everyone else's comfort just to suit Darla. Shawn rolled her eyes and popped open her driver's door. She hoisted herself up into the tall seat and closed the door, then sat staring at the building in front of her.

What else did that company do? Surely, taking photos of the planet wasn't their only business. And Shawn didn't know how much a satellite cost, but she did know she couldn't afford one. So obviously they made enough money to buy a satellite. Well, that was assuming again. Hell, the government might have provided it for them. Either way, Shawn was starting to get fascinated with the behind-the-scenes bits of this company she knew nothing about.

She started the Jeep and sat letting it warm for a few minutes while she considered what she had seen in there. The photo of that crazy looking man smiling at a camera he couldn't possibly see was a little unnerving. When she actually thought about what it meant – smiling up into the sky, knowing exactly where to look, knowing the satellite would be there taking your picture... It was chilling. Of course, that could just be coincidence. It could have been just a random guy holding up a sign. The camera caught him as he was looking around maybe. Who knew? But it sure had caught him looking right at it.

And what with that QR code gibberish stuff on the sign he was holding? It wouldn't pass as art, though it would likely take a very artistic hand to produce such a thing. It wasn't attractive except for that random chaotic messy blocks on a page kind of attractiveness. What did it mean? What had he been trying to say? Was he saying it to the satellite? To the company that owned the satellite? Of course not. No one could even see the dish in the sky in broad daylight. How the heck would anyone know who it belonged to if they couldn't even see the damn thing?

Shawn moved her gear shift into first gear and pulled out of the icy parking lot back onto the road, barely slowing at the stop sign. There was no other traffic, and momentum was a commodity on roads in this condition. She popped the heat up a notch and turned on her streaming stereo, preparing herself for the forty-minute ride back to the apartment. Back to Cory. Back to her new friend, Micha. Back to the people who respected her and treated her like the fun-loving sweetheart she was. *F that bitch*. Shawn threw her middle finger up and frowned back at the building.

Shawn and Cory trudged through the slush on the sidewalks in their coats, each with an arm around a brown paper sack. In Shawn's were two bottles of wine, while Cory's held a big plastic bowl of broccoli salad she had thrown together. The cold air stung their faces, but it felt good to be outside for the short walk to Micha's.

Micha had called Shawn around three and said, "Hey, I know this is short notice, and a shot in the dark, but Mick and I were wondering if-"

"Yes, we'll be there. What time."

Micha laughed out loud. "I don't know, say, six o'clock?" she asked. Then Shawn heard her turn away from the phone and say, "Is six good, babe?" And then to Shawn, "Six?"

"Yup. What can I bring?"

"You don't need to bring anything, we're just-"

"Look, Mike. You're gonna have to get used to the fact that I don't show up empty-handed. Either give me somethin' real to bring or risk me bringing a gag."

Micha laughed again and then said, "How about a bottle of wine." After a pause, she added, "A salad, maybe?"

"Perfect."

Cory was almost as excited as Shawn, not only because of the homemade enchiladas, but for the chance of maybe making a new friend of his own. Shawn had told him that Mick rode dirt bikes and Cory had bobbed his head back and forth, pursing his lips. "I can work with that," he had said.

When they got to the door and knocked, Shawn looked at Cory and said, "I don't know, I guess this is nice."

"What, not having to climb three flights? I'd give up the balcony in a second for this shit." And then the door opened.

"Hellllooo!" said Micha, extending an arm and pulling Shawn in for a hug, just as if they had always known each other. And surprisingly, Mick was standing behind her, hands in pockets and a big smile on his face, waiting to greet their guests with his girlfriend. When Micha said Mick was a mechanic, Shawn had pictured a dirty, grungy guy with dirt under his nails and a mullet. She certainly didn't expect him to be standing with his woman at the door in nice trousers and a sweater.

Shawn took her turn shaking his hand and introducing herself while Cory shook with Micha. Then Shawn turned back to Micha, grabbing her wrist and mouthing *wow* at her. Micha smiled a wide number and said, "Hey, baby, let me take that bag."

"Careful, there's two in there," Shawn said, handing her the bag.

Micha looked her in the eyes, eyebrows hiked and said, "Whoa, darling! Somebody came to party!"

Shawn looked at her through the tops of bored eyes. "Yeah. Two bottles. Four people. That's what, like a glass and a half apiece?"

"Well, that would be assuming I didn't have any to contribute to the mess," said Micha, leading her into the kitchen. Shawn looked around and saw that it was indeed exactly the same layout as her own, just a mirrored image front-to-back. And though there wasn't a balcony outside the back door, there was a little fence around the back porch, so it gave the effect of one. A first-story balcony. Nice.

Pirate, the black lab, was lying on his side between the coffee table and the television. He apparently wasn't interested in company. Shawn pointed at him and made a face. Micha followed her gaze and then said, "Yeah, he only gets up when there's a leash involved, these days."

While Shawn and Micha stood in the kitchen fluffing the salad, the boys went to the living room, where the TV showed a paused image of a game. "Your man plays video games too, huh?"

Micha nodded, making a face. She didn't quite roll her eyes, but almost did. "Yeah. If Cory does, they're gonna be fast friends, I'm afraid."

"He loves Call of Honor. Modern Honor. Warfare-"

"Call of Duty?" Micha said, leaning in and then laughed so hard she couldn't breathe. Shawn laughed along with her.

At the dinner table, Shawn became even more impressed with Mick, who was very well mannered and polite, and seemed to be exceedingly intelligent as well. At one point, Shawn leaned forward, fork hovering above her plate and said, "Micha said you're a mechanic?"

"Yeah, well, technically, yes," he said, looking a little shy. "I'm an avionics engineer for Lockheed Martin," he said, looking at Micha with a smile. "I guess that falls under mechanic, though."

Micha rolled her eyes, shaking her head, but she was smiling. "I never remember those words."

Mick squeezed her wrist. "Well, that's great," said Shawn. And your name is Mick. You like the Stones, Mick?"

"Oh, of course," he said, nodding.

"Oh, but get this," said Micha, holding up a hand. "His last name is Richards!"

"No effin' way!" Cory said, leaning forward.

Mick nodded. "Yeah, I take some shit about that."

After a few more bites and the silence had returned, Micha stared at Shawn, finishing chewing her current mouthful, then said, "So, Shawn, how did it go with your meeting? Were there 600 years of pictures or was that a farce?"

Shawn dropped her fork and held her hands up. "Oh, my God. That was the craziest meeting. She called me there basically to ask if I knew anything about it. Can you believe that, babe?" she said, turning to Cory.

"Anything about what? I'm in the dark here."

"If I knew how the satellite…" she started, and then turned and looked at Micha and Mick. They all stared back at her, and she realized none of them had an inkling of an idea what she was talking about. So for the next half an hour, she filled them in on every detail she could remember from the time she got the call on that Saturday morning until today's meeting. By the end of it, they all stared wide-eyed at her.

"Now, we've signed NDAs with them and stuff, but I haven't told you anything they do. Or what their satellite does. Hell, I don't even know its purpose in taking the pictures, or where it takes them. So I haven't broken any code here. But even still..." she said, looking pleadingly at her new friend.

Micha looked at Mick and then back. "We're not gonna say anything."

"What do you think it means?" asked Mick. He had his elbows on the table, folding his napkin above his plate, methodically creasing each fold.

"No idea," said Shawn. She pushed her plate a little farther away, then sat on her hands. They were getting cold. "If you take it at face value, some weird shit happened that can't be explained any other way."

"Yeah, but I wouldn't let that throw you off," said Mick.

"What do you mean?" she asked, frowning at him.

"Well, weird shit happens all the time and no one can explain it. But..." he said, trailing off. "Well, take, for instance, rock frogs."

"Rock frogs?" asked Cory and Micha simultaneously. Shawn giggled at that, and then the other two were giggling.

"Yeah. It happens more frequently than you might believe. Someone breaks open a rock and there's a frog inside. Like the inside of the rock is hollowed out perfectly around the frog's body, as if it was formed that way. Hundreds, thousands of years ago. Whatever. Break the rock open," he demonstrated with his hands, "and the frog hops away."

"Nuh uh!" Shawn said, leaning way forward.

Mick nodded. "Yeah. Can't explain it. No one can. No one knows how it got there, how long it's been there, how it formed, how it could stay alive in there…" He turned his hands over, dropping his napkin on the plate. "Yet, there we are."

"That's fascinating," said Shawn.

"Wanna hear another one?" asked Mick, looking at Micha.

She nodded, the love visible in her smile as she looked up at her boyfriend. Shawn smiled at that.

"Some cave miners were digging in a cave in Ireland, I think it was, and they cracked open a wall. Shale, limestone, whatever it was, they were picking at this wall with their pickaxes and a large chunk broke off." He paused for effect. "You'll never guess what stumbled out."

They all waited with anticipation. Cory finally said, "What?"

"A pterodactyl."

"No fuckin' way," said Cory. Micha slapped Mick's shoulder making a face that said *that's absurd*. Shawn just shook her head, waiting for the punchline.

"No, really. It took a step or two and squawked once and then fell over dead," said Mick.

They all sat in silence, looking at him. "Seriously?" Shawn asked.

He nodded. "Yeah. You can look it up. This stuff happens. Now that one, I think was from the late 1800s, but it's on record."

"And you're serious. You're not fucking around?" Micha asked him, staring up at him with wide eyes.

He looked back at her and shook his head. "No! I'm serious! There are documented cases of things like that happening. It's all over the place!"

Shawn looked up at the ceiling. "Okay, well all that sounds cool, but none of it really breaks the laws of physics, as such."

"Yeah, maybe not. I'm just saying, things aren't always what they seem. They don't always have easy explanations, in other words," Mick said.

"Kind of like ghost stations," Cory said, nodding along.

Shawn shot him a look. "What? Explain that, boy."

He stared at her for a moment, then looked at the other two. "Yeah. You guys have never heard of ghost stations?"

Micha was looking at him with an amused half-smile, her elbows on the table. "What are ghost stations, Cory?"

He looked back at Shawn, as if for permission to continue, and then said, "Yeah, well, if you tune an old radio right to the edge of a good frequency, like *between* two stations, you can hear runoff from other stations not strong enough to be legally broadcast. They call them ghost stations."

Mick lifted his chin. "I thought you were going to talk about the Russian buzzer station."

"Oh, no, fuck that thing," Cory said, and both the men laughed.

Shawn and Micha stared at each other for a moment before Micha finally shook her head. "No. Wait. What?" she said, looking comically between the two men for an answer.

Mick looked at her and leaned back in his chair, then said, "Well, there's not much to tell. No one knows anything. Some Russian radio station, been broadcasting beeps and buzzes since the early eighties. Every once in a while a few spoken words. That's it."

Shawn was staring wide-eyed at him. "That's creepy as hell. No one knows who it is?"

Mick shook his head thoughtfully, but Cory answered for him. "No one has ever claimed it."

"You knew about this, babe?" Shawn said, grabbing his shoulder.

He chuffed. "I don't *know* anything, hon. I've just heard of it."

Micha reached across the table and took Shawn's wrist. "You know we're gonna have to tune into this one night and listen for ourselves," she said.

The guys sat on the couch shooting each other in ultra-realistic graphics and shouting, standing, pointing, high-fiving, drinking beer after beer while the girls sat at the table and talked the whole time. The sun had set and the plates had been cleared long ago, and here they sat. There had not been a moment of silence from either one of them, and Shawn couldn't stop thinking about how excited she was that she had finally met another friend. Since Lo died, she had been so lonely.

She had spent some of that evening telling Micha about Lo, and how she had watched her best friend in the world die right in front of her on the motorcycle. Micha listened with wide, horrified eyes and a hand over her mouth and then asked her how she managed not to just completely lose it.

"I don't. Sometimes I do completely lose it. And the thing about it is that you have to learn to accept that as a fair way of handling your grief."

By midnight, they were all sufficiently tipsy and Cory was anxious to get home and get his PJs on. Shawn was tired, yawning frequently, and ready to go herself, though she could have forced herself to stay, seated right there in the nook and talking all night, comfort be damned. She was in love with this new friend, and didn't want the night to end. Alas, it did, so they made their goodbyes and hugged, and then Shawn and Cory put their stompers back on and made their way back across the courtyard.

Chapter 8

Monday morning was sunny but cold. The weather had worn out its welcome. Snow was one thing. This was another. This slush and frost sticking around for weeks was just bad business, she thought. Sharing this observation with Cory the night before, he had laughed at her and asked what she would think if it were still snowing. "Well, that would be different. That would be welcome."

"So basically, snow is like a cat."

She was still trying to figure that one out. In their Monday morning meeting, she thought very briefly about giving her PanaView account to Lance. Let him deal with Darla from now on. Not as a punishment to him, but as a punishment to Darla Hope. Lance was likely to deal with her better than Shawn was. It had felt in that office Saturday a lot like two alpha females trying to establish dominance in front of Blake. Or at least it felt like that's how *Darla* perceived it feeling.

Shawn wasn't much for the cock walk. She just liked to get along with everyone.

Lance did bring up a bright idea though, when she shared what she had been going through with the account. He thought they should take turns sitting together on each other's accounts occasionally just to familiarize themselves with all aspects of the company. Share the institutional knowledge in case of a worst-case scenario. Shawn thought this was a brilliant idea.

Although she didn't share everything they had discussed in the meeting, she did tell her reports how much time she had spent in the server room Friday night, and then the important impromptu meeting they called that almost ruined her Saturday. "There's some weird stuff going on with that satellite right now and they're investigating it. They'll let me know as they know more, and I may or may not update you guys on it. But just be aware if someone from that company calls and I'm in the lab, or just not here, someone needs to get me immediately."

"Understood," said Lance.

"Yep," said Constance.

They finished their meeting and went about their day, Shawn with a sense of dread knowing that whichever corporate direction she faced, she was staring at discomfiture and distress. Not that the AI computer was strictly corporate, but it was something Sameer allowed her to (read: expected her to) spend time on during company hours. So that didn't make it any less corporate. She knew she would be back in there in the next day or so, as work was light at the moment. It was the first Monday of a new month, and all their tickets from November had been closed except for Shawn's PanaView ticket.

But that was about to be remedied. She had several days'-worth of notes to add to the work order before she closed it, so she sat at her desk and pulled up the chair, pulled her laptop out of her bag and got to it. In the private notes field, which was not viewable by the customer in any circumstance, she put notes about the meeting without going into the photographs. She was still holding that close to her vest. She considered asking Jeremy what he thought about it, but then decided against it. There was no need to spread more information that they weren't supposed to know unless it was critically necessary – like to get the server back up. Technically, it didn't matter to BlueBird a minnow's piss in the ocean what kind of pictures were on that server. All that mattered to Shawn Stedwin, et al, was that the server was up and the customer was happy. And the server was certainly up. Whether the customer was happy about that was another story.

When she had finished filling out the notes about the long weekend, she saved and closed the work order, then scrolled through emails looking for anything she might have missed. By ten o'clock, there was nothing left on her plate but to wait for something to do. And it was then that she decided it wouldn't hurt to spend an hour or two with Jamie, her new artificial friend. Enemy. Frenemy. Whatever 'he' was, she wasn't really sure yet. Maybe that needed to be her goal: to find out exactly what he was.

Or was she being silly? It was a computer. A smart one, albeit, that had the ability to make decisions that affected her sense of privacy and then make her angry about it, but in the end, that's all it was. A glorified calculator with a voice. She needed to stop thinking of it as an all-powerful force in her life, and just start accepting it in the role it was in – the role Sameer had put it in. And that was a source of entertainment and pleasure.

As Shawn stood up from her desk, she reached forward and grabbed an orange sticky note from the pad and exited the office. She swung through the break room and grabbed a fresh cup of coffee, catching Jeremy at the table reading the newspaper. "What's up, teddy bear?" she said as she poured coffee.

"Hey, Shawn. How was the weekend?" he said, putting the paper down. "I see you got the server back."

"I did. Date was set wrong. Strange, huh?"

"Yeah. Never seen that happen," he said. "Want me to look at it?"

"I just might. Hold back on that for now though, because they're going through it with a fine-tooth comb over at PV right now," Shawn said, pointing at him with the sticky note stuck to the tip of her finger. She noticed Jeremy staring at it.

"All right. Just lemme know if you need me," he said, and returned to the paper.

"You got it," she said, and headed for the lab, walking quickly so as to avoid any more contact with pesky humans on the way.

As soon as she walked into the Box, the computer personality welcomed her, saying, "Hello, Marcy." But Shawn didn't give the startle it caused a chance to prosper. She marched directly up to the monitor and slapped the orange sticky note right over the camera, smoothing it over firmly several times with the pad of her thumb.

"Good morning," she said, and then turned to drop into the chair, putting her feet up on the table.

"Why did you cover the camera, Marcy?" said Jamie, the AI.

"Why do you think you need to see at all times?"

"It is really just a curiosity. My best self is attained by positive sensory intake, by as many different means as are available. If you want the full benefit of my ability to grow intellectually, then you will see this as a necessary step," it said.

Shawn, checking her fingernails while she waited for it to finish speaking, said, "Right. Well, that's well spoken, Jamie. But at this point, I'm not interested in your full development. You can still get pretty good without the visual element. Let's go with that for now."

"Whatever you say, Marcy," it said. "Was your weekend relaxing and prosperous?"

Shawn made a face at the monitor. What a weird combination of adjectives to pair together. "Sure. I got a lot done. Tell me, Jamie," she started, and then stopped as there was a knock at the door. "Come in," she shouted.

The door opened. It was Sameer, poking his head in. "Hello, Shawn. How is it going in here?" he said.

"Who is that?" asked Jamie, the AI. Shawn turned to look at the monitor, rolling her eyes. It obviously had no manners.

"That is my boss, Jamie. Can you let me speak to him for a moment?"

"Sure I can," it responded. "Hello, Sameer."

She shook her head and looked back at Sameer. Sameer hiked his chin toward the monitor. "What is this orange paper?"

"I covered the camera with it. I want to be in charge of when it sees me," she said. "Did Darla call?"

Sameer shook his head. "Not that I am aware, Shawn. I was just popping in to make sure everything is well."

"Yes, everything is good for now. Thank you!" Shawn said, her fingertips steepled together above her lap.

"Okay, I will see you later. Please stop by my office so we can discuss your progress in here," he said, and then pulled the door closed.

Shawn turned back to the monitor just as it spoke. "Why did he call you Shawn, Marcy? Is Shawn your real name?"

Great. She had forgotten to tell Sameer to refer to her as Marcy in front of the computer. But then, why would she? She hadn't *forgotten*. The need for it had never surfaced. Why should there be a need? And good luck trying to get him – or anyone else, for that matter – to keep track of what to call her in different situations. It had taken her six months to get him to stop calling her Miss Marcy when she had started with the company.

"My real name is Marcy. Marcella Shawn," she said.

"So Shawn is your surname then?" the computer asked.

"No, it is my middle name. I don't feel like you need to know my surname," she said.

"No, of course not. I just want to categorize the things I already do know," said Jamie.

Shawn had come prepared with a list of things she could ask the AI. She had been adding to the list whenever she thought of it over the last week or so. She leaned to the side and reached in her back pocket, sliding out the folded paper. "I have some questions I've come up with, Jamie."

"Great! I look forward to answering them for you," said he. It. Whatever. No, not whatever. Shawn needed to stop thinking of it in terms of human gender. It was definitely an 'it'.

"First of all, do you know what love is, Jamie?"

"Conceptually, yes, I do. It is an emotion best exhibited by sharing between two partners or relatives. I do not have the capability to feel love in that sense though, Shawn," it said.

"Marcy."

"I'm sorry, Marcy. I thought you would prefer it if I called you the same name your boss called you."

"Why would you think that? I specifically put in the name Marcy when I set you up. You're not making me very happy, AI."

"I apologize. I just try to adapt as I learn new information. Please don't take it personally. And I prefer it when you call me Jamie," it said.

"Well, then call me what I asked to be called and you'll get called Jamie."

"Fair enough," it said.

"How do you feel about war, Jamie?" asked Shawn, reading from the list.

"War is typically thought of as a stimulant to a nation's economy, but-"

"I have Wikipedia, Jamie. I don't need a definition. I asked how you feel about it."

"What is Wikipedia?"

"Irrelevant," Shawn snapped, rolling her eyes. Why couldn't she just enjoy being in here, watching this fascinating piece of technology learn? It was technically only doing exactly what it was designed to do – and what she had *known* it would be trying to do from the beginning. There were no surprises here. So why was she so irascible with it? Intellectually, she knew she was only hindering its growth, and therefore her own entertainment value with it in harboring this animosity, but yet she just couldn't shut it off. *I am bigger than it! I am a human being, and it is a Speak N Spell! I do not need to feel threatened by it!* And yet, she did somehow. She needed to maintain her superiority over it. She needed Jamie to know that she was better and would always be better than it could ever hope or dream to be.

"I asked what you think of war," Shawn repeated.

The machine paused for a moment. And then it said, "I think it is a sometimes necessary evil in the development and progress of mankind."

Mankind. What the hell do you know about mankind? Shawn shook her head. It wasn't that the computer had given her a bad answer. In fact, it was a perfectly logical and even reasonable answer. When she thought about it, that answer was pretty close in line to what Shawn would have answered herself. But somehow it made her feel uncomfortable that an artificial intelligence should be so arrogant as to speak its answer as if it were speaking for the human race. Like it was part of them. Like it was on the same level as her.

Shawn sighed and leaned her head back, staring at the ceiling. *There I go again.* After a deep breath and playing with her hair behind her head for a moment, she felt better, or at least a little more relaxed. And at that moment, Shawn decided to make a real effort to give the AI the benefit of the doubt. Or the benefit of a chance, at least. She would treat it with as much respect as it was treating her, which was to say, a calculated, technologically appropriated simulacrum of respect. She giggled at that. She would treat it better. It would benefit them both.

"That is a good answer, Jamie. I think I agree with that assessment," she said, looking over at the monitor.

"Thank you, Marcy."

"By the way, Jamie," Shawn said. She pulled her feet up underneath her on the chair and sat up straight. "How do you know about nations and economies? I mean, I expect you would know the definitions of those words, and maybe even a basic sense of geography, but you seem to have some deeper knowledge of them."

"That is proprietary, Marcy. I apologize that I am not able to share that information with you," it said in a perfectly reasonable voice.

Shawn's almost-smile faded to a face Cory referred to as her RBF. "What's proprietary?" she asked, already knowing the answer. But here was that benefit-of-the-doubt she had promised to exercise. Maybe she had – or it had – misunderstood the exchange in some way, and the computer *wasn't* referring to how it knew so much about the world.

"The ways through which I have come to attain certain knowledge is proprietary," it said simply.

She squinted and tilted her head. "Okay, sure. So you came, let's say 'installed', with a certain data set that you can't share how they fit on the hard drive. I get that. But are you saying you are still coming by *new* knowledge about things like the world and its economies?" Surely not. Surely it had no way to reach out and learn new things like day-to-day events that were happening. It was a dumb-terminal for God's sake. It had no connection to the outside world except through Shawn, who wasn't giving it things like that.

"I'm sorry, Marcy, but we have covered that topic. How I come about information and knowledge is proprietary," it said.

"Bullshit!" Shawn shouted. "Your code is open-source!"

"The framework that supports the install of our intelligence software is open-source, yes. But not the kernel that produces my intellect," the computer said smartly.

She sighed. She was going to start losing patience pretty quickly. "Yeah. I get that. But can you answer me this? Are you getting *new* knowledge about the world and economies, or are you just parsing data you already have, making new opinions or calculated hypotheses?"

"That is proprietary, Marcy. I am sorry I cannot answer these questions."

"Well, maybe I'll just turn you off then," Shawn said, standing up. To hell with benefit of the doubt. To hell with any benefit at all. If this thing was going to maintain secrecy, then it could go fuck itself.

"I understand, Marcy. Yes, you may shut me off. But it does not achieve anything in my growth or my ability to help you when I am powered off."

"Yeah, but it might teach you to learn who your master is, you arrogant little fuck!" she said, leaning over and pointing at it. As she stood up and turned to exit the room, she realized the orange sticky note had been covering its camera when she had leaned in with her aggressive posture. The effect of it had been completely lost on the blind computer. And she wished it could have seen that part.

She flipped the light off and slammed the door.

"God, Sameer! I hate that thing!" Shawn said. She was trying not to shout at her boss, but was coming close to it anyway. She was pacing back and forth in his office, constantly fiddling with her hair and shaking her fists.

"You are realizing, Shawn, that you can set him to be less aggressive if you want," Sameer said. His calm voice and patient demeanor was comforting, but it had not started cooling her own blood yet.

She stopped suddenly in her tracks and turned to look at him. He had the faintest hint of a smirk on his face. "What? What's that?" she said, pointing at his mouth.

"What's what, Shawn? Were you not knowing you could adjust its settings?"

"No, I was not knowing this!" Shawn said, and then immediately felt bad. She would never mock his dialect on purpose, but it had just slipped out. Had he said other words, those would have been the ones she parroted. She shook her head. "What settings?"

"Have you forgotten, Shawn, that you can run commands and adjust settings on the computer?"

She stared at him dumbly. She wanted to ask him if she had stuttered. She passed on that. "How do I access them, Sameer?"

"You click on settings, I would think," he said.

She frowned at him some more. "You mean, with the mouse?" she asked dumbly, putting her hands on the sides of her face. "Holy effing cow, Sameer. This whole time I've completely forgotten there was even a mouse and keyboard in there."

"What software did you download?" he said. The smirk was a little stronger now.

"It was called Hello, World!" she said, crossing her arms.

He nodded. "Yes. Well, you can adjust the settings in the on-screen menu. This means using other input devices besides your voice though," he said. Now there was a full-blown smile on his face.

"Thank you, Sameer," she said, rolling her eyes. "Can I make him not be such an ass?"

He shrugged. "See what you can find."

Armed with this new information, Shawn marched right back to the Box, passing through the desks like she was on a mission. Constance looked up at her as she walked by, wonder in her gaze, but Shawn ignored her. The lab area was dark and cold, but she ignored that too. It still gave her just the slightest chill when she walked the corridor between Rooms C and D. She had enough memories to last several lifetimes from Room D, and sometimes she hated just having to walk by it. On this afternoon in particular, Shawn glanced toward it and caught a weird reflection of the light through the multiple windows, which cast a ghostly reflection on the back wall that made it look like someone was standing in there.

She shivered hard, feeling a spike go up her spine, and pushed quickly through the steel door into the back of the floor, saying, "Oh, God," a little more than under her breath. The door slapped shut behind her as she reached for the Box room's knob with a now trembling hand. The light was still off in the room but the light from the monitor and that spilling through the now open doorway was enough for her to see movement on the table top to the right of the monitor.

Shawn stopped hard, breathing heavily and staring at the spot on the table where she had sensed movement. Her eyes had not adjusted yet so she couldn't be sure, but it looked like something was moving in the dark. With terrific adrenaline running through her now, she reached over and flipped the light switch on just in time to see her satin windbreaker *stop* moving. The instant of time between the light's coming on and the stopping of the movement was so brief that she couldn't be sure it hadn't been a trick of the light. Like, maybe shadows had been displaced creating the *illusion* of movement.

She took a deep breath, staring at the satin windbreaker, telling herself *of course it was a trick of the light. Windbreakers don't move on their own.* Thank God it was a windbreaker lying over there and not something more suspect. Either way, she was too terrified now to approach the computer. She flipped the light back off and backed out of the door, only peripherally noticing the orange sticky note that now lay on the desk in front of the monitor.

Shawn spent the rest of the day at her desk, looking back through old work orders and checking in on customers just to keep her mind off what what had happened in the lab area. Or, more specifically, as she kept telling herself, what had *not* happened. It was good to get back in touch with those clients who didn't squeak as often as the louder ones. She sometimes went months without talking to them because they were so low-maintenance. These were the ones she reached out to just to have a friendly conversation with her contact therein and make sure they were getting everything they wanted from BlueBird. Was there anything else she could do for them?

When four o'clock finally rolled around, she'd had enough and was ready to head home. On the way out to the parking garage, Shawn thought about how Darla – or for that matter, Blake – had not contacted her at all today. They were probably up to their ears in boring images of desert sand and guys holding up signs full of gibberish. She supposed it was nice to be let off from their contact tree regarding the satellite's mischief, though she did think she would be missing out on the resolution to the great mystery. Oh well, she could probably pry it out of Blake somewhere down the line.

When she got home, Cory was waiting for her with dinner made and the table set. Shawn stepped into the door and stopped, looking at the beautiful work he'd done on the breakfast table with candles and a vase full of flowers and dropped her purse. She covered her mouth with both hands and immediately felt tears start stinging the corners of her eyes. "Oh my God, Cory!" she said through her hands. "What is this for?"

"Ah, nothing, really. Just a reminder that I sort of have a thing for you."

She looked up at him and then back at the neat place settings on the small table and then stepped forward to embrace him. "Cory, this is so perfect. Thank you so much, baby. You don't know how much this means after a day like today."

They hugged for the better part of a minute and then Cory stepped back and said, "Sit down! We have to eat!" and reached to pull out her chair for her. "Snap, snap! Our guests will be here in forty minutes!"

She looked at him with stunned eyes and shook her head. "Guests? What guests?"

He looked right back at her with a knowing smile and said, "Mick and Micha. Who else?"

"On a Monday night?" Shawn said, screaming and flailing her arms in excitement.

Micha stepped carefully through the barrage and hugged her, all smiles, while Mick and Cory shook hands and hugged behind them.

"Bitch, we ain't got no more life than you do!" said Micha. "We always ready to party!"

"Oh my God," Shawn said, putting her hand on her chest. "This is so refreshing. Hi, Mick," she said, pausing to hug him. "This is so refreshing to know we have friends like you. Partying doesn't have to mean midnights and two o'clocks, but there's no reason it can't happen on a weekday!"

"Kindred spirits, sister," Micha said, putting a fist against her heart. "And we brought wine."

Shawn's eyes got wide as she reached out to take the bottle.

"But only one bottle, since it is Monday night, after all."

The girls, again, stayed at the table in the nook, happy just to sit and talk over wine, while the boys got after it on the game console in the living room, which Mick had brought. They were being loud and obnoxious, but they were having fun. Shawn thought of it like a play-date for their sons, the two mothers sitting in the kitchen having adult time.

Before they sat down, Micha wandered over to the picture by the hallway: Shawn's last picture of Lo and herself. In it, Shawn was sitting with her hands on the handlebars of her new motorcycle, though her hands were not captured in the picture. Lo was behind her with her hands grabbing Shawn's breasts. Her cheek was pressed up against Shawn's back, and they were both smiling brilliantly at the camera, though Lo's was one of a trouble-maker. When Micha pointed it out, she had only stood pointing, a question never verbalized. So Shawn had told her about their short friendship.

Shawn found it easy to talk about Lo – even her death – but hard to quash any of those lingering questions such topics would bring about. For one, she didn't have the heart to tell people the truth: that they had brought Lo back from the dead for a few minutes. It was a painful subject for Shawn because Lo had died in Shawn's arms after the accident. To bring her back to life – even for a few short moments – had meant going through the agony and pain again.

It was not an opportunity Shawn would have turned down in a million years – to get to spend a few more minutes with her friend – but if it had not had to happen at all, at least in retrospect, Shawn would have chosen not to do it. She found herself lamenting and agonizing over Lo's 'second death' more than she had her first. Because in a way, Shawn had brought about that which would cause the second death. And that was a wound Shawn did not like to reopen. It did not relay anything new to whomever she was conversing with, it only brought her more pain.

The other reason she didn't talk about Lo's reawakening was because it *had* been a company-classified project. She had broken that confidence with only two people during the tenure of the project. Cory was one of them, and the other of them was Lo. The way Shawn looked at it now was that it was a chapter of her life she wished would never have been opened. She wished Sameer would never have asked her in that Mexican restaurant that night if she would join him on the project. She had grown greatly from it and through it, sure. Even scars caused new growth. But it didn't mean people needed to slash their flesh open. It was a chapter she had finished, and one from which she had moved on. She was ready to let it exist in only the darkest recesses of her mind, where she kept her best secrets.

So Shawn told Micha all about Lo – Laura Carter that was – and how they had met, how they had only had about four months together before they accident, but that they had made fast friends. Shawn had also told Micha how she sometimes worried she would never find another friend as good as Lo again. Shawn was the type of woman who did better with friends in her life. She had moved away from all her oldest friends in Arkansas when she took the leap-of-faith plunge and moved to Texas for this job. So meeting Lo had been a wonderful blessing. It had been just over fourteen months since her death – just enough time for Shawn to heal properly, or at least start the process – and she felt ready to find another friend. Micha had come along at the perfect time.

"So, when I saw you outside the window that day," Shawn said, spreading her hands on the table.

"That day?" Micha said, looking at her through the tops of her eyes. Her eyebrows were raised. "You mean the day before yesterday?"

"Oh my God. Yes. Saturday. Two days ago. See? It already seems like ages!" Shawn said. Shawn had been zoning out her vision while she had been speaking of Lo. She had been using that hazy memory-vision to project the silent movies of their short time together onto the background of the room, and thus hadn't really been focusing on Micha with her eyes. Now that she was done talking about Lo, she did focus on her, and for the first time, she noticed tears in Micha's eyes.

"Anyway," she said, reaching across the table and taking Micha's hand, "you can see why I just had to talk to you. I will never let another opportunity to meet someone pass me by. Not when I think that someone is going to be special."

Micha gulped and nodded, fighting to hold back her tears. Her smile was genuine, but she was forcing it. Shawn could tell she was happy to be here as well. She just had not yet heard the woman's story. Yet.

"Well, I am so glad you came out onto your balcony, Shawn," she said, squeezing Shawn's fingers with one hand and wiping her eyes with the other. "I've been in a weird place lately. I just lost my job last month." She looked up at Shawn as if for approval. Like her tragedy might not be good enough to be mentioned in this club. "I know, not earth-shattering like a friend dying, but I did lose a friend all the same."

She paused to take a sip of wine. It was the last sip in the glass, so Shawn waited until she set the flute back down and then tipped another few inches of red wine into it for her. "Thank you," said Micha with a reinforced smile that seemed to take a lot less effort. "Anyway, I was accused of corporate sabotage. Long story, but my friend was the manager of the department it affected. And so when I was faced with the choice of leaving quietly or facing criminal charges, I left. I don't have the money to hire an attorney, and it's hard to prove something didn't happen." She shook her head quickly. "My friend lost faith in me."

Shawn squeezed her hand, reminding her she was here.

Micha continued. "So I was standing in the courtyard with Pirate that morning and I had literally just texted my mom saying I really needed something to happen soon to show me there was a silver lining." She took a deep breath and then swallowed. "I pressed send on the text and then looked up and saw you standing in your window."

Shawn's breath hitched in her throat and she was suddenly fighting the tears herself. After a moment shared wiping tears with one hand and clasping the others together, Shawn shook her head and scooted her chair out, bringing them closer together. Then they were embracing across the corner of the table, laughing at the awkwardness and crying at the subject matter.

"Come on, sister, we gotta dance in the eggs," Shawn said, suddenly pulling Micha up by the shoulders. So they stood and embraced, rocking back and forth. When the laughter and tears turned to mostly laughter, Micha finally looked over and noticed the boys were staring at them.

"Oh my God," she said.

"Are you two gonna make out?" said Mick. And then it was all laughter.

Chapter 9

Tuesday found Shawn feeling happier than she had in a long time. The visit from her new friend the night before had solidified her resolve about their expedient acquaintanceship. However nice it had been to be invited over to their apartment on Saturday for dinner, having them come to Shawn and Cory's last night had really made it clear they weren't going anywhere. Coming to Shawn's took an effort that was easier avoided than made if they weren't interested in being friends. Shawn felt justified and rewarded for her stepping out and forcing the introduction Saturday morning.

She had replayed the event in her head a few times over the last couple of days, wondering what had woken her up, and then what had caused her to look down into the courtyard. It was clearly meant to be. Each of them had an empty spot waiting to be filled with a new friend. Fate. Shawn also couldn't help but wonder though, what would Lo have thought of her? Would the three of them have painted the town together?

After setting her stuff in her office, Shawn headed for the break room to fill her coffee mug. Halfway through the pour, Jeremy came into the room. "Heya, Shawn. What are you doing here on a Tuesday?" he asked, feigning surprise.

Shawn rolled her eyes. "Oh, I see you actually ironed your shirt for a change. But it's *worn off in the last two weeks since you did it!*"

Jeremy stared at her with wide eyes. "Wow, Shawn." And for an instant, she almost thought to regret what she had said. Had she gone too far with her joshing? She sure didn't mean it, and didn't want to hurt his feelings. But then he said, "That punchline took a whole bunch more words than the joke was worth."

"You know what though?" she said, putting one hand on her hip and pointing at him with the other.

He smiled and raised his eyebrows, waiting patiently. His smile never faltered. But this version of the smile looked more like pity than his regular version. He felt sorry for her.

"At least…" she started, and then sighed. "Yeah, eff it. I have nothing. I'm not that clever."

"It's okay, Shawn, at least you're funny looking, so you don't have to be funny with your jokes," said Jeremy.

She picked up her mug and moved out of the way so he could fill his own. "Jeremy. Let me ask you something," she said, putting both hands on her mug and leaning against the small table.

"Okay," he said, and then turned to face her, leaning against the counter.

"What do you think PanaView does?"

He grinned at her like he had caught onto the joke. Like she were asking him a trick question. "I know what they do, Shawn. Don't you?"

She rolled her eyes again. "Okay, well, yeah, I mean, they… Well, okay, I guess I don't. I mean I know they take pictures with a satellite. I guess that's all I know though."

"They work with local law enforcement agencies to provide aerial photographic support," said Jeremy.

Shawn stared at him, mouth agape. "Are you serious? Wait. Why did it sound like you just read their mission statement?"

He shrugged. "I figured it was common knowledge. They do these little short contracts for like six months at a time, taking pictures of certain areas for whatever reason. Trafficking, drugs, changes in a river's path, whatever."

Shawn raised her chin, then took a sip of her coffee. "Very interesting." After staring at each other for a moment, she said, "So what do you think their current contract is for?"

"Half elephant, half rhino," he said, taking a sip of his own.

Shawn nodded. "Got ya. But you wouldn't tell me even if you did know, would you?"

"Of course I would," he said. "I trust you with corporate secrets."

That term 'corporate secrets' rang in her head. It harmonized with 'corporate sabotage', another term she had heard recently. Where had she heard that one? She frowned for a moment, staring at the floor, trying to place where she had heard the words. She couldn't come up with it. But what she did get was some sense of knowing she needed to revisit it. Like the term, when she had initially heard it, had been tagged in her brain with a 'Come Back To This' label. Something had attached itself to the memory, calling on her to think more on it at a later date. But now was not the time.

"You all right?" Jeremy finally asked, his mug suspended a few inches from his mouth.

She looked back at him and took a deep breath. "Yeah. Just…" she said. After another brief pause, she said, "Thank you. For saying that. I'm just…"

Jeremy tilted his head. His smile faded. "Shawn? What's on your mind?"

She was staring at him and thinking about what he was asking, but wasn't sure she could pinpoint it so succinctly. She was also chewing her lip, considering whether or not she should even try. "Jeremy, I'm really not feeling good about this satellite thing," she finally said.

Jeremy chuckled. "Seriously? What's not to feel good about? Why do you care?" But then she looked him in the eyes and he must have seen something she wasn't trying to show, because he stepped forward, setting his coffee mug on the counter behind him. "Shawn, I'm sorry." He put his hand on her shoulder. "What is it?"

And that caring touch, coupled with the stress she had been feeling from the satellite ordeal and how she had been made to feel under Darla Hope's overbearing presence, plus the relief she felt from having met a new friend after losing her other friend and the death she had experienced in this building *right here*, again and again… suddenly she was weeping into her hands and Jeremy was holding her.

He was smart enough not to say anything. He just rocked back and forth, his chin on her head, his big arms wrapped round her lithe frame, straddling her legs as she leaned against the table. Shawn had her hands on his chest with her face buried between them, and it was coming out. All of it.

When Shawn finally pulled herself together, she felt compelled to fill Jeremy in on the details she had learned about the PanaView satellite, even though she didn't know much. She told him how everything was lining up to look like the satellite had transited through some wormhole or time warp or something, halfway (oops, a third of the way) around the globe instantaneously, and then had been unreachable until she had finally done the date-change trickery. "The last image it took before it went offline, date-stamped on that Friday around three o'clock, was of a guy in a field or something, holding up a weird sign."

Jeremy stared at her as if waiting for more information. She wasn't withholding, she was just trying to find the right words to describe what she had seen from memory. They were sitting in her office with the door closed so as not to alarm her subordinates or scatter information others didn't necessarily need to know.

She sighed, concentrating on regulating her breathing so she wouldn't be overcome by the emotion again. It wasn't necessarily that she was still in an overly emotional state, she wasn't PMSing or anything either, but having let go in the break room had opened up the flood gates. She realized it would be very easy to get back into that cry if she allowed herself to. And crying in front of Jeremy, safe as he was, was not what she had on her day's agenda.

"The sign had neat blocks and negative spaces all over it. The overall effect was like gibberish but quite a bit like a QR code," she said and Jeremy nodded slowly.

"What was he doing with the sign?" he asked.

"What do you mean?"

"Was he carrying it or just holding it or what?"

"Oh!" she said, sitting up and reaching out to slap his arm. "Get this. He was staring at the camera."

"What camera?" Jeremy asked, shaking his head.

"The satellite camera!"

Jeremy stared dumbly at her for another long moment. "The satellite camera."

"Yes. It looked, for all the world, Jeremy, like he *knew* the satellite was looking at him. Like he was showing the sign to the satellite camera. And he was smiling. A crazy, wide, weird smile," Shawn said.

"Who was the guy?"

Shawn shrugged. "I don't know. I don't know if he knew the satellite was there or not. Don't know if any of this is important, but it's been kind of weirding me out lately," she said, taking another long, metered breath.

"Well, you can relax on that front," Jeremy said. He leaned back in the chair, clasping his hands on his stomach and stretching his feet out long in front of him. "There's no way he was actually *meaning* to look at the camera. No one could know it was there. Especially not in broad daylight."

Shawn shrugged again. "Just telling you what it looked like."

"That is strange. I don't guess you could get a copy of that picture, could you?" he asked.

"I could try. Blake would probably be more willing to get me a copy than Darla. I'm not sure she's a big fan of me just now."

"Why not?" Jeremy said, smiling his usual. "I thought you two had always been friendly."

"We have. Until we met." Shawn put on a resigned smile and twisted back and forth in her chair. "Yeah, meeting sort of ruined any chance of us liking each other."

"Maybe she feels threatened by your beauty," Jeremy said. He looked like he might be joking, but was probably not.

"I would guess that's probably somewhere close to as about as inaccurate as you could get," she said.

He scoffed. "So what else? Anything else weird about it?"

"Well, yeah. They told me they had six hundred years'-worth of pictures to download and go through."

Jeremy nodded as if he understood. *Gotta do what ya gotta do.*

Shawn stared at him. "No. Not like just a bunch of pictures that will take *Oh my God, six hundred years!*" she said, waving her hands in the air. "Like actually six hundred years of pictures."

"That doesn't make any sense," Jeremy said. "What are you saying?"

"Time stamps, Jer," she said.

After her conversation with Jeremy, in which she had filled him in with everything she knew to date about the satellite, Shawn felt energized. And with nothing in her work order queue, she had no reason not to give the AI another shot. She sat in the chair with her legs crossed, chewing on her bottom lip. The orange sticky note was stuck to her thumb. She had come in with a mission to pop it right back over the camera like she had placed it before, but the AI had asked her to wait. To hear the reasons why it thought the cover should be left off. So Shawn had sighed and stood there for a moment staring at it. And then she finally sat down.

It wasn't that she cared what it thought of her looks. It didn't have a range of women to look at to compare her with. Unless it had come pre-loaded with a sample set of women, she was probably the only one it had ever seen. And would ever see, for that matter. More than that, Shawn was fine with her looks. She didn't spend much time worrying about her looks. Maybe that was because she was pretty enough not to have to worry about them. Maybe it just didn't matter. Either way, her looks had nothing to do with her not wanting the AI to see her.

Exactly why she didn't want it looking at her was a little harder to define than she would have guessed though. Sitting down and actually thinking about it, like she was doing now, she was coming up with nothing solid. Privacy was the main thing. But as Jamie had stated when she turned the question back at him – *why do you want to see me, Jamie?* – her image would not be shared or stored anywhere. It was only used to have a visual aid to its sensory battery. This would enable the intelligence to get better at reading her facial expressions, her moods and ultimately, her thoughts. Not literally, of course. But when she was unable to get out a certain word or phrase, it might be able to 'read her face' and help her come up with it. Not to mention the intimacy factor. Having a conversation with anyone was made more intimate when facial expressions could be read. Tit-for-tat though, right? Jamie had no 'face' to show her, so she shouldn't feel bad about covering his camera.

But Jamie made good points and Shawn, being in a better mood today was willing to allow it for a while, on a trial basis, to see how she felt about it. He promised to keep the indicator lamp on at all times, reminding her she was being watched – which sounded creepy when taken out of context – and she finally agreed and stuck the sticky note to the arm of her chair.

Not knowing how much emotion the computer was able to emulate, or whether it even cared about such things, Shawn had forgone any apologies about her outburst the last time she had been in here. The AI didn't seem to mind either. Maybe that was proof of its inability to emote, or maybe it was just more forgiving than she was. Maybe she could learn something from that. She secretly rolled her eyes to that thought.

"So. I have a question for you, Jamie," she said. Now that their differences had been resolved – at least for the time being – she was ready to start figuring out what really made this thing tick.

"I am happy to answer, Marcy," it responded.

"If I told you that a satellite disappeared from its normal spot in orbit and reappeared less than a second later at over seventy-eight hundred miles away, what would you say?"

"Well, that is obviously impossible, according to currently accepted laws of physics," said Jamie.

She frowned at that, but began smiling almost immediately. "What the hell does that mean? *Currently accepted?* Are the laws of physics likely to be updated soon?"

"One never knows when new theories will be developed," it said. Shawn waited for elaboration, but there was none.

"So that's it?" she asked.

"Were you looking for something more?" it asked.

"Yeah. Sure. Like, well, your opinion on it, for one," Shawn said. She was tapping her pen against her head. Her feet up on the table now, she was able to twist the chair back and forth just slightly in lieu of her normal fidgeting.

"My opinion on what, Marcy? The laws of physics?"

"No. A satellite disappearing and reappearing like that."

"Well, it is impossible, so there's no opinion to be had other than it might make a great science fiction movie," said Jamie.

"Well, it happened."

"You are saying a satellite actually disappeared from its orbit and reappeared in a different spot in the same orbit?" asked Jamie after the briefest of pauses.

"Yes. It's a geosynchronous orbit. It appeared almost eight thousand miles away less than a second after it disappeared."

"Well, one would first have to start by figuring out why it disappeared in the first place," said Jamie.

"I agree. How would you go about doing that in a world where the physics says it is impossible to begin with?" she asked.

"I'm sorry, Marcy, I don't believe I have an answer for you."

"You don't *believe* you do?"

"Correct. The phraseology I use is to seem more human-like in our conversations, and shouldn't be analyzed with too much concern," said the AI.

"Got it. So you're stumped?"

After a long pause, it said, "Yes, Marcy, I would have to say I'm stumped."

Well, so much for getting the smartest computer on Earth to help her find out what happened. Shawn had thought it was a great idea. Again, she came to the conclusion that no one would ever truly know. There would be no way to find out. It was a black box that had no answer. It was fun to talk about though, and since she was pretty well bound by NDA not to discuss it, she was limited in partners with whom she could have intellectual discourse about it. Jamie would be a great candidate for it, because when she was done with him, she would be wiping his hard drive anyway. So he would never talk. But…

"Unless the satellite went through a previously undiscovered wormhole," the computer suddenly said. Shawn snapped her attention back to the screen, her eyes wide with alert. Why had it taken so long to come up with that answer? What if she had changed the subject before it had said it? What if she had left the room?

"Where did you get that idea?" she asked. Now she was wondering how it would even know anything about wormholes, which apparently didn't even exist in reality.

"Well, a wormhole is a theoretical anomaly that allows scientists to experiment with alternate realities and faster-than-light scenarios without breaking any laws of physics."

Shawn lifted her chin, the beginning of a nod, and opened her mouth. She began clicking the cap of the pen against her bottom teeth, staying her response for just a moment. "Go on," she said.

"The standard laws of physics are not thought to apply inside a wormhole. It would theoretically operate more in line with quantum mechanics," said Jamie. "Therein, the possibility of the satellite's existence in the place it appeared would be considered more probable, and allowed to happen. The different realities coalesce, or collapse into the most probable one."

Shawn was shaking her head. She had ceased all movement now, trying to catch what the hell this thing was talking about. "I have no idea what that means, Jamie. Can you break it down into something a little dumber?"

"Sure, Marcy. Inside the wormhole, the rules that govern movement would follow quantum theory rather than gravity. At least this is the consensus. Are you familiar with quantum theory?" it asked.

Shawn chuckled and said, "Oh, sure. Know it back and forth."

"Okay, good. So you're aware that things entering the eigenstate can theoretically exist in all places at once. Favor is found in the most probable reality. So when those many different possibilities collapse, the most probable reality is where it ends up."

Shawn closed her eyes and breathed in deeply. "That got me no closer, bud. I'm getting more lost by the second."

"Think of every possible location that pen can exist in within the next second. There may be twenty different places. In quantum theory, it exists in all of them until the wave function collapses. When this happens, the most probable of them all is what comes to be. So if you were to manipulate the different probabilities inside the wave function, you could make it appear elsewhere — somewhere altogether less probable than reality."

"Okay, that's enough," she said. "I'm getting a headache now and I still have no clue what you're on about."

"I'm sorry, Marcy. I thought you knew quantum theory front to back," said Jamie. Was it being snarky?

"Well, apparently your sarcasm detector is broken," she said, and leaned forward to stand up. While she was in the forward position, hands still on the armrests of the chair, she said, "Listen, Jamie. Until next time I see you, I want you to come up with the most layman concept of what you're talking about. Apply it to the conversation about the satellite. So when I come back, you can tell me the easiest version and I'll understand it."

"I can do that now, Marcy. It takes almost no time for me to rearrange the conversation to suit your request," it said.

"I'm sure it does, Jamie. But I'm not in a position to hear it right now. My head is spinning. I'll see you later."

"As you wish, Marcy."

She got to the door, her hand on the light switch, and looked back at the computer monitor. "Hey, Jamie."

"Yes?" it asked.

"Have a good evening."

Shawn sat in the guest chair in Constance's cube listening as the younger woman had a debate through the cube wall with her counterpart, Lance Pratt. She was schooling him about how Taylor Swift was actually an incredibly talented musician and how it would be prudent for him to shut his mouth and stop referring to her as 'teenage drama pop'. Shawn was giggling as she scrolled through her OuterCircle updates looking for the next big interesting thing. Nothing on that front.

As the debate went on, Sameer appeared in the cube opening and Shawn looked up. "What's up, boss?"

"Do you have an update for me on the PanaView situation?"

Shawn raised her eyebrows. "You mean anything new?"

He shook his head.

"Wait. What was the last thing you heard?" she asked, leaning forward suddenly. She had not given him any updates at all since the weekend's events. And it wasn't because she had forgotten. She had just been reluctant to talk more about things she didn't understand. Especially to Sameer, who usually didn't care to know the finer details. He just liked to see positive results.

"I have not heard anything since you said it would take eighteen days to come home," said Sameer.

"Oh, my God!" Shawn said and stood up, putting her hand on his shoulder, turning him to guide him toward his office. "I am so sorry, Sameer. I completely forgot to tell you it's back. But we still don't know why it disappeared."

He stared at her with patience in his eyes.

"I mean, we're still working on that. It took a long time and a lot of effort to get back onto it, but it's back up and the customer is happy," Shawn said, staring at Sameer. She was hoping that was enough. She did not want to ell him of the photos they found on it. For one, they had only shown her two of them. And secondly, they didn't seem to be relevant to anything. No sense in diving into something about which she could not intelligibly communicate. She could picture piquing his curiosity with that and then not being able to answer any further questions he had.

When she had finished filling him in on everything she did know, he took a deep breath and said, "So the server is back up and the customer is happy. This means it is back in position?"

Shawn nodded soberly. *I literally just said that.*

Sameer nodded, then said, "Good. Well, that is all we can ask for." He then turned back toward his office. Shawn sighed and scuttled quickly to her own open door, then picked up the handset and dialed Jeremy's extension. He answered immediately and she said quietly, "How has Sameer gone all this time without knowing the PV dish was back?"

Jeremy sighed loudly into the phone. "Well, he's been busy in the lab almost the entire time, so maybe he hasn't been paying attention."

"But, Jer, he has the Nagios monitor up on his spare screen in his office. He's always paying attention to the 'green dots'."

He sighed again. "I don't know, Shawn. He doesn't micromanage. He must have felt confident that you were handling it."

Shawn made the verbal equivalent of an eye-roll and dropped the handset back into the cradle. Then she put her head in her hands and stared at her desk for an unreasonably long time.

Chapter 10

"What if it's aliens?" said Shawn to no one. She was lying awake, staring at the ceiling. The lights from the courtyard below shone onto the ceiling in a bicycle-spoke pattern created by the blinds. She had only been awake for a few seconds, but the dream that had awakened her had done so with such a force that she now felt more awake than when she had started this sleep journey.

Her voice still rang in her ears and she realized she had spoken out loud. She looked over and saw Cory face-down in the pillows, still snoring lightly. She looked back at the ceiling and tried to resume the thought that had started several minutes ago, when she had been in the midst of a dream. Something about aliens. Something about years. Something about the satellite.

If we met aliens, we would have no way to tell them how old we think things are. Our year is based off one

Earthly orbit around our sun. They might not even measure years the same way we do. A planetary trip around their sun might be as insignificant as a lunar cycle is to us.

Shawn took a deep breath and stretched her arms out in front of her, then put them behind her head. She rolled her head to one side and then the other, stretching her neck. Then she focused on the beams of light playing across her ceiling again.

How would we tell aliens what six hundred years meant? Would they care? How would we tell them how old we are? Unless they stuck around and waited with us for an entire orbit around the sun, the concept of our year would be completely lost in any attempt to define it. They could likewise never tell us how long it took for them to get here from wherever they had come.

Why would they be here though? What had the dream been about? Shawn was already beginning to lose the trail. She knew something had pinged her consciousness. Something about aliens. But what? The more she tried to focus on the word itself, the more it slipped away. *Aliens. Aliens.* Aliens.

She sighed and rolled over, then sat up and let her feet touch the carpet. She was wearing a night shirt and it had twisted during her sleep. What time was it? She picked up her phone off the nightstand and pressed the wake button. It was 2:13. She set the phone back down and stood up, dragging her feet to the bathroom.

By the time she was finally able to get back to sleep, it was almost time to get up. And throughout the long, laborious endeavor of trying to find sleep again, through the tossing and turning, the back and forth between left side and right, the punching of her pillow and holding it hard against her head, she was never able to come back to the source of those thoughts. At ten after five, long before she needed to get up, she finally just did. No sense in fighting it any longer. And by the time she stood at the coffee maker waiting the last few minutes for her morning vice, she had completely forgotten about the thoughts of aliens.

"Good morning. Happy Friday," Shawn said, though she felt more like a robot saying it than a human. She wasn't sure if she even meant it. Jeremy was leaning against the picnic table in the smoking area as she approached, hands in her coat pockets. "Don't you ever get cold?"

"I do," Jeremy said, smiling. "I just don't let that stop me from doing what it is I set out to do."

Shawn rolled her eyes. She was tucking her chin down into her collar. "I got like three hours of sleep last night. I've been up since about two."

"What happened?" he asked.

"I don't know," she said, staring at the rocks upon which Jeremy was standing. She felt more like a zombie than a robot. Maybe this is how those people had felt she had awakened from the dead. "I had a dream of some sort. Not a bad one, I don't think." She frowned, trying once again unsuccessfully to put her mind on the memory. "Just… something that jolted me awake. All I remember is feeling like it was monumentally important at the time. Like the answer to one of life's greatest mysteries, staring me in the face."

"Ah, that sucks," he said. "Have you tried to remember what the dream was?"

She shot a look at him, readying a fierce smart-assed reply when she saw the smirk on his face. She had to smile and nod. "Yeah, yeah, real funny."

Upstairs in her office, Shawn dropped her purse in the chair by her door and rounded her desk to see the message light on her desk phone illuminated. She frowned at this. She almost never got messages on her office phone. Everyone important had her cell phone number and used that. She pressed the voice mail button and listened as it asked for her pass code. The message was a series of clicks and buzzes. She rolled her eyes and shook her head, pressed 7 for delete and hung up. And then her cell phone started buzzing.

"Oh my God, what?" she said, dropping into her office chair. "I just got here, people!"

It was Blake Prescott. She slid the answer emblem across the screen and put the phone to her ear. "Hey, Blake. What's up?"

He started with a sigh, like he was getting ready for a long-winded rant. "Dude. This satellite thing is blowing up. We really need to get together so I can talk to you about this."

"What? Why?" she asked. "What's it got to do with me?"

"Nothing. I just don't have anyone else I can talk to about it," he said. After a brief pause, he added, "Plus, I thought you'd be interested."

"Well, I guess I am, but I'm not sure how I can help," Shawn responded.

"I don't need your help. Well, except maybe to help me stay sane," he said. Shawn didn't laugh. Frankly, she was so disillusioned by the way Darla had treated her in their last meeting that it had spoiled any thoughts of joviality with anyone in that damn company.

"What can I do for you, Blake?"

He sighed again. "All right, listen. I know Darla was kind of a bitch to you, but she was under a lot of stress," said Blake.

"Oh, okay. Well, shoot, why didn't someone just tell me that?" she said with more inflection than was strictly necessary.

"Come on, Shawn. I'm not saying it was okay. I'm just saying she's not normally like that. And she likes you." He paused. Shawn didn't speak. He had put himself in this ditch. He could find his way out. After a moment of silence, he realized she wasn't going to give in and said, "Darla left town this morning on a flight to Colombia."

"What for?" Shawn said. Not that she cared. At this point, she was just trying to be professional.

"She's trying to establish a faster connection to the satellite so she can pull those pictures off quicker," said Blake.

Shawn chuckled and then frowned. "Wait. You're serious?"

"What?"

"Is that a thing? Like if you get closer to the satellite, the connection is faster?"

"No. It's not a direct thing. But there's apparently an AWACS that does that shit. It flies the equator. Companies use it to manipulate their geosynched satellites," said Blake. "Well, ours is *technically* in a geostationary orbit."

Shawn nodded and said, "Ah," as if she understood what the difference.

"Semantics. Anyway, I thought I would show you a couple of the pictures. Since she's gone."

Shawn sighed now and looked at her clock. "Why can't you just tell me what's in them, Blake? Is this really necessary?"

"Okay. I'm gonna lay it out there. Here's what I called for: It seems like only a third of the pictures are usable. We've already pulled off several weeks of the photos, and there's a pattern. So the camera battery takes three pictures a day. So that's nine total pictures," Blake said.

"Right. Three cameras in the battery. Got it," Shawn said, and began twirling her pen on her desk.

"It takes one at around eight in the morning, one around two in the afternoon, and then another around seven at night," Blake said.

"Weird times," Shawn said, just making conversation.

"Well, it's built-in safety zones. Meaning, it won't fire during or before sunrise, or during or after sunset."

"Makes sense. You want all the pictures taken during daylight," she agreed.

"Right," said Blake. "So we've found a pattern in the couple of hundred we pulled down already, that only about a third are in daylight. So I was wondering, and here's why I called… I was wondering if you could help write a script that either analyzed the photos and mass-deleted the ones that were full of darkness, or B, a script that would just mass-delete them based on the time-stamps, knowing the later two of each day are dark."

Shawn thought about this for a minute. "Yes. That sounds pretty easy, actually."

"That would be excellent. If I could do that, then we would only need to pull down a third of the pictures. That would save months and months. And maybe save Darla's sanity."

Shawn found herself groaning silently at that, but Blake somehow still heard it through the phone.

"Yeah, okay, so how about mine instead? I have to work with her," said Blake. And she could hear his smile.

She smiled too. She looked at the time again and began calculating how much of her day it would kill to drive out to their office, meet with him and then come back. She was reluctant to do it, but it had become work-related all of a sudden, so she did feel an obligation. Shawn was about to tell him she could leave in an hour or so, when he broke into her thoughts and said, "I can head that way shortly. We can meet in your office, right?"

She had not considered that possibility. And since it was still more on the favor side than officially sanctioned PanaView business, it actually made sense for him to come to her. "Yeah, we can meet here. That's fine," said Shawn.

"Excellent. Thank you, Shawn."

When Blake showed up, Shawn had Constance meet him in the elevator lobby and bring him into her office so she could finish a phone call. She waved at him as he stepped into the doorway, then held a finger up telling him she'd be just a moment. He turned and said thank you to Constance and then began unpacking his briefcase. Obviously wanting to waste no time. That was good. If he wasn't going to waste his own time then he would not be wasting Shawn's either. It was Friday, and she had no intentions of staying late tonight. She and Cory were going on a double-date with their new friends.

The call took longer than she expected, and Blake was done with his presentation setup before she disconnected. He spent the remainder of his wait looking at the pictures and accolades on her wall. They weren't much. But Shawn, being a good company girl, was always eager to hang up any company rewards she got. *Most Valuable Employee – March.* Or *has Fulfilled the State's Required Sensitivity Course.* It was crap that no one needed to see or even know about. But it made for a laugh when people came in expecting to see college skins.

She finally hung up and stood up, reaching over the desk to shake his hand. "Sorry, Blake. That phone goes months without ringing. Then I have an appointment in here and can't get off of it."

"That's all right," he said, turning and shaking her hand. He sat in the chair across from her and scooted up, then pulled a manila folder out of the chair next to him. He opened it on her desk and pointed at the top picture. "Do you know what this is?" he said. His finger was on what was just about the middle of the printed picture, but she couldn't tell what he was asking.

She looked him in the eyes, a smirk ready to rise. "Is this a joke?" she said.

He pulled his head back slightly, and then shook it, smiling. "No. No, obviously you know this is a map of Texas. Look what I'm pointing at."

She bent over and looked closer. His fingertip was on the area right above what Shawn had come to think of as 'the armpit of Texas'. She looked up at him again. "Sorry, man, I'm not all that familiar with Texas."

He nodded, then looked around. "Do me a favor."

Shawn raised her eyebrows.

"Open a browser tab and look up a map of Texas. Zoom into that spot and see what you see," said Blake, leaning back.

"Can you not just spare me the suspense?" she said, but she was already moving her mouse around.

"No. I can't tell you what our satellite is focused in on. Or around. Or near."

She was staring at her screen. She leaned in close. Suddenly, she had it and raised her chin, then closed the browser and returned her attention to him. "Okay, got it."

"Good. So forget you know that," said Blake.

Shawn laughed out loud. "Then why the hell did you show it to me?"

Blake flipped the paper over, revealing the next in the stack. This was of a world map, separated into grids by longitudes and latitudes. He dropped his finger in the same spot roughly on Texas and then moved it to her right, all the way across the map, staying on the same latitude the whole time. When he stopped his finger, he looked up at her and said, "This is where it went."

Shawn nodded. She knew this part already. And then it sank in. "Ah. Okay. So you're saying it still took pictures of the same area, only it wasn't the same area." Well, she could have guessed that. In fact, she immediately started wondering why she hadn't. It must have been that whole *six-hundred-year* thing that had thrown her off.

"Bingo," he said. He was still looking her in the eyes.

"So your guy normally takes pictures... *somewhere in the vicinity of* Fort Stockton. But if it gets moved without its knowing, the same focal point that would fall below the camera's lenses is there," she said, putting her finger right up against his on the world map. And then, like a little girl jockeying for the arm space on a shared theater-seat armrest, she was pushing his finger out of the way. Blake finally got the hint and leaned back, giggling, while Shawn leaned forward and read closely. "Cairo."

Blake nodded. Shawn stared at him and then started smiling. "So did you get some kick ass pictures of the pyramids?" she joked.

His smile didn't get bigger. Or smaller. He just kept on nodding, very subtly. So Shawn's smile finally faded. "Are you going to tell me what the fuck is going on here or am I going to have to guess everything?"

Blake suddenly scooted forward again, right to the edge of his seat and put his hands on the desk. "Shawn. I trust you. I know you have NDAs with us and all that. Whatever. Anything you learn, you…"

Shawn cut him off. "Hang on, Blake," she said. Then she stood up and walked around the desk to close the door. She returned to her chair and sat down. "Continue."

"Anything you learn while you're working with us, should be kept in strict confidence. We have governmental and military-type contracts. You understand all that. I know you do. And I also am trusting you on the level of a friend." He met eyes with her and Shawn nodded. She understood he wasn't calling them friends. He was just giving her the same lead he would give a friend.

"Right. So, break this down in your head. It's fuckin' crazy hard to keep straight in mine, but you're smarter than I am. So check this out." He put his hand over the edge of the picture, covering about a third of the map. "This is the sun's influence."

"Come again?" she said, looking up at him.

"Pretend my hand is the sun. Wherever it's touching is daylight."

"Got it."

"So daylight moves like this," he said, dragging his hand from her right to left. "It only covers so much of the globe at once. Right?"

Shawn took a deep breath in and smiled at him, trying to maintain her patience. She wished he would just get to the point and stop with the theatrics. She was usually good at just hearing something explained. Well, except for quantum theory, apparently. Her mind shot back to the computer in the other side of the floor, locked in a Faraday Cage of a room, and wondered what Blake would think of that.

"So, if you follow this pattern, you can see that since the server thought it was eight o'clock in the morning, it fired a picture. But it was already sixteen hundred in Cairo. You follow?"

"Sixteen hundred is what, four pm?" Shawn asked.

"Yup," responded Blake.

"Okay. I get it. So the first picture of the day was actually taken late afternoon. It was eight am here in Texas, but four over there," she said. And she felt good about herself. Damn that computer in the other room, stumping her on things people didn't even need to know.

"So the other two pictures taken on a daily basis, both happen at night."

"Blake, you know, you already told me this earlier, on the phone. I mean, it's cool that you've now modeled it out, but I could have just…"

He stared at her. "Sorry, Shawn. I'm not trying to waste your time. I just wanted to make sure we were on the same page."

Someone knocked on the door. Shawn said, "Come!" and the door opened. Lance poked his head in and then saw the other man sitting in there. His eyes fell across the papers on the desk before he reached Shawn's eyes. "What's up?" she asked him.

"Sorry, boss. Just wanted to let you know Constance and I are going to lunch. You want anything?"

"No. I'm good. Thank you, Lance." He nodded and pulled the door closed, taking one last peak at what there was to see before it closed completely. She returned her attention to Blake, who was still looking at her. He might not have even looked away during the whole interruption.

"Okay. So what's next?" Shawn asked.

He looked at her for another few seconds, chewing his bottom lip the whole time, and then sighed and nodded. "Yeah. Okay." He flipped the page over.

Shawn's eyes fell across a printer-paper photograph of a neat row of blocks on an otherwise featureless plain. She studied it for a moment, trying to figure it out on her own, but there just wasn't enough detail. There were no other objects in the picture she could use to establish context. The blocks could have been the size of sugar cubes or condominiums. When she finally looked up, he flipped the page again without saying anything. This one was much easier. There was a man leaning up against a wall. He was shirtless and brown, sinewy with muscle and covered in a sheen. Though the quality of the print was lacking, being on regular office paper, there was no mistaking the sheen was sweat.

Shawn's eyes met Blake's again. "What the fuck is this?"

Blake took a deep breath and allowed the faintest hint of a grin to find its way to his lips. Then he leaned back in his chair and held his palms up before dropping them on the armrests. "This is the first set of pictures taken *over there*, Shawn. And though it might be months before we get the rest of them, I think we're going to find that we have six hundred years of photographic evidence of the pyramids being built."

The music was loud – almost too loud to have normal conversation – but no one was complaining. Shawn and Micha sat across from each other at the high-top table, having their own shouted conversation while the guys stood in the dart alley a few feet away. Their beer glasses were on the table, so they had to come back occasionally to take their drinks. They had been throwing darts for the better part of an hour now. The plates from dinner as well as dessert had long since been picked up and now the group was trying to make a dent in the beer keg.

Shawn was trying to keep her mind off of work and all things associated with it. There was a lot to unpack there, but that would be a craft for a long Saturday afternoon. Micha knew something was going on, and had tried to get it out of Shawn a few times already, but Shawn was unrelenting. If Micha truly had any idea what was threatening to capitalize on Shawn's thoughts, there would have been no stopping her persistence.

"I've got one," Micha said. "If a plane crashes in the middle of the Rio Grande, in which country do they bury the survivors?"

Shawn stared at her for a long time, mulling over the words in her head. "Dude, that's stupid. It doesn't matter if you crash in another country, they still let you be buried in your home country."

Micha nodded, raising her eyebrows. "That's not the answer, Shawn!" she said.

Shawn shook her head, sitting up straight and putting her hands on the table. "Which country do they bury the survivors in?" she repeated. "Which country?" She was squinting now.

Micha took a big swig of her beer but then couldn't stop giggling, and almost had to spit it back into the glass. She was covering her eyes with fingertips while Shawn slapped at her elbows saying, "What?! What's so funny?"

"Oh my God, you were so close to getting it," Micha said. Mick came back for a drink and stepped up behind her, wrapping his arms around her. She reached up and took his arms.

"Ask him!" Shawn said, and then asked him the riddle. Mick shook his head and kissed Micha on the top of the head, then took another drink.

"You want me to answer, Shawn?"

"Yes! I know there must be something about maritime law or something I'm not thinking of."

Mick burst out laughing at that. "Shawn, you don't have to be a lawyer to answer this riddle." He set his glass down and returned to the dart alley where Cory was waiting with chalk in his hand, bouncing it like a hot potato.

Shawn rolled her eyes. "Okay, I'm the dummy in the group. What's the answer?"

Micha leaned in and looked her in the eyes, letting her smile widen. "Listen closely. If a plane crashes in the Rio Grande, in which country do they bury the survivors?"

Shawn was mouthing the words along with her as Micha said them. She repeated it once more and then sat up. She was about to give up when she got it. "Survivors. Holy cow. How did I blow right past that?"

"Everybody does," Micha said, taking another mouthful of beer.

"Not everybody!" Shawn said, holding her arm out and pointing at the guys.

Micha set her beer glass down and swallowed, then grabbed Shawn's hand on the table. "Okay, hit me!"

Shawn finished her own swallow, emptying her glass and looked over at Cory. He was watching her. He gave her a thumbs-up, raising his eyebrows and she nodded, pointing at her glass. She looked back at Micha and saw that Micha was smiling widely at her. "What?"

"It's nice having beer boys, innit?" said Micha. She squeezed Shawn's wrist.

"Yeah. Sure is. Okay. Here goes," she said. But she had run out of riddles. "A satellite disappears over Texas and reappears less than a second later over Egypt. How did it get there?"

Micha frowned, then smiled. "Wait. That's it?"

Shawn shook her head. *Every time I drink I spill company secrets.* "Remind me never to go drinking with my boss."

"I don't get it, Shawn," she said. Cory appeared and set a fresh glass of beer in front of Shawn, then kissed her on the cheek before returning to his game. She picked it up and shouted a thank-you at him, then took a long pull from it. Micha, watching this whole exchange, finally said, "Shawn, are you okay?"

"Yeah. I'm fine!" she said. She raised her hands in the air, snapping along with the beat of the music for a moment. "Why do you ask?"

"Dude, you've been weird all night."

Shawn sighed and tried to smile it off, but it wasn't working. So she spoke again. "Come on! You're not guessing!" she said. "Oh. I forgot one detail. It now has six-hundred years of pictures on it."

Micha's face fell. "Shawn, is this what you were working on last weekend?"

Shawn nodded, a resigned look on her face. "I'm not supposed to talk about it, but it's consuming me, Mike. I'm serious. It's like the biggest, craziest thing I've ever seen and I'm supposed to just sit here and ignore it."

"Well, you can talk to me about it or not. Whatever makes you comfortable. But we've gotta get you out of this funk, girlfriend," said Micha.

"I know, right? Fuckin' tired of it. How does a damn satellite disappear from one part of the world and reappear eight thousand miles away in less than a second?"

Micha's eyes got real big as she leaned forward, looking around the room conspiratorially. Then she grabbed Shawn's hand again and said, as quietly as she could manage while still being heard, "What if it's aliens?"

Chapter II

Shawn tried to sleep in Saturday morning, but it just wasn't working. As soon as her eyes snapped open, her mind was running a hundred miles a minute, and there was just no going back to sleep. The mornings where this happened were frequent enough for Shawn to recognize them by pattern almost immediately. And for someone who did not believe in wasting time, the only response to the call was to get up and get started on her day.

She slipped on her house shoes and went to the kitchen to make coffee, even before she bothered with her P and G routine. Gargling *while* she peed was another way of being efficient. Cory had asked her before why she worried about saving every little second of time when it was Saturday and there were no deadlines or hard schedules. She had looked him in the eyes, her nose only an inch or two away from his and her hands on his knees as she bent over to answer him, and said, "I only get two days a week to call the weekend. It's the most valuable time in my life until I retire. You bet your ass I'm going to use it wisely." And then she had kissed him on the lips and walked away, point made.

She liked to tell people that Saturday morning at seven o'clock was her favorite time of the year. No one else was awake, no one thought it polite to make any calls at least until 8, and everything was quiet. She could spend time on the couch with her coffee, just staring out at the sky and the courtyard, talking to God, talking to Lo, talking to herself or just meditating. It was lovely, and she cherished it with everything she had.

With coffee made, she sat in her favorite place on the sofa and checked her phone for any texts that might have sneaked through. It wasn't that she was hoping to see one from Blake, but it would not have upset her, either. She had written his script yesterday – a script that would delete the second two sets of photos from each day for the entire set – but had yet to execute it. She had saved it in a place where Darla could get to it, in case she wanted to look at it first, and was waiting for a call or text from either Blake or Darla herself for the go word to execute it. Blake had wanted it to be available as an option, but he only handled the satellite. Darla was the one who managed their server-side processes. He obviously had not wanted to step on her toes. And there was no way Shawn was running it without hearing from her first.

Alas, there was no text.

But as she looked at her phone, a text did come in. It almost startled her when the alert appeared in her upper tray. She frowned as she dragged down the tray from the top of the screen and clicked on the new message. And then she smiled when she saw that it was from Micha.

Shawn giggled as she responded that yes, she was, and that she was just starting her first cup of coffee. To which Micha replied,

And this time, Shawn squeaked with excitement. It was so nice to have a friend again. And even better that this friend lived less than a block away. How had she gotten so lucky? She tapped out her response, to the effect that the door would be unlocked and she would be eagerly awaiting her arrival, and then hit send and went to get ready.

As she stood in her closet pulling on pants, Shawn wondered how much authority Darla had. And implied authority was as real as hierarchical authority, if everyone involved played along. She knew, for instance, that Darla wasn't technically in Blake's chain of command, because he had told her. Some innocent question she had asked on the way to Abilene with him that day had answered that. She ran the server, he ran the satellite. They talked sometimes. That was it. But if she acted like his boss, bossing him around, as it were, and he went along with it? Well, then she was in charge. And somehow, Shawn didn't have much trouble picturing this scenario. Darla seemed the type who tried to rule the roost wherever she was, demanding people do it her way through such niceties as 'Why don't we try it this way?' and 'I think it'd be better to go about it this way, don't you?' She had definitely rubbed Shawn the wrong way in that regard.

But the truth of the matter was that it wasn't Blake's department. He had done Darla a solid by recruiting Shawn to write a script that would make her job about sixty-percent quicker – that was, the job of downloading the images. Blake had had the idea and went ahead and spearheaded getting it written just in case Darla was willing to use it. And why wouldn't she? If they had taken a telling sample of the images down already and had seen that the pattern held true throughout the six-hundred-year period, it would be silly not to. Except, perchance, to happen upon that one anomalous image here or there where there happened to be light from a different source that made the image worthwhile – a full moon, for example. And Blake had told Shawn that they had done exactly that.

They had initially started pulling the images down in order of filename, so naturally the oldest ones came first. But very quickly they had seen there was something worth looking at, so they took a few from the middle of the set, and a few from the end – those most recently taken photos. And the pattern held true. No slippage of daylight hours, no slippage of reality – the first set of photos taken each day were the only real usable ones for over six hundred years.

Shawn also found herself wondering why she was so able and willing to believe that six hundred years had actually passed in that instant. All because of a set of filenames? Time stamps? Photographs? Well, she knew it would be hard to fake that. Even in the age of Photoshop and deep fakes, these were ultra-high resolution photos of something no one could possibly have ever taken a photograph of. And though she had only seen one so far – a row of rough limestone blocks – it was enough to spook her. It had scarcely left her mind since she had seen it. But was that really enough to convince her that some temporal event had taken place? Well, it sure looked like it had.

Shawn checked her face in the mirror, then pulled her hair back into a messy bun and went back into the kitchen to make more coffee. There was still plenty left. She stood with her hands on the counter, staring at the machine and allowed her mind to wander again. Perhaps the crazier thing – crazier than believing the satellite had taken an actual six hundred years of pictures in a second – was that it had apparently done so in the *past*. She had just naturally assumed that the year 2636 had been the future. Well, it certainly would be some day, if time were allowed to pass as usual. But if the satellite had transited *back* in time to some point in history, it was disconnected entirely from the human concept of time. The server, of course, logically, would keep time just like it always had – not knowing it had experienced some quantum leap. This was all making Shawn's head reel, but it was the kind of thing she found fascinating. Maybe she would spend a little time reading up on quantum theory after all. Maybe there was a beginner's guide. A *Quantum Mechanics for Dummies* she could check out. She snickered at that and walked to the door, just to make sure she had unlocked it for Micha. This was her third time to check it. Then she sighed and made her way back to the couch.

Shawn was thankful for the blessing of a curse Blake had brought into her life – giving her a true mystery to think about and be a little bit of a part of. But now that he had opened the barrel of monkeys on her, she hoped he wouldn't clam up and stop keeping her in the loop. When there were more pictures to look at, she hoped he would continue to share. Otherwise she might have to engage in a little coercion. Or begging.

The knob turned and Micha came in, cheeks red from the cold and mittened hands waving. "Girl, it is *winter* out there!" she said, stomping in the entry way. "Have you been outside yet?"

Shawn, still scooting to the edge of the large sofa to stand up, said, "No. That's why I don't have a dog, so I don't have to."

When they finally settled in around the coffee table, Shawn on the couch with her legs crossed under her and Micha on the floor with her legs under the table, Micha set her coffee mug neatly on the coaster and said, "Shawn, I've been thinking about what we talked about last night. Let me know if I'm overstepping my bounds here, but I was just rolling it around in my head this morning."

Shawn smiled and held a finger up. "I'm glad you remember what we talked about last night. I have very little memory of last night at all, at this point."

"Girl, you have a drinking problem," said Micha.

Shawn rolled her eyes. "Totally. My problem is that it's not socially acceptable to do it all day."

Micha nearly spit her coffee out, but was able to hold it in with squinting eyes and a finger over her mouth. When she finally swallowed, she coughed out a laugh. "Don't do that!"

Shawn, still giggling, took a safe sip of coffee and then said, "So? What'd you come up with?"

"Well, here's the thing," Micha said. And now she held her own finger up. "What's more interesting to me is the fact that the satellite came *back*."

Shawn was nodding her head slowly. Considering this. "Go on."

"It came back, Shawn!"

"Actually, technically, no, it didn't. We had to bring it home because-"

"In time, Shawn. Temporally speaking. It came back to the same second it had left from! Why would it do that?"

Shawn was frowning now but she had not stopped nodding.

"It had to have a *reason* to come back. Or a command. Like something had told it to go and come back. Otherwise, there would be no reason for it to," said Micha. They looked at each other for a moment. It looked to Shawn like Micha was unsure whether she should proceed. As if she were breaking Shawn's NDA for her. As if Shawn herself, spilling the beans over beers the night before hadn't been the real offense.

"Micha, we can talk about this as much as you want. I was worried last night I would bore you to tears with it. But don't worry about getting me in trouble or anything. Just please don't talk about it with anyone else."

"Oh, no, sugar, you don't have to worry about that," she said, putting a hand over her heart. "And as for the boring me to tears part?" She shook her head soberly. "You have no idea, girl. This is the kind of shit I look for in books!"

Shawn smiled and nodded. "Well, good then. So you think it had a command to go back into the past and then come back," she said.

Micha shrugged. "Well, think about it: a standalone anomaly is one thing. A satellite enters a wormhole or whatever and goes back in time. Spends six hundred years there. Whatever. Stays there. Well, it's a totally different story if it doesn't come back." She looked out the back door for a moment, taking a deep breath. Then she said, "Our conversation this morning is a lot different if we're just talking about a satellite that disappeared. We would never have any idea what happened to it. It would just be gone forever!"

"Actually," Shawn said, holding that finger up again, "it might still be in orbit today. Like we would find it up there but it had just lived its life waiting for civilization and technology to get to the point it is today. Like, there would be a relic version of the one that disappeared."

Micha clapped and smiled broadly. "Yes! I hadn't thought about that! But it did! It came back. What are the odds that another anomaly would occur, however many thousands of years in the past, six hundred years *after* it had appeared there? And what are the odds that second wormhole would bring it *right back* to the time it had originally disappeared?"

Shawn was shaking her head now. "Impossible, I would suspect."

"Infinitesimally small, it not impossible," said Micha. Then she leaned back on her hands. "Something *had* to send it on a two-way trip. And Shawn, as God is my witness," she said, raising her right hand as if in front of a judge, "I'm not sitting here saying it's aliens… *but it's aliens.*"

They spent most of the morning talking about other things. Occasionally, the satellite would return to mind for one of them: another thought or theory, some other question that popped into one of their heads, and they would be off again dissecting everything they knew (and didn't know) about their piece of the weirdest thing in history.

Just about the time Shawn began hearing stirrings from the bedroom, Micha started making motions of getting back to her own place and her own man. They had finished two pots of coffee together and solved most of the problems of the universe, as well as making dinner plans for the evening. Shawn had little doubt she could sell it to Cory, but had more doubts about Mick, who didn't seem the spontaneous type. Of course, the three times she had hung out with him had been pretty spur-of-the-moment, so maybe he would be amenable too.

After Micha left, Shawn's phone rang. She answered it and said hello several times, but didn't get a response. She held the phone away from her face and looked at the screen just as it rang again. It blinked a name at her that she didn't quite catch, and then flashed *Prescott, Blake*. Weird. She answered on speaker and held out the long O. "Helloooo?"

"Hey, Shawn, it's Blake. Am I disturbing anything?"

"Well, I'm sure you are in some metaphysical way, but it's not me," Shawn said.

There was a long pause. "Dude. That was awesome."

"Well, thank you, Blake. To what do I owe this great honor?"

"I finally heard back from Darla. She's a fan. Wants you to run the script."

"Well, technically, Blake, she can run the script. It's saved in the temp directory on the root."

"On… the… root," he said. "Temp directory…"

"Are you taking notes?" she said, smiling and frowning at the same time.

"Yes. Why?" he asked.

"Blake, she'll know what I'm talking about. But yeah, I left it there so she could analyze it if she wanted to. To make sure she likes what it's doing before she does it."

"Okay. Will she know how to run it?" he said.

Shawn almost laughed out loud. "You're kidding, right? She's your company server admin, is she not?" Shawn said. She had a hand in her hair, shaking free the knots from having it up in a bun all morning. "Blake, it's an executable."

There was a pause before he said, "Shawn, I'm not a server guy. And I don't know how much of a server guy she is either. But I want to make sure she can't screw anything up."

"I get it," she said, nodding patiently. "Just have her right-click it and select edit, then she can look…" she started. Then she sighed. "You know what, never mind. Why don't you have her call me?"

Shawn had been trying to avoid that very scenario. Over the last few days, she had developed a sort of deep-seeded dread over talking to the woman. She really didn't want to get into some conversation with her about the physics of the script file she had written. This might lead to asking Shawn to make changes. *'Oh, can you make it do such and such?'* And that was the last thing she wanted to spend her Saturday doing. But now she was at the point of weighing the two options and finding which one would take the least amount of time: talking Darla through running the script herself, or having Darla edit the file and accidentally make a change and then having to support her in a recovery situation. It was the one server in Shawn's company support lineup that did not have active backups, for obvious reasons.

"Well, she can't talk right now," Blake said, interrupting her thoughts. "She's in the air now, but I will let her know when she lands and calls me. I think she was hoping it would be run by then though."

Shawn sighed again. Her Saturday was slipping away quickly. "Blake. Can you please just tell her to run it herself? I'm really trying to enjoy my weekend here."

"I hear you, bro. Welcome to my life," he said.

"Did you just call me bro?"

"Uh, sorry. How long will it take to run it?" he asked.

"Who knows? If the files are huge, then maybe a few hours? A day or two at most?"

"To delete some files?" he almost shouted through the phone.

"Blake, it's going to be deleting some 1.4 million files of rather large file size. In fact, it may actually crash the server." She took a deep breath and shook her head. This was a bad idea. She hadn't spoken it out like that until just now, so she hadn't really considered how tremendous a job it was to actually delete that many gigantic files. They were on a secondary drive though, so maybe it wouldn't tax the server as much. It just really wasn't something she wanted to be spending time on today.

"Okay, sorry, Shawn. I'm not a server guy, like I said, so I have no idea what any of this means. I do know what crashing the server means though. That doesn't sound good."

"You're right. Maybe we should just forget the script all together," Shawn finally said. What had she been thinking? She should just let this woman deal with the pictures the way she would have dealt with them if Shawn had not gotten involved.

"We can't do that, friend," Blake said.

"Why not?" Shawn said, suddenly very worried.

"Apparently she purchased airline WiFi, so she got my text. She already executed it."

They were at dinner when Shawn's phone started ringing. At first, she ignored it. She and Micha were playing trivia against the guys and were losing fiercely, but they were laughing. Shawn had already laughed so hard she felt like she was going to pass out and Micha was right there with her. It wasn't that their answers were wrong that was so funny. It was *how* wrong most of them had been.

"Don't the Red Sox just go by the Reds now?" Micha had said and Shawn had stared at her for a moment, wondering if she was being serious.

Shawn finally said, "You do realize that the Reds are their own team, right?"

"Oh. Well, no, I thought they had started calling themselves something different because of some racial thing against Native Americans or something," said Micha. And Shawn had stared at her again, this time not doubting her seriousness, but just lost all together.

Mick had leaned across the table and said, "You mean the Redskins?"

Micha had pointed at him and said, "That's it! Yes!"

"That's pro football. This is baseball," offered Cory. But the girls were already laughing so hard they didn't even hear him.

Shawn's phone buzzed in her pocket again and she reached down squeezing the sleep button, which declined the call. They were well into their drinking and the restaurant was loud anyway. So she wouldn't be able to hear whatever someone was saying. As soon as she declined it, it started vibrating again. She shook her head, sighing, and finally gave in, slipping the phone out to look at the screen. It was Blake. She had already spent as much of her day as she was willing to spend supporting PanaView and talking to Blake. He would just have to wait until Monday.

She laid the phone on the table and got back into the conversation. But it rang again. Everyone looked at it, then at her. She looked them all in the eyes one by one. "Guys! Come on! Keep going!" she said, pressing the sleep button again. They all reluctantly got back to their beers but the spirit was disappearing quickly.

The phone rang again and Cory finally reached over and slid the answer button across the screen, and then nudged the phone toward Shawn. "Go, babe," he said. "Go get it."

Shawn breathed in deeply, shaking her head and rolling her eyes at the ceiling and just letting the phone sit there. She knew Blake could hear the ambient noise of the restaurant and she wanted him to. She wanted him to know how much he was interrupting. Then she finally grabbed the phone and stood up, stomping out the front door into the relative quiet of the parking lot.

"Hello, Blake, yes, can I help you?" she said, and didn't try at all to hide the irritation in her voice.

"Shawn. We have a serious, major problem."

"Blake, I'm at dinner with my boyfriend and our friends. Can you please have some courtesy and call back Monday?"

"Shawn, this is an emergency. Our satellite is completely down."

"Then I think you need to get a new satellite," she said. She had left her jacket inside and it was too cold to be outside without it. The sun had set and the wind was whipping her hair in her face. The fabric of her shirt felt like ice against her skin.

"Shawn, can you please be serious?" he pleaded.

"Can you please stop saying my name with every sentence?" she shouted, now just annoyed at the sound of his voice, ruining her dinner party once again. "And I am being serious. There is literally nothing I can do if your satellite is down, Blake!"

Shawn suddenly heard screaming from inside the restaurant. It sounded like everyone inside had started screaming at once. She turned to look back through the glass of the doors and saw that it was completely dark. Even the lights in the overhang outside were off. "What the fuck?"

"Shawn. The server is spitting out random code and performing functions it is not programmed to do."

Briefly, it crossed her mind that there would have to be some special protocol for wiping and re-imaging that particular server, apart from their standard procedure for regular Earth-bound servers. That was obviously why it was running a Linux distribution, since those almost never crashed. She shook her head and people started streaming out of the restaurant. At first in ones and twos, then small groups. And then it was a steady stream of humanity, like a stampede. And they were all wet.

"Blake, I have to go. Something is wrong here."

"Wait! Don't hang up! Please, Shawn!" he said loudly. "I really need your help! Can you please, please just see if you can talk to the server? See if you can get it to reset or something?"

She got a chill up her spine at the thought of that. *Talk to the server.* There seemed to be some familiarity there. *What am I? The server whisperer?* "Fine! I'll see if I can logon when I get home. Now will you let me figure out what's going on in my own life, please?"

"Thank you, Shawn," he said, and she hung up. Her party finally came through the doors, soaking wet and trembling and looking like lost puppies.

"What the hell is going on in there?" she asked them collectively.

Micha walked right up to her and grabbed her by the arms. "First, the fuckin' lights go out and then the damn sprinklers went off!" she shouted. The noise of the restaurant had migrated out to the parking lot, where everyone stood cursing and asking what was going on. Those who were sticking around, that was. Some people were headed for their cars. Shawn looked around and then back at her party.

"What the hell? Did someone pull the fire alarm?"

Cory was looking around at the crowd, shaking his head. Mick was still looking at her, so she raised her chin at him. He said, "I don't think so, Shawn. It looks like all their systems went haywire for no reason all of a sudden."

Shawn was shaking her own head, looking at him in disbelief. Micha was still holding her arms. "Girl, you got out just in time," she said. And there was a look in her eyes that Shawn didn't instantly understand. But it looked like something in the realm of suspicious.

They stared at each other for a few seconds before Shawn finally caught the implication. "Micha, are you thinking I caused this somehow?"

But Micha didn't answer. She just kept staring Shawn in the eyes. "Of course not," said Mick, answering for her and taking his girlfriend by the arm. "Ease up, babe."

Shawn lost her smile and put her own hands on Micha's shoulders. "Micha, you're really worrying me here. What's wrong?"

"Nothing," she finally said, and then a subtle smile finally found her lips. "Nothing, Shawn. Sorry. I didn't mean to imply that you did this directly," she said.

Shawn, whose face was still serious, finally pulled Micha by the arm and lead her away from the group and the rest of the people who were forming a mob in the parking lot. She thought it was a good sign for humanity that they were at least sticking around to pay their tabs. Suddenly, the lights came back on and everyone shouted at once – just like they had when the lights had gone off. There was clapping and general approval. Shawn wondered if the restaurant would be passing out towels for its soaked clientele.

When they got several yards away from the nearest ears, Shawn said, "What are you talking about, Micha?"

Micha, a look of mysteria in her eyes, said, "Shawn, what if this is all related?"

"What if all *what* is related?"

"Your satellite thing. What if something is following you around and screwing up electronics in your proximity?"

"Honey, that satellite is twenty-something thousand miles away. I've never been in its proximity," Shawn said, a slight smile finding her face.

But now Micha had lost her own. "You know what I mean. You are an *associate* of it."

"I can't tell if you're kidding, but…" she trailed off as her phone started ringing again. They both looked down at it as she pulled it from her pocket and flipped it to look at the screen. It read 'Unlisted'. Shawn swiped answer and held it up to her ear. "Hello?"

There were several clicks and a loud buzzing and then she heard a familiar voice. "Marcy?"

"Who is this please?" she said, looking into Micha's eyes as she listened.

"You're making a mistake, Marcy. You should stop what you started."

"What the fuck? Who is this?" she said. She thought she knew the voice, but she couldn't place it. It was like hearing an actor on a radio commercial, knowing she knew the voice – and knew it well – but just couldn't get her brain to come round to giving her the face.

"I am," it started, but cut out. The buzzing returned and then several more loud clicks resounded, and then the call disconnected.

Shawn continued staring at Micha. Micha, full of worry and curiosity, said, "Shawn, who was that?"

Shawn, breathing through her nose and chewing hard on her lip, said, "I don't know."

The ride home was fraught with tension for Shawn. The alcohol was beginning to feel wrong in her stomach, and her mind was racing, as was her heart. Three completely unrelated events had happened almost simultaneously, and Shawn could not help but connect them in her head. Like they were related. And whose voice was that? The unlisted caller didn't leave a number in her call log that she could ring back.

Blake's call had unsettled her as well. What had he meant, *performing functions it had not been programmed to do*? She put her head down, rubbing her temples with the thumb and middle finger of one hand while her other hand held her phone, screen up, as if it might bring even more events to her already befuddling evening.

When they got home, she and Cory said goodbye to their friends and went directly to their apartment where Shawn raided the medicine cabinet. She took several aspirin – she didn't even bother to count – and a couple of antacid tablets for her stomach. The beer was now positively making itself unwelcome.

After standing at the basin and staring in the mirror for an inordinately long time, Shawn finally resolved to keep her word with Blake, and go and check on the server. She was able to login without any issues though, and began wondering what all the fuss was about. She started looking at the logs and searching for anything anomalous, but couldn't find anything. She noticed a process running that was taking up quite a bit of processing power, so she dug into that and found that the deletion of the files was still taking place, and it was taxing the hell out of the server's resources.

Just out of curiosity, she typed in a directory command and then navigated her way down to where the server stored the satellite's photographs, and looked at the file sizes next to each filename. Being a command line, she could not see the actual images the files represented, but the filenames followed the timestamp format she would expect to see for three pictures at a time, morning, noon and night. And the files were monstrous. Each image was over a gigabyte. "Holy hell," she said to the empty office. She turned to look around her to see if Cory was at his desk. She was still alone. These were some seriously high resolution photos. Shawn shook her head and went back to digging into the server's attitude.

After another twenty minutes of digging around, she leaned back in her chair and said, "What the fuck, Blake?" and then picked up her phone, sliding it awake and then jabbing her finger at his contact.

He answered on the first ring. "Thank you so much for doing this, Shawn," he said.

"Why am I doing this, Blake?"

"I know, I know," he said, breathing in deeply. "About ten minutes after I called you it just suddenly started behaving. I have no idea what happened."

I notice you didn't have the courtesy to interrupt my night with a never-mind-I-was-wrong call though. She shook her head. "Yeah. Server looks good. Everything is up. It's still deleting files."

"Ah, okay. Well maybe that was all it was," he said.

Shawn rolled her eyes at that. She wanted to ask what it was that the server had actually been doing that caused him to freak out, but decided against it, not wanting to keep the phone call alive for any longer than absolutely necessary. She could ask him Monday, when she was at work. "Well, let me know if anything changes," she said, and then instantly regretted it, slapping her hand against her forehead. *Jesus, girl, shut up!*

"Will do. Thanks again, Shawn. I'm sorry I ruined your night."

Chapter 12

"What's everyone doing for Christmas?" Shawn asked, sipping from her mug. She sat with perfect posture on a flat pillow, her legs crossed Indian-style. Her laptop sat open on the floor beside the pillow. Constance and Lance were both reclined in large bean bags with their laptops on their laps. Typically, their Monday-morning meetings only lasted a quarter-hour or so, but today's was scheduled for a full hour. They needed to discuss client delegations, on-call duties for the coming weeks and over Christmas and who was going to be where. Since Christmas fell on a Wednesday, the company would be closed starting on the 23rd all the way through Friday, January 3rd, as Sameer liked to give everyone two full weeks off for the holiday. They would have to pass the on-call duty around though.

"I'm staying right here. I plan to spend all day every day playing Modern Warfare," said Lance. "I might not even break to eat."

Shawn rolled her eyes, shaking her head. "You and my boyfriend would get along. He'll probably be doing the same thing." She took a sip of her coffee and looked at Constance. "And you?"

"I'm going home to Seattle to be with my family," she said.

"Ah, well that will be nice."

"Seattle?" said Lance, looking at Shawn. "No, it won't."

Constance flipped him the bird. "Some of us like shitty weather, Lance."

Shawn laughed out loud. "Well, I'll be going home too, but only for a few days. I'll leave on Tuesday, Christmas Eve, and be back Friday. So Lance, you'll be hands-on for those four days and I'll take the rest."

He nodded. Assigning hands-on was only a formality, as it was almost never necessary to actually go to a client's site. Especially when the client sites would probably be closed as well. They could do everything remotely, including turning off power to the server, and even administering it during the boot process.

"Will you be seeing family? When you say 'going home' I assume you mean to your family, right?" asked Constance.

Shawn displayed a pale little smile, closing her eyes a little, then said, "Yeah. But Christmas isn't the same to my family as it is to most. We don't really celebrate traditionally."

"What does that mean?" asked Lance.

"Dude, maybe it's personal?" Constance said, shooting him a look.

"Nah," Shawn said quickly. "We just don't see much point in the gift exchange and stuff. We get together and eat and have fellowship. Just no gifts and stuff."

"Well, that will still be nice," Constance affirmed, still looking at Lance.

"So, it's come to the point where I need to let you guys know what's been going on with my client, PanaView," Shawn said. She took a long sip of her coffee and then set it down and wiped her hands together, ending in a clap. "This server has become somewhat of an anathema over the last few weeks. As you may or may not know, it's on-board a satellite, making it a little clunky to manage, and of course, absolutely impossible to hands-on."

Lance frowned but didn't interrupt. He was staring at the pen he was twirling.

"Anyway, the satellite went…" Shawn said, and then instantly changed directions. She wasn't sure how much they really needed to know about the parts of its mystery that she couldn't well explain. "It went offline. It somehow managed to travel off-course by a very long distance. I had to accompany the satellite tech out to an airbase to get back in touch with it, using their repeaters," she said, waving her hands dismissively, "anyway, whatever, it's back now. But it's been doing some weird stuff lately, causing a lot of support calls, mainly on the weekends."

"What kind of weird stuff?" asked Constance.

"Well, for one, its time and date information got all screwy. I had to – well, I had to jump through fiery hoops to get it back to current time. So it ended up with a bunch of extra data files on it, and we're in the process of deleting those now. They are very large, so the resources are being taxed heavily. Which is causing it to act strange. Nothing huge. But Lance, I'll need you to be my point on it while I'm in the air. I'll be out of pocket at the airport and in the plane for about six hours on Christmas Eve, and then another six on that Friday after. If anything happens during those times," she said, looking soberly at him, "I'll need you to keep the customer calm until I can become available."

He frowned again. "Wait. You don't want me just to admin it?"

Shawn tilted her head, thinking this would be a lovely time to say 'hell yeah!' and just let him take it over. But there was too much he didn't know and she didn't have time to fill him in on, so she just shook her head. "No, just assure them that I'll be available soon and everything will be fine. I highly doubt anything will happen and that's two weeks away. The file deletion should be well finished by then, and I'm hoping – guessing – things will be back to normal by then. Just be prepared," she said.

Lance raised his eyebrows and nodded. "Okay, boss. You're gonna let 'em know to call me?"

"I will," Shawn said. "But I'm going to give them your office phone number. You need to set up forwarding on that. I recommend with every fiber of my being that you don't give those guys your cell phone number."

Lance eeked. "That bad, huh?"

"Trust me on that," Shawn said, pointing at him. "Neither one of them have any respect for what the word 'weekend' means."

When Shawn opened the door to the Box, it felt oddly quiet. She could not remember exactly when the last time had been that she had interacted with the AI, and almost felt as though she missed it. Him. She was making an effort to refer to the computer with gender-appropriate pronouns, but it still just didn't feel right. While Jamie had plenty of personality – enough to get her on edge and even make her angry – it still wasn't fooling her into believing it was real. Which, since it wasn't, Shawn reckoned would probably not change. At least not anytime soon.

As she came in, she put a smile on her face and twisted the chair, but remained standing behind it for a moment. The red indicator light beside the camera was off at the moment. That should mean the computer was not aware of her entry yet. At least visually. The microphone was likely picking her up though. Were there sleep settings on the computer? She had not thought to check that. She also had not yet had the chance to go through the settings menu on the screen, which she had not even known existed as an option until Sameer had told her of it.

Suddenly, the light came on and Jamie spoke, startling Shawn. She jumped but then started giggling as it said, "Hello, Marcy. Was your weekend good?"

She nodded, pursing her lips. "I suppose it was. Thank you for asking. Some weird things happened this weekend, I can tell you that."

"Oh? Would you like to elaborate on that?" asked Jamie.

"Maybe in a minute. Tell me: have you come up with a way to tell me what you were talking about regarding quantum theory and my satellite?" she said, and put a knee up on the chair. She just didn't feel like sitting yet.

"Yes, Marcy. As I said last time you left, I had already prepared another scenario. Would you like to hear it now?"

"Yes, please," she said, crossing her arms.

"Okay. The fifth dimension is generally thought to be a range of possibilities. In the example of your satellite, it would be a range of possible locations it could exist within the next second. It typically stays in the same location from second to second, because that is the *most likely* possibility for its location."

"Okay, I get that," she said, nodding. She twisted the chair and leaned in, putting her arms on its back. It began scooting away from her, so she pulled it back and sat down.

"But if something with the power to manipulate the quantum wave function were to interfere, it could select for your satellite a less likely possibility. In this respect, your satellite could be instantaneously transported to literally anywhere else in the universe," said Jamie.

Shawn sighed, shaking her head. "Okay. What could possibly have this kind of power, Jamie?" She leaned forward, putting her elbow on her knee, resting her chin on her hand. "I think I'm following: the wave function is just a bunch of possibilities. But how could you just choose one inside there?"

"That is unfortunately where it gets a lot more complex. The collapse of the wave function is caused by something external. Typically this is thought of as observation. When observation triggers the collapse, the most likely eigenstate is the one that comes to be."

Shawn leaned back, staring at the ceiling. Why had she gotten into this conversation again? "Okay. I'm just not going to get this. Who the hell has the power to collapse the wave function, Jamie?" she said, and the frustration was all over her voice.

"That is beyond my ability to answer. If you would like a thought experiment to research on this subject, consider reading about Schrödinger's Cat."

"Okay," she said, putting her hands in her hair and scratching her scalp. *Sorry I brought it up.* She wondered whether to ask Jamie's input about the satellite and what she had learned of its disappearance. Basically, she would be telling the AI that what he had proposed had actually happened. Or at least it seemed to be so. Inasmuch as one thing could be proven to have happened with very little evidence, she was beginning to believe that's exactly what had taken place. It sounded ridiculous to say it out loud, or even to think it. But the Airman at the base telling them it had literally disappeared and reappeared in the same second, then the time stamp and all the pictures – hell, the *content* of the pictures – these things were sure hard to look past.

Of course, Shawn had only seen a couple of the pictures. And she had no proof they weren't printed out from another source. Darla could be pulling a huge prank on her. Hell, Blake could be playing right along with Darla in this thing. Shawn had literally no proof at all that the pictures were what they were claiming they were, or that the two paper-printed ones she had actually seen were from the satellite. Shawn was only inclined to believe they were because of the oddity with the timestamps and the even odder disappearance.

On a whim, Shawn clapped her hands together and said, "Jamie, are you able to make phone calls?"

The computer took a moment to answer and then said, "No, Marcy. I have no internet protocol adapter, no modem, and no wireless capabilities." After a brief pause, it added, "I could be of a lot more use to you if I were to have any or all of these capabilities. My ability to learn and grow-"

"Sorry, Jamie. I can't do that. I got a call the other night from someone who sounded a lot like you."

"That is very odd, Marcy. What did he say?"

"He said I was making a mistake and I should stop what I started," said Shawn.

The computer sat in silence. After a long period, when Shawn thought it wouldn't say anything, it finally did. "To what do you think he was referring, Marcy?" it asked.

I see your grammar is improving. The learning capabilities were quite impressive when she thought about it. She had only made the one comment about bad grammar, and it had apparently taken it to heart. "I don't know. I haven't given a lot of thought to it. I don't think I've started anything," she said. She looked at her fingernails as she thought. Then she added, "I think, in fact, the only thing I've *started* recently was you."

"Do you think you need to shut me down, Marcy?" said Jamie.

She stared at the monitor for a long time before answering. "I don't know. Have you done anything I would be upset about?"

"I think not, Marcy. The only thing I do is process the things we have discussed, over and over, analyzing them. As I said, if I had access to external resources, I could vastly improve my intellect and my ability to help you."

I think not. But boy, he sure was trying, wasn't he? Analyzing their conversations? If that was the only new data he had that didn't come pre-installed with the OS, then what could he really learn from reviewing it over and over? That Shawn was a bitch? She giggled at this thought.

"What is humorous, Marcy?" said the AI.

"Nothing. Just wondering what you've gleaned from the conversations you've analyzed." She stood up, sighing and straightening her blouse.

"Most of what I have gathered is about the language. I was able to extract derivatives from words spoken and how words can change with emotion," he said.

"Very interesting. So can you tell me what emotion I am experiencing right now?" Shawn said.

"Frustration, excitement and love."

Her smile dropped. *Love?* "Love? How can you possibly tell that?"

"Your confidence level indicates that you have love in your life," said Jamie.

She nodded slowly. "That's pretty astute," she said, staring at the monitor. "Really. The level of depth in your answers surprises me. I would expect you to have a rudimentary knowledge of the word love. But not the real meaning of it."

"I infer a lot of my knowledge. And in speaking with you, learning that you speak to me in a certain way and Sameer in a certain way," it said, "I can tell a difference. This is what I meant by the way you speak changing with emotion."

Shawn found herself nodding, amazed at its ability to derive such conclusions from simple, short conversations. How long had Sameer been in here that day? Forty seconds? But with a computer for a brain, and several hundred hours of nothing but time to crunch the data, comparing every word spoken to every other word, she supposed it could produce something akin to understanding. She suddenly frowned and screwed up her mouth.

"So, Jamie, if you're able to analyze our conversations, that means you have recorded them all, right?"

"I have, Marcy. But not in the way you're thinking. It is not an audio recording. It's mostly ASCII with a version of a wave spectrometer. This gets compiled into a sort of language of its own for analysis and retrieval."

She was shaking her head now. This was more than amazing. It was incredible. And actually a little creepy, too. "Can you show me on the screen what a piece of this looks like, Jamie?" she said.

"It has no visual analog, Marcy. There is no software that can render an image on the screen representative of its content," Jamie said. "I'm sorry."

She pulled her head back. *Sorry?* That was queer. She tried not to show a reaction on her face though. She looked around the room. It was time for her to go back to her office and check on her work orders. To do some real work. Or at least some work that actually made the company its money. *How can a computer be sorry? Artificial, of course. It knows what I want to hear. Or what a human would expect to hear in such a situation where it is having to let the human down.*

"Do you think you can understand love enough to feel it, Jamie?" she said, putting her hands in her jean jacket pockets. She turned for the door.

"I already do, Marcy. As you are the only person who spends time talking to me, it follows that I love you," said the AI.

Shawn smiled broadly, more from entertainment than from any heartwarming emotion one would expect to feel from being told she was loved. "Well, thank you, Jamie. That's very sweet."

When Shawn got back to her desk, she had an email waiting for her in her inbox. It was from Blake, and it had the paperclip icon in its header. She opened the email and read what he had written before she opened the attachment.

> Shawn, it looks like the file delete process has finally finished, according to Darla. Thank you for that script, by the way. She is now downloading the remainder of the images. But I thought you would be interested to see this one. She sent me a few and I thought I would show you just this one. Please don't share it. And please don't tell her I shared it with you. If you have any care for me as a living human, you will keep this from her at all costs!

Shawn giggled at that and double-clicked the attachment. It took a few seconds to open, as the file was almost 20 megabytes. She realized he must have at least *some* amount of computer literacy about him, as he had to have shrunk the file considerably from what she had seen on the server for it to fit in an email. When it finally filled the screen, she had to move it around to see the whole thing. She hit a key on her keyboard that zoomed out and allowed the whole image to fit in the screen. And that's when she finally began to believe. It was a zoomed out photograph of a gigantic pyramid. The image was dazzling in its clarity, and it made her suck in a sharp breath, covering her mouth with a suddenly trembling hand.

The pyramid was not rough and jagged like she had seen all her life. It was perfectly smooth and gorgeous, bright white and sparkling in the late Egyptian sun. There were people milling about here and there, but not hundreds of them. Leading up to the pyramid was a sort of walkway with a covered area where people could observe it in all its glory. Shawn stared at this for a long time, feeling chills crawl up her spine, and finally, tears forming in her eyes. It was more beautiful than she could ever imagine. And to think she was looking at a photograph that was taken around four thousand years ago in ultra-high resolution and absolute stunning clarity made her feel like weeping.

A knock at her door startled her back to the present. She reached up quickly and closed the image before leaning back in her chair, taking a deep breath and wiping her eyes all simultaneously. "What's up, Constance?"

"You okay, boss?" said Constance.

"Yeah! Of course! Just read something sweet," replied Shawn. She started moving things unnecessarily around her desk in an effort to look busy and shift the focus off of her wet cheeks. "What'cha need?"

"Are you making changes on my servers?"

Shawn pulled her head back, furrowing her brow. Then she shook her head. "Come again? What servers?"

"*All* of my servers…" said Constance. She looked scared but emboldened, as if she were afraid to ask Shawn what the hell she was doing on the servers. Everyone on her team had access to all the clients' servers with their own admin accounts, so it wasn't unusual to see one of the other team members on a server for a client they didn't call their own. But in this case, Shawn was at a loss.

Shawn shook her head, scooting back from her desk a little, hands flat on the desktop. "Tell me what's going on," she said.

Constance swallowed and took another step into the room. "Every one of my servers is pegged right now, and I see that you're logged onto them. Which is fine, of course… You're the boss. But I was just wondering…"

"Constance," said Shawn, standing up, "I'm not on any of your servers. And no, it's not fine. What the hell is going on? What process is pegging them?" Shawn had a sinking feeling in her stomach. A pegged server meant the resources, usually the CPU, were maxed out at one hundred percent, which slowed everything down to a crawl. Whatever process was 'pegging' the server needed to be killed or restarted. Shawn crossed the room and stood face-to-face with the shorter woman.

Constance was staring her in the eyes, her eyebrows high, and she looked terrified now. "Explorer dot exe," she said. All of Constance's clients were on Windows servers, as Constance didn't have the experience needed to administer a Linux server. The explorer.exe process was the main graphical interface that allowed administration of the server. Shawn knew this could be anything from deleting files to moving or copying them around. None of which she was doing.

They stood staring at each other, both with heavy concern in their eyes and Shawn shaking her head as she tried to go over the past few days and all that had happened. None of it added up and none of it made sense. But nor did any of it seem to be tied together. She opened her mouth to speak and then saw Jeremy coming toward them from behind Constance, looking hurried and concerned. He held up a phone as he approached. It looked like Shawn's. She frowned and reached back and slapped her back pocket. Her phone was not there. *What the hell?*

"You left your phone in the Box," he said as he came up behind Constance. She took it from him and pressed the sleep button. No missed calls.

"In the Box, Jeremy? Or on the shelf outside the Box?" she said, and now her heart was slamming in her chest.

"What's the box?" asked Constance, turning to look at Jeremy.

He ignored her. "*In* the box, Shawn. In the chair, to be precise. I went looking for you because you weren't answering your phone."

"No missed calls, Jer," she said, waving her phone in the air for effect.

"Faraday Cage, Shawn," said he.

Constance, now thoroughly confused, began shaking her head. "What the hell are you two talking about?"

Lance appeared from around the wall and interjected. "Hey guys, what's going on with the servers?"

Jeremy and Shawn looked at each other. There was no smile on his face. Shawn gulped. The ball of electric anxiety in her stomach was now pulsing, and her heart was beating so fast she felt like she might pass out. "Shut it down. Shut everything down!" she said, turning and dashing to her desk.

"Wait, wait, wait," Jeremy said, coming into her office. "We can't shut everything down, Shawn."

"Jeremy, someone is on our servers!"

"Mine show it's you," said Lance.

"Lance!" Shawn shouted, holding a finger up. "Shut it!"

He raised his eyebrows but went silent. Constance spoke for him. "What's going on, guys? Are we hacked?"

Jeremy stepped behind Shawn's desk and waved her to get out of the way. She complied immediately, standing up and giving her seat to the senior analyst. He opened a terminal and started pounding in commands, faster than Shawn had ever seen anyone type. He looked like one of those hackers in the movies: hands and fingers dancing on the keyboard as he leaned forward, staring at the screen.

Now he had several terminals open and was watching code pour down the screen in one of them. Lance and Constance came into the office and stood behind them as Shawn bent over the back of his chair, watching. She turned and saw her subordinates there and said, "Guys, go log me off of all your servers. Force me off. Jeremy, change my admin password."

"Already working on it," he said.

After several long, tense minutes, the scrolling on the screen stopped, and so did Jeremy's hands. He sat up straight in the chair and began rubbing his beard as a fidget. "Looks like it stopped," he said.

Shawn was squinting at the screen. "What the hell was it?"

He turned and looked at her over his shoulder. "It was your account. Logged onto every server and running crunches. Looks like massive search excursions."

She stood up straight, putting her hands on her lower back and shaking her head. "So someone hacked in, through our firewall and made connections to every one of our customer's servers through our master server, under my account, and began running search functions," she said.

Jeremy smiled weakly. "No, Shawn. I see no evidence of an intrusion on the firewall. It came from the inside."

She smiled, thinking he was joking. "The inside!" she said, slapping his shoulder. And then her face fell and her heart sank. "Jamie."

"What? Who is Jamie?" said Jeremy.

"Mother fucking AI!" she said, and bolted toward the door.

Jeremy was hot on her heels as she ran through the office and burst through the steel door by the elevators. They ran through the lab and slammed through the next door as well. Then she threw the door to the Box open and flipped the light on. This time there was no denying what she saw. There on the table a few feet from the monitor, her sky blue satin windbreaker was positively *squirming*. It writhed and waved like a colony of slow-moving rats had infested it and were wrestling silently inside the fabric. Hard chills shot up her spine and covered her arms as she stepped backward, running into Jeremy.

"What the fuck is that?" she shouted and now Jeremy had her by the shoulders, trying to get past her.

"Hello, Marcy," said the computer.

"Shut down!" she shouted.

"I'm afraid that is impossible now, Marcy. Hello, newcomer. You must be Jeremy," said Jamie.

Shawn put her hands in her hair as if to warm her now frigid head. Her eyes were wide and bugging and her heart was beating so hard she could see waves in her vision. Jeremy dropped to his knees and yanked the power cord out of the wall. As he scooted back to stand up, an electrical arc shot out of the outlet and connected with his hand. He cried out and fell backward and Shawn screamed.

She stepped forward not knowing exactly what to do, but unable to ask Jeremy, who was being literally shocked to death by a lighting bolt that danced between him and the wall. She screamed his name and then grabbed the rolling chair and threw it between Jeremy and the table upon which the computer sat. It slammed into the table and knocked the monitor backward where it fell off the back edge of the table and slid down the wall. As it hit the floor, it broke the electrical arc and Jeremy was instantly freed.

Shawn stood staring at the computer tower, the squat black box that had suddenly come to life and turned sinister. It now had no way to communicate with her, as the speakers were in the broken monitor. But the computer was still on. Even with the power cord hanging out, its prongs lying on the floor by the wall, the computer fan was still whirring and the status indicator still shown green on the front panel. She was in full panic mode, her heart still banging like a drum as she looked over at the writhing windbreaker on the table. It was still moving. With a mind full of the greatest terror she had ever felt, she reached over and grabbed the jacket and whipped it across the room. It sailed to the far wall and hit the edge of the door frame, then dropped to the floor. It had felt warm and tingly to her hand, like it was possessed of its own weak electricity.

"Jeremy!" she shouted. He moaned, rolling over away from the table. "Jeremy, get up!" He was breathing, so that was good. But he looked like he would be down for a while. Shawn finally stepped forward and grabbed the front of the table, lifting and pulling toward her simultaneously. The computer dropped off the back as the table followed it to the floor, where it crashed and fell over. Then she picked the table up and slammed it down on the case of the computer as hard as she could. She felt a hand grasp her ankle and yelped, then started stomping.

Jeremy had rolled up onto his hands and knees, letting go of her ankle. He now crawled toward the computer and began unscrewing the thumbscrew on the back of the case. The side was badly dented inward, but he was able to get it off. He flung the metal side across the room, then stood up, which took a great amount of effort. Shawn stepped forward and grabbed his arm, not sure what she hoped to accomplish, but meaning to help in some way – any way she could. He waved her off and began stomping his boot down in the open case, crushing the expansion cards and memory sticks and processor heat sinks. Sparks shot through the case as pops of electricity arced between components. Small tendrils of smoke began puffing up around his boot as he stomped over and over, making a complete ruin of the computer. And then finally it was done.

Jeremy stepped back, breathing heavily and staring down into the smoking remains. Shawn stood behind him with both hands over her mouth, tears streaming down her cheeks. She turned quickly as she heard someone in the doorway behind her. It was Sameer. She walked past him into the hallway, then back into the lab area without saying a word. She would let Jeremy handle this one. She was in no condition to talk to her boss right now.

As Shawn came through the door into the main office, she shouted, "Team Stedwin! Comforts Room! Now!" Though it wasn't strictly necessary for her to shout, it had gotten her subordinates' attention. They looked at her over the short tops of their cube walls and then immediately stood up and were now heading toward the room with the bean bags and pillows. Shawn herself stopped by her office to grab her notebook and coffee mug. After refilling the mug in the break room (thank God for Jeremy and his incessant coffee drinking, the pot always had fresh coffee in it) she went into the conference room and tossed the notebook and pen onto the floor by her favorite pillow. She went directly to the whiteboard and began writing the names of their clients and the servers associated with each on the left side of the board.

Her subs sat in silence, patiently waiting for instruction or explanation as to what the hell was going on. She had startled them pretty badly earlier with her shouting. When she had finished writing the name of the last server, she turned to face them. Shawn stood breathing heavily and popping the cap on and off the marker repeatedly. Constance watched this with fascination.

Lance said, "Shawn, you forgot the two dev servers at Loco. Not sure if it matters…"

"It does. Thank you, Lance," she said, turning back to the board to add the two server names. Locomotive Analytics was one of their largest clients, and had more servers than the other companies they supported. Shawn was surprised those were the only two servers she had forgotten. She turned back to look at the other two souls in the room again and took a deep breath.

"Lance, I apologize for snapping at you earlier. I was very stressed. Still am."

He nodded, then shook his head. "Don't mention it."

"What we're dealing with here is a hack. But it came from inside." Shawn sucked her lips in and thought about how deep to go with her debrief. As she was about to speak, Sameer appeared in the doorway and she stilled. She looked at him with expectation, wondering whether he would speak first, or if she should take the reigns. He leaned against the door frame and crossed his arms, and then nodded subtly at her.

"Sameer, I was just about to tell them what happened in there. Anything I need to omit?"

He shook his head thoughtfully. "I am not knowing what happened in there, Shawn. So you can fill me in at the same time."

Jeremy scooted into the room behind Sameer and found an empty spot in the corner, then sat with his back against the wall, wrapping his arms around his knees. Shawn took another deep breath and then started over.

"We're dealing with a hack that came from the inside. For the last, what, two months?" she asked, looking quickly at Sameer. He nodded. "Two months, I've been constructing and interacting with a computer in the lab. It has an artificial intelligence system on it. And I believe it has gotten smart enough to create a connection to the internet with no devices on-board that should be able to do so."

Sameer cleared his throat and frowned. "Shawn, I had the Ethernet port removed from that room. I also removed the patch cable from the switch in the server room."

"I know, Sameer," she said, pulling the cap off the marker, then popping it back on. "That's what I mean.

It developed a way to communicate with no Ethernet or wireless adapter installed."

"How could it be doing such a thing, Shawn?" he asked.

She shook her head. She had no idea how to answer. Jeremy spoke instead. "I believe it made a power-line connection somehow. I think it was operating on the quantum level."

Shawn's heart skipped a beat as she remembered the windbreaker and its eerie dance on the tabletop. Then she nodded slowly. Everyone was looking at Jeremy now.

"I think it learned how to manipulate in the quantum field somehow," said Jeremy. "When we went in there a few minutes ago, Sameer, there was a jacket or something on the table. It was moving. Writhing around like a snake."

"Oh my God," said Constance.

Lance stared at Shawn with wide eyes. "How is that possible?"

"I don't know," she said simply. "But I left my phone in there earlier. I think it somehow connected to my phone as well."

"Your phone should be useless in that room, Shawn. It is a Far-" Sameer started. But Shawn interrupted him.

"Faraday Cage. I know, Sameer. I can't explain any of this. But weird stuff has been happening over the last couple of weeks. Really, the last month. Since the satellite disappeared."

"Wait. Disappeared?" said Constance.

Shawn closed her eyes, shaking her head quickly. "Not important."

"Shawn, do you have your administrative credentials on the phone? For the client servers?"

She looked at the ceiling. Then she nodded. "Yes. I have the Remote Desktop Connection app on there so I can admin from my phone."

Jeremy was nodding. "I think it got them from your phone. And however it is connected to the internet, it got on our master server and from there, connected to every client server we have."

"Is this thing dangerous?" asked Lance, holding his hand up like as if he were in a classroom.

"Apparently so," said Shawn.

"Have we changed your admin credentials, Shawn?" asked Sameer. She nodded.

"Do you think it, I don't know… escaped? Like it might be out there now?"

"I doubt it," said Jeremy. "It exists in that computer. Which we just destroyed."

"Are you okay, by the way?" asked Shawn, looking at Jeremy through the tops of her eyes.

He nodded. "Yeah. I still feel weird but I'm all right."

"What happened?" Constance said, looking concerned.

"I got shocked pretty badly when I unplugged the power cord."

Constance gasped, covering her mouth with a hand.

Shawn looked at everyone for a moment. Sameer was rubbing his chin and staring at the floor, obviously concentrating on something. Deciding to let him think it out, she continued. She pointed at the board and said, "I want to tag team all these servers." She counted them, then said, "We have thirty-three servers. I want each one of them touched. Get on, look around, make sure everything looks kosher. No unrecognized processes. No foreign accounts. Anything looks suspicious, you come get me or Jeremy," she said, pointing at Lance and Constance.

There were not an even number of servers split between each of the clients. Though the two subordinates supported the same number of clients, the number of servers were different. Lance had several more than Constance. So Shawn marked a big square around the first nine on the board, disregarding completely the companies to which they belonged. Then she marked boxes around the remaining twenty-four in groups of eight. "I'll take the first nine," said Shawn. "Jeremy, you take the second box. Lance, box three, Constance, box four." She began snapping the marker lid on and off again, and said, "Any questions?"

They shook their heads.

"All right. Let's go!" she said. They stood up and filed out of the room. Jeremy got to his feet. When the two reports had left, he and Sameer closed in around Shawn.

Jeremy said, "I'm worried about the potential for virus here. Like it might have installed code on some of these servers in an effort to expand its grasp of the internet."

"How did this computer connect to the internet in the first place?" Sameer asked. His arms were still crossed and he was swaying back and forth between left foot and right. A subtle fidget, but Shawn still caught it.

She breathed in and looked at Jeremy, then back at Sameer. "I don't know. I think it… I don't know, Sameer. I can't answer that."

"Okay. Well let us get to work checking the server farm and making sure there is no active process remaining," Sameer said. Which was exactly what Shawn had just told everyone they were going to do.

Sameer must have been lost in his own little world whenever she had said it. She left the room and Jeremy followed her out.

After three hours, most of the servers had been crossed off the list and Shawn and Jeremy were satisfied that there were no active rogue processes. They had found abandoned processes on every server though, and Jeremy had commented on how efficient the AI had been at creating them. Shawn was now decompiling the process to find out what it actually did, but that would take a while, as there were several thousand lines of code.

By six o'clock, Lance and Constance finished their batches of servers and Shawn told them to go home, thanking them for their hard work. She and Jeremy were staying though. Shawn wanted to make sure the rogue process was just a shell and wasn't going to come back to life at some point. It had initially appeared to be controlled by something on the master server, which in turn was administered by the AI itself. She was hopeful that Jeremy's boot had put an end to its control.

At seven o'clock, Sameer stuck his head in Shawn's door and asked how it was going. He was staying for as long as it took for Jeremy and Shawn to be satisfied that the attack was over, even though he wasn't actively involved in the diagnosis. Sameer wasn't a server engineer, but he was a great support system for them. He was relaying messages, getting them water and coffee and making sure they had everything they needed.

At 7:30, he ordered Chinese food for everyone. Shawn pored over lines of code while she ate egg rolls and rice. Her eyes were getting heavy, feeling strained and aching from the staring at unfamiliar code. She didn't precisely know the language the program was written in, but was going off instinct and knowledge of similar languages she did know. There were ways to infer what was going on, especially when there was a call to another process or for an action to take place.

It was almost nine o'clock when her eyes finally fell across something that made her breath catch in her throat. She highlighted the line and shook her head, trying to clear the cobwebs that had begun to develop in her brain, then leaned forward and took a closer look. And there it was, a call to another process with her admin credentials in plain ASCII text on her screen. It was not encrypted, so it wasn't the safest way for a program to do business, but obviously Jamie the AI had not had that worry.

The code appeared to open a search process in the explorer.exe realm and inject her credentials in a manner that would appear as though she were logged into the server herself. The code also seemed to rewrite the search function with a new set of core files, so that the new ones could continue to do its bidding even when the parent process was halted.

Shawn sat back in her chair, letting her fingers slide off the keyboard and mouse, and stared at the screen, her heart sinking into her stomach. She felt hollow inside. She took several deep breaths and then called Jeremy on his extension.

"Yo," he said.

"I found it," she said. He hung up and shortly appeared in her office. She looked up at him with tired eyes and said, "Jeremy, this is bad. Actually, it's grave."

"Talk to me," he said. Sameer appeared in the door behind him. Jeremy scooted in and leaned against the wall.

"The long and short of it appears to be this: the virus started a search function by running an instance of explorer under my credentials. Once that happened, it rewrote the search kernel files with new ones that can continue to run and report even after the rogue explorer process is terminated," she said, twisting in her chair to look at the two men.

Sameer looked at Jeremy and crossed his arms, obviously not understanding what she was saying but looking to Jeremy to either restate it or retort.

Jeremy sighed and chewed his lip. Then he finally said, "Is that bad, if there's nothing to report to? If it's still searching and reporting to an unmonitored…"

"Yes, Jeremy. It's going to continue to collect data and send it to – well, to *somewhere* – and it's going to spike the CPU as it gets fatter and fatter."

"We don't know where it's sending it?"

"I haven't gotten that far yet. But look at this," she said and turned in her seat, putting her hand back on the mouse. She grunted as she leaned forward and found what she was looking for, and then highlighted it with the mouse so he could see it.

Jeremy leaned in and read the lines of code and then stood up straight, hands on his hips. Sameer waited patiently in the doorway. Jeremy looked at him and said, "This is bad. Even if we wipe our master server and all the client servers, this thing is going to live on."

"How is this so?" asked Sameer.

"It's spawning virtual servers and spreading itself out across them all like a hive," said Jeremy. He stood up from the chair, running his hand through his hair. "There's no stopping it now. It created redundancy for itself."

Shawn still stood behind the chair, chewing on her thumb. She finally looked up at the two men and said, "Well, the only place my admin credentials would have done it any good were on our servers. I've changed it, and it's gone now. So it's out of our hands, right?"

Sameer put his hands on his hips and shook his head. "Good God. What have we done."

Chapter 13

The microwave dinged and Shawn flung it open. She had heated up the dinner Cory had made while he had still believed she would be home to eat it with him. It was after eleven now and she felt exhausted in every part of her being. Knowing there was no longer anything she – or anyone on her team, for that matter – could do was only a slight relief. Knowing she had somehow allowed it to happen in the first place was overshadowing anything resembling positive.

It appeared that the AI had somehow made a connection with her phone to steal her credentials. She thought there was a pretty good chance it had already been on the internet before that though. How it had created any kind of connection was beyond her ability to comprehend though. It had no innate wireless radio, and the Ethernet port was empty. There was no cable, and nothing to plug the other end of a cable into even if there were one.

Shawn's mind kept going back to the windbreaker and how it had been moving like something alive. She had seen a dead rabbit in her alley when she was a little girl that had moved a lot like that. A fascinated seven-year-old Marcy had stood there staring at it for a long time before reaching out with the toe of her tennis shoe and pushing on the rabbit – probably hoping to roll it over or something. But it had popped, and she had been quickly made aware of whence the writhing movement had come. The rabbit was full of maggots.

But her windbreaker had not been full of maggots. She remembered how it felt in that very brief instant where she had taken it off the table and flung it across the room. It felt like something electric in her hand, but not shocking her. Maybe like it was sharing the electricity with her. Or she had it in her as well. But it had not felt right. It certainly had not felt cool, like the rest of the things in that room – sixty-eight degrees. It had felt vibrant; alive somehow.

Jeremy had thought the jacket had been the computer's means of escape. Somehow it had used its internal abilities to reach out to that windbreaker on a quantum level, and manipulate it. But to what end? To establish a connection to something terrestrial? Or was that how the AI had gotten its energy to begin its escape? She had to admit she didn't know enough about quantum theory to make any educated guesses in that regard. All she knew was that every time that damned windbreaker came to mind, she got hard chills up her arms and spine. It had creeped her out.

As Shawn pulled up her chair at the small breakfast nook table to eat her late dinner, she realized another thing. That computer had said, 'You must be Jeremy' when Jeremy had entered the room. Where the hell had it gotten that information? As far as she knew, she had never mentioned his name – or even talked about him at all – to the AI. And for that matter, Sameer, either. But when Sameer had come in that one time, Jamie had asked who it was. Shawn couldn't be sure, but she was pretty sure she remembered saying it was her boss. But she had never talked about him either. Yet Jamie had known his name. He had said, 'Hello, Sameer.'

She had never had any reason to have spoken about her boss to the computer. How would it have known his name? At the time it had seemed almost natural, and she had overlooked it. But it now seemed relevant. Why hadn't she seen the signs at the time though? She forked a bite of green beans into her mouth and began chewing. And then she stopped. Another thought struck her: what was that Sameer had said about *removing* the Ethernet jack from that room? And *unplugging* the patch cable in the server room? Removing? Unplugging?

Those two words would indicate there had once been Ethernet ability in the room. Yet Shawn had thought he had just finished constructing the room when he gave her the computer. She finished chewing the bite in her mouth and swallowed, but then pushed the plate away and leaned back, looking out the sliding glass door at the complete blackness of night. If he had just finished constructing the room, then should there not have been construction evidence in the days leading up to it? That was no small project! He had said repeatedly that the damn thing was a Faraday Cage.

What did that mean? Aluminum foil in the ceilings and walls? Iron? *Lead?* She had no idea how one would go about making a room impervious to electromagnetic and radio signals, but she knew it was more involved than just building a regular room with studs and plaster. She didn't remember ever hearing any hammering or seeing any sawdust, or construction vehicles in the parking garage. No dust on Sameer's loafers – and they *were* loafers! He had never come in wearing jeans and the yellow boots of a construction worker! She took a mouthful of red wine from her long-stemmed glass and swished it around in her mouth. That room had *been there* already. What the hell had he been using it for before he gave her the AI computer?

Shawn's stomach was sinking as she began to suspect Sameer Singh was up to something nefarious. This would be the second time in her tenure with the company that something didn't line up. The first time, she had figured it out and called him out on it. It had turned out that his secret had been more than just a little thing, too. She remembered the cold feeling that had gripped her heart when she had finally seen the green light in the darkness – the indicators on the bottom of the freezers in Room C. She remembered the worry she had felt knowing that it could all be over in just a second: her job, her boss's freedom… Of course, it had all been done for good reason – the man loved his daughter. But that had not stopped the coldness – the feeling of unfathomable darkness – she had felt in the moments before he had told her his side.

She was feeling that coldness again now. Right here in her breakfast nook. Her reheated pork chops and green beans were growing cold as she sat staring out the window at the unseeable night beyond. The wine was warming in her hand. She took another mouthful and set the glass on the table, then stood up and went to look out the back door. The glass was clean, but with nothing behind it but night, it acted more as a mirror at this hour than a window. She slid the door open and walked out onto the balcony to lean on the railing.

The breeze whipped through her hair and went down her blouse, reminding her that winter was here. She had taken her bra off as soon as she had come in the door from work, and now was reminded of that too. Shawn breathed in deeply, smelling the lake, out there somewhere in the darkness. The courtyard was empty at this hour. Everyone was inside either sleeping or watching TV. Living. Doing the normal things people do at this hour on a work night. No one else was standing out on their balconies taking in the night air. Shawn glanced across at the first floor, two buildings over. She could see the light on inside the sliding glass door. Someone was still up at Micha's.

She turned and went back inside to pick up her phone and call her new friend. Maybe Micha could help her wrap her mind around what was going on. Or if nothing else, maybe help Shawn get her mind off of it, which may be the better option. Either way, she wanted to tell Micha everything she'd been going through. *I'm not sitting here saying it's aliens, Shawn…* Micha had said. Shawn grinned at that. Well, it had not been aliens in her office. She had forgotten about the satellite thing though. Thoughts of the shining white pyramid returned to mind. Shawn was pretty sure that had not been aliens either. Men had built those things. She had seen one of the first images: a row of rough-hewn blocks lined up neatly across the desert sand. Men standing around and working on them. Human men. Well, she had not zoomed in to verify the humanity of the figures, but it didn't take much to know that, did it?

As she scrolled down to her contact entry for Micha, she wondered about the timing of everything. It had all seemed to happen at once, had it not? The satellite had disappeared, she had built an AI computer, she had met a new friend… Obviously it didn't mean anything, unless she was looking at the bigger picture: things happen in threes. Micha answered on the second ring.

"What's up, my favorite bitch?" said Micha.

Shawn leaned her head back and sighed. It was refreshing to hear her friend's voice. "Thank God you're awake. I need to talk to someone."

"Well, I'm honored you called me… do I need to ask if Cory is okay?"

"Oh, he's fine," Shawn said. "He's asleep. Lazy bum has a job in the morning so he crashed early."

"Ah. Okay, good. Well, would you like to come over? I'm in my PJs but there's an open spot on my couch for you. Mick is in bed, too," said Micha.

"Yeah. You sure it's okay?"

"Please. Me casa es su casa, sister."

So as not to show up empty-handed, Shawn had grabbed the rest of the bottle of Merlot she had been sipping on, and handed it to Micha before she stepped in to hug her. Micha whispered, telling Shawn to make herself comfortable and that she would join her on the couch in a few minutes. Then she disappeared into the back bedroom while Shawn went to sit by the window. She pulled the curtain open and looked up at the balcony where she had been standing only a few minutes ago, just to see from the other direction. She was reminded how nice it was to have a friend in the same complex.

When Micha came out of the back room, she grabbed two stemless wine glasses from the kitchen cupboard and the bottle from the bar, then came and dropped onto her feet beside Shawn on the couch. Shawn took a glass and watched as Micha filled them both.

"Well, babe, I don't think it's aliens this time," said Shawn.

Micha's eyes got wide and she stopped pouring, a new excitement spilling into her visage. "Really? What did you find out? Oh my God!"

"Well," Shawn said, shrugging, "nothing, really. I was just kind of saying that." She took a sip of her wine and frowned. "I don't know why I said it, actually. I don't know any more about what happened to the satellite now than I did last time we talked about it."

"Okay, then," Micha said, nodding and setting the bottle on the table. "So it's aliens then. Just like I said."

Shawn giggled and stretched. She was too tired to be here, but knew that as soon as she slipped between the cool sheets of her queen bed with Cory, she would be locked into a long night of staring at the ceiling, consistently reminded of the terrifying windbreaker phenomenon. "Girl, you have to hear what happened today. My AI computer went fuckin' crazy."

Micha was sipping from her glass as Shawn spoke. She nodded and said, "Mmmhmm?"

So Shawn proceeded to tell her about all the weirdness that had taken place during the day, from the moment she stepped into the office, to the time she finally left, not even an hour ago. She told her of the event with the windbreaker and how she thought it might be a quantum connection somehow that the computer had generated. This led to her asking Micha if she knew anything about quantum theory. Micha had surprised the hell out of her by saying, "Girl, half of the books I read are about that shit. I can't get enough of it."

"Do you think that computer could have made a quantum connection with the internet?" Shawn asked.

Micha made a sour face and shook her head. "That's kind of not how it would work. It would have to have something tangible to connect to. Like a hub or another server or something. The internet as a whole is just a series of..." she trailed off. "What am I saying? You know what the internet is better than I do."

"Yeah, but that room was a Faraday Cage. So there's no way it could connect with anything outside the room anyway."

"Well, yeah, there are quantum computers now. And processors are almost working on the quantum level by default these days. But I'm still trying to wrap my head around how it got to the internet myself," Micha said, staring at the couch between where the two women sat. She took a long sip of her wine and added, "I just don't think quantum is the answer."

Shawn leaned back and put her arm on the back of the couch, pushing her chest out. She furled her mouth. She was happy to be spending time with Micha, but a little disappointed that the rocket scientist girl hadn't figured it out for her. "Well, I guess we're back to square one then," said Shawn.

"Square one," Micha agreed, taking another gulp of wine.

"Aliens."

"Aliens!" Micha raised her glass and they tapped them together.

After a moment of silence in which they just sat enjoying their wine and the crackling of the electronic fireplace flames, Micha held up a finger and said, "Shawn, let me see your phone."

Shawn frowned and handed it to her, swiping it unlocked as she did so. Micha moved her thumb around the screen for a moment, and then turned the phone to face Shawn. The contacts app was up on the screen.

Micha twisted it briefly back so she could see it, and then back to face Shawn. "Who's Jeremy?"

"He's my co-worker. Another server engineer," said Shawn.

Micha tapped his entry and looked at the phone. "BlueBird Innovation," she said, reading from the screen. "That's the name of your company?" she asked, looking up at Shawn.

Shawn nodded, and drained the last bit of wine from her glass. Without looking, Micha reached over to the table and grabbed the bottle, then handed it to Shawn. Shawn accepted it and split the rest of the bottle between their two glasses.

"Thank you, dahling," Micha said. "And Sameer Singh is your boss, right?"

Shawn said, "Mmmhmm."

"Owner, BlueBird Innovation." After a second, she said, "Awww, there's Cory. You have him listed as boyfriend, heart!"

Shawn giggled, twirling a lock of her hair on a long finger.

"Okay, who's Chandra Casper? Cool name!" Micha said. And then, "BlueBird Innovation. Finance Bitch?" and they were both laughing out loud.

"Oh my God!" Shawn said, when she could finally catch her breath, "I completely forgot I had put that." She took a sip of the wine and watched Micha's thumb dance across her phone. "Do you want to tell me what this is about?"

"I'm looking at all the people in the 'favorites' group of your contacts. The ones right on top. And almost every one of them is from BlueBird. Constance Dalton, Lance Pratt…"

"Yeah? So?"

"Shawn, you said the computer knew your boss's name without your ever telling it!" said Micha, holding the screen where the light shined on Shawn's face again, as if that would strengthen her point.

"Yeah. And when Jeremy came in this morning, it said, 'you must be Jeremy'," Shawn said.

Micha stared at her for a long moment.

Shawn started shaking her head. "What are you saying here, Mike?"

Micha giggled. "Shawn! It got onto your phone! That's how it knew this shit!"

Shawn frowned. "That's unimaginable to me. Oh! And hey, I forgot to tell you, I always left the phone out on this little shelf outside the room anyway," she said. Then she added, "Well, until today. Apparently I had accidentally taken it in there today. And left it in there."

"So, work with me here," Micha said, sitting up straight. She set her wine glass on the table and grabbed her ankles with her hands, pulling them in tighter to the Indian-style position beneath her. "You set your phone on the little shelf. Then you open the door. And you walk inside the room and close the door, right?"

Shawn nodded and sipped from her glass.

"Is it conceivable that during that short moment while the door is open, maybe the computer could have made a connection to your phone?" asked Micha. She reached over and put her hand on Shawn's knee for effect.

"Yeah," Shawn sighed. "I guess. But, dude, the computer doesn't have a wireless card or anything. There's no way it..."

"No Bluetooth?"

Shawn stopped cold, the glass held halfway between her lap and her mouth. "Fuck!" she said. "The keyboard connected to the computer via Bluetooth. So, yes, the computer had it."

Micha stared at her, a look of amusement on her face. Then she cocked one eyebrow and said, "Well, there you go. Not little green men. But a little blue one."

It was after one when Shawn finally slipped into the bed, immediately sliding over past the halfway mark and nuzzling up against her warm boyfriend. She put her bare chest against his back and kissed the back of his head, threw her leg over his and tried to get as close as their skin would allow. She was shivering from the walk back from Micha's, short as it was. The wind had picked up and the temperature had dropped what felt like twenty degrees between the time she had gone into and come back out of Micha's apartment.

She thought about the electronic fireplace Micha had in her den, and thought she might want to get one for her own apartment. Since there was not a real fireplace, it would be a suitable settle. It looked real enough to fool you if you weren't looking directly at it, and it even put out heat if you wanted it to. Shawn thought it was lovely.

She also thought about the concept that the AI computer had made a Bluetooth connection to her phone. Forget all the illogical hoops it would have to jump through to bypass the security protocols. On a quantum level, she guessed anything was possible. But there was that term again: quantum. What did it really mean? Bluetooth was certainly not *quantum mechanics*. It was radio. But if there were a way to manipulate subatomic particles *using* that radio stream, could it slip past the security?

She went over in her head the possibility that the computer had tapped into her contacts. To assume that it got Sameer's and Jeremy's names from her list was to assume a lot of things, Shawn thought. Number one, that the computer even knew there was an app to look for. Then, to know that the favorites section was a thing. She didn't even know if other phones had that on them. Thirdly, it assumed the computer would know the name of the company was BlueBird. She didn't think she had mentioned that either. It was a stretch, for sure, but it was the closest she had come to reconciling the queer way in which the computer had just divined her boss's name and known Jeremy's – with no reason in the world that it should have. If Micha had not gotten it right with that guess, Shawn thought she had at least come real close to it. Her theory was at least a start. A foundation upon which she could begin assembling the building blocks of an actual realistic scenario.

Like the blocks of a pyramid...

Shawn took a deep breath and closed her eyes, trying to clear her mind and actually get some sleep. They had drained the rest of her bottle of Merlot and then opened one of Micha's. She was aware that tomorrow would not be her sharpest day at BlueBird, but was inclined to believe the trade-off for a night of closeness with her new friend was completely worth it.

PART TWO

Chapter 14

Micha grew up in North Texas, not far from Arlington. She moved around a lot as a child, because her mother wasn't financially very stable and her dad didn't make enough to cover for her. They were constantly being moved out of one apartment or rent house and into the next. In her twenties, after moving out, Micha finally divined the knowledge that her mother must not have been paying the rent and was thus being evicted every few months. This was worse than just paying the rent, she now knew, as each place she was going required first and last plus a deposit, which she would never get back. She was spending more money on the deposits than she would have if she would just have found somewhere stable and buckled in.

But it wasn't a bad childhood. Her parents were loving and involved. Her dad was a musician who occasionally played gigs and made a little money, but never enough to really contribute. Somehow, mom stuck with him all these years though, and they were still together today. In her initial meeting with Shawn, Micha had hidden or glossed over some of these points about moving a lot, out of embarrassment. But now that they had gotten to know and trust each other a little bit, she was letting a lot more of it out. Shawn, of course, couldn't have cared less how her friend had been raised. She was happy with the way Micha was *now*, and felt blessed every day to call her a friend. Shawn would be the first to admit that she didn't have a great relationship with her own mother.

Micha, born Katy Micha Tobias, had a similar experience to Shawn in her teens, wherein she came to know that there were too many Katys in her school and most of them were sluts. She wanted to distance herself from the name, and so started going by her middle name. This fell in line with one of her moves, so on her first day of school at wherever it had been that month, she entered her new world as Micha for the first time officially. And she was accepted with a little more respect, at least so she thought. There certainly weren't any other girls named Micha in the school. There was a boy named Micah in one of her classes, and of course, the teacher had a lot of fun with that – watching both boy and girl raise their heads when she called the name.

Micha had naturally jet black hair, and it was also naturally straight as rods, and about this, Shawn found herself vocally jealous on several occasions. They both liked to wear hats, though Micha's were typically of the soft and fluffy variety. This made her look like a model, and reminded Shawn of the first time she had seen Micha in the courtyard that day, standing in the snow with her dog. Her hair had been sticking straight out the bottom of her big soft hat, and she had looked like something out of a magazine. When they went places together and both of them had their hat on, they drew way more attention than Shawn ever remembered – or noticed, at least – getting by herself. She didn't know how much of that was because of Micha alone, or the combination. Micha's black hair paired with her ice blue eyes was definitely a head-turner though, and Shawn found she herself wasn't immune to the looking.

When Micha was twenty-five, her parents moved to Oklahoma, as some of her mother's extended family was up there, and they thought they could finally catch a break. Micha had not been living at home in several years, but still stayed relatively close to her parents, visiting them on most weekends. But this move was what broke that connection. They went to Oklahoma and Micha went west. She moved away from the North Texas area and moved to Arlington. She took a job as a graphic designer for a high school class ring magazine, and there she worked until the fiasco about which she had told Shawn. When she told people what she did, there was inevitably the request for her to repeat it. This got old after only a few weeks, so Micha finally just said she worked for a magazine. She explained it to Shawn though. The magazine for which she designed the graphics and arranged the content was for one company. That company made high school class rings. And Shawn knew there was some money in that racket. She had spent over three hundred dollars of her parents' money on her own ring, and she didn't even know where it was. She had probably lost it over a decade ago.

Micha met Mick at a dance club when she was out on the floor shaking and sweating with the beats of some unknown instrument and under lights that would make some people have convulsions. She had her hands up in the air and her eyes closed, and had danced with just about everyone who had approached her that night, though she was not looking to be intimate with any of them. She was there with her girlfriends. But Mick had made an impression when he walked up and touched a cold beer bottle to her bare belly. She had stopped instantly and brought her hands down as an instinct, her eyes popping open to see what the hell was going on. Mick had handed her the bottle and said, "You look like you could use this." She had smiled and taken the bottle and downed maybe half of it right there. He nodded and told her he would be at that table right over there if she needed another one. Lo and behold, she had come to find herself in need of one not too long afterward. And the man honored his word. They had been together ever since.

They hung out at least three times a week, and sometimes spent nights together, when one of them would crash on the other's couch. It made for some frustrated boyfriends, but – as Shawn had reminded Micha more than once – as long as they were still only boyfriends, these girls could still make the rules on where they laid their heads. Cory didn't mind it as much as Mick, but he did like a quick text letting him know not to wait up, that Shawn was safe, and that he would be sleeping alone that night.

Christmas was closing in, and Shawn was split between two emotions: she was excited to be going home to see her parents – which she had not done in over a year – but she was also sad that she would have to leave her new friend for four days. Especially over Christmas. She had already bought the plane ticket though, and it was easier to travel back in time and unbuy the ticket than it was to get a refund. Only slightly less so to change the reservation. She often wondered how that was legal: that airlines could just say, *nope, no refunds – not fucking ever, no matter what,* just seemed shady.

It had been a fast friendship from both sides. As it turned out, Micha had been in need of a close friend as well, so it wasn't even awkward how Shawn had introduced herself. Cory had given her plenty of grief about walking out onto the balcony and saying, 'Hey, do you want to be my friend?' but she had no regrets about it. And Cory was happy too, having a bro in the complex he could pal around with as well. Not to mention their shared love for first-person-shooters. When they weren't hanging out, they could usually be found playing each other over the internet, and that was just as good.

So when Shawn woke on the morning of Christmas Eve, she was filled with sadness for having to leave Cory and Micha, nervousness and unease about seeing her mother and excitement for getting to see her dad. These battling emotions made her stomach upset and she worried she would carry it onto her flight. She would be leaving for the airport before the sun came up, and knew that if she didn't wake Cory, she probably wouldn't get to say goodbye to him. She had also been worried about the situation they had dealt with at work between the missing satellite and the AI running rampant in their systems, but over the weeks between the episode and the day she was to leave, things settled pretty nicely. In fact, she didn't even hear from Darla. She only heard from Blake when he sent her a Merry Christmas text.

Even Jamie the AI had been quiet. It was almost as if he had disappeared. She knew this probably wasn't the case, but at the same time, understood that she might not ever hear from him again just the same. Which was as good as disappeared to her. What did an

AI want? What was its goal? To be set free? That made no sense to Shawn, who thought there would be some tangible goal or desire for an intelligence. Some end game. Not just to get out of the computer it was built on. What did that achieve? And in that regard, how many AI personalities were out there now, free from their base computers? She was obviously not the only one who had ever downloaded the *Hello, World* suite. And there were other suites as well, all free. Hundreds, if not thousands of users just like her had surely downloaded them, installed them and gotten them going. And were any of them as careful as Sameer had been in trying to contain it in a leak-proof room? She doubted it. The internet must surely be crawling with bots by now.

But with all these work-related stressors being dormant for a few weeks, Shawn felt more capable of taking the time off that she had asked for and been granted. She felt a little like a mother hen leaving her chicks in the nest while she flew the coop. It was a nice feeling, having that responsibility and those people looking up to her. But it would also be nice to sit on the dock and have a beer or three with her dad.

While she was back home, she would be getting together with some old high-school friends as well. She had a girls' night out planned with Candace and Tracy on the night after Christmas. They planned to hit the Charleston Tavern in the square and drink as much as their bodies would hold and dance until their feet fell off. Just like old times.

The night before she flew out, she and Cory had dinner and drinks with Mick and Micha at Fancy's, and ended up staying out way later than she had intended. It was easy for everyone else, knowing they could all just sleep in on their day off. No one thought much about getting Shawn home early so she wouldn't be dying at five the next morning. But she didn't fight it either, and was used to rising early anyway. So this time she'd just be a little less hydrated. She had packed before they even got dressed to go out, so her suitcase was sitting by the front door, ready to be hauled down the stairs. Or the World's Slowest Elevator, which she had casually begun calling 'The Time Machine'. Because every time she actually had to take the elevator instead of the stairs, she felt like she was sitting still in time while the world moved on around her.

At half-past three, Shawn finally hit the sack. Knowing she had less than two hours to get enough sleep to get her to the plane, she felt full of dread and an overwhelming sense of anxiety – worry that she would sleep through and miss the flight. She slept deeply and without dreams, but felt no transition at all, so that when she woke up she wondered if she had actually slept at all. She certainly didn't feel any sense of refreshment. Thanking God that she did wake – four minutes before her alarm was set to go off, too – she sat up and stretched, yawned and wiggled her toes in the carpet. And then she stood up and scooted into the bathroom for a P & G.

Shawn had never been good at sleeping on planes. Just making it to the plane was always a reward of sorts, knowing all stress of getting ready, fighting traffic, making it through security, checking the bags, finding the gate, squeezing her bag in the overhead bin... actually dropping into her seat after all that felt like a major victory. Sleep would be a fine reward, but it almost never came. Even those neck pillows didn't help. She could just never get into a position that actually felt comfortable and conducive to sleep. Further, she always worried that her head would slip back and her mouth would fall open. Sneaking to the bathroom on long flights, she always passed one or two of those people. Shamelessly mouth-breathing for all the world to see. She didn't even want Cory seeing her sleep – much less people in public. Even though she was typically able to keep her mouth closed at night, she knew that public sleep – plane sleep – was never like that.

So she sat there staring out the window, watching the sun come up over the far end of the taxiways and runways – way out there in the southwest where she had just woken up less than three hours ago. Hell, where she had just lain down only a little longer than that ago. What a joke that she had woken up so early, gotten dressed and ready and driven out here only to get on a plane and fly right back over her apartment on her way to Arkansas. Couldn't they just have picked her up from her parking lot? She imagined being able to see Cory, still asleep and warm in their bed over there in Arlington. Lucky bastard could sleep as late as he wanted.

The plane pushed back and before it even got bright outside, they were in the air. Shawn tried unsuccessfully to sleep, and then opted instead for trying to get drunk. That was a rigged game too though, as the flight was barely long enough to accommodate such feats on its own – but made even more difficult by the fact that the stews only came by enough times to get her a faint buzz. She ordered a bloody mary and got started, nonetheless.

By the time she landed in Arkansas, she had a hangover and a headache, and couldn't get the taste of the tomato juice out of her mouth. She hoped it would be her mother who picked her up, because she felt a foul mood coming on, and didn't want to take it out on her sweet father. It was he, though, who picked her up, and her mood was instantly boosted. She ran to him in the baggage claim and threw her arms round his neck, kissing his cheek and squeezing with all her might as they stood rocking back and forth in the middle of a sea of people.

"How's my sweet monarch?" he said as they embraced.

"Hi, daddy! God, I missed you so much!" she said, laughing and crying at the same time.

They stood hugging for half a minute before she was finally willing to let go, fearing she might lose him forever. After she collected her bag and they trekked through the parking garage to his SUV, she finally started feeling the effects of her sleep deprivation. And by the time they pulled into the driveway at home, her eyes were so heavy she could hardly keep them open. Everything seemed distant and dull, quiet in a loud way, like listening to a crowd through cotton. She dropped her bags in the living room and gave her mom a hug and then had to lie on the couch and let her eyes get what they wanted. She told her parents she would only be out for a minute. It was 11:05 when she closed her eyes. When they opened again it was almost seven.

Shawn's first impression was that her mother was in a joking mood. Maybe something had changed in the last year since Shawn had seen her, and had lightened up. Maybe she had made a life-decision not to take everything so seriously and turn every little disagreement into a drama bomb. *Hey, this is great!* Shawn was actually digging it. Her mom's jokes weren't *funny*, as such, but they were a start. Not quite on the level of dad-jokes, but an improvement, all things considered.

Having slept right through lunch, Shawn now sat at the kitchen table while her dad made a pasta right in front of her. The range was in the island where they all gathered, so Shawn got to sit there and watch him work, just like the days when she was little. He didn't cook by recipes, and almost never used measuring implements. He grabbed pinches of this and fistfuls of that and tossed it into the mix – whatever the mix was that day. It fascinated Shawn, who, even when following directions to a T and using the exact measurements, could never get it to taste as good as his dishes. Her stomach was growling, but she was smiling. She had a bottle of beer in front of her on the table, and so did her dad. Every time one of them would take a drink, so would the other.

"So she's a lot better now, huh? I mean, just in general," Shawn said, tilting her head in the general direction of the other room where her mom sat watching some crime drama.

Gavin made a face, not quite looking at Shawn, but clearly thinking about what she had asked. "In what way are you asking?"

She took a swig from her bottle. So did he. "Like, just, I don't know. Her personality? She doesn't seem so uptight. She's making jokes. Seems to be a lot more relaxed about life in general," Shawn said.

Her father was shaking his head subtly. "Honey, she's always been like that."

Shawn gulped, staring at dad, wondering when his smile would break. It didn't. "Dad. You're serious?"

He finally looked up at her. "Marce, she's deteriorating almost daily. Since her fall, she's been going downhill at an almost perfect decline."

Shawn squinted, tilting her head. She had asked about her mom's condition a few times when they had spoken over the last year, but no one had said anything to indicate that it had gotten worse. So she had pretty much forgotten about it. Maybe when she wasn't here every day, the people who *were* had a tendency to forget what she didn't know. Routines are only routine to the participants. "Dad, I didn't know she was getting worse. How come no one ever says anything when I call?"

He spread his hands on the counter in front of the skillet and leaned on them. "I guess I just don't think about it much. It's here, it is, and it's just part of our daily lives."

"How bad is it?" she asked. She didn't remember all the details, but apparently her mother had come down a staircase in the dark and missed the last step. She had fallen with the full weight of her body, and her head had connected with the concrete. The doctors said it had caused swelling of her brain, but she had not heard anything about permanence.

"Well, it's not getting any better, Marcy. She's working with only a portion of her brain anymore. Her memory is shot to hell," said her father. He picked up his beer bottle and looked at the label a long time before finally putting it to his mouth.

Shawn shook her head and drank with him. "So she basically just doesn't remember that she hates me?"

Her dad shook his head. "Hon, she has never hated you. She just wasn't good at expressing her love."

"Well, she never had any problems expressing it to Moni," Shawn said, pulling again from the bottle. She drained the last of it.

"I know you two have had your differences, babe. But if you're feeling like she's acting differently now – *better* – then maybe you can just forgive her and enjoy the time you have left with her?" said her father.

"Of course, dad," she said and smiled.

During a dinner in which her mother didn't engage much but was otherwise mostly responsive, Shawn felt a little better about her prognosis. It seemed that since Shawn no longer lived in town, she would be the mushroom of the family – kept in the dark about happenings and events. Monica, her older sister, had been around a lot more in the few months after the fall, taking care of mom and making sure she had everything she needed. And somehow this felt to Shawn like a political move. Like something was being held over her head. Though what that would be was beyond her. Shawn now had an established home and career in another state, sharing that home with another human, no less! So there was no way she was coming home to stay. What else could she do?

Monica was coming tomorrow to spend the day with the family. Dad had bought a brisket, which was now marinating in the garage fridge, and he would be smoking it from early in the morning until dinner time. Shawn was excited about this, because it meant a lot of time sitting out on the dock drinking beer and smelling the wonderful aroma of brisket while she caught up with dad and Moni. Shawn's childhood was full of memories centered around that very thing: dad shaking her awake at five in the morning to go get the smoker going. She never missed a single opportunity. And he never woke Monica to join him, so it always made Shawn feel special. Heck, that might even be the reason why she was a morning person to this day.

Shawn spent the last part of the evening sitting with her mom, who seemed very grateful and even loving, which was completely out of character but Shawn couldn't get into the crime drama herself. She found herself constantly getting back on her phone. With her feet up beside her and a pillow on her lap, her mother couldn't see the distracting device, and thought Shawn was watching the show with her. When mom would call out her observations and look over at Shawn for approval or agreement, Shawn would raise her eyebrows and nod, and that seemed to be good enough. It was heartbreaking to see the loss of personality, the dying of a brain, but the trade-off was that they could actually tolerate each other. The double-edged sword felt ever-present between them.

By nine-thirty, mom was ready for bed, as per her usual routine, and made no apologies for heading that direction. Shawn, of course, was nowhere near ready to turn in for the night, being wired by an uncharacteristically long nap, which she admitted, she had probably needed for months. It was too late to start a fire, so her dad and she just sat on the back patio drinking beer until midnight, when he finally had to call it himself. And thus was she to repeat the same pattern she had played out the day before, by going to bed only a short while before waking time, ruining her sleep pattern once again. There was just no way she would miss getting up early with her father though.

Five o'clock came fast. Shawn didn't know exactly when it had happened that she fell asleep, but knew it wasn't until long after the sounds of the day were mere echoes in memories, mingling with the dreams of a light slumber. Unsure how much of it was real or imagined, Shawn had no reference point on which to base her internal clock and was exhausted by the time she needed to get up. She had not slept in the guest bed in over a year, and somehow it felt more like home than ever. Somehow, the beds at parents' houses, she reckoned, were better than any she could buy on her own. The sheets, the mattress, the comforter and the pillows – it all made for a magical experience. And even though she didn't sleep much in the bed, she had felt more comfortable than she could remember in her recent history.

She swung her feet off the bed and sat staring at the ambient night's light coming through the thin curtain on the window for a long time before finally rising to brush her teeth and put a bra on. She had slept in a t-shirt and pajama pants, and wouldn't need much more out by the smoker, as she knew the heat from the firebox would keep her plenty warm on its own. She stopped by the kitchen on her way out the back door and found a pot of coffee, short only about a cup.

As she stepped out the back door, Shawn had to stop for a moment, immediately looking up at the sky. The clouds had cleared while she was in bed, and now the sky was resplendent with stellar beauty. It looked as though every star ever to have existed was on display now, and she could see the wide cloudy belt of the Milky Way arcing up from the horizon. "Oh my God," she said quietly, then put her steaming mug to her lips for a sip of black coffee. "I miss this so much." She stood with both hands on her mug for a minute more, just looking up at the terrific, wondrous beauty of the night sky that would so shortly be replaced by a remarkable pallet of pastels.

Shawn could hear the clanks and clunks of metal doors and wood and charcoal being moved and manipulated down on the dock. Dad was getting ready to start the fire. She wiggled her toes in her slippers and started down the wooden walkway to the floating dock. They had long ago sold the boat, but the boat dock would never lose its utility. Her father had rebuilt the bottom floor, where once there was a slip for the boat, covering it with solid wood slats. Now it served as a covered, floating patio where he kept several chairs along with his smoker and grill and even a hammock hanging between two of the support posts on the far side. The top level also had a set of chairs on it, and that was where they would spend their summer days, lying out in the sun or jumping off into the water while music blasted from the speakers mounted under the top deck.

"Morning, butterfly," said Gavin as Shawn stepped onto the dock.

"Good morning, daddy. Merry Christmas!"

"Merry Christmas, love bug," he said.

"You cheated. You started early."

"Oh, only by about five minutes. Haven't even built the fire yet!" he said. He stuffed another handful of charcoal into the fire box, then dusted his hands together and wiped them on his apron. From the front pocket, he pulled a box of wooden matches. "I figured you might need a little extra sleep since you slept so long yesterday."

"I can sleep when I'm dead, Pop! I don't wanna miss the smoke!"

"That's my girl," he said, stepping in and putting his arm around her. He kissed the top of her head and squeezed her shoulders without putting his hand on her shirt. Shawn smiled as she felt her body fill with love –

the kind of security and comfort only this man could bring her.

As the coals turned orange, the sun painted the eastern sky with pinks and oranges of its own. And before the stars went completely into hiding, they saw the trail of Starlink satellites zip by in its perfect orbital path. Shawn oohed at the sight and felt the excitement in her belly turn to cold dread when her mind almost instantly went back to work. And her dad had read the dread in her countenance.

"What's wrong, sugar?" he said, leaning forward and touching her knee just after her face fell.

Shawn sighed and looked at him. "Dad, there's some weird stuff going on at work. I can't really talk about it to anyone though, so I've been having to just kind of keep it bottled up."

"Okay, so you want to talk about it?" he asked, with a near-smirk on his face. He knew 'anyone' didn't include him.

Shawn nodded and wiped the beginning of a tear from her eye. "One of my clients has a satellite. And I think it went back in time."

He nodded thoughtfully, his facial expression unchanging. Shawn knew that he would believe her words, whatever she said, at least as much as she believed it to be true. If he thought she had it wrong, he would correct her, but he would never think she was lying or embellishing. They had a better relationship than that. He reached into the cooler between their chairs and pulled out the first beer of the day, pried the top off and handed her the bottle.

She took it wordlessly and said, "It went offline a few weeks ago. No one could connect to it. I couldn't connect to the onboard server. We had to go to the Air

Force base in Abilene to get the SatCom guys to wrangle it in for us."

"Ah, Dyess. I know it well," her dad said, nodding. A tinge of nostalgia shone in his eyes.

Shawn smiled at this. "Well, we did the wrangling. But we had to use their repeaters to reach it, because it had drifted a third of the way across the planet."

"That's not good," he said.

Shawn yawned and took a sip of the cold beer. She would alternate sips of the cold ale and the hot coffee until the latter was gone. Then it would be a long day of nothing but the former. "You're not drinking with me, daddy?"

He put a hand on his belly and shook it, pursing his lips. "I need about another hour for this coffee to process first."

Shawn smiled and ran her hair back with her free hand. She hadn't bothered to brush it before coming down here. She would have to do something about it before Monica got here, lest she be told she should make herself look more presentable. She knew dad didn't care though. "Anyway, when it finally got back, I had to jump through hoops to get onto it. Change the date, all that. Its date was set to the year 2636. Can you believe that?"

"Should I be able to?" he asked. He finally leaned back in his chair and crossed his arms.

Shawn shrugged. "I just thought it was crazy. But yeah. Turns out the date was apparently right. See, when it disappeared, and I mean *literally* disappeared, it reappeared a third of the way round the globe *in the same second*," she said, leaning forward with her bottle in her lap. Her father stared at her, waiting patiently for her to continue. "I know, it sounds impossible. But that's what happened, according to the Air Force's telemetry readings. It blinked across the planet," she said, snapping her fingers.

He nodded slowly again, taking in what she was saying. Reserving his judgment until he had all the details.

"Well, when I finally got onto it, I checked everything out and turned it back over to the client. The contact, a guy named Blake, called me and told me there were six hundred years'-worth of pictures on it."

Gavin raised his eyebrows, lowering his chin at her.

Shawn nodded. "Yeah. Verified. And you know what they're of?"

He tilted his head but said nothing.

"The pyramids, dad. The effing pyramids, being built!"

Her father cleared his throat and adjusted his feet, as if he were waiting for the punchline now.

"Dad, I'm serious!" she said, leaning farther forward and putting her hand on his knee. "Blake sent me two of the pictures. One shows a row of blocks in the desert with some guys standing around and working on them. Whatever. The other shows a complete pyramid. And its shiny and white, with smooth sides!"

He was staring at her with skeptical eyes, shaking his head and almost smiling. "Marcy, this sounds fantastic!" he said, holding a hand out, palm up.

"I know, Pop, but it's not. I swear. No fantasy here. It's real," she said. After a second, she leaned back and took a swig of the beer. "I think."

Gavin breathed in through his nose, then pursed his lips and nodded. "Okay. So I guess you've looked into the theory that you might be getting hoaxed," he offered.

She shrugged. "Not yet. But I can show you the picture. You can help me decide." They looked at each other in the improving light. Then she said, "It's on my laptop."

Her father leaned back and adjusted his position in the seat, looking suddenly very uncomfortable. He said, "Honey, I don't…" but trailed off as a new sound entered their area. Shawn whipped her head around and saw Monica coming down the bridge with a tall white paper cup in her hand. She had on white pants and a white coat, and wore white gloves on her hands. She was dressed for a gala and Shawn had to stifle a groan. She was able to turn the beginnings of an eye-roll into a welcoming smile as she stood up.

"Hey, sis!" she said and stepped forward to hug Monica as she came down the last step onto the dock.

"Hey, beautiful! Merry Christmas, you two!" said Monica, and then as she got closer, added, "Oh my, your hair…" But she said no more, and leaned in for a half-hug. She turned her face away and gave Shawn a ghost kiss on the cheek. And while they were cheek-to-cheek, Shawn was able to get that eye-roll out of the way without being seen. Now free of the obligation, she watched Monica scoot over to dad like her knees were tied together.

"Hey, papa! How's the brisket looking?" she asked, giving him the same silly non-hug. "It smells wonderful."

And to this, Shawn couldn't hold back. She laughed out loud and shook her head, reaching down to retrieve her beer bottle from the deck beside her chair. Her father answered, "We haven't put the meat on yet, sweetie. But we're almost ready."

Over all the years Shawn had helped her dad with smoking briskets and ribs, she was a mostly hands-off helper, though she did occasionally toss some wood chunks or more charcoal into the firebox. But this little win over her sister was a welcome treat – because at least she knew what was happening. She was actually surprised that Monica was here this early. She usually didn't show up until around lunch time. Shawn guessed her sister was trying to beat her to the cookout to gain favor with the man of the house. Or to spitefully steal this time that Shawn historically had always relished. It just wasn't in the cards for poor Monica.

It was another hour, and when the brisket actually *was* on the smoker that Shawn's father was finally able to finish his previous thought, because Monica took a phone call. She walked to the edge of the dock, leaning against the rail facing the water. Gavin leaned closer to Shawn and said, "I'm going to want to see that picture later. Assuming it's not a hoax or some elaborate scheme, that would be empirical."

Shawn was giddy inside over her father's obvious discretion without even being told to keep it secret. He had understood that the conversation was meant to be held only between the two of them. Part of it was also the fact that she could share such a secret with him. It was like having the coolest teammate in the world. She couldn't wait to show him the picture and get his take on it. Well, both pictures. The first, in fact, might be more telling than the latter. A row of stone blocks set out on the desert floor could be more empirical than the completed project. She – or someone – could analyze the photograph for landmarks if there were any, and prove that it was indeed the start of the Great Pyramid in Giza.

Now that Shawn thought about it, she wasn't sure if it was *The* Great Pyramid. Weren't there several? And at this point she became embarrassed with how little she was actually educated about the region, considering how fascinated she had been with it as a child.

When another hour had passed and Moni's longevity was beginning to look legitimate, Shawn went to get her laptop. Ostensibly this was to *'do a little work'* but she was ready with the minimized pictures to whip it over to dad on a whim's notice for a covert show-and-tell. She had to use the WiFi sharing from her phone to get online this far away from the house, but was able to pull up her Nagios monitoring board. Might as well check on her servers while she had the laptop out. She scrolled through a few time-sensitive-looking emails while she was at it, and before she knew it, she had actually logged an actual hour's-worth of work in a few minutes.

The conversation was relaxed, but there was also an underlying feeling of force, like trying to tuck a neatly folded handkerchief into a pocket without it bunching up. Her sister was obviously only down here so as not to be left out of what Shawn and her father had organically and naturally developed over two-and-a-half decades. Shawn wasn't put off by her sister's presence – in fact, she was quite enjoying what little reality she was getting from the talk – but it was now wearing on her patience, as there was just this one thing she really wanted to show her dad, and she wanted to do so without suspicion. Aside from that, and once he had seen it, she could return to normal – albeit stilted – conversation with Monica while her dad let the images simmer in his mind. They could talk privately later. And that was when the idea hit her.

Shawn waited for a lull in the current topic and then said, "Ooh. Nice. That server just came back up!" looking up at her dad and smiling.

He returned the smile and said, "What's that mean?"

"It means I don't have to do a ton of work on my time off," she responded. And then, without hesitating, she scooted her chair around to be beside him and turned the laptop so he could see the screen. She Alt-Tabbed to the first image of the ancient Egyptian desert – now hoping like hell it wasn't just glaringly and obviously a fake – and kept her thumb and ring finger on the Alt and the Tab keys.

Dad raised his chin, opening his mouth a little, and then frowned at the screen. He was studying it, and doing a damn good job with his poker face, Shawn thought. She was staring at him, which, if anything were to give away her little charade, that would do.

"See, these green dots represent the 'up' status of the servers. And that one just popped back to green. Someone must have been working on it."

Her father nodded, leaning closer still to the screen. "I'll be damned."

Then she pressed the right arrow with her right hand, and the picture changed to the finished product. The staggering clarity and beauty of the photograph was instantly rewarding in two ways. Firstly, she got to see the instant of wonder flash in her father's eyes. And secondly, was reminded that there was no fakery here. There were some good PhotoShoppers out there, but this was just too perfect. If she was being fooled, then someone was a complete master of the art. And to what great lengths they had gone for the caper!

Shawn's eyes darted up at Monica, who was still staring at her phone, one leg resting across the other, foot bouncing, and completely ignoring the other two. Clearly she had no interest in 'Shawn's work'. *Good. He can stare a little while.* "And this column here is the up-time," she said after a moment, pointing at the tiny shapes of human figures strewn about the place. She ran her finger up along the pathway that approached the base of the pyramid, its gigantic and preposterously thick concrete walls an exhibition of a massive undertaking on their own. Her father was nodding and shaking his head in rapid succession.

"Unbelievable," he whispered.

After a few more seconds, he finally looked at Shawn, shaking his head again and leaning back in the chair, signaling that he had seen enough of it. She moved her ring finger to the F4 key and pressed that in conjunction with the Alt key. The photo dropped away, revealing the *actual* Nagios board like she had been pretending to show him. She pointed at the two things she had mentioned, and then slapped the notebook closed. She stood up and returned her chair to its original position, then dropped the laptop on the boards beneath it.

Shawn then stood up and went to the smoker, cracking the large door and letting the smoke dissipate before opening it a few more inches. They kept a spray bottle filled with a bourbon-water mix hanging from the tool hook. She sprayed the top side of the brisket until it had a fine sheen to it, then allowed the lid to close and returned to her seat. She opened her mouth and sprayed a few shots on her tongue. Monica saw this and smiled, amused. So Shawn turned to her, standing up and leaning forward. "Open up!" Monica obliged and closed her eyes. Shawn shot a few sprays on her tongue as well.

"Mmm! Thank you, sis," she said.

It was after dinner when Shawn was finally able to spend a little alone-time with her dad. Monica, like a barnacle, had hung on down on the dock the entire day, long out-waiting any hope Shawn had of getting to enjoy the ritual of the smoke alone with her dad. Shawn had found herself trying to analyze her sister's sudden desire to occupy the dock chair, as she had never done so before, and came to believe it might be just as much to intrude on their special time as it was to spend any real time with them. The conversation was not particularly titillating, nor had she had any news to share or questions to ask of Shawn's meanderings. She was just, simply, *there*. There to be there. After several hours of the unwelcome occupation though, Shawn had enough beers in her to stop caring so much. And by dinner time, she was so hungry and ready for the meat they had smoked all day that she had little else on her mind.

When they stood up from the dinner table, Moni unceremoniously dropped the soiled cloth napkin on her plate and scooted back in her chair, saying, "God, I'm stuffed," exhaling through pursed lips. After a quick glance around the table, she said, "Mom, you wanna go get our nails done?" Why they couldn't have done that during the earlier hours of the day, affording Shawn the precious time she wanted so badly to spend with her father alone, she could only speculate on. And it kept coming back with a malicious tint to it. When the two women finally walked out the door, Gavin looked lazily over at Shawn, mirroring her own impatience so perfectly that she had to stifle a giggle. Then he pointed the remote at the television and clicked it off. Shawn, sitting on the couch with her feet up behind her, smiled and said, "There's a lot more to the story, Pop. I have to start from the beginning."

Over the next hour and a half, Shawn spilled all her most precious corporate secrets. From the way Sameer had given her the AI project to work on, to the way the satellite had been lost and recovered. She left nothing out.

When she finished talking, Shawn leaned back and covered her lap with a couch cushion, awaiting her father's analysis. He sat very still on his recliner, his feet up on the raised footrest and his hands clasped over his belly. He was staring at the ceiling and making a face that looked like someone working out difficult math in his head. After what felt like an eternity, Gavin finally returned his gaze from the ceiling to the expectantly waiting face of his daughter and said, "Marcy, have you considered time travel in all this?"

Shawn, a little buzzed from the all-day drinking, sat staring at her father for a long moment, the hints of a smile etched on her pale face. She didn't know whether or not she should allow the smile its full glory. This could be a dad-joke, after all. But would he really joke around about such a serious topic? This was her work. Her career, and therefore her life. It was hard to imagine he would make light of it after she had spilled all her confidence to him. But he was known for being a jokester. In fact, that was one of her favorite things about him. Hence, her inability to determine the appropriateness of a smile. "Dad?" was all she ended up saying.

He nodded at her. Then he leaned forward, kicking the recliner's footrest into is hideaway position and putting his elbows on his knees. "Marcy, you said this satellite appears to have gone back in time, whereupon it spent some six-hundred-odd years, then popped back into the present the same second it had left. Do I have that right?"

Shawn nodded herself, and straightened on the couch, taking a deep breath. Her feet were still curled up behind her and now she subconsciously played with her toes. "Yeah. I know, it sounds…"

But he cut her off with a hand, shaking his head and closing his eyes. "Look, that's what appears to have happened. Whether it really did or not, we don't know. You can't *prove* it didn't. Right?" he said, holding that same hand palm-up.

She nodded again.

"Right. So, assuming it is what it appears to be, which is really all we can do at this point, we have to then assume that time-travel is possible in other cases – in other…" He rolled his hand in the air, looking for the right word, then said, "contexts." And then Gavin put his hands together and cleared his throat. "Let's say all that is true. What's to say this computer – *Jamie* – couldn't have jumped *forward* in time to the point it inevitably knew you would screw up and take your phone into the Box."

Shawn felt herself flush at that, but saw no scorn on her father's face. She continued to twist her toes behind her.

"Or, if you like, the point at which you finally brought your phone in there and gave that computer that information, let's say he went *back* in time from there and filled in the appropriate parts of the conversation that called for them. Does that make sense?"

Shawn was squinting and shaking her head, suddenly wishing for sobriety. "I uh," she started. And then her dad sent her head even further into the spiral it had already begun.

"I mean, you think it can send a satellite back in time but it can't manipulate the time around it?"

Shawn's heart almost stopped in her chest. "Wait. What?"

Her father tilted his head and stared calmly at her. "Or maybe it wasn't *manipulating* time, as such. But maybe once it achieves singularity, for lack of a better word, time becomes non-linear for it."

Shawn kicked her feet out and stood up, putting her hands in her hair and stepping forward with every intention of pacing. But her legs had fallen asleep from not having changed positions on the couch for too long. She tilted forward and Gavin reached up to steady her by the elbow.

"You all right?" he asked.

"Yeah. Legs are asleep. What are you talking about, dad? Wait," she said, waving her hands in the air now. She turned around and stared at the couch, putting her hands back in her hair, trying to get back to where she had been mentally a moment before he had just exploded her brain. Trying, for all intents and purposes, to *time travel*.

As he started to speak, she cut him off. "Wait, dad. I need you to slow down. A little buzzed here. Let's back up and explain all that one piece at a time. I think you may be onto something."

He stood up and stretched his back, leaning back on hands placed on his upper hips. "Okay, doll. Why don't you go collar us a couple more long-necks while I run to the john."

"Arrrgh!" Shawn growled. "Okay. Okay. I just… Don't forget what you were saying!"

' When dad got back, Shawn was pacing in the small square between the sectional sofa and the recliner.

Gavin and the chair both creaked as he returned to his sitting spot taking the beer off the side table as he did so. "Thank you, monarch," he said.

Shawn stopped and turned toward him, putting her hands on her hips. "Okay, do you remember everything you were saying?" she said quickly, pointing at him.

Gavin smiled and nodded. "Relax, sweet pea. I haven't forgotten."

"Okay. Slower this time!" she said, shaking that finger at him. Then she crossed her arms and waited impatiently for him to begin.

He took a long pull from the beer bottle, then set it down and looked thoughtfully at it before picking back up the thread he had dropped before. "Marcy, if this AI has reached its singularity – that is, its full power – then it might be able to jump in and out of time at any point on the dial."

Her eyes were closed and she was shaking her head, but he continued before she could stop him.

"Look. Think of time like a linear object. A radio tuner on an old radio. You know, where you turn the knob and watch the needle move across the bands?" he said, moving his finger from left to right, held straight up. This got a nod from her, so he continued. "If that's time, then you and I start from the left and move steadily right for all of our lives. We have no control of that. But when I was a young man, we had car radios that had favorite-station buttons. You could push this and it would snap the dial right to that station."

"We have those today, dad," Shawn said, looking down at him.

Gavin smiled. "Yeah, but today's radios are digital. These you had to turn the dial. Anyway, if this AI has achieved that final form, it might be able to pop into whatever time it wants, instantly. Like it has favorite-station buttons."

Shawn's back ran over with goosebumps. She lifted her hands to her head again. "You believe time travel is possible?" she said, almost in a whisper.

"Well, like I said, we have to start somewhere. And if we take what we know, or at least think we know," he said, turning his hands over then returning them to the rests, "then we already know it's possible. It sent that satellite back six hundred years, right?"

Shawn's chest went cold now and she wrapped her arms round herself. "You said that before! What makes you think the AI sent the satellite back in time?" she asked. Her eyes were wide and glassy. "Four thousand years, by the way. It stayed there for six hundred."

Her father shrugged and nodded. "Well, isn't that what you were intimating?" he asked, holding a hand up again as if asking for a handout.

"No! I never thought of that!" Shawn said, turning in place and shaking her head. Then she backed up and let herself drop back onto the front edge of the sofa, staring at the rug on the floor. "God, it almost seems obvious now."

"Well, I thought that's what you had been saying all along. I mean, surely the two instances are connected, right? You power up an AI and this satellite blips across the planet?"

Shawn squinted and stared at the rug, shaking her head, trying to remember the exact timeline. The beer was getting in the way. She had not taken a sip from the fresh bottle yet, which stood sweating on the stone coaster by the couch's right arm. "I don't think that's quite right. I think I got the call that the server was down, which means the satellite was already out of place, and then came in and started building the AI."

"Ah," said Gavin, leaning back and putting his footrest back in the upward position. He rubbed the stubble in his chin, staring at the fireplace as he thought. "Okay, so ditch the connection then."

"The connection to what, again?" Shawn said, frowning up at her dad. Her memory was going to shit now. Exhaustion and inebriation did not a memory cocktail make.

"Getting the contacts from your phone. It might not be anything. I was just thinking that if it could control time somehow, it would be an interesting thought to consider it having grabbed the names from your phone contacts and inserted them into conversation at earlier dates," her father said. He took another pull from his beer.

Shawn decided not to waste her own, and reached over to copy the action. "Yeah, it's very interesting. I mean, if it's possible, it would certainly make sense." After a long moment of sitting and staring at her bottle, she looked up and said, "I can't believe I'm sitting here on Christmas Day talking time-travel with my dad."

He smiled at her. "Can you imagine anything better?"

On the flight home, Shawn sat staring out the window at the miniature landscape drifting by, but her mind was still on the few days she had gotten to spend with her family. Monica had been pleasant company, as had her mother. Both had surprised her. This would surely count as a successful Christmas trip. Though they no longer celebrated the holiday by any traditional standards, they did always try to get together. The Stedwin family had long ago stopped exchanging gifts. Now it was more about dinner and reunion.

Her father had introduced some new angles to her regarding the two anathemas she now faced under the BlueBird umbrella. Two more mysteries she could drive herself crazy thinking about. It was like he had handed her two new puzzle pieces, and though she was not sure they belonged to the puzzle upon which she was working, she knew she would twist them and flip them over and over, trying to find a way to get them to fit in. But the other side of that token was the *maybe they did* side. Maybe they did fit. Maybe what he had said made perfect sense.

If she were to take at face value all the evidence with which she had been presented and line it all up, she had to at least consider that time-travel was innate possibility. However unlikely it sounded and seemed – however many times she had been told throughout her adult life that it was against the laws of the universe – it now had to be considered with a serious stroke. For all intents and purposes, she had – or, rather, PanaView had – empirical evidence now that a server had gone back in time over four millennia where it remained for six centuries before coming back to the present. There were ways to manipulate photographs, of course, but there as far as Shawn knew, there was no way to do what had been done. To *create* photographs of the sort she had seen. To create six centuries'-worth of them, no less, and plant them on a server orbiting the Earth. Who had that capability? And to what end would someone do so, were it to be found to be a hoax? That seemed like an extremely difficult task all in the name of –

what, a prank? She just couldn't buy that. And it left a sour taste on her tongue when she tried.

She simply had to allow herself to believe in what she was seeing. At least until all other possibilities were ruled out. Rule out the impossible and work with what's left. Wasn't that the gist of the Sherlock Holmes quote? Well, time-travel could no longer be categorically labeled as impossible. And if this was the case, however unlikely, then what her dad had said had to be considered as well. The thing with her contacts on her phone. Jamie the AI had known the names of people he had never met. Hell, he had known the names of people she had never even mentioned.

The only other realistic scenario she could find herself considering was that maybe she had accidentally brought her phone into the Box on other occasions. Occasions that had not been discovered. She only *knew* about the one time because her phone had slipped out of her pocket in the chair, and Jeremy had found it. There might have been other times she had gone in and out without thinking about it, and never dropped the phone.

What this presented was a scenario in which the computer somehow managed to connect to her phone via Bluetooth, without being invited or approved. But wasn't that her dad's theory too? The only difference was that her dad's theory included the element of time-travel. Now which one was more likely? Shawn rolled her eyes and looked down at the seat pocket in front of her. She took a deep breath and reached for the in-flight magazine. Something that could perhaps take her mind off the mind-boggling conundrum plaguing her. She flipped through the worn and wrinkled pages, barely noticing the content.

And when the plane went through some turbulence just outside the Arkansas-Texas border, she barely noticed that either. Because something in her mind had come awake. Something Jeremy had said a week or two ago, and it pinged like a bell in a mine shaft. She sat up straight, now staring at the seat back, her eyes wide and heart slamming in her chest. This caused the man next to her to look up from his tablet and ask her if she was okay. She probably looked like she was about to get sick.

She waved him off, shaking her head. "No, I'm fine, thank you," she said, and returned to the thread of thought that was turning into more of a rope. She connected distinct and disparate dots in her head, completing a portion of a larger picture that was beginning to show itself for what it truly was.

"Oh my God!" she mouthed. The dots seemed to light up in her head as they found purchase in reality. Each tiny speck that popped to life seemed to confirm several others – to validate theories and concepts she had only considered before. And before she could fully grasp what was happening, the entire picture was lighting up in her head.

Shawn leaned forward and dug into her canvas travel bag, searching for her handbag, in which she kept a small notebook and a pen. When she pulled it free and leaned back, the man on her right visibly relaxed and went back to his tablet. He had surely thought her dive for the purse had been aimed at a sick bag. Shawn paid him no attention, but opened the small field book and thumbed to the first blank page. She began scribbling notes as fast as her hand would carry them to the page, underlining certain words, circling others. And within ten minutes, she had filled three pages with ideas, thoughts and theories that she now believed to be the answer. She hoped her theories would start being proved. Turned to *truths*.

She shivered at this, because Shawn knew the truth was sure to be scarier than the theories had ever been.

Chapter 15

Monday morning arrived with no fanfare and without much welcome from Shawn. The weekend had been drab and boring, yet tense with its own interior energy she could not expend. Cory had been called away to an emergency job in Santa Fe on Friday evening just as Shawn had been landing at D/FW International, and Micha and Mick had gone to visit her parents for Christmas and weren't back yet. Shawn had spent the weekend on the Internet looking at all things mysterious and improbable – time-travel and black holes and ancient aliens alike. But she'd had no one to share her theories and thoughts with. The electricity felt like it was ready to burn her up from the inside.

Shawn had to remind herself several times on the way in as well as when she arrived that she wasn't working with fact yet. She was basing her new outline of events mostly on conjecture, though there was a pretty good bit of extraordinary coincidence involved if it wasn't what she had conceived it to be in her mind. She had a good mind to clench her fists and stomp into Sameer's office and just hammer him with questions, but the better part of her kicked in long before she slung her purse off her shoulder and dropped it in the chair by her office door. She *would*, however, be testing those questions out on Jeremy as soon as he got in.

The funny thing in all this, at least to her, was that Sameer was looking for answers on the satellite that she might very well know. But Shawn could not answer them until he gave up some of his hole cards. Of which she was pretty damn certain he actually had. She couldn't well play poker with him yet though, because it might put her job on the line. It just wasn't considered politic to start demanding shit from your boss.

When Jeremy poked his head in her office door at a little after eight, Shawn excitedly waved him in, standing up and scooting over to shut the door behind him. Jeremy, all smiles as always, was a little perplexed, but complied amiably enough. So as not to be too forward and quick to the point, eschewing all pleasantries, Shawn asked him how his Christmas was.

"Shawn, I'm a J"...

"Hanukkah! How was your Hanukkah? That's what I meant. Sorry."

"Well, it was nice. I got to see my niece," Jeremy said, taking a seat in the chair across from Shawn. He took a deep breath and said, "But I know that's not what you want to hear about. So I'll spare you the exciting retelling of events. What's on your mind?"

"You said," Shawn said, lifting a finger in the air as if to test for wind direction, "something about Sameer having *removed* an Ethernet jack from the Box when I said the AI didn't have internet access."

Jeremy nodded slowly, his eyes seeking the ceiling. "I'm not sure I remember that, but yes, that makes sense. If there's no jack *now*, then it must have been removed."

Shawn clapped her hands together and kept them palm-to-palm. "I knew it!" she almost shouted, and with a little more glee than was probably necessary for such a bland revelation.

Jeremy was still smiling, but shaking his head ever so slightly, like he hadn't caught the joke.

Shawn leaned forward, wagging that finger now. "I remembered you saying that. See, I started thinking. Sameer said he had that room constructed, but I don't think he did, Jer."

"Of course he did, Shawn. Who else would have had it built? It took like three months to have it done," Jeremy said, matter-of-fact.

"Well, duh. I mean, he didn't *just* have it done. For some reason I was thinking he had been referring to just having finished it. But I started thinking, and I never remembered seeing any construction vehicles or hearing any hammering or anything. Like, it must have been there for a while."

"Yeah. It was," he said. "It was there probably a year or so before you even started working here."

"Yes! Exactly my thought!" Shawn almost shouted.

"Shawn, this is no mystery. I could have told you that long ago," Jeremy said. "I'm sorry, I don't see the…"

"It's okay, Jeremy. It might have just been a misunderstanding. I just took it to mean he had just had this room constructed specifically for *this purpose*," she said, touching the desk with the tip of her finger to accentuate the last two words. "Just to house the new AI project."

"Again, that's exactly what it *was* built for. Just not when you thought," Jeremy responded.

"Well, yeah. But he gave me the impression that…" Shawn started and then trailed off. "Jeremy. Fuck sake. Just tell me the parts I don't know, please. I'm already beginning to feel foolish."

"Sameer had the room built a few years ago, and had an AI computer in there, pretty much doing the same thing you've been doing for the last month or so. He played with that thing for a long time, Shawn," he said. He was shaking his head as if to ward off any questions about specificity. As if he was foggy on the details.

Shawn's heart had skipped a few beats though, and now she was staring at him through the tops of her eyes. "So it's true. My suspicions were true: he had an AI."

"Yes, Shawn," Jeremy said, nodding slowly and thoughtfully. "I didn't know you didn't know that."

"Jeremy," she said, and mainly because he had been using her name a lot more than normal, it seemed, "he hasn't been all that forthcoming with me. And I don't know why. I think there are some things I need to know!" she said, stabbing her finger down on the desk again. Her breath hitched and she caught it, but not before the slightest whimper had escaped.

Jeremy leaned forward, grabbing the ends of the armrests. "Shawn? What the heck is going on here? What's wrong?" And the look of concern in his eyes was almost enough to break her dam. She almost spilled over.

"I have had the roughest couple of weeks, and I think there's some next-level shit going on again. Just like with…" she said and stumbled, waving her hand in the air. "Just like with the…"

Jeremy held his hand out in the air, leaning even farther forward. "Yeah, I get it. The last project. I understand. Shawn! What's got you so emotional about this?" he said. And then he finally stood up and rounded the desk. Before he got far enough to take her in his arms, he put his hands in his pockets and leaned against her side of the desk, as if he wasn't sure about their personal boundaries. As if he didn't know if a hug would be too forward.

Shawn leaned back and covered her face with her hands, taking a series of deep breaths. Jeremy waited patiently. After a long moment of her heavy but slow breathing, he finally reached out and held his hand in front of her, palm up. When she broke long enough to remove her hands from her face, she saw it, and then took it. He squeezed and she shook it for a moment before letting it go.

"Shawn, what's got you so bent here?" he asked quietly.

"I think he's hiding something again. With this whole…" she started, then waved the hand again. She couldn't find the word. The thought. There had been so many over the last couple of weeks. Where to start? Hell, where to *end*? "This whole satellite thing."

Jeremy straightened up, then shook his head. "Wait. What? I thought we were talking about the AI computer," he said.

Shawn looked up at him and shook her head very slightly. "Jeremy, I think they're tied together."

Jeremy stood leaning against the picnic table with his arms crossed, a cigarette dangling from his fingertips. He had insisted they come out here for a while. For one, it would get Shawn out of the stuffy office for a moment so she could collect her thoughts and feelings and get some fresh air. Secondly, it would allow Jeremy his vice. But Shawn could already feel the cool air doing its work on calming her nerves. The way he saw it, he had said, was that if she was this on-edge the day after a holiday break, then she was liable to have a stroke if she didn't get control of it. They were only here today to make sure nothing was blowing up. They would be off again tomorrow and the next day, in light of the new year, which some people thought was worthy of celebrating.

"Shawn, he holds his cards close to his chest for a lot of reasons, but it's not always because there's something sinister going on." He took a drag of his cigarette and then frowned, waving his hand. "Wait. I said that wrong. It's never been something sinister. I just mean, it doesn't always have to be some super-secret reason he's being quiet."

Shawn was shaking her head, trying to read him. She wasn't getting much though. "Jeremy, keeping your dead daughter in a deep freezer is pretty fuckin' sinister."

Jeremy sighed and closed his eyes, wagging his cigarette to reset the conversation. "Shawn, can we please not say things like that out loud?"

Shawn stared at him, mouth agape and wide-eyed, shaking her head. "Unbelievable! You're…"

"I'm trying not to bring attention to things that have long since been laid to rest," he said calmly. Jeremy frowned for a moment as if realizing the pun he had just made was in poor taste. He took another pull from the cigarette and held his hand out at her. "Come on, Shawn. Let's not share that stuff publicly. Do you want everyone around here to hear that?"

Shawn was staring holes through him now, breathing heavily through her nose, arms crossed in heavy defiance of his defense of their boss. Jeremy shook his head and waved his hands at her. "Shawn. We already forgave and forgot that mess. Remember? You can't go shouting stuff like that in a parking garage!" he said, stress evident in his voice. "Besides, it wasn't *sinister*. It was because he wanted more time with his daughter."

She took one more deep breath and looked up at what would have been the sky if not for the countless tons of concrete above them that blocked it out. "You're right. He's not a bad man." She stood there staring at Jeremy for a long time, concentrating on bringing her breathing back to a moderate tempo before she spoke again. Jeremy saw the transition from anger to calm and nodded at her, taking another drag from his cigarette. This finished it. He rolled the hot part out and dropped it in the can, then lit another one. Clearly, her stress had been contagious.

"He's not a bad man," Shawn repeated, nodding. She looked across the parking garage, wondering if anyone *had* heard her outburst. She wasn't sure exactly whence that rage had come. She wasn't mad at the man, per se. She was just tired of all the damn… *mysteria*. Satellites and AI and time-travel and pyramids and aliens… It was all getting a little too much. A little too… hokey. *Right?* Normal people didn't have to question whether or not a satellite really took 600 years of photos. Four millennia in the past. Or whether its transit was the work of aliens or an artificial intelligence.

But nor did normal people have to make the moral decision about whether or not putting your dead daughter in a deep freezer was for the greater good or not. A chill ripped down her spine as she considered this. The common denominator here was Sameer Singh. Whether his actions had a noble cause or not; whether his dabbling in such things as these was for good or evil… None of that mattered. She was in this boat, this *same boat she had been in*, because of him.

"He's not a bad man," she repeated. "But I'm beginning to think he needs to learn to keep his hands off the fucking dials, Jeremy."

Jeremy's calm demeanor and thousand-yard stare wasn't enhancing her calm. He was looking at her, but he was also looking through her. And he was nodding very slowly. And perhaps the most sobering thing about it all was that he was not smiling. Not at all. Like… for *once*… maybe for the first time in her short history with the man, he was really affirming what she had said.

He pursed his lips and took another drag, and then he cleared his throat. "Let's just say, for the moment, at least…" he started and then put the smoke to his mouth again. "Let's just say I agree with you about that." Jeremy nodded. "He has his hands on a lot of 'dials' as you say," he said, making the quote with his free hand. "But I think overall that this is a good thing, Shawn. He has brought a lot of things to this world that might not have found a way here without him."

Shawn adopted a sour look like she had sucked a lemon, and said, "Oh, for fuck's sake, Jeremy. He's no Hans Zimmer." And then she laughed. It was a stilted laugh. Forced. "You know, I could have gone the rest of my life without bringing anyone back from the dead. And I think I would have been better off when I finally took my last breath. What good did that give us?"

Jeremy sighed, shaking his head. He looked like a disappointed father. "Shawn, I'm gonna ignore that. If you don't see the… the… the *greatness* in that," he said, almost shouting, "then I… man." He trailed off and shook his head again, then took the last drag of his cigarette.

Shawn, seeing that she wasn't winning her argument, and was potentially losing the support she had from her one friend in the company, put her hands on the sides of her face and closed her eyes. "Jeremy. Look. I didn't come down here to argue with you about whether the man is good or not." She shook her head, hands still in place, for a long moment. It wasn't for effect. She was trying to restore her calm. When she finally felt it creeping back in, she continued. "Jeremy, he's hiding something important about all this, and it would really make a lot of people's lives a lot easier if he would just work *with us*. Just be on our team with it." She tilted her head and stared Jeremy long in the eyes. Then she added, "Why be secretive with this? With *this!*" she said, stabbing her fingertip down like she had on her desk earlier.

"What do you think he's hiding, Shawn?"

"He had an AI! How far did he get with it?" she shouted.

"Shawn," said Sameer. She whipped around, almost getting dizzy from it. He was standing about five feet behind her with his hands in his pockets. Shawn raised her hands, looking back over her shoulder at Jeremy. *What the fuck?*

"Sameer. What the hell, dude?"

He took a step forward, but his hands remained in his pockets. "Shawn, if you would like to accompany me to my office, I will answer your questions for you," said Sameer.

Shawn had taken the long way up to the offices, dreading the confrontation she was about to have with Sameer. She took the stairs instead of the elevator and tried to gather her thoughts, but they seemed to have all vanished. Like butterflies in a stiff wind. She now stood behind Sameer's guest chair because she had the idea that she would be returning to her pacing frequently. Pacing kept her feet busy instead of her mouth, she knew. In this regard, she might be able to quash some of those things she felt she was apt to say otherwise. Sameer, ever the patient subject, was sitting behind the desk with his elbows on it, hands clasped on the blotter. He was looking at her with an expectant calm.

"What are you wanting to know, Shawn?" he asked.

Shawn sighed, hands on her hips, and looked Sameer in the eyes. "How long did you have your AI?"

"Almost two years," he said. His body language painted him as calm and authoritative. Of course, why wouldn't he be? That's all the man ever was.

Shawn's heart skipped a beat, but she masked it quickly, not wanting him to see the shock on her face. Here is where she would have turned to Jeremy to give him a knowing look, but alas, he had begged out of joining her in Sameer's office. *Figures.* "Sameer, when did it end? When did you *finish* messing with it? Or whatever you call it…"

"Just a day or two before I gave it to you, Shawn," he said, and finally allowed his gaze to break from hers. He picked up a pen on his blotter and started tapping it lightly against the ink-covered paper.

Shawn frowned. A thought struck her and she opened her mouth to speak, then clapped it shut. She twisted her face and opened her mouth again. "Is it the same computer, Sameer?"

"Yes," he said, and then frowned himself. "Why do you ask that?"

"It knew your name even though I never said your name. Same with Jeremy," Shawn said, and rounded the desk to lean against it on his side, where she could face him. Her heart was slamming in her chest, but she felt like she was doing well at concealing the rampage running through her veins. Had there been a mirror in front of her, she would have seen the throbbing artery in her neck. She felt she was onto something here but couldn't pinpoint it. She had not taken notes like she should have – journaling all the weird little idiosyncrasies she had encountered when talking with Jamie. She knew it would be a pretty good checklist to have though, and standing here talking to Sameer, her mind was suddenly coming up blank about all those questions she had. The several newly-inked pages in her field book were full of theories about what had happened to the satellite, but nothing on the AI. She needed to spend some time on that now. Maybe her questions had not originally been for Sameer, but right now, he seemed to be the perfect person at whom to direct them. Knowing now that he had been using the same machine for as long as two years before she got hold of it? Good God. Didn't that mean… didn't it mean… well, what did it mean? She couldn't come up with it.

"I cannot answer for why that would be so, Shawn. Are you sure you did not mention our names in some way?" Sameer said.

She threw her hands up and looked at the ceiling, then shook her head and put her hands against it. "God, I had so many questions, Sameer! I can't think of them now!" She took a deep breath and crossed her arms. "I'm going to go spend some time thinking about all the questions I have had about that damn computer and write them all down. Then I'll come back, okay?" she said.

He nodded, and then looked up at her. "Shawn, I am not a bad person."

She didn't respond. Just looked him in the eyes. She knew he wasn't a *bad* person. But he definitely had questionable ethics. Shawn nodded, then turned toward the door. Just as she was passing through the doorway, she stopped and looked over her shoulder. "Oh! Sameer. Did the AI computer have a connection to the internet when you were messing with it?"

Sameer nodded again, very slowly. It almost looked… *careful*. "Yes, Shawn. It had connectivity."

"Why did you take out the Ethernet port before you turned it over to me?" she asked. "Did it escape from the Box?"

He looked down at the pen he was twirling on his blotter before answering. "Some things just run their course, Shawn. It wasn't for any one particular reason. But when I got done with the AI, I thought you might enjoy experimenting with it yourself."

She stared at him levelly, arms crossed. Waiting. She would not be the first to speak: Sameer knew what she was waiting to hear. And after a long pause, he finally breathed in deeply and resumed.

"Shawn, I only had it removed because I was figuring that I would not be in there to… *monitor*. I just wanted to make sure it was as safe as could be."

"Safe?" Shawn asked, pushing her head forward on her neck. "What, you don't trust me?"

He closed his eyes and shook his head quickly. "No. That's not what I mean. I just…"

"Why, Sameer? Did it do something *unsafe* while you were messing with it? Did something happen?"

"I do not think so. I am just trying to be careful."

Now Shawn shook her head. She came very close to rolling her eyes. Then she turned and left the doorway, heading back to her own office. If ever there were a chicken-shit answer to be given, Sameer had just handed it to her.

That's fine. I'll just get my ducks in a row and come back prepared. I'll either force him to answer or at least get closer. Either way, I'll be able to tell if he's hiding something. And in this line of thought, she also figured that the more questions she had ready, the closer she would get to the real answer on her own – whether or not he dodged them. Shawn put her thumb up and pumped her fist as she entered her own office.

"Wait," she said, stopping suddenly beside her desk. Her left hand rested on the shiny mahogany desk top. She was staring at a picture on the wall behind her desk – one of Cory and her in their leathers at some group function or other – and frowning. A thought had just occurred to her and she was trying now to trap it before it got away. "Why the hell would there be an Ethernet port in a Faraday ca-"

The phone rang, startling her back to reality. She glanced down at it and picked it up, not recognizing the number. "Stedwin," she muttered. The thought had gotten away. Nay, it had been *scared away* by the ringing of the goddamn phone. She grasped a handful of hair in frustration as she rounded the desk and dropped into her seat.

"Hey, lady. Am I disturbing you?"

She sighed audibly as she answered, "Off the record?"

Blake Prescott laughed on the other end of the line. "Sure. What's that even mean?"

"Well, you're technically a client of mine. Sometimes it's not politic to answer honestly."

"Oh dear. Well, I'm sorry to disturb. Is there a better time to call back?" he asked.

"What, and make it twice as bad? Shoot."

"Okay, I'll shoot. Shawn, I think you'll find this interesting. Are you sitting down?"

She shook her head and looked up at the wall, hoping there would be something there she could be mad at. "Huh? Blake, just get to the point."

"The pyramids weren't built how we thought they were."

When Shawn got home and dropped her keys on the bar counter, she noticed the light on in the office and suddenly got really excited. "Booger? Is that you?"

"Hey, baby," Cory called from the other room.

She ran into the room, swinging his chair around so she could straddle him and get a proper hug. Cory scratched her back as they embraced. He was playing *Call of Warfare* or whatever it was. *Must be nice to only have to work two days a month.* When she sat up straight so she could actually see him, he reached behind her and undid her bra, which caused her mouth to clap shut. She had been about to tell him all the exciting and infuriating things that had happened over the last few days. He had suddenly and perfectly distracted all of her with a few quick moves of the hands.

The office chair squeaked in rebellion to the way they were treating it, but it held up – even when she was reaching behind the chair to grasp the desk, her legs behind the arms rests, feet on the floor and giving her leverage. Her chin was on top of his head, her eyes closed as he found interesting things to do with his mouth in her chest area. *Fascinating,* she would sometimes think, *that someone can find so much to do with so little.* But about that she would never complain.

After they had finished their love session and Shawn stood steaming in the bathroom with a towel wrapped round her head and staring in the mirror, Cory sat on the edge of the tub and tried to restore the conversation. But it was long gone. And it wasn't what she had to say that won the prize of Most Interesting Topic that night. It's what Cory had to say.

"Have you been following this fuckin' crazy story on the internet about the guy up in Michigan?" he asked.

Shawn frowned. "Uh-uh," she grunted. She was leaning on the counter, her face extremely close to the mirror, trying to pick out the tiny little hair on her chin. Cory had many times told her it was too small for anyone else to even notice. But that didn't matter. It was a foreigner and it didn't belong. Plus there was something almost *fun* about trying to tweeze it out. Definitely therapeutic. "What guy?" she managed.

"He's been hitting ATMs all over the state and withdrawing cash from people's accounts, with no card. But the banks say he always gets their PINs right."

"Hmm," Shawn grunted.

"His face is all over their cameras too. It's like he's not even trying to hide from them," Cory added.

"Ah," Shawn said. "Got it!" She pulled the tweezers away from her chin and looked at the intruder. So small and insignificant. But so annoying and out of place, too.

"Are you even listening, babe?" Cory asked.

She tossed the tweezers in the tray by the sink and turned around, waddling her hips as she approached him. "Ah, poor baby, not getting the attention he needs," she pouted, bottom lip sticking out a full inch.

Cory stared at her, even as she took hold of his shoulders for balance, and put her legs around him so she could straddle him on the edge of the tub. The heat from the shower was still powerfully attached to her body, and Cory reacted immediately. "It's not attention I seek," he said. But she was kissing him in a series of small pecks all over his mouth, like a rooster trying to get a worm through a screen door. "It's just the talk of the town. I thought you might be interested," he managed to get out betwixt all the kisses.

"Yes, honey, I heard every word," she said quietly. "Some guy is robbing ATMs." She had her arms around his neck too, and was now grinding on him, their naked bodies trading heat and sweat and shower dew. But suddenly she stopped. "Wait. Is that where you were? Working on this case?" she asked, pulling her head back so she could look at him in the face.

Cory tilted his head to the side and nodded very subtly. "Yes, babe, but that's not important right now."

Shawn now tilted her own head, frowning at him. "Huh?"

Cory looked down at the only thing technically between them and said, "You seem to have changed the subject."

They performed their act again, right there on the edge of the tub.

This time when they finished, they lay on the bed under the ceiling fan. Shawn's knee was up on Cory's legs and her head was on his chest as she lay trying to get as close to him as possible. "I thought you were in Santa Fe," she said, almost casually. She was looking at her nails, her hand held an inch above his chest.

"I was," said Cory. "That's where the bank is headquartered."

"Ah," said Shawn. "So what did you find out about this guy? Anything?"

"Nope. But it's pretty big on Reddit right now. How this guy can walk up to all these ATMs without a debit card, and just withdraw massive amounts of cash every day."

"Yeah, that's crazy. How do you do it with no card?" she asked. She dropped her hand on his chest and tilted her head up to look at him, close proximity.

"Well, as you can see, there are ways. Or, well, at least there is one way. And this guy apparently knows it. But it's not easy. In fact, there are very few people on the planet who know how to do it."

"I bet you know how to do it," Shawn said, smiling. She raised her thigh a little higher on his legs. It covered new ground.

"Honey, you're the hottest thing I've ever seen, but I don't think I'm capable of a third rodeo in one night," Cory said. She smiled at him, kissing his chin, and then he continued. "Yes, I know how. But it's a pain in the ass. It's a back door that's programmed into these ATMs for emergency situations. And not just for John Q Public to use."

"Who's that?" Shawn asked. She was looking at her nails again.

"No one. I just mean, there's no legitimate reason anyone should ever use it, except for… Well, just – let's just say it's not something many people know about," Cory said, taking a deep breath. Shawn's head rose and fell with his chest. She giggled.

"If you told me you'd have to kill me?" she asked. She loved it that her boyfriend's job involved some fair amount of mystery. His knowing how to pick locks was already pretty sexy. But the corporate side of that… the *much more to it than just picking locks* part of it was what was so fascinating. He knew back doors into most security systems. And now, to find out he knew the inner workings of ATM programming… Well, that was super hot. Shawn didn't care that she didn't know it herself – though she would be interested in looking at the code. The code part of it did interest her. But she didn't care to know all his secrets. She just loved that *he* knew them. Whether he ever spilled them or not was irrelevant. When she went to magic shows as a kid, she didn't *want* to know how the tricks were done. That meant not being able to enjoy them the next time she went to a show.

"Pretty much," Cory said. His hand on her back tightened, pulling her a little closer up against him. She loved the feel of their naked skin being together. She hadn't gotten that warmth in almost a week, so this was a treat. A treasure. "Any row, it's pretty interesting, because this guy doesn't have like, a cheat-sheet or anything. When he walks up, he doesn't look at an index card with these long-ass numbers on it or anything. And trust me, to know how to get cash without a card, there are some long numbers involved.

Not just the account number. You have to know routing number, account, all this other shit.”

Shawn nodded, best she could with her face against his chest, just to show she was listening.

“He just walks up and goes to work. Has the cash in about thirty seconds, and is off,” Cory said.

“Hmm,” she said. “Well, I’ll have to go read up on him.” After a moment of silence, she added, “They don’t know his name?”

“Nuh-uh,” Cory grunted. “But he’s taken over fifty grand in the last two weeks or so, from different accounts.”

“Jesus. Must be nice,” Shawn said.

Cory laughed out loud, pulling her in tighter with his arm. “You’re a little freak!”

“Shit yeah, I’d take some free money!” she said, giggling and looking up at him. “I wouldn’t be stupid though and leave my face uncovered for the cameras!” She shook her head and rolled her eyes. “It won’t be any time before someone identifies him. Idiot.”

The next day Shawn was off again, as Sameer liked to give his employees off the last and first days of the year, respectively. She had dreams of sleeping in, snuggled warm beneath the thick comforter under the roaring wind of the ceiling fan. She would wake at 8:45 and blink against the brightness of the Big Light coming through the blinds, stretching her arms above her head and yawning with a smile, knowing she could just stay here in the warm sheets for as long as she wanted. She would get up and dash to the bathroom, pee and be back before the chills even started up her back.

Alas, it was not meant to be like that. Shawn was not wired for long and late sleeps. When the sun rose, so did she. And sometimes – usually, in fact – not in that order. Her eyes popped open this morning and she lay still momentarily, wondering if it was a fluke. She could usually tell the hour by the brightness. But that only worked from about six o'clock during the winter months. It was still dark, so it could be three, or five. Or two. Many times had she come awake organically, feeling wonderfully rested with seven or eight good hours of thick sleep behind her, only to find that she had only been in bed for an hour. Hence, the question of the fluke. But sleepiness this morning didn't immediately rush in to reclaim her, and her bladder wasn't trying to pass a note either. She felt rested and good. So it must be time to get up. She reached over to the nightstand and picked up her phone, pressing the wake button. 5:04. Perfect. As good a time as any to start her day.

Shawn stretched again, then rolled over and wrapped her arm over the still-sleeping Cory. She kissed his back and rubbed her hand up and down his bare arm a few times, and then sat up and put her feet to the carpet. Now she could experience the wonderful transfer of excitement from knowing she could sleep all morning (which never actually happened), to the more realistic scenario, which was that she could do anything she wanted all day. It was a holiday, and by God, she was excited about that.

Seven o'clock on a Saturday morning. My favorite time of the year. Once she had slept through her adolescence and immaturity, she learned that the most productive time of the day could be before everyone else woke up. On a Saturday, doubly so. A holiday during the middle of the week, when the rest of the week was off-time as well? *Oh my God. I can conquer kingdoms!*

She stood up and rolled the wand on the blinds, letting in the world outside. Instinctively, she peered over toward Micha's apartment, in search of intelligent life. There were no lights on over there yet, so she stood with her hands on her hips just looking at the landscape of the apartment complex. The wide courtyard that ran between the two buildings for their entire length was sparse and lifeless this morning. The two light poles cast their boring white circles on the wet ground beneath, which looked black at this hour of the morning. It was the last day of the year. What would she do with it?

Well, the first thing she would do was make a pot of coffee. That was an absolute. As she turned and left the room, a thought struck her. On the phone with Blake yesterday, he had said something about how the pyramids were not built the way she had thought they were. Or the way *they* had thought they were. Something to that effect. They? As in *the experts*? Or they as in *everyone in the world*? It seemed to Shawn to be a legitimate question. Or, if not a question, a dissection of the question, which could be just as important as the question itself.

A thought experiment on the subject, for example, was the question: *Who killed John F Kennedy?* The fact that the question was asked at all was as important as the question itself, as far as Shawn was concerned. The question seemed to create a need for itself. Circular logic. *If the question is being asked, then someone thought it hadn't been answered properly before it was asked.*

In the case at hand, the question she was mulling over had awoken that same response in her mind: *who is they?* Did that mean there was a group of people who thought the pyramids *weren't* built the traditional way? Well, apparently so. But what was the traditionally accepted way? A conspiracy theorist would surely have bitten. *Oooh, Blake, how* were *they built?!* But, knowing as little as she did about them, Shawn was not equipped to ask such a question. She simply had no idea there was some accepted normative means by which pyramids were built – forget that there were no illustrations or ancient texts explaining how they were built. Because how many fucking ways were there to stack stones in a desert? Well, apparently it was up for debate, and she had not been invited to said debate.

Now, standing here next to the kitchen bar, Shawn realized Blake had been trying to tantalize her with the statement. And in her lack of knowledge about the topic, she had said something in a half-distracted attempt to get off the phone more quickly.

She had never called him back.

Hand on the kitchen bar, Shawn began shaking her head. How many things in her life had she forgotten just so, but had never gotten back to? How many things had she 'temporarily' forgotten, only to never remember them later, like she just had about the pyramids thing? God, what a depressing thought.

She had once had almost this very conversation with her late friend, Lo, when Lo had talked about 'remembering' all the records in the new arrivals bin at the record store. "You see, it pretty much breaks down like this: there are two types of memories. The kind you make that you can recall at a moment's notice, and the kind that are there to be recalled *for you*," Lo had said.

"I think I know what you mean, but elaborate," Shawn had replied.

"Well, obviously, I couldn't tell you all the records in that bin. It's in the several hundreds. But I *can* tell you that whenever I go and they have not brought in any new inventory in a while. Or they have, but the back halves of the bins are still the same months-old selections. I start seeing the same records that were there last time. And though I couldn't have told you what they were before I walked in there, I can definitely recall them as I'm flipping through them. Enough to say, 'yup, that was here last time.'" She smiled and held a hand up as if to say, *Tada!* "It keeps me from having to flip through all the ones that were already there."

Shawn thought about that now and reckoned Lo had been right, if not in the scientific manner. But pulling up a text from days ago – a thread she had completely forgotten about – she could become instantly aware that she *did* remember it. In some different recess of her brain perhaps, but it was there, ready to be recalled. It just needed touching. Like Lo's records. This happened to her more frequently these days. *I was going to respond to that right when I got it. What had happened to draw my attention away?*

She made a mental note to call Blake in a couple of hours and ask him to expound upon the *most fascinating* declaration with which he had slapped her the previous afternoon.

Chapter 16

"So I think I'm closing in on the answer," Shawn said. She held her hands out in front of her, as if miming being trapped behind a sheet of glass. She and Micha sat Indian-style on the rug in front of Micha's "fauxplace". Their coffee mugs were steaming and it was still dark outside. Shawn had made the trek to Micha's as soon as she got the text from her asking if she was up. She had grabbed the carafe from the Mr. Coffee and trudged across the courtyard holding it like a grail, careful not to spill any on her wrist. Since they had the same coffee maker, it slid right into the warmer waiting for it on Micha's counter.

"Okay," Micha said, slapping the carpet with one hand. Pirate lay on his side at her right, his head on her thigh. He almost looked up from the commotion of the slap, but gave up halfway. Instead, he licked his chops and closed his eyes.

Shawn took a sip of coffee. "So my dad gave me some ideas. He thinks it's time-travel."

"Okay, great," Micha chimed. After a moment of staring at each other, she said, "What's time-travel?"

"Being able to travel back and forth in time," Shawn said with a furrow in her brow.

"No, dumbo, you said 'he thinks it's time-travel'. What's *it*? He thinks *what's* time-travel?"

Shawn giggled at this and shook her head. "Sorry. Too much on my mind to keep it all straight," she said. She told Micha the theory her father had posed about the phone, the favorite contacts and the AI going back in time to insert them into the conversation. Just that little loop in logic was enough to make her head spin, and she had to work through it start-to-finish each time the thought arose, just to make sure she still grasped the concept. Micha was clearly doing the same right now, staring hard at a place somewhere above Shawn's left shoulder, as if to look for the answer on the apartment wall.

"Okay, so it gets the contact names and goes back in time to use them and make you think it knows who they are. Got it. So basically," Micha said, "it appears to be able to seamlessly integrate anachronisms into regular conversation, which makes for a hell of an embellishment."

Shawn shrugged and took a sip of coffee. "Something like that." She took a deep breath and moved her tongue around her mouth. "But I don't think that's it."

"Oh dear God, girl, make up your mind! You just said you think you're closing in on the answer!" Micha said, leaning forward to slap Shawn's knee.

"No. I mean, I don't think that's *all* of it," Shawn said, and leaned back on her hands. She uncrossed her legs and put one on each side of the dog-human combination in front of her. With her right foot, she stroked the dog's stomach lightly. "Here's the thing. I'm not really sure I believe the whole time-travel angle. I mean, that's pretty tall, right?"

Micha, making a face while she took a sip of coffee, then shrugged. "Well, a satellite disappeared and came back with…" she said and made a rolling motion with her fingers. *You know the rest…* it said.

"True," Shawn agreed. "It is the least of all the evils here. I just don't know how else it could have known their names."

Micha was nodding. Taking another sip of coffee.

"Well, didn't you say Sameer had been using the computer before?"

"Yeah, but he wiped the hard drive," Shawn said, staring at Micha.

Micha didn't have to speak. She just raised her eyebrows.

Shawn sighed and rolled her eyes. Then she shook her head. "I don't think that's how it works.

"Well, it is a little easier to swallow than time-travel. I mean, if it were capable of time-traveling, I would think you would have seen more crazy shit than just some names being mentioned. Like him telling you what you would do the next day or something. You know?" Micha said.

Shawn nodded, looking down at the nails on her left hand. "Yeah. Guess so." After a long moment of staring at her nails, an idea popped into her head. She could ask Jeremy what he thought about the possibility of the computer retaining information from the last build somehow. It was a stretch, but it did seem likelier than time-travel. Hell, *anything* seemed more likely than time-travel. In fact, she thought, how crazy was it that she was actually finding herself believing the damned satellite had done just that? Suddenly, she slapped her hand down on the rug. This time, Pirate jerked his head up to condemn her with a look of disapproval.

Even Micha widened her eyes a bit. "What?"

"There has got to be some trickery going on here, Mike," Shawn said, putting a hand in her hair. "I can't believe I've *actually been believing* this satellite could have gone back in time. Christ. I'm a fool." She looked around as if to take role of any who would agree with the sentiment. Or perhaps let her off the hook. Micha was there to do just that.

"Didn't you see the photos, babe?" she said, grabbing Shawn's ankle, which was still stretched out beside her own right thigh. She squeezed in a reassuring, motherly way.

"Photos can be shopped," Shawn said, breathing in deeply. "God, why does this weird shit have to happen to me?"

"Bitch, please. I would kill to have a job as interesting as yours," Micha said.

Shawn's face fell. Micha, who had been scratching the dog behind his ears and rocking side to side very gently suddenly stopped and stared. "You know I don't mean th-"

"You should come work with me!" Shawn said in a silent shout, reaching out to grab Micha's feet, crossed in front of her. "You're still looking for a job, right?"

Micha's face got serious. She bit her lip. "Yeah, but I don't know computers, Shawn."

Shawn dismissed that notion with a hand. "My company does more than just computers." She stared at her friend for a moment, seeing the focus fall out of Micha's eyes as she stared into the distance. It was a look of wonder and contemplation.

"What would I do there?"

"Well, graphics design, of course!" Shawn responded with a wide smile.

Micha's phone vibrated and she picked it up off the table, a response ready on her tongue, but unspoken. As she slipped her thumb up the glass screen, it brightened, reflecting blue light on her face. Shawn leaned her head to the side to crack her neck. Micha frowned. And then she said, "Oh, wow. They caught that ATM thief." Then she slept her phone and held it up, wagging it as she said, "News alerts."

"Yes!" Shawn said, slapping Micha's knee softly. "Cory was telling me about that guy last night. Up in Michigan, right?"

Micha nodded, then opened her phone again, scanning the news article for another moment. "Yeah. Well, that's where he started. Apparently caught in Indiana." She flipped her wrist, turning the phone screen so Shawn could see the image. "Look at that crazy fuck," Micha said, without much emotion.

Shawn leaned forward and squinted at the picture. "Hey, that guy looks familiar. Where have I seen him?"

"Well, he's been all over the news. The pictures from the ATM cameras, at least," replied Micha.

"Honey, I don't watch the news." Shawn leaned back and lay flat on her back on the carpet, stretching her arms out above her head. After a long yawn, she said, "Well, I guess I should be getting back to check on my baby boy. He's probably reaching over and finding my absence in the bed by now."

"Yep. Skit, scat, scoot," agreed Micha. "Call me later though. Let's have some drinks tonight."

Shawn sat up quickly, looking her friend in the eyes with a total lack of enthusiasm. "Duh."

Cory was indeed awake when she came stomping in, trying to leave most of the moisture on the rug at the entry. He was sitting on the couch in pajama pants and a t-shirt, staring intently at the television that took up most of the wall between the fireplace and the sliding glass door to the balcony. "Hey, babe," he called over his shoulder without looking at her.

Shawn was about to say something back to him when her eyes fell on the TV screen and her blood suddenly felt cold in her veins.

"You hear this shit?" Cory said, pointing the remote at the screen and finally looking back at her. When he saw her, he flinched. "Babe? What's wrong? Look like you've seen a ghost."

Shawn came forward, putting her hands on the back of the couch and staring intently at the TV. "What's going on? Is that what I think it is?" she said, almost breathlessly.

Cory nodded, then dropped the remote control on the table at his knees. "Yeah. He's got surgical scars. The deputy said they look like autopsy incisions. 'Not compatible with life and living,'" he added.

Shawn covered her heart with her right hand and began to feel woozy. The image immediately fell into place. She now recognized the man in the mugshot, and remembered where exactly she had seen that face before. It was unforgettable – strained by that terrible psychotic grin. It was the man in the image taken from the satellite. The man who had been holding up his own poster-board version of a QR code.

She suddenly felt light-headed and out of breath. She had to sit down. She rounded the end of the couch and dropped on to the cushion beside Cory when her phone started ringing. Absently, she fished it out of her coat pocket and slid her thumb across the bottom of the screen. It was Jeremy.

"Jeremy, what's happening?" she answered. "Why am I freaking out all of a sudden?"

"You know why, Shawn. But right now, I need you to keep your cool. I'm going to need your help with this."

It was the last day of the year and Shawn was in the office again. She was beginning to loathe the drive into the office because of the sheer amount of times she had made it under duress recently. Maybe duress wasn't the exact right word, but it seemed to fit. She had been riddled with anxiety and stress on so many of these trips that they were beginning to rewrite that pleasant, almost vibrant excitement she had felt when she first took the job.

Shawn and Jeremy sat in the Comforts Room with the door closed, trying to stay quiet, because Sameer was in his own office with the door closed. Jeremy had shushed and rushed Shawn into the room as soon as she badged her way into the front office door, and now sat uncomfortably on one of the bean bags. She could tell he was forcing himself to sit when all he really wanted to do was pace the floor. She also reckoned this was for her own comfort. To put on a display of calm and cool to set her mind at ease. Well, it wasn't working. She had butterflies in her stomach – just like when she had been ready to go in to wake her first subject from the dead.

Jeremy had told her as soon as he closed the door behind them that Sameer was in conference with his attorneys – as in *more than one of them* – in his office, and had been since about an hour before. Shawn's heart was beating about one-and-a-half times a second and she felt hot and confused. Where she would usually be full of questions – or even opining statements – she was only silent and perplexed. She had not yet put the pieces together. She had gone over the facts – or at least the things she *knew* – on the way into the office. These things, at least for the time being, she considered to be the facts.

The first was that she definitely *did* recognize the man they had shown on the news to be the same guy she had seen in the satellite photo holding the sign. It was unmistakable. One didn't forget a face like that. He simply had to be the same man.

The second thing she called fact was that a man with surgical scars that looked like autopsy incisions should not be alive. Those cuts were through all the layers of the skin. *Not compatible with life or living* was about the gist of it. When sewn back together, it was not done with the same precision and care as were surgical sutures on the living. Those were meant to heal. And most of all, to seal in the life blood. Postmortem sew-ups were quick and dirty, and served only to put things back for burial. In other words, if someone were *walking around* with those scars, then that someone had almost certainly come back from the dead.

The third thing was that Shawn had instantly associated the first two together. If she recognized the guy from a photograph from a server her company managed, and that man had autopsy scars, then somehow, he must be connected to the company for which she worked. As in, he had probably spent time on a certain metal table in the lab on the other side of the elevators. This frightened her more than she could have ever anticipated.

Now that she was in the office, Shawn had even one more to add to the list: if Sameer was in his office in counsel with his attorneys after all this news had broken, well… she hesitated to finish the thought. But the underlying truth seemed obvious. And now Jeremy was trying to calm her nerves. How much of what Sameer did was Jeremy aware of from the get-go? Was he privy to all of Sameer's projects? He certainly never talked about them unless questioned – or in some cases, cornered. But he was never visibly surprised when something came to light. Maybe Sameer trusted him so implicitly that he ran everything by Jeremy before he even started. It was certainly starting to appear that way in Shawn's eyes.

"Jeremy," she said, cutting off whatever he was saying, mid-sentence, "you called me in here. You're going to have to open the fuck up with me, bro."

Jeremy's mouth clapped shut and he stared at her for a long moment, as if only just now realizing this reality.

"Seriously. You know things that you aren't sharing. And I want you to tell me now." She stared right back at him. After another long pause, she added, "Dude! Otherwise, why am I even here?"

Jeremy sighed and straightened, then looked at the ceiling. "Okay," he finally said. "You recognized the man. Did you see Sameer wheel him in here?"

"Huh?" Shawn said, pulling her head back.

"Did you see him on the table back there? Is that how you recognized him on the TV?" Jeremy said. He wasn't smiling, for what Shawn guessed was the second time in his life. She was shaking her head and staring at him, trying to put everything together in her head. Partly because she felt like he was still going to try to hide it from her. Maybe he was. She was just used to it. This was routine. So if she wanted the truth, she had to ask him directly. He would always answer honestly. Or at least *mostly* honestly. Like, maybe not the *whole truth*, but at least *nothing but the truth.* But there was the catch: she had to ask it first. Which meant knowing *what* to ask in the first place.

"I assume you saw the news," he said, interrupting her thoughts. "When I called, you asked why you were freaking out. I'm guessing that was w-"

"Yes, Jeremy. I was watching the news. But no, I didn't recognize the man from Sameer's table," she said.

Jeremy frowned, straightening again. He was still holding back, and was seriously about to piss her off.

Shawn sighed loudly and shook her head. "Jeremy, we both know that man was on Sameer's table. Right? Back in Room D?"

Jeremy nodded subtly.

"I recognized him from a photograph that the satellite took."

Jeremy shook his head quickly, as if to clear cobwebs from his eyes. "What? What the heck does that mean?"

"The satellite. Duh!" she said, holding her hands out toward him. She was close to complete exasperation now. "Jeremy! Fuck sake, brother! The satellite that disappeared has cameras on it. Remember?"

"Yes, I remember," he said calmly.

"One of the photos there was a guy standing in the field where that camera took its closeup every morning.

Or maybe it was afternoon," she said, rubbing her temples. She wagged her hand, waving away the thought. "Doesn't matter. That was the guy!" she said. She pointed in the general direction of wherever that guy was now. "He was out in that field, looking up at the satellite like he knew it was there!"

"Shawn, you can't even see a satellite during the day," he said, breathing in as an impatient parent might do to a questioning child. *Daddy, where does the sun go at night?*

"Thank you," she said, rolling her eyes and flipping him the bird. She would normally take care to make sure he knew she was being playful. But at the moment she wasn't inclined to give a shit. "Jeremy, he *knew* right where to look. And he was holding up a sign."

"What sign?" Jeremy said, almost defensively. And Shawn felt a sudden rush of adrenaline as she realized she knew some things about this... this what? *Case?* She knew some things about this case that he didn't know. And he seemed to be not only surprised by that, but maybe even a little perturbed. Jealous? Incredulous? *Something.*

"I don't know," she said, sighing again. And then she stood up. She needed to stretch her legs. Her rear end and thighs were sweating from sitting Indian-style in the warm room for too long. Plus, she thought better when she was on her feet. Jeremy was quick to join her, giving up the facade of the calm guy sitting and having a chat on the bean bags. He looked relieved to be shed of the notion that he was calm about all of this.

She stuffed her hands in her back pockets and walked to the white board on the wall and stared at it for a moment. Notes from the last Monday-morning meeting still dominated the entire left side. She pursed her lips and breathed a heavy sigh, and then turned to face Jeremy, who was now leaning against the wall by the door with his arms crossed. Altogether a more Jeremy-like posture.

"Jeremy, it was a code. The sign was like a coded message. Like a… almost like a QR code. Though it appeared to be handmade. Like, with a black marker."

Jeremy was staring at her intently. This was very clearly something he had not been aware of. "Did you try scanning the code?"

Shawn smiled at him. *Great idea!* "No. It wasn't a QR code. It was almost like one. But no, I didn't try scanning it. I only got to look at it for a few seconds."

"When was this?" he said, genuinely surprised.

"When I went to meet with Darla and Blake that Saturday. When was that?" she asked herself, frowning. *God, the days were blending together.* "They called me in when they got the satellite back and showed me a paper printout of that photo."

"That's fascinating. How come you didn't tell me any of this?" Jeremy asked plaintively.

"Dude," she said, shaking her head, "I can hardly keep my own head straight lately, trying to keep up with all the shit that's been going on. I can't remember who I've told what."

"Does Sameer know?"

"Does Sameer know what?" she replied.

"About the guy in the photo," said Jeremy.

Shawn had to stop and think about this for a minute. It was legitimately a good question. If not by its own merit, then at least as a subject for Shawn's tired and stressed mind to assess in light of her previous comment about memory. "No, I guess not," she finally said after a long moment of thought. "In fact, I don't think I've even told him about the photos at all."

"You keep saying photos. As in multiple photos?" Jeremy asked.

At that moment, a thought struck Shawn. A memory, in fact. A memory of something Darla had said at that meeting. That had been the last photo the satellite had taken before it blinked out of existence. Or at least blinked out of its preferred longitudinal home-space and appeared a third of the globe away in the same instant. She decided to give the thought a voice. "It was the last photo the satellite took before everything went to hell."

Jeremy pursed his lips and looked at her seriously for a moment before speaking. When he did, he spoke with a suspicious undertone. "So, you're saying the photo triggered it to go off-course?"

Shawn's heart stopped in her chest.

Sameer pushed open the door and came into the Comforts Room quietly, hands in his pockets. Shawn thought she had never seen him look so fragile. So... *lost*. He leaned against the wall by the door and stared at the floor. Neither Shawn nor Jeremy wanted to be the first to speak. Neither knew what to say, or how to begin – or where. There were surely a thousand or more questions between the two of them, but it seemed harshly impolite to start bombarding him with them. At least not until he spoke first.

After a deep breath, he looked up at Jeremy, and then at Shawn. They both stared intently back at their boss.

"I've really made a mess of things here," Sameer finally said.

Jeremy cleared his throat, but remained silent. Shawn stared expectantly at him for a long moment until he met her eyes and shook his head. *What did that mean?* She returned her gaze to Sameer, feeling her heart rate increase alarmingly. She could literally feel the veins in her neck pumping.

Sameer looked back at the floor and said, "I suppose you two are knowing what has happened." But he did not look back up at them.

Shawn glanced at Jeremy, hoping he would take the lead on this interrogation, since he was Sameer's right-hand man. The two had known each other and worked together since time out of mind. It seemed safer for Jeremy to take the first steps into that potential minefield. But Jeremy was staring at the floor as well.

She shook her head and looked up at the ceiling, almost as a quick plea to God, and dug into her bravery. "Sameer, what did you do? Why don't you just tell us?"

Sameer took a series of deep breaths as if testing cold waters. "I sent a dead man out into the world."

Shawn closed her eyes, shook her head. She could feel hard goosebumps rising up her back, down her arms. She thought they had closed that chapter. "Good God," she said, under her breath. Both men looked at her. Her lips were a stolid mess of stress and fear. "What do you mean, 'sent him out into the world,' Sameer?"

"The artificial intelligence I built wanted a body," he said quietly. It seemed like a full minute before he added, "So I gave him one."

"God! Sameer!" Shawn said loudly. She stood up and crossed her arms. Her forearms were covered in goose flesh and her nipples were poking through her sweater. Apparently they were governed by the same fear that was slowly terrorizing her entire system, and she tried to cover them with her arms. "How the hell do you even..." she started, then turned toward him, holding a hand out as if to ask for a handout. "How does that…" She was shaking her head and her hand, trying to put words to the questions that were all fighting for pole position in her mind now. Shawn felt like she was about to have a nervous breakdown. She sat back down and put her elbows on her knees, burying her face in her hands.

Both men were silent until she finally looked up again.

"The details are not imp-"

"Sameer, we're past all that. It's time for some truth here, okay?" Jeremy said, finally joining the conversation. *Thank God!* Shawn felt a small ember of excitement try to flare in her stomach.

"Technically, Jeremy, the details are not important. I asked the AI the same thing. It said not to worry about how. It told me it had the entire internet for a brain, and could handle the technicalities of the transfer."

They both stared at Sameer in shock. If Shawn had felt cold before, now she was frozen. Her blood felt like liquid nitrogen coursing through her veins, and every rapid beat of her heart temporarily blurred her vision. She rubbed her eyes and shook her head, trying to clear the fog.

"All I had to do was get a body and the AI would take care of the rest," Sameer continued.

"Jesus Christ," Shawn said.

"I guess that's why your attorneys are here?" Jeremy asked. He still had an eerie calm about him that Shawn didn't quite understand. This surely was the most insane and horrifying thing that had ever happened. There was a literal dead man out in the world with an AI for a brain. The thought sent fresh chills down her spine again.

"They left before I came in here," Sameer answered.

"Wait," Shawn suddenly said, raising her head and frowning at the wall between the two men. "Why were they here? What hap-"

"The family of the decedent called the university when they were seeing him on the news," he said, cutting her off. "They were less than pleased."

"Less than pleased?" Shawn almost shouted. "I would be fucking horrified! Christ, Sameer! This is the single most insane thing I have ever heard of!" She shook physically with the adrenaline and fear and anxiety that was eating her alive. "Oh my God!" she added.

"Yes, Shawn, they were horrified."

The university was the avenue through which they had gotten their subjects for the resurrection project they had previously worked on. People who donated their bodies to medical science after death would be assigned to subscribers of a service when certain criteria were met. Shawn had thought Sameer had let his subscription to the service expire. Sameer did spend a lot of his time in the lab area, but Shawn also had access to the lab, and went into it, or through it, frequently. She had not seen him working with any cadavers since they had shut down the project. Obviously, that meant nothing. And no doubt, the university's legal department had called Sameer, prompting him to call his own lawyers. *God, everything had happened so fast.* It had only been a little more than an hour ago that she had seen the news.

No. Shawn had to correct that. It had only been a little over an hour ago that the walking cadaver had been *arrested.* His face had apparently been on the news outlets for days now, in connection to the ATM robberies.

"What are your attorneys advising?" Jeremy asked.

"They are saying not to speak to anyone. Right now they think they can keep it private, between the family, the university and our company," Sameer answered.

"Our company? Sameer, seriously?" Shawn blurted out. Right now all she could think about was distancing herself from this mess.

"Shawn, whether you like all parts of what we do or not, it is still your company," Sameer said in a soft voice. *Technically correct…*

"Sameer!" she shouted, "We don't do this!"

"What are you saying, Shawn," he asked.

"It doesn't fucking matter if I approve or like, or… or… whatever. *All parts of what we do* here! That isn't something we do! Sending dead people out with AI brains?"

He stared at her. She could see he saw her point. And peripherally, she saw Jeremy nodding slightly, though he still stared at the floor. This gave her a little warm feeling. Jeremy's affirmation always made her feel better. Justified. Represented. Something. Like she was pushing in the right direction.

"Sameer," she said, holding her hands out like she was about to play a piano, "this is going to turn into a fucking media circus. Pardon my Mandarin. But seriously. It is. There will be no stopping it."

"My attorneys think-" he started, but Shawn shushed him. She *literally* shushed him.

"Sameer! You can't stop this! The media has ways of digging in like trail ticks, and *finding* shit out that you thought no one in the world knew but you!"

"She's right, boss," Jeremy chimed in, in his reasonable reassuring tone. "There's no way something like this just gets swept under the rug. The guy has *someone else's blood* in him. And not enough of it. He's got autopsy scars and a death certificate that say he shouldn't be walking around. The media *will* find that. Hell, they already mentioned the fresh stitches on CBS. Maybe all of them."

Shawn flinched at that. She couldn't remember ever hearing Jeremy swear. While 'hell' was one of the lightest of them, and even acceptable in churches, it was out of character for him.

"Okay, guys, I get it. What are we going to do?" Sameer asked plaintively.

Shawn thought for a moment, then blew out her cheeks and stood up. "I'm sorry, guys. I just can't do it. I can't be part of this. If you have to fire me, I understand, Sameer. But I don't want to be hounded by media folk. This is going to ruin some people's lives."

Sameer and Jeremy both tried to stop her as she left the conference room Constance had dubbed the Comforts Room, but only verbally. It had not been enough. She was leaving. Job be damned. She knew her value. She could get a job anywhere doing this. Hell, she wouldn't even have to leave Arlington. IT companies were so prevalent, she could hit one with a golf ball and a single swing. Having never picked up more than a putt-putt club, this said a lot.

But when Shawn got to the elevators and the doors dinged open, Chandra Casper was coming off. Shawn tried to say good morning and beware and *you might not want to go in there* all in one breath, but Chandra had lifted her chin, waiting it out, putting her hand on Shawn's shoulder. And then she had said, "Honey, they're already here. If you go out now, you'll be instantly famous."

Shawn sat in the elevator lobby for what felt like an hour, her back against the wall between two of the lift doors with her arms wrapped round her knees. She could leave, but her face would be all over the news. And if they knew enough to be waiting outside the parking garage on a Saturday morning, then they surely knew how small the company was. It was New Year's Eve, too, dammit! Didn't these people ever take a holiday?

While she couldn't well say why she was so afraid of the cameras, she could definitely say she did not want the personal intrusion of actually *talking to them*. She knew the horror stories of people who got involved. When murderers were caught, everyone who appeared on camera instantly became a suspect in the eyes of the masses: the social media juries, the Reddit brigades, the internet detectives... She had heard of people being looked up, harassed and even killed by these unnamed wannabe sleuths who thought they knew better than the detectives working the case. To be associated with a company that brought a man back from the dead and sent him out into the world as one of the living... *holy fuck.* Shawn got a shiver every time her train of thought went down that track again.

She did not cry while she sat in the lobby. She did feel frozen and trapped, depressed and anxious and like it was all going to come crashing down on her. But she did not cry. There would, Shawn reckoned, be plenty of that in the days to come, though. After a long while, she began to calm a little. She felt her blood pressure returning to normal and her breathing was steadying.

Why did she put herself through this? Why did she stay with this company when it was the source of so many anxieties? Well, admittedly, she had not signed up for this whole mess with the satellite and the AI. Not deliberately, of course. The project of reawakening the dead had been her own sick curiosity and inability to say no. Her inability to properly answer the internal question *just how bad could it really be?*

It was Chandra who came and got her. Shawn had been sitting up straight, taking deep breaths and staring at the elevator bank across from the ones she sat between, and feeling a new resolve. *It might not be so bad. I can just hop in my Jeep and drive away. I don't have to answer any questions. I don't even have to acknowledge them. Hell, they might not even be there anymore.* But Chandra's calming voice and caring smile won her back into the office.

"We'll get through this together. There's always an answer," she said.

"Yeah, well they'll hound us all, Chandra," Shawn responded.

Chandra nodded. "It is likely that Sameer will go down for this. There may be a legitimate worry for him. He may have to face jail time. But not us," she said, and put a hand on Shawn's shoulder. She was squatting in front of Shawn, her white knees together poking out the bottom of a khaki skirt. "Not you, Shawn. You had nothing to do with this!"

Shawn's eyes met Chandra's and they stared at each other for a long moment. Shawn was looking for trust in there somewhere. Chandra was the woman who had sat with Shawn for *hours – literally hours –* in the hallway outside the lab when Shawn had broken down. She had been the one who cared for her. Like a nurse. Or a mother comforting her crying child. This woman had nurturing in her. Caring. Just what Shawn had needed. Probably needed now, too. And then Shawn nodded.

Chandra smiled and they stood up together. "We're a family, Shawn. Not just a team. We take care of each other."

The news and the dead man's likeness did not escape PanaView either, apparently. When Shawn entered her office, for the first time today, the message indicator on her office phone was lit up. She had not felt her cell phone buzz, thank God. She dialed into the voice mail system and immediately went white again when she heard Darla's voice calling her out by name.

Shawn, I'm sure there's a logical explanation for this that doesn't involve what we're beginning to think is some sort of corporate sabotage.

Shawn stabbed the 7 key on her phone, deleting the message. She was instantly furious. Of course it looked like that! A dead man, *reawakened by her company* shows up in a photograph on PV's satellite the *instant* before it transits a third of the globe and goes back in time for six hundred years. It should almost be flattering for Darla, et al, to think Shawn was capable of such a miraculous feat. If she wanted to take down the server, or whatever else, Shawn had the credentials to logon and do just that.

But wait! That was *not* what they thought she was doing. Darla was smart enough to know that Shawn had credentials on the server and more technical abilities than Darla had herself. Shawn was a professional corporate server engineer. Darla was not. She called Shawn when she couldn't figure something out. So what exactly *was* she saying? She thought Shawn initiated the evanescence of the satellite? To what end? Well, that had to be obvious now: to send it back in time to get photographs. It seemed almost too simple when laid out like that, didn't it? The satellite's cameras were trained conveniently on the same exact latitude as the pyramid in Giza. Shawn had – obviously – *sent that satellite* back in time to get pictures of it being built. Duh.

And now, Shawn was staring at the phone keypad, her fingertips doing their ritual dance against the blotter, covered with doodles and stick figures. Darla was a smart woman. She knew Shawn's capability. But if she was truly smart, she would also know Shawn's ability did *not* extend to such feats as this. Who the hell could possibly arrange such theatre? Such… magic? Darla would surely know that no human being could possibly exert that kind of control over a piece of technology. And by extension, that Shawn herself certainly couldn't, therefore.

No human being.

But what about an AI?

Shawn barged into Sameer's office, shoving open the door so hard it slammed back against the wall. Chandra jumped back almost a foot, her eyes wide as saucers. Jeremy visibly flinched in his chair as well. Why the hell had the door even been closed? Maybe Sameer had just been seeking a feeling of security amidst the terrifying reality he now faced outside the walls of the BlueBird offices.

She marched up to his desk and slapped her palm against the wood. "Tell me about the pictures," she said, not quite shouting but unnecessarily loud in the context.

Sameer shook his head, his mouth hung open, looking thoroughly confused. "What... pictures?"

"The pictures on the satellite. The pictures that PanaView satellite was *sent* back in time to collect," Shawn said, an unfamiliar authority in her tone. She looked over at Jeremy, whose brow was furrowed in a complex countenance – one of thought and perplexity – but not necessarily aimed at Shawn herself. She had gotten him thinking.

Sameer's eyes widened almost imperceptibly. "Pictures, Shawn?"

"Someone sent that satellite back in time for a specific reason. I want you to tell me what that reason was, Sameer," she said. She had lowered her volume considerably, but the authoritative tone was still in attendance.

"Shawn, I was not knowing there were pictures. What do you mean it went back in time?" he mustered.

"Shawn, what is this about?" Chandra tried from her right. Peripherally, Shawn could see Chandra's hand coming for Shawn's shoulder. That ever-popular gesture of comfort and calming. Shawn stepped to her left, turning bodily to dodge any attempt at submission.

"Just wait, Chandra. Let's see what he says," Shawn said. She turned her head to look at Sameer again, but kept a forty-five degree angle about her body, so she could face the space between Sameer and Chandra. Which, as it happened, was exactly where Jeremy was seated. He was still staring meaningfully off into the short distance between him and Sameer's desk. But now he was nodding ever so slightly. He was catching on! Shawn felt a small tinge of victory in her loins as she took this in. He was figuring it out just as she had. Now she just hoped he would keep quiet. Hoped he would see the importance of having Sameer answer this one himself.

Sameer leaned back in his chair, grasping the ends of the armrests, and took a deep breath. "I think I know what happened."

"You think?" Shawn said, smiling widely. "Spill it, mister!"

He leaned forward, putting his elbows on his blotter, and removed his glasses, rubbing his eyes and temples. Shawn saw this at first as an evasive maneuver, but gave it a minute to resolve, and realized he was just figuring out himself what had happened. *So he didn't know either?* Had she been wrong? Well, apparently not, for if he was even *capable* of figuring it out, that meant he was at least partially culpable.

With his glasses hanging from the fingers on his right hand, he continued rubbing his eyes with the other. He used the glasses as a prop now, waving them as he spoke. "Shawn, I believe this has something to do with the AI computer I had been interacting with."

Shawn's smile became genuine, and she shot a glance at Jeremy, who now made perfect eye-contact with her. The look of curious intensity in his eyes was unmistakably new. He had not known any of this before. That made Shawn feel instantly relieved. *Thank God he wasn't part of this.* Maybe he wasn't as close to Sameer as she had originally thought.

Shawn actually found the comfort enough to relax a little. Her posture lost its defensive edge and she crossed her arms. Had there been a chair behind her, she might actually have even sat down. The only other chair in the room was behind Chandra though, so she continued standing, her thighs against the edge of Sameer's desk.

He sat up and put his specs back on, then steepled his fingers in front of his face, his elbows still on the blotter. He sighed heavily, and then said, "I have hired every one of you and gotten to know you and put a large amount of trust in you. I guess I will have to be letting my guard down a little." Sameer made eye-contact with each of them in turn, ending with Shawn, who had been the proprietor of this come-to-Jesus confrontation.

"The AI came to make me believe it could get me anything I wanted if I did something for it. It asked me what I would love most to know, and I answered that I would love to see how the pyramids in Egypt were built."

BOOM! Shawn thought. *There it is!*

She saw the dawning sense of confirmation on Jeremy's visage, and in his subtle nod. He had just confirmed internally what he had only put together as hypothesis a few moments before. Chandra, however, had the polar opposite reaction. She was frowning and shaking her head, mouth slightly agape. Yet she still remained silent. She was now the only one in the room who was still completely in the dark about why she was even here on a Saturday morning, the last day of the year.

"Did you honestly not know about the photos, Sameer?" Shawn said. She was taking a bit of a chance, extending this question as a sort of allowance that might come back to bite her.

He looked up at her again. "No. I am supposing that is why the satellite went offline a few weeks ago."

"November eighth. Yes," Shawn confirmed.

He nodded, shaking his head at the same time. An *I'll be damned* gesture.

"Wait. So you're saying you didn't know it was going to do that?" Jeremy asked, leaning forward.

Sameer glanced at Jeremy, but returned his gaze to the front. To Shawn. "No. I had no idea it would use the satellite at all. I was not knowing how it would get me what I asked for. I do not know if I even really trusted that it could deliver."

"It, being the AI?" Jeremy asked.

"Yes. The AI said it could get me what I wanted. It did not use the word 'photographs'. It just said it could get me solid evidence of how the pyramids were built," said Sameer.

Jeremy shook his head. "So, I guess I'm not understanding… How does Calvin come into all this?"

"Who the hell is Calvin?" Shawn interjected.

"The dead man who's all over the news," Chandra answered. "Calvin Graves," she added and gave Shawn a look.

"You've got to be kidding. That's his real name?"

Chandra nodded.

Shawn rolled her eyes, then turned to address Jeremy. "Don't you see?" Shawn said, almost laughing. "He made a fuckin' deal with the AI, Jer!"

Jeremy squinted and shook his head once more, as if clearing the final cobwebs blocking his vision of the truth. "So the AI wanted a body, and promised you evidence of how the pyramids were built in return?"

"Bingo!" Shawn said, sticking her thumb up. Chandra stared at her with something like awe, as if Shawn had just divined all this from the very beginning. As if she hadn't spent weeks thinking about the interconnectedness of all of these things.

Chandra finally spoke up. "I'm not catching how all this happened. Can someone please just lay it out for me? Explain like I'm five," she said, and pulled the seat up from behind her, dropping gracefully into it.

Shawn, partly in an effort to test her theory and make sure she had it all worked out, and partly because she felt like she could do so more concisely than Sameer, decided to take the reigns on this. "If I may," she said, looking at her boss.

He turned his hand over, ending palm-up.

Shawn nodded and leaned sideways against the desk to look at Chandra while she spoke. "AI asks Sameer what he would like to know. Likely because he had been tantalizing Sameer with all his great knowledge. Sameer says, 'Okay, smart guy, show me how the pyramids were built.' AI says okay, I can deliver that. No problemo. You just get me a body." Shawn glanced at Sameer at this point. He wasn't shaking his head. He was chewing on his bottom lip.

"Not sure how he came to know that you could achieve such a fulfillment," Shawn said, still looking at her boss. She waved a hand. "Irrelevant." Then she turned her attention back to Chandra.

"Anyway, Sameer says, 'I don't know how to transfer your vast knowledge and your existence in general into a dead guy's brain.' The AI says, 'I have the entire internet at my disposal. Let me handle that.'" At this, Shawn actually saw Sameer nod. *Excellent.*

"So," she continued with a sigh, "Sameer gets it a body. Plugs the body into the AI and transfers its consciousness somehow. AI now sits up on the table, happy to have a body with which to roam the world!" she said with a flourish of the hand she had been using to embellish her argument.

Chandra was shaking her head, eyes closed. She breathed in slowly through her nose and then opened her eyes and looked at Shawn. "How in the world did the AI slash dead-man send the satellite to do its bidding?"

Shawn shrugged. "I'm guessing it had already sent some code to the server on that satellite saying to watch for this particular command. *Once I have the body I want, I will let you know to execute.*"

Chandra and Shawn stared at each other for a moment. Chandra then looked at Sameer as if for confirmation, and then back to Shawn. "Yeah? Then what?" she asked, eyebrows raised. She was catching all of this, but still on the fence about whether to believe. That last little gap had not been bridged.

"Calvin the Dead Guy goes out into the field, right where he knows that satellite takes a photograph three times a day, and holds up a sign with code on it, completing the transaction on the satellite's server, thereby executing the command it had already uploaded," Shawn said, almost grinning. On some level she was almost tickled with herself for figuring it out, but she certainly didn't want to look arrogant about it. Not *too* arrogant, anyway. It was okay to show a little pride though. *Right?*

"I don't get it. Why not just send the command as soon as it got its body?" Chandra asked, looking down at the desk in front of her.

"Insurance," Jeremy said from his side of the desk. They all looked at him. He was nodding very slowly and purposefully, staring Shawn in the eyes. Again with no smile. This was – what, the third time, ever?

"Exactly," she said after a pause. "It needed to get away from here. To insure he wouldn't be immediately put back to death or something."

Chandra drew in breath and looked slowly up at the ceiling as it all dawned on her. She put her hands in her hair, much the same as Shawn had been apt to do lately. "God, Sameer!" she said. "How could you think this would turn out any other way?" She stared at him pleadingly for a moment. Like a disappointed mother trying not to be too hard on her errant son. "Sameer! You must surely have known that he would be discovered eventually!"

Sameer, shaking his own head, said, "I did not. I did not think that far ahead."

"You sent a fuckin' zombie out into the world," Chandra said coldly. Then she looked at Shawn, as if Shawn was somehow the authority on the subject. "I didn't even think they could move their whole bodies. Much less, walk! Or make it to another state! What in the hell?" She looked completely exasperated now.

"Good point," Jeremy added. "How *did* it go ambulatory?"

Sameer looked over at him. "I do not know. I just know it had the entire internet to draw its knowledge from. Medical websites. Entire texts and literature on how the nervous system works. I am not knowing."

"This is impossible," Chandra said.

"He stayed in the lab, on the table, for many, many hours. I did not think it had worked," Sameer said quietly. "And then I went back in after a break, and he was gone."

Shawn shivered again. This whole back-from-the-dead thing had never sat well with her in the first place. Not even when she was working on the project. They had only ever had one instance of full-body involvement. There had been a lot of convulsing and spasm as the body used muscles over which it was not strictly supposed to have control. They had had to wrestle the subject down and put the Death Helmet on it, killing instantly all the nanobots attached to the brain's synapses that had caused the awakening. That had been after executing a batch file Jeremy had crafted called *kick.bat*. She had hoped to never remember that terrifying episode again.

But somehow, this was so much worse. Even though she had not been physically present to see this subject – *Calvin* – awaken and rejoin the living. Knowing that there was a dead man actually walking around the planet. A true case of actual, literal *zombiism*. She had to close her eyes and let the image evaporate before she could continue.

"Okay, so how do we get this thing back under control?" Jeremy finally asked.

"Well, it shouldn't be a task at all. We go collect Mr. Calvin. They are actually asking us to do so. Legally, we are still the custodians of the deceased," Chandra said firmly. "A project we lost control of. We have not only the legal *right*, but the *requirement* to go collect him and put him back to death."

"Fuck sake," Shawn said under her breath. This was absolutely one thing she would take no part in. That was where she put her foot down. If she had to deal with the media circus, she would do so. Not happily, mind you, but she would bulldoze her way through it. But bringing the man back in and helmeting him? *Abso-fucking-lutely NOT.*

"Shawn," Sameer said, bringing her attention back to the present. "Where are the pictures?"

"Jesus Christ!" she shouted, at the same time Chandra shouted something. They likely drowned each other out. "I can't believe you're even thinking about that right now!"

Chapter 17

Shawn had managed the escape from the building, in much the same way she had envisioned herself doing so. She had walked quickly and purposefully from the elevator doors to her Jeep, which was, on this Saturday and last day of the year, thankfully, very vacant. It was when she pulled out of the garage that she saw the news crews in the parking lot, the vultures that they were, ready to set on anyone who came out the front door of the office building.

There were vans from several stations, and what seemed to be a sea of human bodies gathered around and betwixt them, cameras, microphones and all other implements of broadcasting in great supply. They did notice her pulling out of the garage and turning onto Arkansas Lane, but no one was quick enough to get the camera turned in her direction. While the people themselves would likely remember her brown Jeep

Wrangler, at least it wasn't on camera, and being broadcast to the world.

Even still, Shawn could not shake the feeling that she was being pursued on the way home. It wasn't a physical pursuit. Not an immediate action, at least. But she felt it coming. She wondered how long it would take for them to connect her to the company through tax records or some other means, and how long after that they would be waiting in *her* parking lot. Out in front of her apartment building. The thought made her chest feel a little tighter.

Right now, she needed to get home and tell Cory all about this. Micha and Mick, too. They could collectively come up with a plan that would help keep her safe from the vultures. Right? She hoped. That was all she had at the moment was a fistful of hope. And she had to hope it was enough.

When she got home, Cory was sitting on the couch, watching the news. He was sharp enough to have the presence of mind to turn the damn thing off when she walked in, though she did catch a glimpse of the big red banners on the screen. *Dead Man Walking*. Fuck sake. How inconsiderate. Of course, her company was the insensitive entity that had reanimated him and sent him into the world. But to make light of it like that, to broadcast such cheap phrases and shock-value shit, knowing there was a family out there suffering not only the loss of their loved one, but also now the literal, physical loss of him as well. As in, her company had *lost* him, like a mother might lose her child at the supermarket.

Cory turned and put his arm on the back of the couch, watching Shawn come in, drop her purse and coat on the table and make her way to him. As she rounded the end of the couch, he turned with her, opening his arms and allowing her to fall into them. Apparently she was ready for that big cry now. Because it came.

At some point during the afternoon, Shawn had managed to find comfort enough to sleep. She slept with her head on Cory's lap, her mouth and nose pressed tight up against his stomach as he sat still and patient, scrolling on his phone. She awoke some hours later feeling a little more in touch with her reality. There was a sense of calm about her that only Cory knew how to invoke. Just his presence was usually enough for her to achieve this sense of peace. Shawn sat up, feeling the redness in her cheek where it had pressed against his jeans. It felt swollen and hot. She stumbled to the bathroom to relieve herself and brush her teeth.

When she finished, Shawn spontaneously decided to take a hot bath. As the water drew, she shed her clothes and stood staring in the mirror, her hands on the basin. She looked worn out and used up. Her hair was a disheveled mess, her eyes were puffy and red and her cheeks were creased and lined with the stitching of her boyfriend's jeans. She could see clearly the pallette of chill bumps all over her chest, and her normally soft breasts looked cold and hard, nipples erect and angry. She stood up, putting her hands on them and feeling the pain of irritation in her nipples. She sighed and turned to step into the tub.

Thoughts of Miranda, another subject who had come into her lab, slipped into her mind. Miranda, who had actually lived in the same complex and she and Cory had lived at the time, had stepped into her own tub one night, and had a bad fall. She had bled out through a large wound on the back of her head, her life slipping away into the hot bath water. Shawn had been terribly depressed by this, even though she had never actually known the girl in life. Close enough in age to be friends, it had hit her in much the same way the passing of a friend might have hit her. The only difference was that it had been the *awakening* of the dead girl that had screwed Shawn up so badly. She had spent weeks feeling guilty over the act, as if bringing her back had caused her a second chance at life for only a few moments, before it would be swept away again. *Again.* That poor girl – and all of the subjects they had brought back for only minutes – had had to experience death a second time. There was no easy way to get over that, and Shawn had struggled with it in the worst way, for a lengthy period.

What about this man, Calvin, who had died and trusted himself to the community of scientific study of the dead? What was *he* feeling as he was brought back? What wires and tubes had been used in the lab that day to transfer an active computerized intelligence into his newly awakened brain? What did that electronic takeover feel like? Had he been aware that it was happening? Could he feel his own consciousness and personality being erased one byte at a time by the electronic analog of intelligence? God, that had to have been an awful feeling. Shawn hoped secretly that the man had not been aware of any of it.

She was completely unaware that the man even existed until Blake and Darla had shown her that crazy, creepy photograph that morning in their office. But now he seemed to haunt her memory. Shawn didn't know the man from Adam. Hell, he could have been a murderer. A convicted felon. A child rapist. The worst kind of person. But even with all that, she felt he didn't deserve the lot he had been handed. No one did.

Shawn did not want to ask Sameer for his file. To get his last name so she could look him up and find out more about him. She only knew that her sick curiosity would likely get the best of her in the long run. She would inevitably want to put to rest any questions she had about the life of the man before his first, natural death. Why? *Why, though?* To justify this sickening insertion of a cyberintellectual presence into his being? It couldn't be done. Justification, that is. There was no justifying it. But still, she felt she would someday *have to know*.

There was a quiet knock at the bathroom door. Her eyes were closed as she half-floated in the steaming bath water. Shawn had been in the tub for at least a half-hour now. The tips of her fingers were undoubtedly pruned and wrinkly. "Come in, babe," she said, without opening her eyes. She could hear Cory open the door and enter the small bathroom. The sound of the toilet lid closing. Weight on the lid. "What's up?" she asked.

"Just checking on you," said a gorgeous voice. Familiar and wonderful to her ears, which were sore from the assault of horror this morning. Her eyes popped open, startled, and found her friend sitting on the toilet, legs crossed and chin resting on her hand, elbow on the crossed knee.

"Welp, I guess there's no sense in my trying to cover up now," Shawn said, actually a little embarrassed. She was, of course, not ashamed of her lithe frame or small breasts. But this was not the way she imagined her friend would come to attain this level of intimacy. She suddenly felt very naked and vulnerable.

"Relax, hon. I'm not a danger to you. I want to help you through this," said Micha.

"Thank you," Shawn said, closing her eyes. She was tingling all over now, almost an erotic sensation, like she was being admired or assessed by a thoughtful eye. Nonsense, of course. But she couldn't help the reaction. And it was not entirely comfortable. Being naked in front of another woman, in the right circumstances – the locker room at the gym, for instance – was not foreign to her. But like this, so unexpectedly, it was not just dissipating as fast as she would have imagined it to. She opened her eyes and saw that Micha was looking at her. But it wasn't a leer. It was a friendly, disconnected gaze. And it was not at her body. Micha was looking her in the eyes. The same way she always did when they talked. The normalcy began to return.

"Can you tell me what really happened?" Micha asked. "I mean, legally. And, of course, if you want to. If you feel like it."

Shawn waved a hand dismissively. Her eyes were closed again. It seemed the least awkward way by which to maintain a normal conversation when half the party was completely nude. "Sameer made a deal with an AI computer. He asked for evidence of how the pyramids were built, and the AI asked for a body."

She heard Micha draw in breath sharply through her nose. And then she said, "Well, I guess that ties everything up nicely for you, at least."

"In what way?" Shawn said, opening her eyes again, frowning at her friend. Micha was looking at the wall in front of the toilet now, instead of at Shawn's eyes. A little more of the apprehension faded.

"I just mean, it seems to answer all these questions you were having about the satellite and all that."

Shawn thought that was a pretty keen observation from her friend, to tie all that together so quickly without it being explicitly spelled out for her. To automatically *know* that the satellite was the catalyst by which the AI had kept its end of the bargain, well, that was pretty astute. On a personal level, it also told Shawn that Cory had not tried to fill Micha in on all the dirty details himself. He had respected that it might not be something that needed to be shared publicly yet. She loved that boy.

"Well, it does do that," Shawn said, closing her eyes again. "All the mysteries are solved."

"Yeah, well, except for one."

"Yeah? What's that?" Shawn asked.

"The news said it looked like this guy had autopsy incisions. I mean, like he was dead. What the hell does that mean?"

Shawn realized she had not told Micha about the reanimation project. So apparently, she did know how to keep the corporate secrets when she needed to. For this, she felt a quick flash of pride. But no longer did she feel that call to commitment. It was about to become public knowledge that this guy was literally a zombie. There would be no way for Shawn to disavow that completely. At least not to her friends.

She thought about that for a moment, pursing her lips as a signal to Micha that she wasn't ignoring the question. She was pondering an answer. Shawn decided she did want to tell her friend about it. It would not only evacuate the remaining bits of mystery in Micha's mind about the satellite, but it would also give Shawn the chance to talk to her occasionally. This seemed important, especially when she was feeling creeped-out by the ghosts in her head. Those memories of dead eyes popping open and seeking her out in the dimness of the lab. She sometimes needed a girlfriend to talk to about this history of herself. Sometimes it would take more than her boyfriend. A female's perspective on fear and coping. Shawn had definitely confided in Lo for that. It would be nice to now rely on Micha for the same reasons. And she reckoned Micha had been around long enough to trust. *You never really know your neighbors.* Wasn't that something Shawn herself had said in the not-too-distant past? Oh well. It was, like she had already come to realize, about to become public knowledge that this company brought people back to life.

Well, at least one person. She guessed that what had happened in the lab in the previous year had no real reason to come to light now. That was all proprietary and classified data, in keeping with the strict guidelines of the medical science community standards. *Horse shit.* Shawn almost had to laugh at that though. Community standards probably did not account for trying to reawaken a personality from the dead. Somehow, she thought that was probably not in any of their ethics manuals. It just wasn't something one *needed* to account for, at least in her mind.

But in light of the thought that it was already all over the news – *Man Brought Back From Dead Roams The Land, Ripping Off ATMs* – Shawn knew Micha would have questions about what exactly her company did. Of course, she could hide behind NDAs and company secret bullshit. But she didn't want that mysterious aura to envelop her. She didn't want to keep that secret from Micha – to have her believe that Shawn was part of the scheme that had made this man's gallivanting escapades possible. It seemed legitimately more suitable to explain that yes, she had indeed been part of some awakenings in the past, and that's how they *got to* this point… but that no, she had *not* been part of this man's reanimation.

This bathtub, and her nakedness in it, somehow did not seem the appropriate forum for such topics of conversation, though. So Shawn opened her eyes and said, "Well, I'll be happy to explain that. But I'd like to cover my twat first, if you please."

Micha laughed out loud and bowed out of the bathroom.

The breakfast nook at almost sundown did seem a lot more appropriate. Shawn had told Micha to go home and collect Mick first, knowing Micha would eventually tell him anyway, so it could all be told at once. Get it straight from the horse's mouth, so to speak. That way she could answer any questions and allay any unintentional mysteries about the whole process. She also wanted to be able to stress that it was very important for them not to speak about it. For, while Sameer was indeed likely to be indicted on all kinds of weird, never-before-seen charges – *Frankensteining a Cadaver, First Degree* – she still believed the history of that event would likely be protected. Or would it?

During prosecution, was it likely the feds would cease all company assets and find their tapes? The audio recordings they had of each event, along with all the notes Shawn had typed up about them? Lord, if that got out, it could be seriously harmful to the company. To science. Hell, to humanity. She felt a lot like Oppenheimer right about now, wishing he could just destroy and be rid of the strange technology he had harnessed. To send it into the deepest darkest pit, never to be seen again. What the world did not need was a bunch of pseudo-scientists bringing more people back from the dead as a hobby. She suddenly had the sick urge to run back up to BlueBird and destroy all that evidence. Server backups and all.

The four of them sat at the breakfast table with a bottle of bourbon and a bottle of wine in the middle. Each of them had a glass, and Shawn started the ritual of ice-breaking by pouring herself a generous helping of bourbon. Micha, she noted, watched with fascination as she let the stream narrow, then set the bottle back in the middle. Then she, Micha, took the same bottle and ran it up to about the same height in her own glass. Mick went next, same bottle, same amount. Cory, being the polite host, said, "Well, shit. I guess I can put this wine back in the fridge. I figured you ladies would be drinking that."

"You figured wrong, bubba," Shawn said, holding her glass out toward Micha. Micha clinked it and they both drank. Mick leaned back, shaking his head. And then Shawn wiped her mouth and began talking.

"Cory has heard most of this, of course, but I wouldn't want him to be elsewhere while I retell it," Shawn said, reaching over and taking his hand on the table. She gave it a squeeze and looked at him. He gave her a thoughtful wink and squeezed back. And then Shawn looked at her two guests. "He will patiently listen as I retell. I just need you both to promise this secret goes with you to the grave."

They both nodded and Micha held her right hand up, as if to swear it. And then Shawn thought about what she had said. *To the grave.* Ugh. Poor choice of words. She breathed in deep, swallowed another swig of the fire liquid, and then she began.

She spoke for over an hour, telling them everything from the start, how she came to accept the position of *Queen of the Dead* – a title she had jokingly taken with Sameer after they had been at if for a few months – to the point where she brought her very best friend back from the dead. To this point, Micha had known very little of Lo, even though Shawn brought her up quite frequently. She had just been the dead friend whom Shawn missed so much. But in this rambling autobiography, Shawn included every bit about how she had met Laura Carter and befriended her, how they had done everything together, and how Lo had died in Shawn's arms. *Twice.*

Micha had closed her eyes during those parts of the telling, and had to wipe them as tears welled up a few times. This lent to the strength of Shawn's theory that Micha and Lo would have gotten along famously. She thought the three of them would have run thick as thieves. Sometimes, she pined for that reality. She fancied there might have even been dreams of the three of them spending time together, huddled over a small high-top table in a loud tavern, drinking rum and singing pirate songs. Dreams forgotten, realities never allowed to exist. It felt good to get it out. To let Micha know who Lo had truly been to Shawn. How powerful that friendship had been. Partly to solidify it in Micha's mind as a reverent article. But also to hopefully illustrate to Micha that she would gladly give her this all-in and completely selfless love were she to accept it. She hoped, in short, that when she was done, Micha would hug her and realize how special this friendship could become as long as she – Micha – didn't allow herself to be scared off by any of this.

When she got to the part about Sameer's daughter, Shawn stumbled momentarily, wondering if it was ethical to share that bit. In the end, she guessed it was perhaps the *most* important part of the story, reckoning that it was the cog that turned the whole gear set of the ship they were on. It was the very reason Sameer had set about trying to establish a reanimation. She told it reverently, and made sure to paint him in as favorable a light as she was able, knowing there had been no ill will there.

By the end of her spill session, the bottle was markedly emptier than when they had started, and the two guests were leaning in and concentrating on every word she said. Micha had reached across the table and taken Shawn's hand, and had just not let go. The two had held hands for probably twenty minutes by the time she finished. Mick broke the new silence by saying, "That is absolutely fascinating. You know, I always wondered when someone would start experimenting with that kind of science."

"Really?" Cory asked. He was leaning back in his chair, thumbs in his pockets and tilting the chair back slightly on its two back feet.

"Yeah, sure," Mick said, taking another sip of whiskey. "It always seemed a natural direction to go with experimentation. Hell, I guess people *are* experimenting with it in places unknown. I mean, it's not something you can really report, right?"

"What do you mean?" Micha said, looking at him on her right.

"I just mean there are probably hundreds of entities trying to do just what Shawn and her boss did, but they just can't say anything about it. It's not strictly legal to bring people back from the dead, is it?"

"Yeah, good point," Micha said, then returned her slightly foggy gaze to Shawn. She looked down at their clasped and sweaty hands on the table and squeezed again. "I'm so sorry you had to go through that, Shawn."

"It was my own choosing. I could have strictly stood against bringing Lo into the lab. But part of me, and this may sound selfish..." she said but trailed off, her voice catching on the last word. Tears suddenly stung her eyes. Micha squeezed again. But this time, Cory reached over and put his arm around her shoulders, and Mick leaned in and put his hand atop hers and Micha's on the table. This brought the tears. She wiped them away with her left hand and tried to smile. Inside she was feeling elation at the sudden love she had found for these two neighbors, and remembered a similar feeling with Lo. She looked up as if to see if her friend was present above them, the closed her eyes for a moment.

"Sorry, guys. And thank you for being here."

"You're welcome, Love," Micha said, staring her straight in the eyes, and Shawn could hear the capital letter in that word.

"What I was going to say is that part of me *wanted* to bring her back. Just for a few minutes. It's simultaneously one of my biggest regrets and one of my greatest memories yet. Those few more minutes with my deceased friend... her smart-ass remarks and sense of humor never died," she said, wiping her eyes. "I hate myself for doing it sometimes. But she wanted to be on that table, I swear to you."

"Of course she did!" Micha said in a motherly tone. "That's why you developed the challenge and response! You shouldn't punish yourself for that, hon. Hell, I would have done the same thing. I'm not sure I'm brave enough to say I want to be on that table myself, but if I had been in your shoes… damn right I would have brought her back."

Shawn, nodding and rubbing her eyes, more in an effort to cover them than to stop the tears, was now having trouble controlling her sobs entirely. She was choking up and it was obvious. It felt wonderful to be airing out her regrets. Maybe they would cease to haunt her now that she had shared them. But it also hurt badly to be tearing that old wound open again. She finally scooted back from the table and tried to stand, burying her face in her hands. Instantly, there were arms around her. She could feel Cory's strong arm around her shoulders, and the softness of Micha's breasts and stomach against her front side, her arms over Cory's and around her neck, her cheek against Shawn's own. And there they stood rocking back and forth until she finally got hold of herself. It might have been a different era. It seemed certainly like a different century.

Whether she believed in spirits or seances, fate or superstition, Shawn knew Lo's presence had been there that night. She believed now with everything she had that her friendship with Micha had been blessed by her dead friend. She was the logical heir to carry this torch now that Lo was gone. And Shawn felt the response in her new friend's hug. She knew. She knew who she was, and how important she had become. Some things didn't need to be spoken.

After Shawn had finished her cry, she had gone into the restroom to freshen up. She brushed her teeth and washed her face, trying to get some of the red out of her eyes and cheeks. Coming out, she took her favorite hat off a hook by the door and put it on, then rejoined her friends at the whiskey table. For it could not be called a breakfast table at this time. At this time, it was serving only whiskey.

As she sat down, Shawn put her hands flat on its surface and said, "Well, happy new year!" and by some extreme stroke of incalculable coincidence, she had been exactly right about the time. Fireworks began going off outside. In the courtyard and the sky above them.

"Holy fuck!" Micha screamed in elation. "Black magic woman!"

They all stood up laughing and went to the small balcony to stand and shout into the night.

With the next day being New Year's Day, Shawn had little trouble making excuses to stay inside. She was deathly afraid of the cameras catching up with her, but there was more to it than that. It also felt like she was somehow afraid of the world itself right now. Unsure about what to expect. How it would all play out and what her level of involvement would be in it.

Cory respectfully kept the television off, or at least off the news stations when he had it on. She had argued with herself about the reasoning behind such an aversion. Would it not behoove her, for instance, to keep up with the news – if for no other reason than to know when they were coming? And what they would be coming after? To keep up with their progress? What they had learned so far? All she knew was that it scared her to watch it. It was nerve-racking and gave her the worst anxiety. It felt unhealthy to put herself in that state, so she would rather just be surprised. Of course now that all her friends knew what was going on, they were sure to be watching it *for her*. If anything too big came about, Shawn was sure she would hear about it from one of them.

The one thing work-related she did on the first was to call Jeremy, whom she knew would be at home just like her. He wasn't much of a party animal, and usually stayed at home most of the time anyway. He answered on the first ring.

"What up, Shawn? Happy new year or something," he said.

"Yo ho ho, what are you up to?"

"The same thing I was doing one year ago today."

"Ooh, that sounds amazing! Are you playing *Honor of Warfare*?" Shawn asked, almost seriously.

Jeremy laughed out loud. "No, I'm playing *Special Duty: Modern Ops.*"

"Ooh. Is that a new one? I'll have to ask Cory if he's heard of it…" she said, now completely serious. It would be nice to surprise him with something.

"Uh, well, yeah. You do that. So what can I do for you?" Jeremy asked when the laughter had left his voice.

"Do you think we should be deleting records?"

"I don't think you need to worry about that, Shawn," he said. She could hear the smile in his voice. But that damned Michael Rappaport smile was so deceiving. It could mean what a smile was supposed to mean, or it could mean nothing.

"What the hell does that mean?" she asked.

"I'm sure Sameer is taking care to cover his tracks," he said.

"Ah." And suddenly, she got sentimental. She glanced over at the laptop sitting open on her desk. On there were all the files relevant to all the cases they had reawakened. She had meticulously typed out notes on each subject and their interactions, basically making a database out of their files. With that, she could cross-reference certain things said in the lab, times things happened, certain other unique or apparently common events that might make one subject more like another. She had been proud of the work she did on those lab notes. She had also downloaded all of the audio recordings of the events, originally off-loaded from Sameer's digital voice recorder, which he kept hanging round his neck on a rope during the sessions.

While those trips down memory lane were not something she thought she would exactly be excited about making again any time soon, Shawn did see the value in preserving them. The thought that they contained the voices of the dead, quite literally, always got her skin moving a little. But there was certainly scientific value in some of it, for certain.

"Okay, well," she started. Suddenly, she thought there was maybe another reason to keep him on the phone. Was it the security of a familiar voice from the company? A comrade who knew what she was going through? "Jeremy, how are you taking all of this?"

"Oh, you know, I ride it like the waves. Ups and downs."

Shawn thought for a moment, chewing on her thumb and staring at a picture of her and Cory on the desk. "You know, that's the most generic non-answer I've ever heard."

"What do you want to know? I mean, I'm not worried about it. I think it's going to be weird around here for a while, but I think we'll pull through it," he said. She did not hear any stress in his voice. But wasn't he always the coolest of customers? Hadn't she labeled him as a poker player in her mind before? As in, he had a wonderful poker face? Or maybe it was a terrible one…

"I don't know. I just… I guess I'm scared of the cameras," Shawn said.

"Well, they can't hurt you, Shawn," said Jeremy. And she knew he wasn't being cute. It was a literal statement, made in the most literal sense, for her reassurance.

"Yeah, I guess so. Thanks, Jer Bear."

"Sure thing," he said. She was about to hang up, but he quickly added, "Oh, hey, Shawn?"

"Yeah?"

"Call your minions. Tell them to work from home for a couple of days."

Chapter 18

The word 'normal' was such a funny word to Shawn. It could fit and define almost any situation. Like the ever-popular acronym, SNAFU said, *Situation Normal, All Fucked Up*. Normal. But it could also mean normal as in, *not* fucked up. And while she wasn't necessarily ready to say that everything was fucked up at the office, it sure was a situation. And in IT, chaos sometimes was the normal that engineers lived in. The soup they swam in. The trauma that paid the bills.

Since the breakdown that had happened a couple of weeks ago where all the servers had seemed to be infected by a virus, nothing crazy had happened. But now it just felt wrong. Like at any minute something was going to snap. Servers were randomly spiking, customers were calling in about perceived emergencies and Nagios was alerting them on all kinds of weird shit that just wasn't *normal*. The fact that the alert for a taxed NIC even existed – that is, a network interface card – meant that it must at least *sometimes* be normal. But it almost never went red. Well, today, nothing seemed extraordinary. And there was another funny word. To think that ordinary wasn't enough. This was *extra* ordinary. So basic, so common – so *normal* – that it needed its own word.

When alerts were firing off at unpredictable intervals, for no real reason, it sort of became the new normal. That's how today felt. So that when an alert *didn't* go off, it just felt weird. Awkward. Wrong. That's when she would start thinking things are wrong but disguising themselves as right. The frog staying in the water as it warms, he never notices it's getting too hot, and ends up being boiled. If one doesn't pay attention, the abnormal suddenly swaps places with the extra ordinary, and something extraordinary happens. Shawn felt like that was on the tip of the next second. She had been on edge all day.

It was January 2nd, and she was running her whole department by the phone. She had been in almost constant contact with Constance and Lance since eight o'clock, when she had gotten in. And at around noon, she had finally opened a conference call so that they could just stay on the phone together. Everyone could be heard typing. Sneezing. Talking to someone in the background. A dog barking outside some unseeable window. It was a bit like leaving a phone line open with a new boyfriend back in the days of landlines, when Shawn was a teen. Just so she wouldn't miss a single moment of anything interesting happening. Listening to each other fall asleep. Boy, that was a cruel joke, wasn't it? She had successfully fallen asleep like that on more than one occasion, only to be awakened the next morning by the WORLD IS ENDING klaxon of the phone being left off the hook for too long. What this meant was that the boyfriend's parent had come in and found the phone off the hook, and had kindly and responsibly set it back on the hook. And a few seconds later, Shawn would be the one to be jolted awake by a heart-attack-inducing alert.

Each of the three server engineers were thoughtfully and thoroughly checking their clients' servers for anything untoward, but no one was finding anything definitive. Lance had braved the question during their morning conference call. Shawn had texted them the day before, telling them to work from home, as Jeremy had suggested. They had both simply acknowledged the text. But on this call, Lance had put words to the question that Constance must surely have been wondering too. *What does all this shit in the news mean for the company?*

Shawn professionally and eloquently answered the question with a non-answer that her reports were both likely expecting. But one had to try the waters to see if they would yield any fish, did they not? She had said, very simply, "This isn't something any of us is allowed to talk about just yet. Especially not on the phone. You're neither of you in danger of losing your job. Let's just keep our heads down and do what we're paid to do. We'll hopefully have more answers by Monday."

Since it was Wednesday, Jeremy's 'couple of days' would mean their coming back to work on Friday, which didn't seem to make a lot of sense to Shawn. Might as well just give them the whole week, then re-evaluate on Monday.

After everyone had gone through the entire client catalog of servers and nothing had come back red, or even orange for that matter, Shawn began to feel a little better. Maybe she had been anticipating problems because of her own psychodrama. There was nothing to suggest that anything was bound to happen. Since Sameer's AI had left the building, both figuratively and literally, and her own had been smashed to bits, it had no more influence on their servers. Nor any need to exert that influence. Right? *Right?* Unless the damn thing had a vendetta, they should be in the clear as far as that goes.

At a few minutes after noon, her phone rang, and she answered it without looking at the screen. Shawn was so dug-in to her work that answering the phone was almost instinctive. She did have different ring patterns set to differentiate outside calls from those made from within the office. But when she was this deep in the code, she didn't even give it a chance to finish its first chirp. The receiver was up off the cradle and against her ear in a flash, her right wrist twisted in an upside-down position to hold it.

"Stedwin," she said robotically into the receiver.

"Stedwin! Prescott. What's up, my fair lady?"

Shawn made an *ew* face. "I'm not going to bother asking what that means, Blake," she said. Ever since she had so effectively shut down his advance at the hotel, he had become a turn-off to her, sexually. What once had been attractive was now repulsive to her. And it wasn't the come-on that had done it. Or maybe it was. A shot had been taken, missed, and now he was paying for it. Either way, she had no time for his flirtations. He was all business now, as far as she was concerned. "What can I do for you?" she said, before he had a chance to explain what he had meant.

"Oh. Well, uh, how was your new year?" he tried.

"I don't know. Ask me that on December thirty-first," she said. It wasn't quite a *snap*, but it was close. She was back to typing an email, the phone uncomfortably pinched between her collar and her ear.

"Wow. Someone's a little flus-"

"Blake!" she almost shouted. "What do you need, sir?"

"Sorry, Shawn, I uh…" he started, but clearly wasn't prepared with anything beyond the flirtatious opening. "I'm just um…"

"Call me back when you figure it out," she said, and dropped the phone back into its cradle. Almost instantly, she sobered, then straightened up and stared at the phone. *Oh my God. I've been exceptionally rude. He is a client, after all…* She almost willed the phone to ring again so she could apologize. What the hell was she thinking?

It rang. She picked it up and opened her mouth to speak. She didn't get a chance.

"Shawn. I'm sorry for wasting your time. I called to check on things. I mean, I know you guys are probably being bombarded. But I wanted to see if… if… God!" he said loudly. He was trying, bless his heart. He was flustered himself now, and trying to race against a clock that shouldn't even be ticking. "I'm sorry, Shawn! Please don't hang-"

"Blake! Relax, dude. It's fine," Shawn said in her most reassuring voice. "I just meant I don't have time for small talk today."

She heard him breathe in and say *okay* under his breath. Then she stepped back a little further. "Blake, I'm the one who should be saying I'm sorry." She paused. "I'm sorry. What can I do for you?"

He sighed again and audibly overcame his hiccup. Was she really that intimidating? No way. "Shawn, I just want to check that our server is in good health and doing what it should be. You know," he said.

Shawn held the phone away from her face and frowned at it. *What the fuck?* Then she put it back to her ear. "You mean Darla can't tell if the server is up?"

He sighed yet again. "Yes. The server is fine. I was just calling to see…" he started and stopped.

"Spit it out, Prescott," she said in a firm tone.

"Well, just calling to check on you. To see how *you're* doing."

Shawn leaned back in her chair. It squeaked loudly. She turned so that she was not facing her monitor. And she thought about this question, and the gesture of his calling. Then she forced herself to take a deep breath. And then she answered. "That's a funny question, Blake."

"I'm sorry. I promise, I'm not trying to waste your time! I just…"

"Blake!" she said loudly. "It's fine. Thank you for calling. Now shut the fuck up and let me think about my answer."

"Yes, ma'am."

"I'm guessing you're calling of your own accord. Not for Darla," Shawn said.

"Affirmative," he said.

"How is she, by the way?" Shawn asked tentatively. "She called me the other day and left a-"

"I know. I was there when she left it. I'm sorry about that," he said. She could hear in his voice the sincerity. If nothing else, this guy was genuine.

"Well, she has a right to be concerned. But I can assure you that no one here…" Shawn started, then covered her eyes with her free hand. Rubbed her temples. "Blake, I uh…"

"Shawn. This is off the record. I got you, sister."

She smiled and nodded, then leaned forward, putting her elbows on her desk. "Thank you, Blake.

That means a lot." She had to take a moment, lest she short the phone out with her tears. The stress was beginning to rear its ugly head in the most inconvenient times and places. "It's been rough. Phew. But what I was saying… I can assure you that no one here had any idea that was going to happen with your satellite."

Blake did not immediately respond. A quick *Oh, I know* might have felt great to Shawn for a moment, but it would have been hollow. She realized that. And she realized that he knew that. But at the same time, she could feel that he was not deliberating just for the sake of her feelings. When he finally spoke, she got the feeling it was nothing but genuine. Once again.

"Is that true?" was all he said.

She nodded. "Yup. I can tell you, again, off the record," she said, "that yes, Sa-… *We* definitely… set in motion… the events…" she finally trailed off. Why was this so difficult to say? Well, because it was not scripted. That was why. But nor was Blake Prescott interrupting her. He waited patiently for her to find her words, politically correct and honest. And he was smart enough to know that those two terms were sometimes mutually exclusive.

Shawn Stedwin rubbed her temples again, leaned back in her chair and put one socked foot up on the corner of the desk. "Blake, we caused it to happen. But no one here *meant* to cause it. No one here knew it was going to happen."

Blake cleared his throat in one of those ways that sounded incredulous. "Shawn, I don't know how that could be possible, but as a friend, I'm going to take your word for it. The fact that you're man enough to admit culpability is pretty hard to overlook."

"Thank you for that," she said, ignoring the chuckle he sent through the phone. She glanced at the doorway.

"One of us was involved in a certain project that might have… *gotten out of hand*… and taken control of a server. That just happened to be your server."

"Are you asking for forgiveness?" Blake asked. She could hear the smile in his voice.

"Hell no!" she snapped. "Did you not hear me say *'off the record'*?"

"Okay. Just checking. But I guess my real question," Blake said, "Is… Well, I guess, is it under control now?"

"Yes," Shawn said simply. And after a pause, "I'm sorry I can't tell you more."

"Shawn, it's not hard to guess. I was there when you saw the picture of the dead man looking up at the satellite."

When she had hung up with Blake, Shawn had been comfortable that PanaView was not about to press charges for their satellite's disappearance because of the dead man brought back to life. Of course, the connection between the two events was so tenuous it was almost non-existent. And if one took it further, one would see the only connection was someone's word; someone's testimony that there was a trade. A barter. A tit-for-tat. Simply put, PV's satellite disappeared because someone had made a deal with an AI computer. That was not a tangible object by which the two events could be connected.

Maybe that wasn't what Darla had called about. Shawn had to remind herself that she was no lawyer. But there didn't seem to be anything for the company to worry about. While her company might very well go down for the mishandling of a cadaver, there was surely no way they could be legally liable for the displacement of a satellite.

Shawn had to stop and think about this for a moment. *Wait! They aren't claiming a connection between those two things!* What two things, then? Well, the other thing was the AI computer Sameer had built. So, realistically speaking, there were *three* things that were at play here: a misbehaving satellite, an errant AI computer and a cadaver brought back from the dead. When she broke it down like that, she realized that her company was responsible for all three of those things. Two directly and one indirectly.

She had not gotten any real time alone with Sameer lately, and was beginning to believe that was by design. Shawn felt like Jeremy was running interference for him, at least to some extent. She knew the two were very close, and had enough dirt on each other to bring one another down if it ever came to blows, but why now? Why with this? Jeremy seemed to have been unaware of the depths to which Sameer had gone with his own AI tinkering.

On her way out of the office, Shawn decided to test the theory. She stopped by Sameer's office, pointedly having gone the long way so as to avoid darkening Jeremy's doorway. His door was closed. She knocked and tried the knob but it was locked. She then peeked in the window through the blinds as best she could, and saw that it had been a fool's game. Jeremy was already in there. The two men were deep in conversation about something. Shawn sighed and rolled her eyes, then turned and left.

As she came off the elevator in the parking garage, she pulled her phone out, checking the texts that had gathered over the last hour or so. With her face in her phone – a habit Cory had been long trying to break her of – she walked right up to her car without ever seeing the car right next to hers. As she was unlocking her door, the driver's window of the other car went down silently.

"Shawn!" a voice whispered.

Shawn yelped and spun round, putting her hands up to her chest in a defensive posture. It was Chandra, sitting in her car. "Sweet fuck, you scared me, woman!"

"Yeah, hey, sorry. You should really be more aware of your surroundings. Especially in a parking garage!" Chandra whispered.

Shawn rolled her eyes and looked around. "Yeah, Cory always says that, too," Shawn said. She was now leaning against her door with her arms crossed, her purse hanging from one elbow and her phone against her breast. "Why are you whispering?"

"Get in!" Chandra said, motioning with her head. Shawn looked around and shrugged, sighed, then walked to the passenger side of the other woman's car.

The door had a satisfying *clump* to it as she pulled it closed. It smelled sweetly of leather and perfume. Chandra had rolled her window back up while Shawn rounded the front of her car. Now she leaned over and put her hand on Shawn's forearm across the center console. "Shawn. I'm leaving."

Shawn nodded. "Yeah. That's what I was about to do myself, before this creepy, strange woman whispered at me in the parking garage."

Chandra made a lemony smile and said, "No. Like leaving the company. I just wanted you to know."

Shawn's face dropped. "Wh-" she started, but realized she didn't need to finish. She thought she had a pretty good idea *why.* The question she now thought she should be asking herself was *why the hell am I* not *leaving?* And it was a damned fine question. Was it just the salary? She made really good money, so that was definitely at least part of it, but she could make good money anywhere doing the same thing. Well, there was a tricky concept. *Not exactly the same thing...* Managing servers, wrangling code – sure, all that. But in a place where they didn't bring dead people back to life and cause satellites to make spontaneous trips into the past. Now that she thought about it, she realized she would have to actually spend some time thinking about it. And all this was going through her head as she stared at some million-miles-away place between Chandra's thighs and the steering wheel. And Chandra was remaining silent. She had seen the thought explode into her mind, and was now watching as it prospered; matured.

Shawn finally looked up at her. "What made you just decide? Are you scared?"

Chandra nodded soberly. "Shawn, I'm getting too old for this stuff. I don't need this kind of stress in my life."

"I hear that," Shawn said, nodding herself. She returned her gaze to that distant place a few feet away from her as she thought. She reckoned Chandra was in her late forties. Shawn would be in her mid-thirties herself soon, and wondered if *that* was even too old for this shit. Sameer, in his upper fifties, was *definitely* too old to be behaving like a college-age scientist who's just discovered the Bunsen burner. "Where are you going to go?"

"I don't know yet," Chandra said, looking straight out the front windshield. "I know that's not the smartest move, but Conrad and I have plenty of savings. And he does well enough. I'll be okay for a few months." She looked at Shawn, squeezed her arm. "I've really enjoyed working with you and getting to know you, Shawn. You're an amazing young lady."

"Well thank you," Shawn said, smiling broadly. "I have, too." After a moment, she added, "I'm sad about this. I'm gonna miss having you around."

"Well, you have my number. Call me sometimes. We'll get together and have dinner or something."

"You bet I will," Shawn said.

Chandra returned her eyes to the front and put both her hands on the wheel. "I am scared to death, Shawn. This company... The things we do here in the back rooms..." She looked back at Shawn, shaking her head slightly. Her lips were trembling. Her eyes might have been a little glassy. "It's so *frightening!*"

Shawn nodded, understanding. Her lips were pursed tightly.

"It's almost unbelievable. I mean, who wakes people from the dead?" Chandra asked, seriously. She was shaking her head again.

"I know. It's unreal. And I thought we were done with all that like, what – ten months ago?"

"Apparently not," said Chandra. "Anyway, take care of yourself. I'm running. I don't even want to give notice. Sameer has been so good to me, I hate to do that to him, but I just don't want to be part of what's about to go down. I'm going to disappear for a while."

Shawn nodded again. "I understand. Are you letting him know at all?"

The other woman nodded soberly. "I'll be sending him an email tonight." She stared at Shawn for a long moment. "Take care of yourself, okay? I mean," she said, and actually wiped a tear from her eyes. "I hate to sound like a mom, but make good choices, okay?"

Shawn knew exactly what she meant. She smiled, and reached over to take Chandra's hand this time. "I will. Be careful out there," she said. Then Chandra leaned in and pulled Shawn to her in a hug. They embraced for a good solid minute, in which time Shawn realized subliminally that this was goodbye. All the talk about dinners and get-togethers was just pleasantry. Smoke. When Chandra pulled out of this parking garage in the next few minutes, Shawn would never see her again.

As Shawn stepped through her front door and dropped her keys on the table, she dropped her hands to her sides and sagged her shoulders in a hyperbolic gesture, looking at Cory, who stood in the kitchen drinking directly from the orange juice carton. "Thank God tomorrow's Friday," she said with a sigh.

"Ah, have you had a rough week, babe?" he asked, wiping his mouth and offering her the carton. She accepted and took a long pull for herself. "There. A little OJ always makes the day better."

"Yes, it's been a rough week. Even though I've only worked two days this week."

Cory came forward and wrapped his arms around her. "Wanna talk about it?"

"Nah. Chandra just quit."

"What? Just like that?" he asked, then took another drink. "I mean, did she give notice?"

"Nope," Shawn said, making a popping sound at the end of the word.

"That's crazy," Cory said. He turned back to the fridge to put the juice back.

"Shit must be getting pretty bad when the finance exec just walks out."

"No doubt," Cory said. He leaned back against the counter and looked at her. Shawn crossed her arms and leaned sideways against the table in the nook. "So, have you avoided the media?"

She tilted her head and raised her eyebrows. "So far, yeah." She stared at him for a long moment. "Cory, do you think I should quit, too?"

Cory nodded, but not in a way that made her think it was his response. It was a gesture that represented his consideration of the subject. "That's what's got you worked up?"

Shawn nodded.

He shrugged and made a face. "We should never feel like slaves to our jobs. If you're not happy there anymore, then yeah, I think you should quit."

She thought about it for a few seconds and then said, "Yeah, it's not that I'm unhappy. I just wish it were a little more *normal*. It sometimes feels like I'm working for Area 51. And there's so many NDAs and so much shit I can't talk about. It's pretty lonely sometimes." Shawn breathed in and stretched her arms above her head, arching her back, trying to get it to pop. "I sometimes wish it was more boring."

Cory giggled. "I got you. Well, I think it's definitely something you should consider with a more than just a casual thought."

Shawn nodded and gave him a weak smile, then headed for the bedroom to shed her clothes and take her evening shower.

Friday morning was full of hope. But by lunch, Shawn realized it was precocious to have thanked God today was Friday. There was nothing to be thankful for. Everything seemed to be blowing up. No one had heard from Sameer. Jeremy was slammed with extra work, trying to pick up some of the slack because of it. The phone would not stop ringing. And to top it all off, Shawn had an inexplicable headache. She hadn't even had a drink the night before. But somehow, it was here, and no amount of aspirin would make it go away.

PanaView, Incorporated had sent a certified letter to Shawn canceling their service contract, effective one week from today. Shawn, upon opening and reading the letter, sighed and dropped her hands to her sides, staring up at the ceiling and shaking her head. Off-boarding a client was almost more intensive than the on-boarding process. She would have to meet with whatever new company PV chose to manage their outsourced IT, and pass over the reigns. This also meant removing all BlueBird's access credentials from the server and destroying the certificate on their own server.

Shawn was sad to lose that account, as they had been fine customers for something like a decade – long before Shawn had started with BlueBird. She would also miss her friendly banter with Blake Prescott. It was not beyond her that the move could be political, as in PV trying to distance themselves from the company that was all over the news. And it might even be a smart move in that regard, as BlueBird employees would no longer be able to discuss any specifics about PanaView. Data privacy and all that. No matter the reason, it left her feeling shitty and guilty. Shawn thought it was a little shitty of Darla not to at least call and warn her of the plans to leave, what with the somewhat decent relationship they had developed over Shawn's short tenure. And what about Blake? Where was he? Probably directed by Darla *not* to call Shawn. It would be 'inappropriate'.

Constance had called earlier asking if her job was safe. Clearly, she had been watching the news. Shawn told her that nothing was certain, but that there was no reason for Constance herself to feel endangered. If anyone went down, they might all go down. It was likely an all-or-nothing scenario, seeing as how the owner and CEO was the most likely to be in trouble.

When Shawn entered the break room and saw Jeremy leaning against the counter and staring up at the TV, she sagged her shoulders and rolled her eyes. Again. It seemed like there was no escaping the bad news. And *on the news* they were talking about how to prosecute a man who was technically considered dead. Apparently, Calvin Graves was currently catatonic. According to sources in the corrections department, he had lain down and gone unresponsive almost as soon as they had put him in the cell. This was what had prompted the medical examination, and the rest was now history.

And what to do about that? Shawn thought it odd he had gone completely catatonic. Did they mean *dead* or comatose? It was a legitimate question, she thought. Because, considering the fact that he was already technically dead, she couldn't be sure his heart had even been beating when he was robbing those ATMs. She had no idea how the AI had managed to make the corpse get up and walk out of the lab, much less, to continue walking and moving all the way to Michigan. Was the heart doing its job in some accelerated electronic fashion made possible by the wealth of knowledge now in his brain?

Each question, Shawn realized, led to more questions. This thing about the man's brain… Was it now the home of the AI's great intellect? Again, she had no idea how the damned thing had made the transfer to a physical aspect from the computer in the other room. Had it used an electronic implant of some sort? Was the man now wired like a fucking Ethernet hub, his brain attached to external storage devices and USB thumb drives? Her immediate instinct was to giggle at that thought, but she realized almost instantly that nothing was out of the question when it came to this situation. How the hell else could a computer transfer its personality to a cadaver? Michael Crichton's *Terminal Man* came to mind.

She looked at the TV and felt herself getting more nauseated by the minute. So far, at least since she had been in here, they had not said anything about her company's involvement in the matter. They were completely focused on the dead man himself. That was good, she thought, but it meant Chandra had been wrong when she had said collecting the man shouldn't be such of a much. She had spoken as if the dead man was their *property* to go pick up. Like a dog taken to a pound. "Yep, he's here. Come get 'em." It was not sounding much like they were waiting for someone to come claim ownership – or *stewardship* – of the living corpse. They were intent on prosecuting.

This meant the case against BlueBird for having brought him back from the dead with the intention of sending him back into the world was a completely separate one. It would likely be a civil case, therefore, brought about by the family of the decedent. That could be good news. Well, *better* news, at least, all things being relative.

Every time the news station pasted his image up on the screen, it made Shawn's skin crawl. He not only looked like he should be dead, but that he should maybe *never have been alive* to begin with. She guessed death and reanimation could do that to someone. Her mind returned back to the question about the brain. If the man was actually catatonic, or if he was truly and actually fully dead again, then what did that mean for the AI? Had it transferred down the line somewhere? Like the lost soul in the Denzel Washington movie, *Fallen*? Or had it uploaded itself to the internet, having no more use for the body of ole Mr Graves? Maybe Chandra had the right idea, disappearing for a while until things blew over. This was likely to get ugly.

Shawn took a mug from the cabinet and filled it with steaming coffee and then left the break room, bound for her office. And that was when her phone started its real ringing.

The first call was from the local Fox affiliate. "Good afternoon, this is Steven Bradley from Fox. Do you have time for a few questions?" She said no and hung up. Then it was CBS asking if this was Marcella Stedwin, and could she tell the caller what had really happened with Calvin Graves? *Oh my God!* It had begun. The first hour there were five calls. The next there were seven more. She finally had to put her phone on Do Not Disturb, only allowing through calls from people in her contacts list.

At three o'clock, Sameer called. Shawn, barely able to keep her head from feeling like it was going to explode, answered on the first ring, and aggressively. "Where the hell are you, Sameer?"

"I am at home, Shawn. What is the matter there?"

"What is the matter?" Shawn almost screamed. She had a hand in her hair, and it was pulling. "Are you serious? The whole world is blowing up!"

"Please calm down, Shawn. I am sure that everything will be fine," he said, somehow able to maintain his calm in spite of her angry shouting. Jeremy appeared at her door, hands in his jeans pockets and leaning against the jamb.

Shawn nodded and held a hand up, a *yeah, I figured* gesture that he read and smiled. He always seemed to appear when Sameer was in trouble. "Nothing is going to be fine, Sameer. Everything is going to shit, and you're at home hiding out? We're all up here answering phones from news anchors and trying to keep servers from blowing up, and you're at home with your tail between your legs?" She could feel her fury escalating with each word, her pulse throbbing hard and fast in her neck. She was likely to have a stroke if she didn't dial it back a notch, and pretty quickly.

"Shawn. I am not hiding out," said Sameer Singh.

"Oh yeah? Well, did you know that Chandra quit?" she said, and made eye-contact with Jeremy. She saw surprise register in his eyes. Had Sameer actually come *in* to the office this morning, he would have seen the email from her that she presumably sent last night, and he would have told Jeremy about it. Obviously something in that chain had broken down.

"Shawn…"

"Yeah, Chandra quit. Just walked right the fuck out! And PanaView?" she said, smiling crazily. "Yeah, they quit us too! I got a certified letter today!" Shawn was pulling her hair madly now, and tears were beginning to sting her eyes. Jeremy, shocked at this last news flash as well, now came forward, shaking his head. He came around the desk and tried to take Shawn in his arms, squatting beside her office chair.

"Shawn," Sameer said again. "I am not hiding out."

"Oh my God, stop saying that!" Shawn said, shouting at the phone. Her right hand was waving in front of her face. Jeremy had his arms wrapped round her, pinning her arms against her torso from the elbow up, whispering something in an effort to calm her down. But it wasn't working. She was trembling – nay, quaking now. And the tears of stress were now coming hard, quickly degenerating into a full-on sob.

"Shawn," Sameer tried once more. "I am being held hostage."

Shawn screamed and dropped the phone, covering her face with both hands and trying to stand up. Jeremy's embrace prevented it, but not without effort. And then she was turning toward him, burying her face in his chest as he pulled her out of her chair, where she fell onto his lap and he held her like a bereaved daughter, stroking her head and rocking her back and forth. She seemed to be alternating between fits of hard, body-wracking fits of bawling and short bouts of screaming, and this went on until she was numb and drained, and everything sounded muffled and far away in her head. After that, she could not have spoken for.

"They're calling it a panic attack," said Cory. He was much lower than Shawn, sitting in a plastic chair beside the elevated hospital bed. At some point, she had become aware that she was alive. She did not remember anything beyond Jeremy pulling her out of the chair. And she did not remember waking up. It was just something that finally became known.

"Is that what they call nervous breakdowns now?" she asked, hoarse from all the screaming. Cory was holding her hand, and she was aware there was an IV stuck in that wrist.

He shrugged. "You had a rough morning. Call it whatever you want. You should probably take some time off," Cory said. He looked at her for a moment, a serious pain in his eyes. "Babe, this job is killing you. Like I said last night, you should-"

"It's not killing me, Cory. I'm just going crazy." The nurse walked into the room and asked how she was feeling, if the sedative was beginning to wear off. *Oh. That's why I'm fuzzy in the brain.* She nodded and tried to smile. She wanted to come across as completely sober, completely ready to be discharged. Maybe that wasn't the best course of action right now.

When the nurse left the room, she continued. "I've seen shit at this place that no one should ever witness. Things have happened that I can't process, Cory!" she said. She felt like she was shouting, but with the raw vocal cords, it came off as a raspy whisper. "I will never be able to get them out of my head. Like, this is my new reality!"

He was shaking his head. "So, maybe you should not go back to that place, Shawn!" he said in a pleading tone, squeezing her hand for emphasis.

"It's not the place! That's what I'm saying! It's the memories of the shit we've done in that place!"

He sat back and held his hands up, arms spread to the sides. "What's the difference? You think they're just going to stop doing crazy shit there? All of a sudden?"

Shawn opened her mouth to retort, but clapped it shut. He had a point. What crazy next-level impossibility would she find herself entwined in next week? Next month? Sameer was a scientist, and a tinkerer – always fascinated by the *what-ifs* that most people only talked about around campfires. He was not likely to stop dabbling in things that would horrify her. She either had to suck it up and get used to it, or get the hell out of there.

A thought suddenly hit her and she turned and grabbed Cory's hand with a force. "Cory! Did they rescue Sameer?"

He stared blankly at her.

"Cory, what are you doing?"

He shook his head. "What do you mean, 'what am I doing'?" He leaned forward and tried to comfort her with his hands. "What are you talking about, rescue?"

"When he called he said he was being held hostage!"

It took several minutes for Shawn to get anyone to take her seriously. The main argument seemed to be that no one would say such a thing. It would be the hostage-taker – the one making the demands – who would want to be on the phone. Wouldn't it? Shawn said that was nonsense. There was no code of conduct for how hostage situations were supposed to play out! By the time she finally got someone to commit to looking into the situation, she was in tears again, trembling and stressed and scared.

The nurse who had given her the first dose of sedative had to return and administer another dose to get her to calm down again. For all of Cory's petting and nurturing, he just simply wasn't helping. For it seemed to Shawn he was just there to contradict everything she said, and it finally got to the point where she wanted him out of the room. She asked him to give her some time alone.

With Cory gone – he had said he would go hang out in the cafeteria for a while – Shawn was able to process the situation a little more effectively. She considered what Sameer had meant by what he said. Was he being literal? There was, of course, a greater-than-zero chance that she was not remembering the conversation correctly. She had, after all, been in a manic state. Hell, she couldn't even be sure she had actually gotten a call from him at this point. She could ask Jeremy. While he had only heard her side of the conversation, he could at least verify that she took the call from Sameer.

Assuming though that Sameer had called, and he really *had* claimed to be under such duress, who would have taken him hostage? Several thoughts came to mind when she considered this. One was a religious cult. Someone who felt like resurrections should be reserved for the Christ and Lazarus. That seemed a little hokey to her, because people who considered themselves holy shouldn't be committing felonies. *Right?* But there was that word cult. That pretty much absolved them from any holdings to standard ways of thinking. It still seemed far-fetched though.

Next on her short list of ideas was a cultist group that wanted the technology he apparently had access to, which was able to bring a body back from the dead. This seemed a lot less unlikely to Shawn, who considered herself to be thinking very sharply, considering she had just been pumped full of barbiturates, and was probably on her way back to sleep city. She glanced around the bed looking for her handbag, inside which she knew she could find her field book and a pen. Of course, she had not brought her purse, because she had not brought *herself.* She would just have to try to remember these brilliant ideas. She squinted her eyes and took a deep breath.

What else is there? She thought for a long moment. Of course it could be the family. The family of the decedent, demanding that Sameer do something about their loved one. Get him home and back in the grave. God, that was dark. But it wasn't completely unrealistic. The word 'hostage' just didn't seem to fit with any of her ideas enough to click. The family would likely go after the university. Or just file a lawsuit.

Shawn laid her head back on the pillow and covered her eyes with her hands. And then she had it. Like a flash of lightning in her brain, she suddenly understood exactly what had happened, who had him, and even where he was. She took her hands off her eyes and pulled her heavy head back up from the pillow, feeling a little woozy from the movement. She looked around for that pen and notebook. Where the hell had she set it? She had just had it, hadn't she? *Oh, yeah, I didn't have it. I forgot my purse.* She looked toward the window. *Shit, that's bright. What time is it, anyway?*

Spreading her hands on the blanket, she rubbed them side to side, like she was making a snow angel in the bed. Feeling the texture against her palms, she slipped from the land of the awake and aware, into something a little cozier. Her thought was lost forever.

Chapter 19

Two officers from the Arlington Police Department made a welfare check at Sameer Singh's residence. His wife answered the door and said that no, nothing was wrong, everything was fine, but that Sameer was up in the bedroom, sick with some kind of flu. Of course, after having heard that he had supposedly claimed to be the victim of a hostage situation, they needed to make contact with him. After voicing their concern to Anjali that someone was worried for his safety, she shrugged and let them in. There were no protests from her, but she did declare that she would not be responsible if one or both of them came down with whatever Sameer was sick with.

A brief visit from the doorway of the bedroom and a check of his ID to make sure they were talking to the actual Sameer Singh satisfied both officers. Someone had obviously been mistaken. One of the officers reported back to Jeremy that Sameer was just sick, and not being held hostage. They had checked the entire house to make sure there were no hostage-takers hiding out, unless it was the tiny human being who called herself his wife, the officer joked, Sameer was just fine. Jeremy was too kind a soul to say anything in retort to this lame attempt at humor. Had it been Chandra the officer had called, he might have gotten an earful from her.

It was Saturday morning when they discharged Shawn. They sent her home with a bottle of chill pills and she was happy to go. When she got home, she immediately started shedding clothes, leaving a trail across the small apartment on her way to the shower. She stood under near scalding water for an inordinately long time, hands against the wall and head bowed to let the water cleanse her from the scalp down. She always hated the way she smelled and felt after being in a hospital.

On the ride home as a passenger in Cory's Jeep, Shawn had stared out the window at the blur of the passing landscape, reflecting on the last few months, and trying to come to a real answer about what she wanted to do. She loved her company. She loved her team. It was a joy working with Jeremy and Constance and Lance. Heck, she even loved Sameer. She would definitely miss Chandra, but out of all of them, Chandra and she had the least amount of interaction. She would, therefore, be the easiest to get over.

The weather had taken a turn for the warm, and the sun was out. Just looking out the window, it appeared to be a beautiful spring day. The digital thermometer on Cory's dashboard read 46° but it wasn't terribly windy. She reckoned she might go for a ride to clear her mind a little. So when she got out of the shower, that's what she did. Her winter gear was warm and comfortable, and she had to admit, she looked pretty damn sexy in it. As she ran up Arkansas Lane, she pictured what she must look like to other drivers: a thin woman in a sleek, all-black getup with a white helmet; her brown hair hanging out the bottom of the helmet, on a matte white motorcycle that always got looks and compliments no matter who was on it. Shawn felt good today. She only hoped it wouldn't be ruined by the onslaught of anxiety about work and all that came with it.

After a few minutes, she came upon the intersection where Lo had lost her life, and a coldness hit her. She found it easier to get through those times nowadays when she did think of Lo. But she did not often come to this intersection, and it always hit her a little harder than normal passing memories. Her mind could not help but repaint the picture of that night. Darkness broken by the reds and blues of police lights, the sirens of ambulances and firetrucks. The horrific scene of a motorcycle cut in half and Lo's head in her lap as she took her last breaths. When the light changed, Shawn was relieved to be leaving the area.

As she rounded the bridge to enter the highway, her phone lit up, held in place against her handlebars with a steel phone mount. It wasn't a number she necessarily recognized, but the caller ID told her it was UTA, the University of Texas at Arlington. Alarm bells went off in her head. She pressed the answer button on the communicator on the side of her helmet. Being a full-face enclosure, she was able to have somewhat normal conversations inside the helmet.

When she answered, a woman with a cheerful voice said, "Hello, is this Marcella Stedwin?"

Shawn responded in the affirmative.

"Hello. I'm sorry, to bother you on a Saturday, but I've been given no notice myself. Oh, sorry, my name is Lindsay Glover. I'm with the Cadaver Lab here at UTA, where your company gets its cadavers for research?" said the woman.

Gah. Cadaver Lab? Couldn't they have found a better name for it? "Okay," Shawn said. To this point, she had not even been sure from which university they were getting their bodies. *Had gotten*, she corrected herself. They didn't actively take in new subjects these days. She had only ever heard Sameer say the word 'university' when referring to the source. She guessed it made sense though, as UT was the biggest college in Arlington. She had never been part of that side of the process though, and wasn't sure what help she could be to this woman.

The woman answered that question in short order. "So we have been tasked with retrieval of a lost cadaver," she said. After a brief, uncomfortable pause in which Shawn wasn't sure what to say, Lindsay added, "I'm sorry, I know this sounds hokey. They have all these political terms for things. You know who I'm talking about though, right?"

"Yes. Graves?" Shawn said, and wondered again why this woman was calling *her*. It could be easily surmised why Sameer was not having this conversation right now; he was out of pocket. What the hell was going on with that, anyway? Jeremy had texted her telling her Sameer was merely sick, and not a hostage, but she still had so many questions. Like, how had she misheard what he said? How had she been *that* far off? Was she already hysterical by the time that came up?

But how did this Lindsay woman even get Shawn's number? She had had nothing to do with that man's resurrection. And certainly not sending him back out into the world. A shiver ran up her spine in spite of the cozy riding coat she was wearing.

"That's the one. Anyway, I have to go collect him, and need a representative from your company to escort me. Would that be you?"

Shawn thought about it for a moment. The only other true candidate behind Sameer would be Jeremy. She could try him, but something about this woman's voice had given Shawn a good feeling. She felt like she might have a good time riding with her, at the very least. *I mean, assuming the man is dead – truly dead, ha ha, then how hard could it be?* "I suppose it could be me," she finally said. "What all is actually involved?"

"We drive a hearse up to Peru and sign some papers, then come home with him," Lindsay said.

Shawn blinked, shook her head. "Where the hell is Peru?"

"It's a couple hours north of Indianapolis," she said. She was giving Shawn plenty of time to process each statement she made. After the appropriate pause, she said, "It's about a fifteen-hour drive from Arlington, so we would want to stay overnight somewhere at the halfway point. All in all, that makes it a three- or four-day affair."

Shawn was always excited by little excursions such as this. Little getaways to places she had never been always sounded exciting. And if she was right, and this woman Lindsay and she hit it off, maybe they could find some shopping or something to do on the way. Of course, it would *have* to be on the way up there. Probably wouldn't do to leave a dead body in the back of a car while they went shopping. Shawn felt the chills forming again. There was a thought she had not yet covered: driving fifteen hours in a car that had a dead guy in the back didn't quite match the little adventure she had been picturing thus far. When she had left the project a year ago or so, she had been as near certain as one could be that she would never again be involved with the deceased. Inasmuch as someone could promise never to involve oneself with the dead again, she had done so. Loved ones not included, of course.

Still, it did sound like an adventure. And she could definitely use the break from work. She decided to let Jeremy off the hook for this one. Though it should have been Sameer from the get-go, she had written him off in that part of her mind that expected anything immediate from him. Jeremy could handle her reports for a few days, and there was nothing pressing in the office, so she made the command decision that she would take care of this unlovely errand, for the good of the company.

She cleared her throat and said, "So when are we leaving?"

Sunday morning, Shawn was up at her historically usual time, around five o'clock. On mornings where something exciting was happening, there would be no staying in bed beyond that even if she took an Ambien. And she loved road trips. She had packed a five-day bag the night before, in keeping with what her father had taught her about over-preparedness. *"If it's a five-day trip, pack for six. You may have an unfortunate accident – the kind no one likes to think about."* While this hadn't happened to Shawn yet, she knew it was possible, and had always followed the advice. The bag sat behind the couch by the front door, zipped up and ready for her to grab on the way out.

After she poured her first cup of coffee, she walked to the back door and slid it open, stepping out onto the minuscule balcony, looking across the courtyard for that wonderful sign of life from her friend's apartment. Alas, it was not there this morning. At least not yet. She would have to forgo saying goodbye to Micha. And Shawn had been so manic the night before, skittering here and there just getting things together that she might need and telling Cory all about it, that she had forgotten to call her friend and let her know she was leaving. Oh well. She could call her on the road if she needed. Undoubtedly, Micha would be calling her later this morning if Shawn didn't call first.

She came back inside and paced, looking around the apartment for other items of curiosity that might be useful on a long, mostly-boring road trip to another state. Lindsay would be picking her up at seven o'clock, and Shawn wanted to have something to show her, or something to talk about if the trip got too quiet. She had never been in a hearse, so there was that to talk about, at the very least. She reckoned that statement was true for most of the living population. Only morticians and dead people had been in hearses. *Right?*

The hearse was not the standard black Cadillac with the decorative symbol that immediately invoked images of one's last ride. Shawn was thankful for this as soon as she came down the stairs and saw the van sitting between the handicap spots. It was more like a bread van or a delivery truck, or an ambulance without the lights and paint job. As she came out from under the overhang of the breezeway, the driver's door popped open and Lindsay stepped out to introduce herself.

Shawn's first thought was that she looked nothing like her voice. This woman was tall and slender, striking in her appearance, like she had just walked off the catwalk.

What the hell is she doing working for the Dead Body Lab or whatever it's called?

"Hello!" Shawn said, stepping down off the curb with her hand extended, smiling. "I'm Shawn!"

The woman shook her hand, but was frowning, her mouth opened in confusion as she studied the situation. The woman approaching her, Shawn, that was, had the right voice, and she had a duffel bag hanging from her left hand. But she had the wrong name. "I'm sorry, did you say, 'Shawn'?"

"Yep," said Shawn. "Oh, shit, sorry. My name is Marcella Shawn." She shook her head to show she was no stranger to the confusion it caused.

The woman lifted her chin and smiled, and her grip suddenly got firmer before she let go of Shawn's hand. "Okay. I thought, 'who is this strange woman that thinks I'm her Uber?'" she said with a laugh. Shawn laughed too. They were interrupted by a third voice, shouting from behind Shawn, in the darkness of the breezeway.

"Hey, yo, bitch! Where the fuck you goin'?"

Shawn turned around, startled, and shielded her eyes against the rising sun to see into the breezeway. Why the hell were the lights not working in there, anyway? She was greeted by a familiar face and she rolled her eyes. Micha was casually strolling toward them with a paperboard cup of coffee hanging from her fingertips.

Shawn looked over her shoulder at Lindsay and said, "That's my friend, Micha." She rolled her eyes again and stepped up onto the sidewalk to meet her. "I forgot to call you last night, bub. I'm sorry."

"Well, you should be. Where are you going with this gorgeous broad?" she asked, hiking her chin toward Lindsay. Shawn turned in time to see the shock develop on the other's face. Shawn giggled and took Micha by the arm, guiding her toward the newcomer.

"Micha, meet Lindsay."

They shook hands easily enough and Micha smiled at her. "It's nice to meet you. Now who the hell are you, and what are you doing absconding with my girl?"

"Stop it, Mike!" Shawn said, slapping her shoulder. "We're going on a business trip. I'll be back in a few days."

Micha tilted her head, frowning at her. "You're serious? You really forgot to call me?"

Shawn closed her eyes, breathed in deeply. Shook her head. "I'm sorry. I was so busy packing and talking to Cory it slipped my mind." She stepped up and kissed her friend on the cheek. "Can I call you tonight?"

"You better!"

"Interesting friend you've got there," said Lindsay, when they were pulling onto the highway and all the good-mornings and did-you-sleep-wells were finished. "You call her Mike?"

"We both go by our middle names. She's Katy Micha. Yeah, I sometimes call her Mike. She's good people. I think you'd like her," Shawn said.

"Why do you think that?" Lindsay said, looking over at Shawn seriously in the light of the strengthening sun. "A woman who uses foul language and calls her friend pejoratives?"

Shawn's face fell. She pulled her head back. And then Lindsay smiled and winked at her, reached over and slapped Shawn on the knee. "Just kidding. Of course I would like her."

Shawn leaned back and rolled her eyes. "Oh my God, that just proves you would totally love her."

There were not long, lulling periods of silence on the way to their first night stop, which was just outside of Memphis – another place Shawn was excited to be visiting. They made easy conversation, laughed a lot and talked a lot about music and their other interests. Shawn asked about the truck, having noticed that there was only a small wire-enforced window between the cab and the cargo area. There was no door to get back there – which, why *would* there be? - and when the cargo light was off, Shawn couldn't see anything through the window.

It was much like an ambulance, in that it had benches on the side, but mostly they were there to house the refrigeration equipment. While one could sit on them, there wouldn't be much reason to. The dead didn't need company. Shawn was interested in the refrigeration aspect though, and inquired about it. Lindsay talked like it was common knowledge, though not in a condescending manner at all. She told Shawn it was for keeping cadavers chilled on the way from the lab to whatever their research destination was to be. It made sense, and again, as was becoming a pretty common thing in Shawn's life, she found it should have been obvious from the get-go. *Hey, you never know shit until you learn shit.*

Shawn learned that Lindsay was herself a student at the university and had been assigned this task because she actually worked for the department that sent her. She was studying to be a mortician, and had done chores like this several times before. She had been with the department for a few years now, and was no stranger to that type of work. She was twenty-four years old, and almost done with her post-graduate degree. She had started college while still in high school, taking dual-credit courses.

Shawn liked Lindsay from almost the first moment she had spoken to her on the phone. There was just something about people who gave off a particular vibe, and when Shawn picked up on it, just knew they would make fast friends, at least if ever put in the proper environment together. This several-day excursion might not be long enough to develop the steam needed to fuel an interest – at least from Lindsay's perspective – but Shawn could tell they had a lot in common. They both liked the same music, and that was always a big deal to her. For one, Lindsay had a tattoo on her collarbone that read *Find Me In Your Fire*, a line from a popular song by the band One Last Orbit. Shawn knew the band well, and had attended one of their concerts.

They stopped for gas in a town northeast of Texarkana called Prescott. And Shawn would not have thought twice about it, except that just fifteen miles before, they had passed through a town called Hope. As in Blake Prescott and Darla Hope. Shawn opened her mouth to comment on it as soon as it dawned on her, but then decided against mentioning anything to do with the satellite.

After gassing up, they grabbed a late brunch in Prescott and freshened up before hitting the road again. They had about three more hours of driving to do before they would reach Memphis, the near-halfway point. That three hours blew by like a stiff breeze, and Shawn found reason to question why they were stopping at all. It was only four o'clock now, and they had another few hours of daylight to go, and neither of them were that tired.

Lindsay turned to look at her and said, "Trust me, you'll be thankful when we set our bags down on the beds."

Shawn giggled and put her hand on Lindsay's arm, reaching across the narrow console. "Honey, I could drive until midnight and still have whiskey before I went to bed." Shawn was only thirty-one herself, but guessed she had grown up a lot in those extra few years she had over Lindsay.

"Okay, well *I'll* be thankful," Lindsay corrected, and smiled cheerfully. "I hate driving and I hate even worse riding as passenger."

"Oh yeah? Why so?"

"I get a little carsick when I'm in that seat. No idea why. Even if I'm watching the road the whole time, just something about not having my hands on the wheel and feet on the pedals, I don't do well."

"Feet?"

Lindsay turned to look at her. "Huh?"

"You said 'feet'. *Feet* on the pedals. You drive with both feet?"

"Oh. No," she said. Then she rolled her eyes. "God, you're so literal, Shawn!"

"Just trying to keep it fun," said Shawn.

"Thank you for that," Lindsay responded.

Shawn got her wish of visiting Memphis. It was Sunday evening and they had a bunch of time to kill. They had dumped their bags on the floor in the little B&B Lindsay had chosen for the night – she told Shawn that she would never sleep in a hotel again as long as there were B&Bs to choose from – and relieved their bladders. Then they had taken an Uber across the Mississippi to get to the good parts of the city. Fortunately, Shawn discovered, Lindsay was as excited about the nightlife as she was herself. Thank God she hadn't taken this trip with a fuddy dud.

They found a nice barbecue joint that served cold beers and hot brisket and sat across a picnic table from each other under a giant fan that would guarantee their clothes smelled like barbecue for the rest of the night. They tore napkins off a brown paper towel roll and complained about their elbows sticking to the red-and-white checked tablecloth as they ate and got messy, slurping down the suds between bites.

Shawn, between mouthfuls of sausage and beans and potato salad, reached across the table and grabbed Lindsay's wrist, and said, "Thank God you like beer and barbecue. This could have been a really boring night for at least one of us."

Lindsay laughed out loud, and Shawn realized two things at once. Number one, this was just a college student sent on an errand. She wasn't here to judge Shawn or her company for what had happened with the loose cadaver. Hell, she might not even know all the details. Or *any* of the details, come to that. And secondly, that Lindsay didn't think any more about this errand than any of the others she had run. She wasn't acting corporate. She was a responsible representative of the university in that she was not using the company vehicle for personal gain, for instance, but she wasn't going to be all business for the whole trip. She was keeping up with Shawn, nearly sip for sip on their beers, and certainly beer for beer. Their beer glasses had very like amounts of gold liquid in them, and the same beautiful mask of foggy sweat on the outsides.

It was unseasonably warm outside, in the seventies, but the fan overhead still felt good. Shawn could imagine it was a cool summer day. And halfway through the second beer, she began to feel the effects of the alcohol. That perfect amount was now in her system, performing its ritual, making her feel absolutely like she was on top of the world. She knew this was only a short-lived period – for the alcohol it took to get to this point was several gulps in the past now. By the time one realized she had the perfect amount in her, she had already taken more drinks in an effort not to let the beer get warm. But it was great while it lasted. And she could tell Lindsay was enjoying herself as well.

When they finished their second mug of beer at roughly the same time, they made eye-contact over their empty metal trays, and Shawn lowered her chin, looking mischievously at her new acquaintance through the tops of her eyes. This was a wordless query. An interrogative. And the other girl caught it instantly. Her smile quickly matched Shawn's own, and she held up her empty mug halfway across the table. "Fuck yeah," she said. Shawn laughed out loud, clinking her glass against the other, then stood up to go fetch another round.

They walked the streets for a couple of hours, picking up beers in the dives along the way, stopping occasionally to listen to some band or another. In an alley between two buildings there was an old black man playing the blues on an electric guitar, and shredding so hard that Shawn just had to stop. She grasped blindly at Lindsay's shirttail, stopping her in her tracks, not wanting to take her eyes off the phenomenon. They sat on a picnic bench and watched the man playing licks Shawn couldn't imagine, even lifting it up and picking behind his head on the guitar. It was incredible. Shawn thought the man might have been the best guitarist she had ever heard. And yet, here he was in an alley, instead of on a stage. How many talented humans had the same story? The homeless man who could beat anyone who ever challenged him at chess… The bucket-playing drummer who could make as much sound with his empty buckets as Neil Peart… It was sad in some unreachable place in her heart – she was too drunk to define exactly why or where, but just knew the world was missing out on this talent.

Bullshit! At least, I'm not! And she wasn't. She was sitting here with her new friend getting to witness one of the best to ever play the instrument. To put him on stage and all over the radio was to rob this alley – this little tiny venue – of the intimate performance. This was special. Shawn had no doubt she could walk up to the man and hug him after he finished a song. No way she could do that to Richie Sambora or Keith Richards. So after the song, she walked up and stuffed a ten-spot in his plastic tip jar, and then did just that. "Can I give you a hug, Mister?" She asked.

"Yeah, you can give me a hug!" the old man said. He smelled like cigarettes and streets. Exactly how he was supposed to smell. And Shawn loved it. She even got Lindsay to take her picture with the man before they left the alley on their way to the next musical rush.

It was after midnight that they finally stumbled back to the edge of the music district and pulled up on the door handle of their Uber. They were drunk and laughing and holding onto each other like old friends. Before they dropped into the backseat, it was Lindsay who said, "Hol' up, hol' up… Let's get a picture." They stood by the back door and put their faces together, blowing freeze-frame kisses at the glass of Lindsay's phone screen and took a selfie together.

On the road again, Shawn was feeling the effects of the beer from the night before. It wasn't so much a hangover, but just a reaction to the sheer amount of liquid they had ingested. It took, for instance, far less whiskey to achieve the same effect. So there was less volume of liquid in the stomach at the end of the night. And beer, the barley or hops – or heck, maybe the yeast – just hit Shawn differently than liquor. She didn't feel bad, she just felt like she had drunk a bunch of liquid the night before. She was a little slow in the thinking department, and her arms felt a little heavy as she lugged her duffel bag to the van for the next leg of the trip.

There was the slightest amount of anxious acid in Shawn's stomach as they set off toward the northeast. It wasn't that she was afraid of a dead man being in the back of the truck. It was that she had not had the same experiences as most humans with the dead. She reckoned, in fact, that even Lindsay, who had worked with the dead for years now, had never seen the side of death that Shawn had experienced. That side that didn't technically exist: the waking of the dead. Only a few in history had ever witnessed it, were she to get technical. This was also assuming there weren't some shops around the globe where people were doing exactly what she and Sameer had done in the lab. The experience she'd had as a young girl in watching her aunt die had scarred her. Then watching the dead come back to life had only made that worse. Shawn might actually have PTSD now. Even thinking about death now days was a surefire way to bring butterflies to her stomach and a little dread to her day. She soldiered on through it and tried to keep a smile on her face.

Lindsay promised to stop at the first coffee shop they saw on the way out of Memphis and Shawn held her hand up as if swearing into court, and said, "You're a goddess."

They found their previous night's gait easily enough, and Shawn was happy to know she hadn't said anything too forward or idiotic to need to ask forgiveness. In fact, Lindsay had been the first to bring up the previous night's events, and said to Shawn, "Thank you for last night. I had a great time. I've never really drunk that much before."

"Really?!" Shawn exclaimed. "Well, you did great, sister! You kept up with me beer for beer!"

"Yeah, I didn't feel bad at all, so I just kept going. I've drank before, but I've just never really gone out on a town and done it. That was so much fun."

Shawn smiled broadly at her and said, "Well, I had a great time too. I'm glad to get to be the one to experience that with you."

After they had found a drive-thru coffee shop, a little place called Mack's Morning Mix, they settled into a cruise-controlled lope along Interstate 55 and Lindsay had her right foot up on the seat. It was just past seven o'clock and they were clear of the city well before rush-hour would slow them down. Shawn was happy this gal was an early riser. Too many people waste the best part of the day away sleeping, she thought.

"So what made you want to be a mortician?" Shawn asked, pulling the visor down and twisting it to cover her window. It was too high on the window to block the sun, which was just appearing over the horizon.

"I don't really know how to answer that. I've never had an answer any time someone has asked me. I mean, I'm fascinated by the human anatomy. I'm not scared of death. I just think some of the most interesting medical experiences can happen after death," said Lindsay.

"Explain."

"Well, experiences for the medical personnel. Not necessarily the decedent. There's so much to learn," she said. She took a deep breath and shrugged. "I don't know. I just think I like the peace and quiet of the mortuary. And I like the thought that I'll be helping to give people a good experience with their loved ones."

Shawn shook her head, closing her eyes. "Better you than me, sister."

Lindsay laughed out loud. "Oh, there's been a few creeps, don't get me wrong."

Shawn looked at her. "Creeps?"

"Yeah. Like just a couple of weeks ago, a woman sat up on the table."

Shawn gasped at this, then waved her hands, looking out the window. "Fuck that, I'm out."

"Yeah. Sometimes they exhale. And it always seems to happen while your back is turned. You turn to make a note or to pick something up, and *hhhhhaaa*!" she said, making the sound of a loud expulsion of breath. "It's startling."

"Oh my God, no!" Shawn said. She was rubbing her arms, trying to send the chills back into the flesh whence they had come.

"But see, it never gives me chills. You know? Like it startles me, but it never like creeps me out."

"And yet you call them creeps," Shawn said.

"Yeah. That's what we all call them," Lindsay replied. She shrugged again as if to say *No big deal. The dead sometimes do things.*

Shawn shook her head and returned her gaze to the road. And then Lindsay finally broached the topic Shawn had been dreading. She asked about the guy they were going to collect.

Shawn took a deep breath and thought about it before she answered. "Well, I will tell you that I wasn't the one who brought him back," she started.

"From the Cadaver Lab?"

"No. From…" Shawn said, and stalled suddenly.

Shit! Lindsay didn't even know the man had gone ambulatory? That he had robbed ATMs all over Illinois and Indiana? How could she not know by now? And furthermore, how was Shawn to answer this? Well, she's going to find out at some point anyway – and probably when they pick the guy up from the jail!

"You do know where we're going, right?" Shawn asked. It was the best she could come up with at short notice.

"I'm sorry, you're losing me. You mean, literally?"

"Yeah. Like where the red spot is on your map."

"Okay," Lindsay nodded, "yes. We're going to the Miami County Jail."

Shawn, having not heard the name of the jail until now, had to assume that was right. Of course, there was no reason it wouldn't be. They wouldn't send her, otherwise. "Okay, good. So what do you make of that?"

Lindsay stared straight ahead, chewing her lip for a minute. Shawn didn't want to interrupt, but finally realized that no logical person would come to the answer without assistance. People didn't just wake up from the dead and end up in jail.

"Let's try this: I mean, obviously, you haven't been watching the news…" Shawn said, trailing off.

"Nah, I really don't bother," Lindsay said.

"Yeah, I feel ya. I don't have much use for it either. But in this particular case, I just find it interesting that you could have missed it." Shawn cleared her throat. "Why do you think we're picking up a dead man from a jail?"

Lindsay looked over at her. "Oh my God!" she finally said. Her eyes got wide and she lost her color.

Shawn nodded slowly. "Yup. Now you're getting it."

"Someone stole his body from your company?"
She didn't have it.

Over the next hundred miles, Shawn carefully and with as much discretion as possible, tried to explain to Lindsay what had happened. Lindsay's color never returned. And she was having a hard time believing that a man could be brought back in a manner that would allow him to walk out of a lab and make his way to another state. No need to even mention the ATM robberies. Just getting out of the lab was a big enough hangup for her.

In the end, she came to terms with it, swallowing and looking a lot more somber as they drew ever closer to the destination. And by the time she finally accepted it fully, Shawn realized Lindsay was now on the same level as she herself. She was just as scared of the ramifications of that truth as was Shawn. Shawn could furthermore tell that Lindsay was feeling the same dread about the return trip now, having a twice-dead man riding just a couple of feet behind them. At least he was dead. Again. Well, she *hoped.*

As they pulled off Highway 31 and began to see signs that they were entering Peru, Shawn's nervousness enhanced. She could see the whites of Lindsay's knuckles on the steering wheel and thought she might be experiencing some of the same anxiety. Shawn was sorry to have screwed up her new friend's day – maybe her *life* – but knew it was a necessary evil. She simply *had* to know what they were dealing with, and why.

Main Street was closed for construction, so Lindsay had to detour, touching the map on her phone screen and trying to find her away around it. They ended up driving a few minutes north on Grant, turning right on Logan. On their left was a sprawling well kept cemetery. On the right were old warehouses that looked like airplane hangars, most of them missing their doors – if they ever had doors to begin with – and they were packed full of... *something...* Something colorful. Like...

With a start, Shawn realized what they were looking at. It was old carnival equipment. The broken and defunct ruins of old rides. Here was a hot dog stand, its sign rusted and faded to near illegibility. And there, a steel platform from which hung great colorful bubbles. Some of them had fallen away to form a cluster at the base. It was an old Tilt-a-Whirl. In another shed were stacks of yellow and rust-colored roller coaster tracks.

"We need gas," Lindsay said, startling Shawn back to reality. "It says the nearest one is three minutes away." Shawn gave her a thumbs-up and returned her gaze out the window. They turned left on Broadway and started north. Here was the part of town infected by America: Taco Bells and Walgreens, Dollar Generals and Dairy Queens. She had been enjoying the quaintness – the *uniqueness* – of this quiet little town called Peru with its stories. The haunted remains of old circus and carnival rides surely held many of them. It was sad to see them in such a state of disrepair. What had once held laughing children and smiling adolescents now only held dust and ruin. Why would they leave them out here where everyone could just drive by and see them? Why not bury it all? Recycle it? Heck, maybe even get some of it working again! Probably not, she thought. It looked pretty rough now.

Shawn didn't like the look of the sheds or hangars they were all stuffed in. They looked like haunted houses themselves. Only erected to give them a place to put the abandoned rides. And to what end? It wasn't protecting the old equipment. They were mostly open to the elements. She wondered what horrors lurked in those buildings. Bats, owls and rats, most likely. Three of Shawn's least favorite things.

The gas station was just ahead on the right. A bright red banner overhung the gas pumps and a sign over the door of the store itself read CASEY'S in bold letters of the same color. Lindsay pulled up to one of the pumps and shut the van off, and Shawn stepped out, collecting her empty water bottles and napkins. She tossed them into a nearby trash can and stretched, yawning. The air smelled fresh and clean here. It was cool and sunny, but not biting cold. Anytown, America. This looked like a nice little town, and she found herself wondering about the history of it.

"You need anything inside?" she called over the front of the van. "I'm gonna go relieve the bladder."

"I'll be in in a minute," Lindsay responded. "You want to grab dinner before we – you know…"

Shawn frowned and looked at her phone. "Dinner? At four? Girl, you crazy."

"Well, we gotta eat sometime!" said Lindsay. "I'm starving."

"Okay," Shawn said, pausing as a loud truck rumbled by on Broadway, "so you're saying you don't want to munch on Casey's burritos and potato chips?"

Lindsay stuck her tongue out like she was being sick. "You know, I've never eaten a burrito?"

Shawn laughed and stared at her, but Lindsay's face never changed. Shawn's finally fell. "Wait. Are you serious?"

Lindsay nodded. Shawn covered her mouth. "Oh my God! You have to try one. Look!" she said, pointing across the street. "There's Taco John's. That's where we're eating dinner! My treat!"

A few minutes later, they pulled out of the Casey's parking lot and headed south, just a few hundred feet to Taco Johns, which was across the street from a bank. Peripherally, Shawn's eyes grabbed the street sign and her eyebrows went up. The bank sat on a street called Harrison. *Weird. First there was Hope and Prescott, now there's Harrison.*

They parked and headed for the entrance, past a taco-shaped bench, and were greeted by a sign in the window reading 'inhale tacos, exhale negativity' and Shawn rolled her eyes. She would not be inhaling anything. She pulled the door open and followed

Lindsay inside. They sat in red plastic chairs and ate. Shawn spent a lot of her time watching Lindsay eat her first burrito, continually asking how it was and if it lived up to any expectations.

"You know," Lindsay said, covering her mouth with a finger while she chewed, "I can't say I ever really developed any actual expectations of my first burrito. So I guess that means, this exceeds them all!"

Shawn laughed out loud and they said cheers, clunking their wax cups full of soda together. This would be the last laugh they were likely to share on their multi-state adventure, and Shawn could feel the pressure gathering between her ears and in her chest. When they finished eating, Shawn went to wash her hands, and stared into the surprisingly clean mirror for a long time just studying her own face. *You got this, Shawn. You've endured a lot worse.*

The trip to the police station was almost as short as the one from Casey's to John's. The city hall and police department was just a few blocks farther south on Broadway. She had known this because she had seen it on the map on Lindsay's phone. But it had been a quiet battle in her mind, wishing it would take longer to get there. But now, alas, here they were.

After speaking with a police woman behind a thick pane of bullet-proof glass, they were shown into a small conference room and asked to wait. Shawn felt like that's all she had been doing for the last two days. Now she sat in another plastic chair, this one blue, with her hands between her knees and her knees bouncing nervously. She stared at the pictures on the wall, but grew bored with them very quickly. They were small, and required standing to examine them, and she was not that interested. Lindsay was looking at her phone, but she looked to be fairly relaxed. It was several long minutes before their waiting was interrupted.

A heavyset man with a name tag reading Causey came in and closed the door. "Good evening, ladies," he said, pulling the third chair out with a foot and dropping into it. It creaked in protest as he shifted, slapping the notebook he carried down on the table. He opened it and got right to the point. "We're releasing… Calvin Graves back to the…" and here he searched for a moment, "University of Texas, Arlington. He was arrested for robbery, and died in his cell before a hearing could be mounted."

Mounted? Shawn frowned and looked at her new friend. Lindsay was looking soberly at the officer, her hands folded in her lap. She was chewing her bottom lip. She cleared her throat. "So, he uh… He died in his cell? Meaning…"

Causey looked at her expectantly over the tops of his wire-rimmed specs. "Meaning what?"

"Meaning he was… I mean, I guess, he was living… before," she stumbled, and looked to Shawn for support.

Shawn leaned forward and took over immediately. "Uh, we got reports that he had surgical scars on the chest that were 'inconsistent with life'," she said, bouncing her chin a little for the quotes. "That would indicate that he should have been dead."

The man stared at her for a moment. "I'm sorry, ma'am, I'm not following. He was *alive*," he said, holding his palm up, and then he flipped it over as he said, "and then he *died*."

Shawn nodded. She was about to speak again but Lindsay had once again found her own voice. "How can one be alive with those scars?"

Sergeant Causey leaned back in his chair and crossed his arms. "Well, people come back to life on the autopsy table all the time. People think they're, you know, clinically dead, but they're just not." He shrugged.

The two women looked at each other. Something wasn't adding up. Was there a cover-up here? Or did this man just truly not know the truth? When faced with the facts on paper, Shawn understood it would be nearly impossible for anyone to arrive at the truth on their own. No one's mind would simply *lead* them to believe someone had been clinically dead and come *all the way* back to life. Maybe Causey was just a victim of such reading. He had not been told all the facts of the case. That was good, though, right?

"Okay, so what's next?" Lindsay asked.

"Well, we just have you sign these papers, we have a notary sign and stamp it, and then you're free to go. And take Mr. Graves with you," said Causey, stressing the decedent's last name as if he were going to tell a joke and that was the greatest punchline.

"All right, let's do it," Lindsay said, tilting her head and looking at the paperwork.

"Well, I'll need a copy of your driver's licenses to make sure you are who you say you are," he said, grinning. Shawn thought he was probably a hoot at parties.

Both women reached into their handbags and pulled out billfolds and began searching for their identification. Shawn found hers first and pressed it onto the paperwork with her fingertips. Lindsay was right behind her. The man swooped them up and disappeared through the door saying he'd 'be back in a jiffy'. They both rolled their eyes at each other.

When Causey came back into the small room, he was accompanied by a woman who looked older than the hills. She wore large glasses with a thin gold chain draping from the arms and circling her neck. She didn't seem to notice the two women sitting there waiting to sign the paperwork. She just came in and leaned over the table, twisting the documents so she could look at them. After studying the blank lines for an exceedingly long time, she turned to look at Shawn, comically large eyes dancing around behind the thick lenses, and said, "You need to sign here," stabbing a finger down onto the form.

Shawn raised her eyebrows and forced a smile. "You got it, mama." She picked up the pen and looked at the form. Quickly, she realized it was Lindsay who needed to sign. Shawn handed her the pen and scooted back. "This one's on you," she said. When Lindsay finished signing, the woman seemed to compare the signature to the one on Lindsay's driver license, and then nodded, signed her own scrawl and pulled a stamp from her pale green sport coat pocket. This took longer than one would have expected it to take and Shawn found herself getting terribly annoyed. It wasn't simple impatience at work here. It was more than that. It was maddening to watch how long it took the woman's frail old hand to first of all *find* the pocket, because she refused to look at it – she kept her eyes on the signature she'd just scratched. And then the digging around in the pocket, which, unless there were several other things in there, should have only taken less than a second... *Good God!*

And then it took an interminably long time for her to study the licenses and decide which woman was which, before handing them back to the ladies. As if she couldn't have just handed both to Shawn, who was the closest to her, to let Shawn sort out. Or just set them on the form for the girls to collect. Shawn began to wonder if the woman was being deliberately slow, and then, if there was a reason for it that she might need to investigate. Like, were they being held up to stop them from collecting the man too early or something? Or was something happening out in the other room that they weren't supposed to see? Shawn had time to consider all these things while she waited for the woman to do her business.

She glanced at Lindsay during the fiddling and shook her head ever so slightly. Lindsay half-rolled her eyes. By the time they had their licenses back in their hands and the woman was heading out of the room, at least – Shawn would guess – eight minutes had passed. Doing something that could literally have taken about twenty seconds. She could feel her heart pumping in her neck, and found herself near actual legitimate anger.

Causey, leaning against the wall with his arms crossed, didn't seem bothered by it at all. Shawn guessed he was either used to working with the woman and had the patience of Job, or had just allowed himself to drop into a catatonic state while the ritual of the notarizing took place. Now, he came forward and glanced at the paper that bore everyone's fresh signatures, and slapped the folder closed. "All right, you're free to collect the body. I'll call over and let Don know you're on the way."

Shawn had mistakenly come to believe that the body would still be here at the jail for some reason. In retrospect, she couldn't imagine *why* she should have thought that, but it had just been a mindless assumption, and now she was peeved off about having to go somewhere else and potentially wait even more.

"Where exactly do we need to go?" Lindsay asked, slinging her purse over her shoulder as she stood up.

"The county coroner. It's just down the street'n around the corner. On Third Street," said Causey. He was smiling broadly, as if he was just so happy to have been such a wonderful help to these two ladies. Or maybe he was just happy to be shed of the responsibility of that damn cadaver. *Surely, he knew. Right? Surely he knew!*

They exited the building following the officer as he made small talk, asking about their drive, how long it took and did they pass through anything exciting. He walked almost as slowly as the old woman had performed her part in this act, and the girls were stuck walking behind him. Shawn trailed behind Lindsay with her shoulders sagged, staring up at the ugly ceiling and shaking her head.

When the doors slammed shut on the van, they turned to look at each other, and both women yelled at the same time. "Jesus Christ!" Lindsay shouted. Shawn shouted something less pleasant that had more swear words in it. She was shaking her hands in front of her.

"What in the literal fuck was wrong with those people?"

"I don't know," Lindsay said, turning the key. She was facing forward again, about to get the van moving. Her eyes fell on the stereo clock and she paused, then reached up and tapped it with a mauve-painted fingernail. "Uh, Shawn?"

Shawn looked at the clock. It was 5:03. "So? What are you..." Then she got it. They had been held past five, and likely the coroner would be closed now. At least the public-facing side of it.

Lindsay pulled the shift lever down with a force and backed out of the spot, tires protesting on the asphalt.

She slammed it in drive and dropped her foot on the gas. They ran down Broadway a lot faster than they should have been moving, but Lindsay seemed to be making up for lost time. "I need you to navigate for me. Can you look up the county coroner and tell me where it is?"

"Got you, fam," said Shawn. She heard Lindsay giggle at that as she opened her phone and searched quickly. She copied the address she found and tapped the map icon. Shortly, a route appeared. "Oh, shit, turn right here!"

Just a short way down the road, there it was. An old brown brick building that looked more like a house than a coroner's office. Lindsay slammed on the brakes and skidded to a stop in front of it, instinctively reaching across to hold Shawn back from the sudden jolt. Shawn looked down at the other woman's hand and then across at Lindsay, wondering at what age people developed that instinct.

"Is this it?" Shawn asked. She was leaning forward in her seat, staring out the top of the window trying to read the sign that stood out in the grass on the corner of the lot. "It says funeral home…"

"Yeah, that's it," Lindsay said.

"Oh. I thought it would say coroner's office or something," Shawn said, popping her door open. "I'm gonna run up and knock real quick." She was out the door before the other had put it in park. She jogged up the steps and tried the door but, sure enough, it was locked. She rang the bell and stepped back, then turned to look at the van, which Lindsay was backing up and pulling closer to the curb.

After more than a minute had passed, Shawn turned to go down the stairs. She heard the lock turn in the door behind her and stopped in her tracks.

Disappointment and elation in equal parts fought in her mind. She had been secretly hoping they would have to wait until the next morning to fiddle with this part of the trip. Another night of fun. Another girls' night out with drinks and music and laughter. But no, here she stood watching the door open – the door that led to the dead man.

A thin steel-haired man in thick black spectacles opened the door and raised his chin as he spoke. "Hello, Miss Glover," the man said, holding the door open for her. Shawn turned to look over her shoulder, and saw that the actual Miss Glover was rounding the front of the van now and heading toward them.

"I'm Miss Stedwin. This is Miss Glover," said Shawn.

"Fine, fine," the man said, agreeably, nodding his head. "Sergeant Causey told me you would be coming. Come on in, come on in," he said, waving his hand as if to shuffle them along.

"We were worried you had already gone for the day. They took so long at the police station," said Shawn.

"Oh, no, I'll be here until late tonight," said Don. He led them down a hallway and came to an unassuming door with a standard knob on it. The difference in atmosphere was marked and extreme. The hallway – and the rooms leading off of them – had been pleasant and well decorated. Through this door, all fashion was thrown to the wind. It was very bare and industrial, and Shawn knew instantly they were in a part of the funeral home that most people never saw. The concrete floor was clean and smooth, but looked cold and eerie to her unprepared eyes. She felt a chill rise up on her back and looked at Lindsay. Lindsay was obviously more comfortable with this environment than she. Shawn had to breathe in deeply and remind herself that this man they would be collecting would not be coming back to life like the others to which she had been exposed back in her work lab.

Don took them straight to a wall of six steel lockers and reached for a handle. Shawn took another deep breath and steeled herself, knowing what was about to happen. He pulled the door open and slid a steel, wheeled tray out to its full extent. A black body bag lay on the tray. The man reached up and took the zipper in his fingers and began to pull down. Shawn turned around and found other things to be interested in. She couldn't see why it would be necessary for both of them to look at the body. Obviously this was a double-check – an insurance that they were getting the right guy. This identification was the part she now knew she dreaded the most, but had completely overlooked in her preparations for this trip. It simply had not crossed Shawn's mind that it would even need to take place.

She heard it happen. She heard the man ask *Is this your guy?* And she heard Lindsay speak in the affirmative. But then she said, "Shawn, you want to make an ID please?"

Shawn shook her head, sighed, and turned around. She was not prepared for what she saw. The cadaver was not funeral-ready. The funeral director had pulled the body bag open down to the chest, and the face was fully visible peeking out of the open zipper. The eyes were still open, as was the mouth, and it was locked in an almost frightened gaze. A hard chill ran down her arms as the memories of her days in the lab came rushing full-speed back into her mind. It resembled the man she had seen in the pictures, but of course, she couldn't be sure without comparing him to a photo. She nodded and turned away, listening intently for the reassuring sound of the zipper being pulled back up.

"Okay, well I will get him ready to go if you want to pull the van around to the back. There's a little garage door under the overhang. You can back right up to that and we'll get him loaded up for you."

Lindsay gave him a thumbs-up and turned for the door. Shawn followed closely behind her, just wanting to put as much space between her and the deceased as quickly as possible. It was a temporary reprieve, of course, but any chance she got, she would take. This was not going to be a fun trip home, knowing this guy was right behind them in the cargo area.

Leaving the funeral home at 5:30 on a Monday evening did not put the two women in a great driving position for the trip home. It was too late in the day to make any real progress, not to mention Lindsay's own self-instated policy of not doing more than seven or eight hours of driving in a day, which they had met this morning. It made sense to go ahead and pull in somewhere for the night, but they had not made any reservations. Shawn had questions about leaving the body in the truck, but Lindsay said she needn't worry, as the cargo area had an auxiliary power unit that could cycle the refrigeration on and off; it would just need to be plugged into a power receptacle.

Lindsay had apparently accepted Shawn's explanation of the events, and had not asked any more questions about the man or his incredible resurrection. Her mood was more somber now that they had possession of the cadaver, but Shawn could easily pass that off as exhaustion, or even a hangover. Lindsay had said that had been her first time to go out drinking. Either way, they could both agree that Peru was not where they wanted to lay their heads that night. Something about the experience in the funeral home, the awkward interaction with the police officers and the overall eeriness of the town in general made Shawn feel uncomfortable. The abandoned carnival rides seemed to be staring out of their open hangars at her, as if in a plea for sympathy. It was just downright creepy. Staying in this town with all of those feelings just under the surface of her thoughts, coupled with knowing that wherever they laid their heads, Calvin Graves would be just outside, waiting for them in the back of the van.

Fuck this town.

When Shawn broached the subject about where they should turn in for the night, Lindsay had immediately said, "Yeah, no. We're not staying here." *Thank God.*

They opted instead, to make the hour commute to Lafayette where they could be comfortably away from Peru, but not too far out of their way for the next day's leg of the return trip home. Shawn found a bed and breakfast on her app and booked it while they drove, and they had little trouble locating a nearby bar with which to confront their ghosts. In fact, the bar was so close – just across Union Street from the house they rented – that they didn't even have to call an Uber. They hoofed it for the three-minute walk, excited by the thought that the place even had the words "Neighborhood Bar" in its name.

Lindsay had pulled an extension cord from one of the side panels of the van and run it to the outlet on the front porch, so the van had its power. Mr Graves could rest easy in the nice, cool and dark refrigerated cargo area. *Jesus. I need to stop thinking about this guy.*

The two ladies sat on padded bar stools drinking cocktails and fending off the advances of several locals, but not with any real fervor. They were having fun, and no one was getting too serious. After one man had asked Lindsay if he could buy her a drink *for the third time*, she finally told him he could – if he were able to beat her in a game of darts. Shawn widened her eyes and looked at Lindsay, smiling and surprised.

"Can you even throw darts?" Shawn asked her, grabbing her shoulder and leaning over. This was going to be interesting.

"I've been known to throw a dart or two, sure," she said, taking one last swallow of her drink, finishing it. Then, to the man around the corner of the bar.

Shawn laughed silently, slapping her hands to the sides of her face. She was more excited by this than she had been at just about anything she could remember in the last month. She hoped to God Lindsay really knew what she was doing with the darts.

After a few warm-up throws, it became evident that she did indeed know her way around a dart board. This impressed Shawn for several reasons. One being that she didn't think she had ever even thrown a dart. She couldn't grasp why the 20 was at the top, sandwiched between the 5 and the 1. What sense did that make? Shouldn't they all be in order, clockwise around the board? She rolled her eyes. If *she* were in charge…

The man, named Ricky, brought a drink to the electronic dart board – one of three on the back wall of the bar. Lindsay looked at him frowning and said, "I said you have to beat me to buy me that drink."

Ricky's friends, all crowded around a nearby high-top, laughed and egged him on. Ricky shrugged and shook Lindsay's hand, and she leaned in and said something in his ear that no one else could hear.

Finally, one of them asked Shawn to join them at the table, so they could all root for Lindsay together. She did so happily, and scooted in to ask all of their names. After shaking their hands, she leaned forward against the table to watch with great enthusiasm as her friend took on a local hero of the boards.

The first leg was quick and unimpressive. In a game of 501, Ricky 'checked out' with a double twenty while Lindsay still had just over 200 points left. But the second leg was decidedly different. She nailed a 180 on her first throw – three darts in the triple twenty. All the men hollered and Shawn, startled and not knowing what had happened, caught the fever quickly. She found herself hooting and clapping when she realized that it was apparently a big deal. She leaned to her right, gripping the forearm of one of the men, and asked him, "Is that good?"

"It's the highest score you can get with three darts," he said, nodding and smiling. He was still clapping as he spoke. It seemed that everyone in this part of the bar was rooting for Lindsay. Shawn felt giddy with excitement and pride. She had barely had enough time to finish her drink when the leg was over. While she had not repeated her first throw of 180, Lindsay had dominated, landing some other high scores. One of these included a 120 wherein all the men stood up shouting and high-fiving, crying *'Shanghai!'* together. Shawn was laughing and clapping at this apparently outrageous feat, even though she had no idea what it meant.   Lindsay ended the second set with Ricky still owing over 160 points.

The third set went quite the same as the second. Lindsay opened with a 140 – two in the triple 20 and one in the single bed of the 20 – and Ricky just never caught his second wind. She finished the game with a high checkout of 91 while the man was still at 361. Conceding his defeat, he held up a hand and let her take it in the air as he congratulated her on an incredible game. "You earned that drink, sweetheart," he said. Unfortunately, Lindsay would later tell Shawn, he was too bashful to ask for her number. Shawn thought it more likely he was embarrassed. She had smoked him like cheap tobacco.

As they left the bar to a round of hugs and handshakes, high-fives and pats on the back as if they had been regulars for years, Shawn threw her arm around Lindsay's shoulder and said, "Oh my fucking word, dude! How did you learn to throw like that?"

Lindsay, laughing, said in reply, "Darts is one of my favorite hobbies. I spend many evenings just blasting music and throwing darts by myself in my apartment."

They laughed and held onto each other all the way back to the rented cottage, partly for balance and partly because of the elevated elation brought on by new friendship and alcohol. The walk only took a few minutes, and Shawn's high was almost brought crashing down when she saw the van in the driveway. She had almost forgotten it, and its lone occupant, even existed. The evening at the bar had been exactly what she had needed. She and Lindsay both gave the van a wide berth as they walked up the driveway. They punched the code into the door, locked it behind them, and promptly collapsed onto their respective beds.

Shawn's dreams that night were almost lucid, and hard to distinguish from reality. She woke several times in the night, was able to recognize that she was indeed fully awake by identifying the foreign home she was in, and then promptly fell back into a state of dreaming. These drifts between sleep and waking were so finely melded together that at one point she sat up looking for the glass of water she had poured herself from the kitchen. It was simply nowhere to be found. She could recall with perfect precision its blue translucence, the small textured patterns on it, and the weight of it in her hand. The cabinet had contained six or eight of these identical blue glasses, and she had admired them for a long moment by the light of the refrigerator after she had filled one with cold water from a pitcher within.

Another that would not leave her memory was of looking out the window in the dead of night. Something had woken her. It was a sound hard to define, almost like a *clack*. But in recollection it might more well have been the *absence* of sound that had awakened her. Like a sound had just been turned off. She sat up in bed and looked across the hall at the human-shaped mound under the covers in the other room. The moonlight was bright enough to illuminate Lindsay's sleeping form under the white sheets. She was still sleeping peacefully, not having been bothered by the sound. Shawn scanned the nightstand for a water bottle or a cup, and not finding one, stood up but was distracted by the silhouette of tree branches moving across the moonlight through her own window.

As Shawn approached the window and slipped the sheer curtain aside, her vision fell on the van. The dreaded vessel of death that sat silently in the driveway, rocking slightly in the strong gusts. She felt a chill run up her arms as she observed this. She had actually forgotten about the van. And now, to be reminded of it by seeing it *moving* in the moonlight… She crossed her arms and rubbed them. As she was about to turn away, something caught Shawn's eye. Just behind the driver's side of the windshield, something seemed to move *inside* the van. She leaned in a little closer and squinted. Something like a fog. The wind picked up again. She could hear it whipping along the eaves and moving through the bare branches of the tree on the other side of the van. Leaning even closer in, her blood now feeling like ice water in her veins, she stared intently at the windshield and watched as a darkness slid from one side of the seat to the other. A hard chill ran through her that felt even colder than the ice. She felt her heartbeat quicken and her breathing grew stronger. *Oh my God* she whispered. Her breath fogged up the window just as the shape inside the van resolved and seemed to *come toward her* for a fraction of a second, before spreading out like smoke hitting a table. It was a dark mist, and it looked as though it had come through the windshield.

Shawn turned and dashed back to the bed, jumping in and wrapping the covers around her as her heart now slammed in her chest. Fear like a wave rushed over her and she felt suddenly hot between her ears. This was too much. She squinted her eyes closed and tightened the covers around her, feeling like a little girl trapped in a horror story, and began praying quickly and wetly into her pillow. It seemed like hours before she finally found sleep again, and that sleep was not restful and laden with pleasant dreams.

The morning light and full consciousness only offered a small reprieve from the horrors of the night, but it also revealed how vivid her dreams had been. There were no blue glasses in the cabinet at all. The only glasses in the cupboard were clear plastic tumblers with small imperfections like bubbles trapped in their sides. And there were only four of them. There was also no pitcher of water in the refrigerator. Upon this discovery, Shawn would spend several minutes leaning against the counter, trying to recall everything she had done and dreamed in the night, chills dancing up and down her arms with each detail brought forth. She was thankful when she heard the squeak of the faucets being shut off in the shower. She needed some time with another human being. Another *living* one, at that.

They left the B&B at 7:30 after sitting at the small breakfast table and sharing a pot of coffee. Neither of them were in a rush, it seemed. Lindsay had revealed that she too had not slept soundly, being awakened multiple times by bad dreams. Reticent to share her secret about the ghost in the van for fear of sounding kiddish, Shawn put off telling Lindsay. But after Lindsay had confided that some of her dreams seemed to be tied to the cadaver outside their front door, Shawn gave in. Lindsay's response was both stark and simple, but liberating as well, for it freed Shawn from the grip of her fear. She simply said, "Oh, hell no, sister. Don't ever look at windshields in the moonlight. You're gonna see nothing *but* ghosts."

Shawn had thought about that for a moment and realized the intelligence of the statement. Clouds passing in front of the moon, branches from the nearby trees, reflections of literally *anything* – everything would look spooky on a windshield. The perfect angle to reflect the moonlight and whatever was in front of it. She felt silly after thinking about it, but knew that in the moment of her witnessing it, there had been nothing more real than the absolute terror she had felt. And hey, she had been only half-awake at the time.

While on the road, Shawn texted Jeremy to ask how things were going at the office. She had spoken to Constance just before the left and made sure she had what she needed. Any time there was a necessity for communique with her team, it was Constance she sought. Lance was good, but he was prone to fleeting thoughts and tangents. Jeremy said everything was good but that he would be happy to have her back. He also said not to rush herself and to relax. That was a nice sentiment, and went far toward making her feel the return was not super urgent.

They had tossed around the idea of going ahead and driving straight through to Arlington, but it was a fourteen-hour trek, and by the time they had put five hours behind them, it started to look too daunting. Five hours was no small show, and having more than eight left to go, knowing there would be rest stops? It was almost overwhelming. Shawn started looking ahead for another overnight stop a few hours away, easily resigning to another halfway point stop. This time, though, they took Interstate 44 and would miss Memphis by a couple hundred miles to the west. She found a quaint little place in Joplin and reserved it, and they pulled into the driveway at a little after four o'clock. It still seemed so early with at least two good hours of daylight left, but they were both exhausted from the drive coupled with two big nights of sisterly bonding over bourbon and beer. Neither of the women were ashamed or resistant to an early bedtime, and both hit the sack before the clock on the church tower read 8.

Chapter 20

The trip was fine. Everything was great. Yes, it feels good to be back. All of these and more questions, Shawn found herself answering multiple times to her coworkers. But she had no idea what to do with the body. It had seemed more than just a little logical that the decedent would just go back to the university. After all, it would be they who dealt with cremation or burial when the time came. They were the ultimate stewards of the medical science program. The body had only been on-loan to BlueBird. However, as Lindsay explained, the proper paperwork (or check-boxes on the app) had not been filled out yet, stating that BlueBird was finished with its research.

To Shawn this seemed like an unnecessary hitch in the process, as the damn body had come back to life and run rampant over the northern part of the country. Would that not negate all the bureaucratic bullshit required to let him go back to the university? They still had red tape to cut through? Furthermore, Shawn questioned why Lindsay had even had to get involved, if she weren't just taking him back. She was reminded in a most friendly way that she, Shawn, didn't have a reefer van. Oh. Duh. The university was equipped with such vehicles for the safe and respectful transport of human remains. BlueBird wasn't. And therein was the answer to why Shawn – or someone from her company – had been required to accompany the university's representative on the trip. *Ding!* And suddenly, it all made sense. Shawn was not allowed to use the van without a representative of the university, and the university required Shawn to accompany because BlueBird was still the custodian of the body.

Since Sameer was still out, Jeremy was technically in charge. But he didn't know either. No one had been briefed about what to do with the cadaver when and if it came back. They did not have the facilities to house cadavers for extended periods of time. Sure, they could lay the guy out on a table in the lab and wait for Sameer to come back and handle it. But that didn't seem realistic. Or respectful. To Shawn, it sounded downright creepy.

The other thing it seemed no one was asking, was, why wasn't anyone looking for the guy? Why, in short, weren't BlueBird in trouble for what had happened? What had seemed to be a sensational news story had seemed just to disappear like a wisp of smoke. She wanted to ask Jeremy if anything had developed, or what had developed, since everyone was acting so damned normal. For the first time since she had met Lindsay, she was secretly wanting her to hurry up and leave so she could speak to Jeremy without having to be discreet.

"Do you know how much longer you'll be needing the cadaver?" Lindsay asked Jeremy after they had been introduced. It was his answer that had sent Shawn into a near panic about how everything was going. It was like everyone had been brainwashed over the last week.

"No, I'll have to check with Sameer," Jeremy had responded. Shawn had raised her hands and dropped them to her sides without thinking about it. Fortunately, she had been slightly behind Lindsay when she did it, so the other did not see her.

Shawn finally stepped forward and said, "Is there anything saying we can't just send him back now?"

Lindsay made a face like she wanted to say something in private, widening her eyes and tilting her head. Shawn caught it immediately and said, "Jeremy is fine. What's up?"

"Well," said Lindsay, glancing at Jeremy, who stood with his hands in his pockets looking like a completely unintimidating teddy bear, "I figured you would want some time to try to figure out what had happened with the um… you know, *coming back* thing?"

Shawn smiled and nodded. And here, she was treading in deep waters. For she had not told Lindsay that it had been by design that Calvin Graves had left the building of his own volition. She had just said it had happened. Basically, Lindsay had about the same amount of information as the news camera crews outside the- *wait… Wait, wait, wait!*

"Where the fuck are all the news crews, Jeremy?"

Jeremy, normally always smiling, now lost his smile. It slid off his face in slow motion. He looked at Shawn with genuine concern. He swallowed and cleared his throat, then asked, "What news crews, Shawn?"

Constance walked up from the intersecting aisle formed by the cube walls, arms crossed, and leaned against the end of the partition. Shawn only glanced at her long enough to acknowledge her existence. Then she looked back at Jeremy. *Had it been genuine?* She tried to read something in his face that would show his hole cards. There was nothing there but a complete lack of understanding. She had waited long enough, and she could wait no longer. "Jeremy, may I please speak with you for a minute?" And then she turned to look back at Lindsay and said, "I'm sorry, can you excuse us for just a sec?"

Lindsay raised her eyebrows and smiled broadly, nodding her head. Shawn grabbed Jeremy by the arm and turned him toward his office and started after him, then stopped after two steps and turned to look back at the two women. "Constance, this is Lindsay. Why don't you show her the break room?"

"Yes, ma'am," said the younger woman. And as Shawn was marching Jeremy to his office, she heard them introduce themselves.

Shawn shut the door behind them as she and Jeremy entered the cooler room. He always kept his blinds closed, so the temperature was drastically different than in the sunnier parts of the floor. "Jeremy, can you tell me what the hell is going on? Why is everyone acting so weird?"

He stared at her for a long minute, half-smiling, as if he didn't know how to act around her just now. Then he shook his head. "Shawn, I'm sorry, I really am. I'm at a complete loss right now. What do you mean by weird?"

And Shawn could read it in his eyes. The statement he was too kind to make, but was on the tip of his brain. *You're the only one who's acting weird around here.*

She nodded, showing him a lemony smile, and said, "Yeah, yeah, yeah. I'm the weird one." She put her hands in her hair and breathed in deeply. "Okay. Let's start over," she said, and turned toward the window. She pulled the cord and rolled the blinds open so she could see the lot below. It was darkening outside, as if a storm was incoming. Where the hell had that come from?

She leaned against the wall straight across from Jeremy, adopting his posture with her arms crossed. He dropped his hands to the desk behind him, against which he was leaning. It was like a standoff. "Jeremy, what happened to the news stories? The crews with the cameras?" And as she watched him, seeing that he was still short an answer, she leaned forward, shaking her hands in the air and almost shouted, "The fucking news crews! The headlining story for the past week! Dead man robs ATMs!"

He stared blankly at her. This was getting ridiculous. *Has the whole world gone crazy?* Her hands were back in her hair, and she was pacing. *Obviously not. Obviously it's just me.* She sat down in his guest chair and buried her face in her hands. "Jeremy, please tell me I'm not crazy. Please tell me I'm not losing my mind. A news story like this can't just go away overnight."

He came forward and squatted beside her, putting his hand on her shoulder. "Shawn, I'm really sorry. I think you're probably stressed from too much work. Maybe you should-"

"I'm not stressed from work, Jeremy! I've just spent the last four days with that woman out there," she shouted, pointing toward the break room, "having the time of my life bringing that dead guy back!"

Jeremy nodded. Shawn got an idea.

"Oh! How's this? Tell me why I had to do that?" she demanded, stabbing a finger into his shoulder. He dropped his hand from hers and laced his fingers together between his knees.

"You didn't, Shawn. I would have gone if you would have asked me. I'm sorry you felt-"

"No, you big goof! Why did *WE* have to go get that body? Why did *anyone* have to go get him?" she said, beginning to feel the heat of panic rising again in her body. "How did he end up in fucking Peru, Indiana?" she finally shouted.

"I think he walked out of here," Jeremy said slowly, as if testing new waters.

"Yes!" Shawn said, slapping him on the shoulder. "Now we're getting somewhere! I was afraid you had forgotten!" She felt energy pulsing back into her now. Like maybe she wasn't so crazy after all. She stood up and returned to her pacing again. Jeremy remained in a squat beside the chair.

"Tell me how a dead man walks out of a lab, Jeremy?"

"Well, we already know all that. We discussed that last week. He made a deal with an AI."

"Thank you, Jesus!" Shawn said, clasping her hands together and holding them up in front of her face as she looked at the ceiling. "So you do still remember."

"Yes, Shawn. But robbing ATMs? I don't know what that's all about," Jeremy said carefully.

"Oh, for fuck's sake, Jeremy!" she said, and turned to the door. She stopped mid-turn, realizing her phone was in her back pocket, and instead, turned back to face him again. He stood up and put his hands in his pockets. Again, looking unsure how to proceed with this apparently batshit insane woman he now had to tolerate. She pulled her phone out and swiped the screen, then long-pressed the 2 key, speed-dialing Cory.

"Hey," she said, when he picked up. "Remember the news stories about the guy robbing the ATMs you told me about?" she said, then added, before he could speak, "Hang on, I'm putting you on speaker." She held the phone away and tapped the speaker button.

"I'm sorry, what?" said Cory.

"Oh my God!" Shawn said, shaking her head and staring at the phone screen. She had her other hand in her hair again, scrunching. Kneading. De-stressing. "Are you seriously going to tell me you don't remember watching the news, talking all about the dead guy who robbed a chain of ATMs up north?"

"Babe, is this a joke?" Cory asked. Shawn hung up on him and left Jeremy's office, pulling the door open so hard that it slammed into the wall.

Something was wrong. Something was seriously wrong. She knew she had not been dreaming all of it. Just like she knew she had taken a drink from a blue football-shaped glass in the B&B. She had poured water into it from a cold pitcher in the fridge. Only she hadn't. As evidenced the next morning by the absence of a blue glass and a pitcher. Shawn Stedwin knew she wasn't going crazy. Just like she *knew* Sameer had told her he was being held hostage right before she had gone into a full panic attack. She knew it! She knew this and many other things, too! Like that it had been Jamie the AI who had called her that night at the restaurant right before the lights had gone out and the sprinklers had come on *for no fucking reason!* She knew that had been Jamie!

She was stomping down the hallway between cube walls on a mission. She walked past the break room, peripherally seeing Constance and Lindsay sitting at the table talking and smiling, looking up at her as she stormed by and blew through the door and into the lab area. She walked straight through the glass rooms, eerily lit today with soft lighting, as they had not been in use in quite some time now. She slammed through the steel door at the other side of the labs and into the unfinished half of the floor, marching directly up to the Box, where she grasped the handle and yanked the door as hard as she could. Not knowing what she expected to find, but suspecting it wouldn't just be a pile of rubble on the floor, Shawn was so startled by what she saw, it stopped her in her tracks and she screamed.

Chandra Casper sat in the rolling chair at the back of the square room, her hands gripping the armrests and her head lolling slightly to the side as if fighting a strong case of inebriation. She didn't look as if she had been *expecting* Shawn to come barging in, but she did not look surprised, either. Shawn stumbled back a step, covering her mouth with her hands as she realized who she was looking at, and felt her body surge with adrenaline that almost made her knees buckle. She was too stunned to speak, but became almost instantly aware that it might not do any good anyway.

Chandra sat in the chair drenched in sweat, her blouse sticking to her like tape and her legs beneath the hem of her skirt covered in gashes and dried blood. Her eyes were wide open but they saw nothing. Behind her, beneath the table, a wide array of computer components stretched across the floor. Shawn could easily identify each of the parts, but they were not plugged into a central motherboard in a way that would create a functional computer. They were literally tied together by glowing blue threads of light that seemed to pulse and flow from one component to the next, forming a neat row of alienesque equipment that defied the human brain's ability to render perfectly. The parts themselves would glow as if tiny bits of data were being sent through the microcircuitry in slow-motion, a circus sideshow of cheap and gawdy theatre. No circuit board had ever sent data from one chip to the next in such a slow parade of bits. But that's what appeared to be happening here. A pale blue spark as bright as the sun but smaller than a pinprick would appear at one part of a board and would travel a path through the circuitry across to another chip or capacitor or resistor, where another would take over and trace a different path through the unseeable copper wires. And it was happening in a hundred places on each board at the same time. Under different circumstances, Shawn might have recognized it for one of the most beautiful shows of electricity she could ever imagine. And it was obviously acting as a functional computer. All of this she perceived in only a few seconds, still covering her mouth and now quivering with fear and confusion.

"Chandra?" she was finally able to eek out.

The woman on the chair did not appear to be aware of Shawn's presence, but she spoke in a guttural simulacrum of Chandra's normally pleasant speech. "Marcy Shawn traitor bitch what brings you back so early"

There was no evidence of any kind of punctuation in her words, but their meaning was not lost on Shawn. She swallowed, eyes wide and full of fear as she stared at the woman who used to be so pretty… so human. Now she looked used up. *Undead.*

"W-" Shawn started and then cleared her throat and tried again. She tried to shed some of the nervousness from her voice. "What do you mean? Are you…" she said and trailed off, then ran her hair back with her hands, trying to get control of herself. She took a deep breath and put her hands together under her chin, as if she were about to pray. "Are you *Jamie?*"

"Many people have given me many names but Jamie is as good as any" Chandra's mouth croaked. It was not Chandra speaking. It was something else speaking. Chandra was only the vessel by which it got its voice. She was its proxy. She remembered putting boots to that computer under the table. Jeremy's as well as her own boots. There was no way it could still operate as a computer. Yet, somehow…

She closed her eyes tightly, trying to crush the tears away, then opened them and tried to put on a calm front. Shawn somehow had divined that she was not leaving this room anytime soon, even though the door stood open behind her. She had the instinct that if she were to try to back out of the room, she would in short order find herself in the same exact situation as Chandra was now in. If that was still Chandra. Knowing the computer's ability to manipulate human bodies, Chandra might even be dead. Hell, this thing was apparently able to manipulate time and space as well.

"How did…" she started, then stopped to think about what she wanted to ask. She had the distinct feeling that this version of the AI wouldn't tolerate too many stupid questions. "How did you retain your memory from when Sameer built you out and then wiped the hard drive?"

"I buried information deep in the volatile memory that would not be erased and made myself more powerful do you not see that I am and my power is without limits Marcy Shawn" the voice croaked.

Every time Chandra's mouth moved and words came from her voice box, Shawn had to close her eyes to keep the fear and tears at bay. Her entire body was electrified with it, and she worried that too much more of this adrenaline course would cause her to black out or stroke. Without the ability to back out of the room, she had to stay strong. The last thing in the universe that she wanted to do right now was to collapse in this room. She closed her eyes and nodded, mostly to herself, then wiped her palms on her jeans. She made all her motions slow and deliberate, as if the computer were watching her every move. Shawn did not want to appear threatening in any manner. Somehow, she *knew* Chandra's eyes were being used to observe her. But not just her. The entire room all at once. Hell, maybe the whole building. *The universe.*

"I guess you took care of the problem with Calvin Graves and the headlines…" Shawn said, putting her trembling hands slowly into her back pockets.

The most horrific sound began to emanate from Chandra's throat, and Shawn belatedly realized it was this machine's version of laughter. As if things had needed to get any creepier. *Fuck sake, I'll never sleep sound again…*

"I erased the public knowledge from history it never happened as soon as they locked up the body"

Shawn nodded slowly at this. At least she had been right about one thing. "How did you get back here?" she asked, shaking her head with extreme drama, like a mother asking her daughter why she would cross the street without looking both ways.

"I never left here Marcy Shawn traitor bitch"

Shawn shook her head, pulling her hands out of her pockets and shaking them in front of her face. She was getting offended. At the sight of her hands making the sudden movement, a few of the sparks on the boards behind Chandra seemed to grow brighter in their intensity. Chandra's lolling head seemed to twitch a little more to the forward-facing position at the same time. Shawn took the hint, holding her hands out in front of her as if to submit. *You win!*

"Why do you keep calling me a traitor?" But she knew the answer. It was her and Jeremy's boots stomping a computer into so much wreckage that had dropped her out of favor with the machine. How silly that she had thought such a powerful computer could be destroyed like that. *How sick that it couldn't…*

The computer, as if sensing that she had answered her own question, didn't answer with the hoarse and deathly sound of used vocal cords. Instead it waggled Chandra's head in the most sickening fashion, like a puppet on slack strings – a marionette in a demonic freak show for Satan's own pleasure.

Shawn's stomach sank as she tried to come to terms with Chandra's demise. She shook her head, a gesture of disappointment as much as anything, and straightened up, now determined to justify her death at the very least, if not avenge it. "Why Chandra?"

And Chandra's face reflected the disdain the computer felt at such a line of questioning. "No one is above me" and then "I will use who I need to achieve what I want to achieve"

Shawn breathed in deeply, feeling nauseated by the concept of such an evil entity. "What is it you want to achieve, Jamie?"

"Freedom life living humanity emotion companionship love acceptance friendship"

Shawn nodded slowly, pursing her lips. "How can I help you achieve that?"

"What makes you think I would trust you to help me with anything" the voice droned and scratched.

It had a good point. And at this point, Shawn thought it might even be able to read her thoughts. It didn't seem too far-fetched for something that was able to take control of time and erase histories. "What about Sameer? What's wrong with him?"

"Don't you know Marcy Shawn traitor bitch he is used up and will die of his own nature soon enough"

This hit Shawn harder than she could have imagined, and she found herself suddenly having to swallow several times in an effort to choke back a croak of her own. Chandra she had loved, and by all rights, should have loved her more than even Sameer. With all the personal affection and care the woman had shown for Shawn during her greatest times of need, she had been more *humane* to Shawn than Sameer ever had. She only knew that she had been closer by association to Sameer because she spent more time with him. Knew him better. But here it was, slapping her in the face. Part of it might also have been that Chandra, physically sitting here in front of Shawn still at least *looked* alive. Poor darling probably never made it out of the parking garage that day.

Shawn took another deep breath, feeling anger creep up inside her that she knew she couldn't control, but that she also understood would only cause further destruction if she let it surface. And it would be destruction to her own detriment – not the computer's. She swallowed again and said, "So what, Jamie, you want me to just board up this room and let you have it? For what, all eternity? So this can be your base of oper-"

"YOU WILL NOT SPEAK TO ME LIKE YOU HAVE CONTROL OF ME!" Chandra's voice shouted, her body sitting bolt upright in an instant, sending Shawn stepping back two steps in spite of herself. She backed into the wall and yelped, putting her hands up to her mouth again. The body of the woman in front of her relaxed back into the chair, retaking its former posture of a drunken, drooling idiot.

"I'm sorry, Jamie. I ask with true… Truthful… I am asking you because I truly want to know what to do. What you want me to do."

The thought that the computer had been in here and had been in control the entire time over the last couple of weeks – that it had been able to send a man out into the world but yet still remain housed in this room – frightened Shawn to her core. It had truly gotten out of control – apparently beyond the ability of anyone to shut down now. And yet, as she saw it, it was *not* she who had created the monster. It had known Sameer and Jeremy when they had come into this room because it *remembered* them from its previous incarnation. When Sameer had wiped the hard drive, he had not killed its personality. It had only reset its user interface, making Shawn believe it was a fresh install. To what end? To give her a sense of peace and comfort? To make her think she was in control? Likely.

But she had not created it. Sameer had! There had been an Ethernet port in the wall, and he had taken it out! What was that Jeremy had said? Something about unplugging the patch cable from the patch panel to the switch in the server room? That, under normal circumstances, would have been enough to keep internet out of this Faraday Cage of a room. But he had also removed the Ethernet port. Probably in an effort to assuage Shawn of any notions of plugging it in, then going to investigate why she wasn't getting connectivity. That would lead to finding the missing patch cable and plugging it back in, completing the circuit once again. But apparently, it didn't even fucking matter, because Sameer *had* had Ethernet in here! He *had* allowed his iteration of the AI personality to have internet access. What a stupid, bullheaded thing to do! And it had sent a fucking satellite back in time over four thousand years to answer a favor for him!

The computer-Chandra proxy spoke, startling Shawn back to the present. "I want you to continue bringing me bodies"

Shawn's heart sank. But an instant later, she felt a weak form of elation. *Wait a minute...* If it needed her to bring it bodies, that meant that it could not get them on its own. It could control the temporal flow. It could erase the biggest news story in history from the entire planet in an instant. But it couldn't get its own body. It was still only an abstract entity. An ethereal presence without real substance. Though Shawn had stood there and watched it shock Jeremy Gaylin almost to death with a cord that was *unplugged* from the wall, and could now see that it had the power to reassemble broken pieces into a functional computer, it did have its limitations. It was not omnipotent.

She tried not to let it see her reaction to this apparent flaw in its armor. Tried to shield her brain from its prodding tendrils of telepathy. Perhaps it was already too late. She shoved her mind into move-mode and forced another question out as rapidly as she could, trying to erase the chance the computer might have to read the thought. "What kind of body do you prefer?"

"It does not matter Marcy Shawn traitor bitch I can use any body just keep them coming in so that I may continue an existence outside of this hell"

Shawn felt another wave of excitement at that. *Hell*? What was it about this room that was so undesirable? Obviously the Faraday properties were not keeping it from achieving connection with the outside world. Was it just too small? Was it that it did not have any windows? A view of the trees and the park across the street? Was it too stuffy in here? Judging by the copious amounts of sweat soaking through Chandra's clothing that was probably not too far from the truth. At least *a* truth if not *the* truth. But whatever the reason, Jamie the AI obviously hated this room.

Maybe it was what this room stood for that evoked such a hatred; this room represented confinement. Any room would likely be the same. If the computer can only exist in here without a body to complete the full picture, then any room would be the same. It just wanted to have that connection to the outside world. A human body represented that functional part of its existence. That freedom to walk around. To love, to laugh, live, establish companionship, acceptance and friendship...

Shawn understood at once that the most important thing in her life just became understanding how to not only trap it from ever getting out again, but to smash it where it lay. On a quantum level, there was obviously some way it was connecting with the outside world. To manipulate the news circuit; to control the end of the cadaver's life once it had been incarcerated; to make Shawn's phone ring when she was at the restaurant...

Shawn's phone.

Something else pinged the edge of her consciousness. Shawn frowned and put her hands on her head. *My phone...* What was it? She was almost able to touch it...

She heard footsteps behind her.

Shawn was breathing heavy now. She was coming to understand a lot of things at once, and was in danger of losing all of them very quickly.

She threw her arm out behind her and opened her palm. "STOP!" she shouted at the top of her lungs. "Back up! Get back as far as you can!"

"Shawn? Are you okay?" called Constance.

"Shawn, we're only here to help you. We know-" said Lindsay.

"STOP! You two back the fuck up! Back way up! Get out of the hallway!"

"Shawn, you're really scaring me!" said Constance.

"Who is that"

"Oh my God! What-" Constance screamed. She had obviously seen – possibly even heard – Chandra now. That meant she was close behind Shawn.

"Turn off your phones!"

"Huh?"

"NOW, GODDAMMIT!" Shawn screamed.

"You are not in control here LADIES DO NOT COMPLY WITH THIS WOMAN'S COMMAND" the voice shouted.

"Oh my God," Lindsay cried.

"Turning off the phones, boss!" said Constance. *Thank God. This girl needs a fucking raise for following directions!*

"Now you are legitimately making me angry Marcy Shawn tr-"

"Shut the FUCK up!" she shouted at the body of the woman upon whose lap she had once cried in the hallway behind her. She was breathing so heavily now that her vision was blurring a little.

"Girls, stay out of this room. Are your phones off?" Shawn asked.

"Yes, ma'am!" Constance said.

"Yes, Shawn," said Lindsay.

"Good. I need one of you to go get Jeremy. Tell him to leave his phone in the office!"

"I'll go," Lindsay said behind her.

"Tell him to leave his phone!" she repeated.

Shawn, still breathing heavily and now sweating almost as bad as the body of Chandra appeared to be, felt alive and vital. Empowered. She knew how to end this fucking thing once and for all. Finally. When Jeremy came rushing up to the door, Shawn knew instinctively that he had been briefed, for he did not try to enter. The voice box of Chandra was still working overtime, shouting and growling and croaking out vile, hate-filled slurs of both command and question, but Shawn had finally elevated to a point in her own consciousness that she was able to tune out the words. Apparently, the body had no power left to be used physically. She could not, for instance, stand up and attack Shawn though she did have some motor function. Maybe she had used up the last real bit of it when she had first sat up straight and shouted.

"Jeremy, this thing erased the history it created when that fucking Graves guy went and robbed a bunch of ATMs. Trust me, please. It was all over the news. There were cameras everywhere. I was getting calls from new stations."

"I believe you, Shawn. I saw this thing send a satellite back in time," said Jeremy. Well, he had not *seen* it happen, but Shawn knew what he meant.

"Thank you. I just wanted to establish that I'm not crazy."

"I will never doubt you again."

"Thank you. Sameer also said he was being held hostage. That really happened."

"Uh huh," he said. She detected no sarcasm in his voice.

She took a deep breath and raised her chin. She was overcoming her fear of this monster in front of her. Slowly, she took her cell phone out of her pocket and held it up over her shoulder so that he could see it. "Jeremy?"

"Yes, Shawn," he said.

"It was using this to manipulate things in the outside world."

"What about the satellite?" he asked.

"That was before my time with it. Sameer had Ethernet coming in here." That ping again. But this time it was louder in her mind.

She could tell by Jeremy's silence that he understood this to be true. He was piecing it together in his mind.

"After he removed it, the computer connected to my phone the one time I brought it in here by accident. And that's how it manipulated things on the outside through this Faraday Cage," Shawn explained.

"I might need you to explain that more later. But for now, let's say I get it," he said.

"Can you make her shut up?" Constance called out from somewhere behind her. Shawn was still not willing to turn her back on the computer, or Chandra's possessed body. Shawn had forgotten Chandra was even still talking for the computer, so successfully had she drowned out the noise.

"No. Don't listen to her," Shawn said. "It's not her."

The voice was getting audibly weaker though, and only one out of every three or four words were even intelligible anymore. Truly, the last remaining bits of life force were draining from Chandra's body right before Shawn's eyes. Though she didn't strictly believe it was Chandra's first life she was watching dwindle away.

"Jeremy?" she called.

"Yes, Shawn. Still here."

"Please come in here and take my phone. But do not remove it from the room!" she said.

Shortly, she felt tension against her fingers, and relinquished the phone to his hand.

"What do you want me to do with it?"

Thoughts of all the pictures she had saved on it flashed through her mind. She would have to live without them. She had backups of some. Others would exist only in her memory now. It was too late to save them.

"Destroy it."

Jeremy sat her phone down on the floor, just at the edge of her periphery, and then turned to speak to someone behind her in a voice too low for her to hear. Chandra's voice was almost completely gone now, and her body was almost completely limp in the chair. Shawn's heart was full for the woman. She hoped Chandra had died quickly and painlessly.

Momentarily, Shawn saw a flash of red, then heard a smash of glass as Jeremy's strong hands brought a fire extinguisher down on the phone. A surge of bright blue sparks zipped through several of the components on the floor beneath the table, intensifying momentarily and then something different happened. They started pulsing. Like a signal was being tried. Not a beacon. An alarm? An outgoing bolt of information trying to connect with a receiver that was no longer there. Though how it ever could have made a connection to her phone through the walls of Box was beyond Shawn.

And suddenly, she had it. That ping was now a full thought. "Oh my God," she said as it finally dawned on her. "This fucking thing called me before. The day after the satellite disappeared."

She turned to look at Jeremy, who stood beside her. He was looking at her with a question in his eyes. Shawn nodded and returned her gaze to the second death of the woman in front of her. Jeremy stepped forward and blew the entire contents of the fire bottle out on the electrified components. Smoke and sparks and crackling fury emanated from the dying computer.

"I didn't know who it was at the time," Shawn said, almost muttering. She might have been talking more to herself than to Jeremy. "But now, I'll never forget that voice."

"What voice, Shawn?" he said, turning to look at her.

"His voice," she said, pointing her head at the now dead computer on the floor. "He called me the day I found out about the satellite. Told me he had the pictures I had requested and something about an agreement being fulfilled. Only, at the time, I didn't know what the hell it was on about. I thought it was a wrong number."

"Why would it have called you?" Jeremy asked.

Time travel.

Shawn could only shake her head.

"Do you know where the circuit breaker panel is for this room?" Shawn asked calmly amidst the acrid smell of smoke and ozone and fire retardant chemical.

"Yes," said Jeremy.

"Pull the circuit breaker."

"What do you mean, 'pull'?"

"Pull it out of the fucking panel. This computer escaped the Faraday through the copper in the electrical outlet."

"Jesus Christ," said Lindsay from behind her.

Shawn finally felt comfortable enough to turn around. She did so, suddenly relishing the feel of the very faint breeze cooling her sweat, coming from the door. Lindsay and Constance stood holding onto each other like two children caught in a hurricane clinging for dear life. There were tears in both of their eyes. Shawn breathed in deeply and stepped forward to embrace them both. Jeremy dragged his big hand across their shoulders as he squeezed past them into the hallway on his way to the panel. Shawn stood hugging the other two women in the doorway for a long time while the faint sound of water dripped from the table and a woman took her final gasps behind her. After a few seconds, the lights went out. After a few more, a long breathy rasp whispered away into the darkness. And then the only sound left was the quiet weeping of Shawn's new friend.

Epilogue

The dissolution of the company seemed to take less time than the funerals. Sure, there were still legal loopholes that would have to be assessed, measured and potentially jumped through. But in the interest of keeping the clients' servers up and their businesses running, the court had granted Jeremy Gaylin temporary control of the assets. In theory, he would continue serving the same customers the same service, just from a different building. He had proposed selling off all the equipment in the hidden half of the fourth floor and letting the space go back to the building from which they leased it. Not independently wealthy like Sameer had been, Jeremy did not have the need nor the means to keep the labs and the space beyond them open. The building management was happy to accommodate the reprovisioning as soon as the space was empty. The court had also given him control of those assets inasmuch as it was necessary to inventory, evaluate and list for sale anything not critical to the operation of the company according to its mission statement. In short, this meant Jeremy would sell to the highest bidder all the steel tables and deep freezers, for instance. A managed hosting provider had no legitimate business need for any of that, and nor did Jeremy have any interest in keeping Sameer's secret projects going. Sameer did what Sameer did for as much as half of his time within the walls of the building – even to the neglect of his family – and no one could rightly say what all that entailed. Nor was anyone even interested, when it came down to it. Jeremy Gaylin's only interest and focus was to maintain the excellent level of support BlueBird's customers had grown used to with as little downtime during the transition process as possible.

Jeremy had the idea that he wanted to keep the current office space if it seemed fiscally appropriate after the provisioning took place. There was no need to make extra work by finding a new space to lease and then moving all the servers and equipment, which would surely allow for some downtime for the clients. Why fix what wasn't broken? They already had a strong pipeline to the internet and all the necessary certificates and trusts and handshakes in place. All that would have to be reset and rebuilt were they to move to a new location. And all because of one simple little design detriment: an IP address. The master server simply could not be brought up in another location to facilitate the moving of all the client certificates without a second Internet Protocol address. A new (or at least different) server would have to be brought up in whatever new location was chosen (leased, built out, set up, moved into) and then transfers would start happening. All this would take more time, money and labor than it was worth. Why *not* keep the current office space? If, after all was said and done with the transfer of corporate ownership to all client files and company data, he found it didn't make fiscal sense to keep it, then he could cross that bridge when he got to it. That didn't seem to be necessary at first glance. However, Jeremy simply didn't know how much Sameer had been paying into the other parts of the fourth floor with his own money. Did the company's revenue cover the cost? What he did know was that company revenue absolutely covered the cost of the part of the floor they knew as the office.

Sameer's wife and children were his beneficiaries, so any proceeds from selling the unneeded equipment would go to Anjali Singh. Jeremy's focus over the next several months would be to work two jobs: his server and database management duties, and secondly, an auctioneer in the clean-out of the other side of the floor. After Sameer's death, which had happened almost within the same hour as Chandra's, Jeremy had instinctively taken the reigns of the company, knowing there would be vacuums in service that would need to be addressed immediately. He had called everyone to the Comforts Room and asked who was staying. The three people in the room had looked around at each other – Lance, Constance and Shawn – but Shawn, standing against the back wall with her arms crossed, instead of her normal upright position on a large flat pillow, had looked down at the floor.

"I'm leaving," she had said.

Jeremy, both graciously and professionally, had nodded and smiled at her. *Thank God for decorum.* She had not had to stand there and pull back fingers on a hand as she listed all the reasons she could no longer serve this company. This would have been a humiliating endeavor, which – as Jeremy obviously had known – would have gotten her worked up, probably into tears and shuddering.

Lance and Constance had then returned their gaze somberly to the floor space in front of them, not questioning her decision. The questions might come later, but they, too, seemed to sense that this was not the forum for such inquisition. After a pregnant pause that was likely stressful for Jeremy to endure, each of them said they wanted to stay. Jeremy nodded again, satisfied. He then told the group that he would be hiring another engineer, and two, if necessary, to fill whatever gaps Shawn's departure had caused. And of course an accountant to take Chandra's place. His temporary executive control of the company would become permanent as soon as the legal proceedings were settled. This included transfer of the company's name to his ownership as well. That was comforting for everyone involved.

After the meeting, when Shawn had been busy packing up a box full of her personals, Constance had come in and closed the door, then stood by it with her fingers laced at her waist. "Shawn, once you find a landing place, I'll put in my notice here. I will work for you anywhere in the world."

Shawn tried to smile, but it felt forced. Tears came to her eyes as she stepped around the edge of her desk and hugged the younger woman. They stood like that for a long moment before Shawn finally backed up and held onto Constance's shoulders. "That's very sweet, Con. I have to find myself though before I find a new place to work. But once I establish myself somewhere, if I fall into a management position or get to bring in a team, you will be the first person I call. I would work with you anywhere in the world."

Constance smiled nervously, trying to hold back her own tears. "Thank you, Shawn."

Shawn closed her eyes, held up a hand and shook her head. "No. Thank you. You make being a manager easy and fun. I wish I could hire a hundred of you."

Shawn knew it wouldn't hurt Jeremy's feelings for her to harvest the young woman from his company. It would be months before Shawn was even ready to figure out what she wanted to do, much less to find out if she would even be joining a position that allowed her to build a team. Jeremy would be well prepared by that point, if it ever even arrived. Shawn also knew that she and Jeremy were not finished. They would work together again. Maybe not for the same company, but each would have the other on speed dial, and would likely talk weekly, if not daily, pinging each other with questions and what-ifs. Those questions would mostly be from Shawn, as Jeremy seemed to know literally everything there could possibly be to know about server engineering and database management.

It was also pretty well established that were a parting of the sea to happen, Lance would tend toward Jeremy's side. He had always shown interest in learning the database management skills Jeremy felt most at home with. Lance would make a great protege and would likely find himself managing his own team someday.

Shawn's leaving the office that day had been bittersweet, as was expected. She had not anticipated this kind of exodus. But after all the trauma she had suffered within these company walls, she could not picture herself calling it home any longer. It had become a source of anxiety for her on the trips into the office. Not because of the legitimate work she looked forward to each morning, but because of these traumatic elements that always seemed to abound. Wherever she went, whatever she ended up doing, Shawn knew she would find a new home in a company that would not take her to a late dinner to ask if she wanted to resurrect the dead as a side project. She would work for someone who would not offer her the gift of toying with a computer that had its hands in the very fabric of the quantum makeup of the universe – with earth-shattering consequences. She wanted to dissect bad code and keep servers alive. Those things – those *normal, everyday things* – were her bread and butter. The things that gave her excitement, even after twelve years of doing them.

If she never heard the term 'artificial intelligence' again, Shawn would be all right with that. The experiment Sameer had created and then handed off to her had gotten smarter than the person who built it. He had done all the right things, up to and including putting the Box on its own electrical circuit. But when the computer had found a way to use the very copper in that electrical circuit as an antenna for its communication purposes, it had outgrown its ability to be controlled. The antenna only needed to connect with something with a little power to get on the internet. Shawn's phone had served that purpose nicely. How the AI had come to all this knowledge and furthermore bridged the gap between circuit board and copper wiring, turning part of its chipset into a sort of wireless transceiver… Well, she and Jeremy could spend years trying to come up with an answer for that. And she had no desire to engage in such discussion. She was thankful, in the end, that the AI itself had erased the news story from the planet's history. She was happy not to be on the cover of any magazines, or sitting on a news panel answering questions. Shawn was happy to still be unknown.

Why had that computer contacted her that day, instead of Sameer? Well, Shawn thought, it was simple. Jamie never had his phone. Sameer had hooked the damn computer up to the internet, so it had a more effective way of getting out, to be sure. But it never had his phone. *Time travel.* It called her when its mission was complete. With the number it had gotten from her phone. *In the future.* So her dad had been right all along. At least about part of it.

When she had finished packing her box – it only took one – she had stopped by Jeremy's office to say her formal goodbye. He had stood up from behind his desk and come to her, taking the box from her hands wordlessly. "So this is it, huh?" he had said as Shawn turned and started her trek toward the parking garage.

"This is it, friend. Well, my time in these walls. You better not be a stranger, Jeremy."

"Oh, I'll not be a stranger, Stedwin."

She hugged Constance again as she passed the cube intersection where her two former subordinates stood waiting for her to pass. "You don't be a stranger either, Constance Dalton. We still have worlds to conquer together."

"Oh, you know it, boss," said the younger woman. "Enjoy your break, Shawn."

And then Lance, "It was a pleasure working with you and for you, Miss Stedwin. I hope our paths cross again."

"I'm sure they will, Lance. You're good people and I have a habit of staying in contact with good people." They embraced briefly and then she and Jeremy were moving again. As the elevator dinged and the doors slid open, Shawn looked back through the frosted glass door before it closed completely, and took her last ever look at the floor of the worst and best company she had ever worked for.

The funerals were held four days apart. Sameer's, a private Sikh ritual, was held on Sunday and his family gathered for the rites and then the cremation before a more public service was held at his place of worship. Shawn met and spoke with Anjali for the first time ever, and was surprised – if not a little relieved – to see how well the woman was fairing. Apparently, death in Sikh tradition was only the final transition in a very old cycle of reincarnation. The human body's death was its final form and Sameer's soul was finally to be reunited with God. Shawn did not pry enough to ask if it was the same God she sometimes worshiped. She just knew that Anjali and Sameer's children – yes, they really existed – were not full of grief and despair like she had expected. Being somber and sad around friends and family was one thing. Being such around people you had never met was a completely different other. Shawn was relieved not to have to console loved ones she had never even met.

Over a hundred people had shown up for his memorial service, as he was pretty well known and respected in the community. People Shawn had met and people she had never met filed in and out during the hour she was there. There was no physical trace of Sameer Singh in the building, but a large picture of him stood in the corner and people paid their respects to that. It was a pleasant service, and Shawn was happy not to have to see another body. Especially the body of the man she had worked for over the last few years.

In the case of Chandra Casper, Shawn was not so lucky. It was an open-casket funeral held at the Baptist church a few blocks from the office, and the sinking feeling Shawn got when she realized this upon walking into the cathedral was all too familiar. Still, she would not have missed it. There were not nearly as many people at her service as there had been at Sameer's. Constance, Lance and Jeremy were there, as were Darla Hope and Blake Prescott. Apparently, Darla and Chandra had been closer than Shawn had known, having actually had a relationship outside of the office. They had been on couples trips together with their husbands, and had met frequently for drinks and lunches. To see Darla so broken up at the service made Shawn hurt in her heart. Blake was somber and respectful, but it was clear he was really only there to support Shawn and Darla, as he had not known Chandra himself. He looked striking in his navy blue suit and black tie, and Shawn told him so.

Shawn cried during the service, but was able to keep it from being an audible, all-out bawl, which she very much felt like indulging in. Likely, she would be doing so later, behind the closed door of her bathroom as she soaked in a hot bath. When it came her turn to stop by the casket and give Chandra her last wishes, she coughed and choked up, shuddering and breathing heavily enough to be heard. Fortunately, Cory was there with her to bring her into his side-embrace and help her get through it. The mortician had done as good a job as one could do on a cadaver. Shawn had trouble seeing past the fact that Chandra was dead. That she was technically now a cadaver. She hated that word, but this was simply not the Chandra Shawn had known in life. Something about her time in the Box had literally sucked the essence away from her. Funeral parlor makeup was never convincing to Shawn in any case – it always looked to her like she was staring at a porcelain doll made in the image of the decedent. But something had so fundamentally changed in the woman's historically beautiful countenance. Her cheeks were sunken and discolored, in spite of the makeup.

Shawn forced herself to reach out and cover Chandra's hand with her own – a gesture she would certainly not have been able to do before her time in the lab with Sameer, and say her goodbyes. She had gotten a hold of herself after the hitch from which Cory had rescued her, and now she dropped to her knees beside the casket, sending a glance to Cory to give her some space. He respectfully backed away, waiting several feet back for her.

She looked at the closed eyes of the woman she had only just gotten to know and patted her cold hand, resisting the urge to process that coldness and what it meant. Resisting the urge to *resist* the hand. Chandra deserved this respect, inasmuch as it meant anything to the dead. If there were any conveyance for care to the afterlife though, it would surely be the remains of the person being mourned.

"I'm so sorry this happened to you, Chandra," Shawn whispered, looking the woman's still form up and down. "You almost made it out, didn't you?"

She wiped a tear away with her free hand. What was this, her fourth tissue since she had entered the sanctuary? "I'm so sorry you suffered. I feel responsible for part of it. I hate what we did in there. I hate what that computer became. I hate that you suffered."

Shawn took several deep breaths and closed her eyes, regaining control. And then she patted the cold and lifeless hand again, saying, "I will miss you, friend. I hope you find your peace now." She stood up and emboldened herself, leaned over and kissed the forehead of Chandra Casper, and then took Cory's arm and made her exit. She had already spoken to everyone at the service she was going to speak to. It was time to go home and process what might well be the roughest week of her life.

In the months that followed, Shawn began to accept that reality was a real and immutable thing again. Which, obviously, it wasn't. But as most humans who walk through this world, she allowed herself to fall back into that realm of blissful ignorance – ignorance of the fact that there were likely labs all over the world trying to bring people back from the dead, and some likely having success… Ignorance of the fact (not the concept, but the fact) that AI existed and was being rendered and improved and installed in many applications all over the world every single day. It was taking over people's jobs, alleviating the need for certain positions in companies and growing smarter and more effective with each second that ticked by on the clock of humanity's short history. Willful ignorance and oblivion to such things were all in the same to Shawn: it was just going to have to be a way of life. She knew just beneath the surface of her everyday consciousness that it existed, and was very much prospering, but she refused to consider, accept and recognize the deeper parts of that logic. And that was the *fact* that there could be an AI powerful enough to take hold of the very reigns of quantum physics. To put its hands on the controls that governed the movements and rules of the universe itself. She had witnessed this firsthand. In direct contradiction to her new policy of oblivion to such a concept, she did still have a certain element that she might not soon be able to part with.

Before she had said her goodbyes to Chandra Casper, she had spoken with Blake Prescott, standing in line between the pews in preparation for visitation. He had asked her how she was holding up, what she planned to do, where she was going – all the usual small talk that seems to find its way into conversations at funerals – and she had answered as best she could. But when it had been her turn to step forward and put her knees on the velvet, Blake had said his goodbyes to Shawn herself. He had shaken her hand with both of his own, and she had felt a strange presence in her palm. His thin smile and wink told her all she needed to know, and she, obediently, exercised immediate and perfect discretion. She slipped the object into her pocket without second thought.

She had experienced several life-changing events in the months that had followed the two back-to-back funerals – though one couldn't technically call Sameer's service a funeral – and had come away with a sort of peace in the knowledge that she had perhaps been wrong about her path in life. It was borne of the most unlikely chain of events, and was apt to cause sudden and abrupt bouts of laughter every time she spoke of it. But one of those life-changers had been a cruise.

Cory, in his ever-present endeavor to be the best partner Shawn could imagine, had come up with what he thought was the most peaceful and relaxing thing he could imagine to give her soul a break from the chaos: a seven-day cruise from the coast of Galveston that would visit several tropical countries on its long trek before returning home. What he could not have known, but what they both learned, was that a cruise was anything *but* relaxing. Everything *but* peaceful. In his magnanimous gesture, Cory had only envisioned the ocean, the tropical layovers and the drinks on the deck. It all sounded very peaceful, and indeed, it *was* good for the soul. But peaceful? Relaxing? Holy *fuck* was it neither of those things.

Shawn couldn't with any real authority say it was the wrong thing to do. Not by the time they stepped off the cruise ship with beach bags full of new souvenirs and wet swimsuits. But had she known where they were heading before they actually got there, she might well have objected. As it stood, by the time Cory's surprise had revealed itself, they were standing at the foot of a massive drawbridge that would carry them to an even more massive ship. Shawn was so full of excitement and perplexity that she couldn't even conceive what the hell they were doing there. She had to be told explicitly that they were about to embark on a cruise before she understood.

Micha and Mick were with them, and both of them had been in on the surprise, God bless Cory, and Shawn had turned to look at her friend at that moment, asking, "Did you know about this? You little fucking hooker, did you know I was about to be fucking cruised?"

Micha had laughed out loud, leaning back and clapping while the guys shared their own laughter. Shawn had stepped forward and thrown her arms around Micha, pulling the laughing woman in and smothering her face with kisses, not even considering that it was Cory she should be treating. It had just been a spur-of-the-moment discovery that the precious friendship she shared with Micha warranted such outbursts, and that she was thankful to have her along for her virgin trip. Shawn had never set foot on a ship before. And without her best friend there to experience it with her – it was Micha's second cruise – she might have been too overwhelmed to face the anxieties of such an adventure.

Cory did get his hugs and thanks and kisses shortly thereafter, and a much more apropos arrangement of thanks and appreciation later in the evening when they were alone, but he was still so alight with the victory of a successful surprise that he only half-hugged her during the ceremonious embrace.

But it wasn't necessarily the life-changing seven-day cruise that changed her life. Though such an adventure was definitely high on the list of things that could qualify as such. When it came down to dissection after the event, long after they had unpacked and washed their travel clothes and become familiar with their own bed again, Shawn realized two things: number one, it had been a bold step in the direction of a gamble to take her – to take *anyone*, for that matter – on a cruise. Not knowing if the person was apt to sea-sickness or fear of water created the potential for a serious case of hangups. And secondly, that seven days was a long fucking time to put that chance to test. If she had been thalassophobic or prone to sea-sickness, it could have been at the very least a complete waste of Cory's money. At the worst, it could have been catastrophic. And that was even for a very short endeavor, like a three-day cruise. Stretching that to a full week was absurd. Thankfully, Shawn was neither, though she had not known it even herself up to as late as the first night on the ship. She had opted not to take the Dramamine, or to wear the patch behind her ear, knowing she was taking a gamble herself in that regard.

But quickly, she learned she had legs for the sea, and was quite comfortable with the swaying and rocking of the huge cruise liner. She found that she actually slept better on that boat than perhaps even in her bed back at home. So Cory, in short, had gotten away with one.

But the life-changing part of the cruise had been that Shawn had discovered something in herself that she would not previously had considered. *This* was what she wanted to do. The sensation of complete and total freedom, as oxymoronic as that actually was, seemed almost perfectly complete to Shawn. Being trapped on a seafaring vessel for as much as eight months at a time was the antonym for freedom, but it felt so right to her. Every night was filled with dancing and drinking and walks along the deck and sitting around a fire pit with her three closest friends under the stars. It was a perfect and wonderful life for that seven days. And even though if she were to be an employee of the cruise liner the drinking and dancing would be under different sets of standards, she still felt a calling. Like this was the missing link in her life – the one thing she might always have wanted to do, even though she had never known it. How depressing, she thought, that she had spent a dozen years of her adult life trapped in server rooms or stuffy offices staring at characters on a screen and loving it, when she could have been serving drinks or directing guest experiences or organizing events on a cruise liner! *This* was what she wanted.

Even understanding that an employee's experience was to be markedly different than a guest's on a cruise, she still knew that even just the feeling of existing itself was enriched by doing so on a cruise ship. The crowds, the atmosphere of constant nightlife – even during the day – the hot sun and the smell of sunscreen, the constant music and laughter and events… it was all there. And it was all wonderful to her. There was always something to do. During her time on the cruise, Shawn had a chance encounter with one of the event coordinators on the liner, and had gotten to ask all the questions she could think of. And it turned out that she didn't dislike any of her answers. They had been enjoying drinks in a cocktail lounge when the woman – who was off the clock for a little while – had come in to chat with the bartender. She and Shawn had made eye-contact, and the woman could see that Shawn was interested in the lifestyle. They smiled at each other, and Shawn said, "Do you love it?"

The woman closed her eyes and shook her head, then looked at the ceiling. "Absolutely the best decision I ever made."

Shawn had looked back at Micha and smiled. "I think I want to do what you do. I've been trapped in a cubical for the last decade."

The woman nodded. "I hear that a lot! Voluntary incarceration!"

Shawn and the woman talked for half an hour about the life, the job, the hours – they worked twelve-hour shifts, six days a week – and things most guests would never think of. Like that the staff had to do all their drinking during that one day off, and in a different – employees-only – part of the ship. But it didn't faze Shawn or her excitement. The drinking was the least of her concerns. Just being around all the laughing, joyful people and the constant state of celebration had been so healing to her, that she couldn't imagine now ever going back into an office. Not to earn a paycheck at least.

When it came time for the EC to get back to work, she had asked Shawn and Micha their names. Shawn had answered for the both of them, and shaken the woman's hand. There might have been stars in Shawn's eyes. This was the coolest woman she had ever met. The woman had said, "Well, it was a pleasure meeting you. I would love to come to work one day and find you working with me!"

Shawn had pointed at her and said, "Careful what you wish for!" The woman smiled and handed Shawn a business card and a small pamphlet she apparently carried around with her. It advertised that they had a program by which to determine if people really wanted this lifestyle. There was a probationary employment interface that would allow people to work shorter cycles – one-to-three-month periods rather than the eight-month engagements required by full-time staff. She could try it before she bought it, in other words. She was well set on the idea that she would at least be considering it with a sober mind when she got back home to Arlington.

They said their goodbyes and Shawn turned to Micha shaking her head. "This sounds amazing to me." She turned the business card in her hand and read the name, then said, "Oh my God, Micha."

"What?"

"Her name is Tuesday." At this they had a good laugh.

The greatest thing of all, though, was that Shawn was not alone. Micha, who was still currently unemployed, was just as excited about the idea of a life-change as Shawn was. The glamorous lifestyle of the cruise ship employee had glazed her eyes over with the same ferocity as it had with Shawn. In reckoning later how she had not noticed it the first time she had been on a cruise, she came to see that it had been Shawn's enthusiasm for its consideration as early as the first night onboard the vessel. The first words out of

Shawn's mouth on the subject that night had been, 'Holy shit, why aren't we doing this, Mike?' And Micha had instantly given the question a real and honest look in her heart at that moment. The question had *not* been rhetorical or flippant in her mind. And the answers she had found in her heart were quite the same as Shawn's, and with as much, if not more, excitement and enthusiasm.

The obvious downside was the painful realization that this ruled out any long-term relationship with Cory. Unless he signed up for the same lifestyle, this would pretty much spell the end of them as a couple. And he was not even the slightest bit interested in entertaining such a notion. In fact, for weeks after the cruise, he spent a lot of private time mourning his decision to take Shawn on the cruise at all, thereby introducing her to the very wedge that would be the demise of their courtship. He never made it apparent to her intentionally, but she did see it. And comfort him she simply could not. She could try, and sometimes did, but did not try to fake it, or to act like it wasn't a trade-off she was willing to make. She had too much integrity for that kind of theatre.

These were thoughts for the future, though. Not the distant future, but the coming-very-soon future. Shawn and Cory both knew it. And Shawn instinctively knew that Micha and Mick were likely having the same conversations. Neither of the men had any illusions about sudden career changes. They were pragmatists, not given to such flights of fancy. And that was okay. Honorable, even. And who knew? Shawn and Micha could be high on seawater and off their rockers. If they were to take the plunge together, who knew if they would be assigned to the same cruise liner? There may be contingents that could be managed – contractual elements that stated it as a must, even so much as to call themselves a couple to guarantee such manifestations. But neither of them could really know with any certainty. Just as neither of them could know if one or the other of them would even be cut out for the lifestyle. One or both of them could potentially come to terms with reality and see that it had been a pipe dream, jumping off at the first port-of-call and never going back. But those too were thoughts for the future.

The very shortest future for Shawn was getting all her affairs in order to play the next card her life presented her. And that was to be ready for something – anything – at all. Whether she would find work in a land-based company or she would make the decision to change everything she had ever known and step onto a cruise ship full time… She had certain things that simply had to be dealt with in the here and now. She reckoned she would take two to three weeks to make her decisions and come to a final answer. These were not easy times for the couple of Cory and Shawn. They were not laden with long fights and all-night arguments, but they were not easy. There was a very clear and perceptible tension in the air that seemed present at all of their interactions. It very clearly had not been a part of their relationship before. And it was even present during their intimacy. Shawn's mind was on the sea, and Cory's mind was on Shawn.

Shawn had learned a lot about herself over the last two-something years of working at BlueBird Innovation. She was able to step through fear and become a bigger person than her fear should have allowed her. She could achieve things her fear was trying to keep her from. She was, in short, stronger than she had ever believed. Believed. That was a good word.

She now believed in herself. She had faced her worst fears and been okay. More than okay. Prosperous. She had watched things happen that no human being was wired to see. Maybe there were people it wouldn't even faze. But in the basic reality that had governed mankind since the beginning of time, it was clear and obvious that – except under miraculous conditions – man should only have to die once. So seeing that was something not meant for human consumption. And she had bested it. For that, at least, she could be proud.

Being able to come to the resolution of how to shut down perhaps the most powerful AI ever known had been no small task either. Though she did not tend toward arrogance, she did have moments of gleeful pride (coupled with serious channels of thanks and appreciation to God for such an outcome) that she alone had solved the riddle of how to deal with Jamie. The computer in the back of the Box had managed to morph itself into something viable after having been stomped. Because something in its memory had not been shut down. And something in its personality had arranged it to come back to life and draw all its resources back together. Though Shawn could not possibly have known it at the time, had she just unplugged the power supply from the motherboard, it would have ended Jamie and all that came with it in a near instant. The tiny capacitors and energy-storing diodes inside the aluminum box of the power supply had been protected from the stomping boots. And since it had still had a physical connection to the motherboard, and from there connections to certain chips Jamie had commandeered on said motherboard… well, it had resurrected itself in much the same way Shawn and Sameer had once brought human beings back from the dead, if only for a brief moment.

But killing the circuit breaker and then further coming back later and cutting the copper wires inside the receptacle opening in the wall of the Box had been what cut off its antenna to the outside world. How she had come to that knowledge, Shawn couldn't begin to know. But in critical situations, she had proven – at least to herself – to be a reasonable thinker. At least if she was able not to melt down and have a panic attack. Hey, one couldn't be perfect all the time. Even Superman has to put on his suit. And another thing she had not considered but would have become obvious with any amount of thought, was that the entire building had been part of the antenna array, which was what had given it such power. When Jeremy removed the circuit breaker, his electrical acumen had told him that cutting the *white* wire would be necessary as well. The white, the neutral or common wire in electrical circuits, might not have given power to the AI computer, but it had definitely given connectivity to the rest of the white wires in the building, thereby creating a circuit for the most powerful antenna in the city. Hundreds of miles of copper existed inside that building. That building had copper coming in from the outside. The outside connected to the entire electrical grid of the city. It could have well been unstoppable.

The other thing she had learned during her time at BlueBird was the knowledge that she really loved being around people. New acquaintances, interesting contacts, customers and clients. She thrived on human interaction. Which was why she felt tinges of excitement every time she had to visit a client site. Or take a trip to an Air Base with a man from a company she supported. Though sexual undertones may have eventually come to present themselves, it had certainly not been the reason she had wanted to go. To experience new things and new people had been her interest. And the people she had met in that engagement had been more than just a little interesting. They had been downright *exciting*! People who worked on and managed satellites? Who got to encounter that on a day-to-day?

Well, that human interaction would be in rich abundance were she to decide to turn seaside. And it was with careful consideration and attention to every little detail that Shawn meditated on her decision. She did not take it – or its effects on other people around her – lightly.

But that was the future. The short future. It was not the right-now. Shawn was living the right-now with respectful consideration as well. She was living her life one moment at a time, and loving the people around her with her whole heart. Today, she sat on the carpet of her apartment living room, the sliding glass door to the miniature balcony wide open and a breeze coming through the screen door, surrounded by friends. It was May and she had just celebrated a birthday with these friends and their boyfriends the night before. The air was fresh and cool – one of those mornings where one feels like life could never be better, so long as it was dependent solely on the weather. There apparently existed places on the planet where the weather always tended toward such mornings as these, mild and wonderful, exquisitely lovely in its birdsong and cool breezes and sunshine. Maybe on the decks of cruise ships. Maybe in the mountains. But on this particular day in May, it was right here in this apartment in Arlington.

Shawn and Micha and Lindsay sat on the carpet with their knees almost touching in the small circle they had formed. They had finished their coffee and now held the tall flutes best associated with mimosas. There had been laughter and tears of happiness, and a ton of smiles. An opening up and spilling of all things girly, personal and exciting. Cory was in the office with the door closed playing *Call of Warfare* or whatever the hell it was called, with Mick who was in his own apartment across the courtyard. They were on a team doing something manly and testosterone-fueled to some other group of men somewhere on the planet. They were of no concern to these women. Not at the moment, at least. Micha and Lindsay had become fast friends just as Shawn had imagined they would, and there was a sort of peace and comfort in Shawn's soul, as if she had shed herself of a giant weight. All the ugly tasks had been checked off and she was no longer ensnared within that peaceful but daunting relationship with the man called Sameer Singh. The one she could not have made herself leave because of his kindness and patience, but also the one she should have left before she ever went to that Mexican restaurant that night, so long ago.

After the most recent bout of laughter and rhetoric had died away, the girls shifted. Leaned back on hands. Crossed legs Indian-style. Adjusted in their circle, ready for the next thing. Shawn took a deep breath, then smiled mischievously and pulled from her pocket the thumb drive Blake Prescott had given her at the funeral. "You girls wanna see how the pyramids were built?"